CLOAK AND DAGGER

by NENIA CAMPBELL

Cloak and Dagger by Nenia Campbell

DEDICATION

To those who said I could.

Cloak and Dagger by Nenia Campbell

Chapter One

Honor

Michael:

The man in the cell was called Itachi Watanabe. In Japanese,
Itachi meant weasel. He looked like one. Greasy hair. Pinched,
rodent-like features. Slanted black eyes constantly shifting, never
meeting one's gaze. On the security monitor he paced like a caged
animal, pausing periodically, restlessly, to stare in the direction of the
camera with a pleading expression.

I'd read his file. He'd built up quite a thick one over the years.
He was a Japanese programer, thirty-eight-years-old. Attended
school in MIT, as an international student, until he was kicked out
for hacking into the administrative system and changing the grades
of his ex-girlfriend and her new lover. A series of similar
transgressions resulted, from various insults both actual and
imaginary, causing his subsequent firings at various technological
institutes. Following his expulsion from Apple for leaking corporate
information to competitors — for a price — his public career went
under and he disappeared underground like the rat he was, where
he continued to hone his skills. Antisocial, but highly intelligent.
Insecure and possibly schizophrenic. They say that genius is closely
linked with insanity. Allegedly, Watanabe could hack into even the
most sophisticated of firewalls. Including ours.

4

Cloak and Dagger by Nenia Campbell

It had been a silent entry. A silent escape. If he had kept his mouth shut, he might have even managed to remain undetected. Watanabe had made a fatal error: he'd bought a round of sake bombs at a sushi bar in San Francisco and then, hungry for praise, made drunken boasts to his new-found companions. One of those companions had been an ex-client of ours. Out of a duty-bound sense of honor, he made an anonymous call from a local payphone. My men came for Watanabe that night.

I stared at the pathetic man on the screen, at the mess he had been reduced to over the last twenty-four hours. I'd seen men lose their backbone before, in his position, but Watanabe had nothing to lose; he was spineless. The computer was both his shield and his sword — and it had also been his downfall.

Yesterday morning a handful of computers in L7 had crashed, all of them part of the same network. One of the technicians immediately discovered the cause: a computer virus in an e-mail, opened and released by one of our employees. The infected computer transmitted the virus to every linked computer, rendering the entire network unusable. *Pandora*, the e-mail read, *She's a curious girl*. There hadn't been a sender. L7 was chiefly responsible for the archival of our weapons database. The network that had been targeted by the virus cataloged the imports that had transpired between 2000 and 2009. The items and their prices were encrypted, but Watanabe managed to crack some of the code.

Our IT people had checked out his home computer, which he had been stupid enough to use. In addition to a couple megabytes of porn stashed on various flash drives, they found several of his current hacking projects, including the encrypted import logs he'd been deciphering using pirated software called Skeleton Key that worked by implementing several thousand different decrypting algorithms a minute until one that fit the code was found. Before wiping his computer clean with a high power magnet, they had managed to determine that the e-mail had been sent from his e-mail account but not from his computer. And, since he hadn't installed a time-release, that meant somebody had helped him.

I was going to find out who.

On the monitor his lips were moving as he spoke with a wild-eyed desperation that implied he was ready to talk. Or just begging again. The video had no audio; I couldn't be entirely sure. He might be a nut. I swung around in my chair to face the hovering technician. "What's he saying?"

"I'm not quite sure. From what I've been told, he's been babbling for a while."

"Coherently?" I wanted to know what I'd be working with, whether he'd be delusional.

The technician shrugged. "I don't know. I manage the audiovisuals. Probably as coherent as can be expected given his current situation. One of the psychologists evaluated him earlier, I think. He's terrified, but sane."

Good. "Give me the computer read-outs. I'll speak with him."

"Last guy didn't have much luck," he warned me as he handed me the papers. They were still warm from the copier.

"Who was the last guy?"

"Ricky Morelli."

Ricky Morelli was a thug, with inside connections to the Italian mafia. His sister was married to one of the dons. They were old friends. Went way back. Morelli had helped the don dispose of some evidence implicating him in a major drug bust. The don was grateful, so grateful that he had made some debt collectors mysteriously vanish, and introduced him to my boss — yet another friend who had been kind enough to help him in his time of need and just so happened to be searching for another operative.

I love happy endings.

Morelli did not like me. I had the habit of making him look like an idiot; something that wasn't difficult to do. I was pretty sure he'd tried to have me killed — I hadn't stopped to chat with the hired goons that had tried to shoot me after one such humiliation. The bullets they fired spoke for themselves. Subtlety isn't Ricky's style, nor mine. I left the spent bullets on his desk along with a condolence card that said, "I'm sorry for your loss…" He never said anything about the card, but it was gone the next day. So were the bullets. He focused on his other competitor instead — Adrian Callaghan — which was like abandoning a fight with a mean dog for an even meaner dog with a taste for human flesh: further proof he wasn't the brightest bulb in the box. Callaghan was amused and all too eager to play along. Morelli was hoisted by his own petard; how could he get Adrian to back off? The solution became clear when a notebook filled with dirt on Callaghan, and his ties to the IRA, magically appeared in his locker. Their power play ended in stalemate, and Callaghan searched elsewhere for victims.

I like to think that Morelli and I have reached an understanding.

Shaking those thoughts off, I grabbed the papers. "I don't need luck."

I took the elevator down to B1. Unlike the upper-level rooms, which were virtually indistinguishable from run-of-the-mill office cubicles, these underground rooms had steel doors with key cards. I swiped mine through the requisite slots and entered Watanabe's cell. Except for a wooden table, a chair, and a cot, it was empty. A strong, pungent smell hung in the air. From the way he avoided my eyes, I knew the man had soiled his pants.

I set his file down on the table and rolled up my shirtsleeves. The smell was foul, but I'd been through worse. "Sit *down*."

After a wild look around the room, he plunked himself down in the chair. I pulled the computer printouts from my coat and set these down, too, ignoring him for the moment. One was from the IMA database — it showed the page he had accessed, staying up half the night to decrypt like a kid with a fucking decoder ring. The second printout was a copy of the infected email. When I looked up his eyes were locked on the pages, his face pale.

Schooling my own expression, I held up the first printout. "Look familiar?"

He stared bleakly at the page for several seconds before shaking his head no.

I had anticipated the lie but it still pissed me off. My interaction with the inept technician and the burden of Callaghan and Morelli had eaten up what patience I had; I didn't like playing second fiddle, or cleaning up after others' messes. Before Watanabe could get any further denials in, I shoved the desk forward, knocking him out of his chair. With a cry of alarm, he landed in a graceless sprawl on the floor. "Do you consider yourself an honorable man?"

"I…" He trembled like a leaf. "…why — what do you…?"

"You're protecting someone." Watanabe opened his mouth. "Don't lie to me. I *know* you're protecting someone. Hackers rarely work alone, as I'm sure you're aware. Do you honestly believe you are the first to have attempted to gain entry through our firewall?"

"No."

"So you're not a complete fool."

Color rose in his face. "I do believe that I am the first to succeed," he muttered.

"Then you should be more cognizant of the level of trouble you are in." I knelt down. "Would you put a price on honor? How much is your allegiance worth — your life, perhaps? The life of your... associate?"

I saw the gears turn in his head as he began to understand. The blotches of red in his cheeks receded, as though sucked into a vacuum, rendering his face even paler than before. "Honor is worth more than blood money."

"No, I'm afraid honor is worthless. Honor won't save you now, and whatever pathetic comfort you derive from it will do little to ease the pain I am about to inflict on you. Maybe you fear your associate will retaliate. Maybe you think he can save you. He can't." I paused. "Do you know what we do to liars here?"

He swallowed with visible effort. "No."

"In the next room there is a man waiting to show you. The prisoners at our internment camp call him *el tiburón* — the shark — because they say the scent of blood excites him. He takes great pride in what he does" — I paused again, indicating a small, hand-held radio — "do you want me to call him?"

No response.

"Well?"

He managed to raise himself to a slumped, seated position on the floor. "No…"

"Then I'll ask you one more time. Do you recognize this? Does it look familiar?"

He nodded wearily. "It's the code."

"The code to what?"

"I don't know. I'm not sure." He stared at the paper, as if willing the encryption to reveal itself before his hungry, desperate eyes. "I swear."

I shuffled the papers, revealing the second printout of the e-mail. "And this one?" He frowned, leaning closer. I held the paper just out of reach. I didn't think he was foolish enough to make a lunge for it, not with me armed, although he was spry enough — and desperate enough — to do so, but there was no need to tempt him. I let him take a good look before prompting him, "Yes or no?"

He started to speak, then closed his mouth and shook his head. "No."

I pressed the button.

His eyes shot open so wide I could make out the yellowed whites of his sclera under the track lighting. "Wait! What are you doing? I am telling the truth!"

"You have lied to me twice already. I will not be lied to again."
To the radio, I said, "Get Callaghan on the line — "

"No!" Watanabe made a wild lunge for the radio from across the table. I kicked him in the diaphragm. He hit the ground like a sack of cement and started sobbing. "Please — "

"Subject is being uncooperative."

"No," he wheezed, "I'll talk. I swear — "

"You'll lie."

"No! I'll tell you anything you want to know. Anything!"

I held my thumb off the button. "You have a minute. Starting now."

"But — "

"Fifty-three seconds. Do not argue with me."

For a moment he looked like he was intent on doing exactly that. He wet his lips, then spoke in a rapid burst, "Okay. I — I might have come across something similar to this once, a few years ago — though I swear I've never seen that one before!"

"This?" I brandished the second printout.

He flinched. "Not exactly. But they're similar, ah — the other e-mail I saw also made references to Greek mythology, and it also contained a virus."

"I never said it contained a virus."

"It's obvious. There is no sender, and just the way it's laid out…"

He shook his head, not repentantly but in admiration. "It's quite intricately done. The message provokes curiosity. If the user acts upon their curiosity, it becomes their own undoing; it's a clever homage to the myth of Pandora. There's so many layers to study and analyze — " slowly, unconsciously, he reached out toward the paper

"That's *enough*." I folded it away. "Tell me about the other e-mail."

He drew his hand back as though he'd been bitten. "I-it was about Hephaestus. The god of technology. I don't remember much more than that. It lacked the same level of sophistication, but there was a similar trap, also based on myth. I-I remember it contained a form of malware — called Alloy, I believe. At first it seemed to improve the computer's performance speed, but at the same time it was infecting other, less frequently used, files." He paused, scratching at the inside of his wrist. I could see the reddish imprint of rope bindings. "I believe it was supposed to be an allegory to the arsenic added to copper to smelt bronze. It seemed like a cheaper substitute at the time but caused serious health risks from repeat exposure to those who used it."

"Who is he? Where does he live?"

"I don't know. It was…speculation."

"You seemed pretty sure a moment ago," I growled.

"He's from America. I think he's from the west coast. He doesn't quite have the right...mentality for a southerner, or someone on the east coast. And the weather — what he mentioned of it — fits the description of Oregon, northern California, or southern areas of Washington. Temperate. Damp. I notice these things. I like to know who I deal with." Watanabe paused, thinking hard. "If he is who I believe he is, he goes by Hephaestus. It's a pseudonym."

"Where does he *live*?"

He blanched, wary again. "I-I don't know his address. We were never close, only acquaintances. Distant ones. But we moved in the same circles. I respected his work. We chatted, on occasion. Shop-talk mostly, or chit-chat, like the weather or — or our..." His face scrunched up. "I can give you his name. His real one. At least" — he frowned — "I think it is. I was surprised he introduced himself...so forthrightly. I gave him a fake name. In hindsight, it seems likely that his was fake, as well."

"I'm losing patience." I stepped toward him. "The *name*."

"Parker. Rubens Parker."

As the doors whooshed closed behind me, I pressed the button on the radio once more. "Get Mr. Watanabe some water. If he remembers anything else, inform me at once." I waited until the woman on the other side of the line assented before shutting off the device for good. When he discovered that no food accompanied the drink, he might have another bout of hypermnesia.

I'd managed to get through to a difficult subject, establishing my reputation as a great field operative and investigative agent. I was feeling pretty satisfied, cocky even, until a familiar voice stopped me dead in my tracks. "All work and no play makes Michael Boutilier a dull boy. Just where do you think you're going, hmm?"

Adrian Callaghan was one of the few men I had to look up at — 6'7" at his last physical. He was also a sadist, a sociopath, and our chief interrogator. And he reported to me: a fact I had to remind him of constantly.

Like now.

"What do you want? I didn't think you had clearance for this sector."

Callaghan smiled, revealing slightly crooked teeth. He came to this country too late to lose his both his accent, and his overbite. The violence he'd wreaked in his home country against the English had earned him a death sentence, making him an expatriate at eighteen. I knew far more than I liked about Adrian Callaghan and his personal life. Like Morelli and his don, we went way back — but our relationship was far from friendly. I'm pretty sure he knew who had revealed his shady origins, and he had never quite forgiven me for breaking his nose.

"You called me."

"I no longer have need of your services. You're dismissed."

I resumed walking. He followed. "The weasel decided to talk then?"

"Yes."

"How disappointing. Oh, well. I prefer them stubborn, anyway." At my silence, he continued, "It's a bit like a game. You played Battleship when you were a lad, right? Choosing random spots, never knowing when — or what — you're going to hit. Guessing their weakness is like getting that hit, Michael; in that instant, you own them. And they know it."

The holding cells were separated from the main building by a steel-doored elevator with an access panel: a kind of fail-safe should a prisoner manage to do the impossible and escape from his or her cell. I punched in the code and could not hide my annoyance when Callaghan tagged along. "Don't you have something you need to do?"

He lifted an eyebrow. "No use trying to get rid of me. I'm your backup in this assignment. Your business is my business, Michael, my boy."

What? The doors parted with a hiss of air. I stormed out of the elevator.

"Why the hurry?" he mocked, keeping pace with my brisk stride. "Did Richardson forget to tell you?"

Goddammit. This was beginning to seem an awful lot like

16

punishment: the last couple of cases I'd had were complete rot. Traitors. Petty thieves. Cases nobody else wanted, which gathered dust in the filing room until Richardson could find an appropriate stooge to do the field work. But maybe it wasn't the personal attack I was taking it as. Maybe Richardson hoped that we would monitor each other more closely than two more amiable colleagues.

And maybe pigs would also grow wings and perform aerial fucking cartwheels.

"Hennessy," I snapped. "Get me everything you can on Rubens Parker."

She looked at my face, then at Callaghan, nodded, and raced out of the room.

"Parker, hmm?" Callaghan mused, watching her leave. "Anyone I know?"

"Doubtful." I did a double-take. "Wait. Didn't Richardson debrief *you*?"

"Maybe." He grinned, pleased that he'd caught me off-guard. "However, a second opinion never hurts."

Bullshit. He just wanted to annoy me. "He's the hacker that caused the network to crash if Watanabe isn't lying."

"You mean you aren't *sure*? If I'd had my way, there would be no uncertainty."

"You would have destroyed him. Richardson wants to keep him.

He may be a blubbering imbecile," I added, "But he's useful behind the keyboard. I can see why a waste like him might be considered valuable enough to keep alive…for the moment."

Callaghan shook his head — but didn't argue; we both knew I was right.

The mousy woman returned a few minutes later with a sheet of paper. "Here," she said breathlessly. "Everything I could find about Rubens Parker. As you asked."

"Thanks." A glossy eight-by-ten color photograph topped the stack. My target was the middle-aged man. His wife and daughter sat on either side of him like bookends. The wife appeared Filipino — or maybe Latino. So did the daughter. Hard to tell. I wasn't sure if this would be relevant or not, but I filed it away just the same.

Rubens Parker. I was sure he'd do anything I'd asked him to.

The wife, on the other hand, could be a problem. There was a fierceness in her expression, drawn in the lines around her cheeks and eyes. I'd have to find a way to get her out of the picture so she couldn't influence her husband.

Callaghan craned his neck to look over. "Oh look, fun for the entire family. And they've got a kid." He smiled. "I love kids."

I gave him a sharp look. "You stay out of this. You're *backup*."

"Yes. I'll be right in back of you. Watching your every move." The smile hardened. "Oh, I know about your understanding with

Ricky Morelli and the others. Don't you know, Michael, that everyone is just as afraid of you as they are of me? They're glad to help you now, but if you fall…" His voice dropped to a whisper, "Unlike you, all they say about me is true. Deep down, you're soft… weak…and so very inferior to me."

"I'm your superior officer, Callaghan," I snapped. "This is insubordination."

"Would you kill her?" Callaghan asked, running his finger down the image of the girl. "She *is* pretty, isn't she? And so young. Could you kill her for no reason, other than getting in your way? Could you hurt her? Could you do it with your own two hands? You might. But you would hesitate. And that, Michael, is the underlying difference between us. Because I wouldn't."

"Get out."

"I wouldn't," he repeated. His mouth smiled but his eyes remained dead. Callaghan lied about many things but this wasn't one of them. "Don't get into pissing contests you can't win, Michael Boutilier. Especially not with me."

"Get *out* and let me do the job that *I* was asked to do."

He clapped me on the shoulder. "*Well*. Don't screw up, then." For one brief instant, as his arm drew away, his hand closed around the back of my throat and squeezed — not hard enough to cause any pain, but there was power behind it. I whirled around, my hand on the butt of my gun, just in time to see his shirttails disappear around the corner.

Fuck.

Christina:

In pop science, there's this phenomenon called the butterfly effect. You know, that a butterfly flapping its wings can cause a hurricane on the other side of the world. Well, on the day that my life changed — forever — it all started with me not doing my Spanish homework.

It was stupid, careless — completely *unlike* me, in other words — not to have finished it the night before. I was responsible. On top of things. The kind of child parents were referring to when they told their own offspring, "You should be more like so-and-so." I spoke Spanish *fluently*. It would have taken all of ten minutes.

But I hadn't done it.

I looked down at the text that had woken me up. It was from Renee. The message remained the same, taunting me: *What did you get for number six on the Spanish homework?*

Had the instructor even mentioned homework? He had spent the entire class period on Friday blathering on about the subjunctive and its uses. I remembered that much because I had been staring out the window at the empty soccer field, bored to tears, wishing *futbol* was in season because at least that would have given me something to focus on.

Havent done it yet. Maybe l8er.

The response was quick. *What? You? Not doing your homework?*

Please. If I was a good student, I wouldn't have teachers breathing down my neck, waiting for me to make a mistake. I was just...predictable.

Maybe too predictable.

I stared at the window and sighed. The icy light glazed the windows like a thin layer of frost, casting my room in a pale blue glow that turned the walls the most delicate shade of lavender. My room always looked best in the early mornings because the walls were baby pink — a color whose true hideousness was best revealed, like that of most horrors, in broad daylight.

I tried to complain about this, but most of my friends were unsympathetic; they couldn't understand why I was making a big deal over something as unimportant as the color of my walls. Sometimes, if they were feeling petty enough, they called me spoiled. My friends didn't get that it wasn't about the *walls*, not entirely. It was about what they represented — and that was my mother's determination to have control over every conceivable facet of my life. I called it *my* room, but that was just a formality. It was really my *mother's* room.

Oh, there were traces of my presence if you knew where to look. The books were mine — *Don Quixote* (in English), the Oz books, a signed collection of Julia Alvarez (in Spanish), *The Phantom Tollbooth*, and Harry Potter — as were the baseball pennants, and the collection of plush owls on the window seat. If you were really determined, you might find my trading card collection (hidden underneath my bed in three thick binders), some programming manuals (stolen from my father), my grandfather's chess set (missing a rook), and a couple of old game consoles from when I was a kid. My tomboy proclivities were otherwise banished from the household, as if my mother believed she could eradicate them by sweeping them beneath the pink rug. It wasn't my room she was trying to change. It was *me*.

I dressed quickly, avoiding the mirror. I'd pigged out on a bag of open chips someone had left on the counter last night and I could still feel the fat clinging to my thighs. I didn't want to *see* the evidence, as well. I hid the bag in my room because I was pretty sure that my mother snooped in the rubbish bin to spy on what I ate.

"Happy thoughts," I muttered, grabbing my bag from my desk chair. It was a pretentious thing — the chair, I mean, not the bag; an early twentieth century dining chair that had been reupholstered and repainted. It was so uncomfortable, I kind of suspected that it wasn't meant to be sat on. In that sense, the Victorians and my mother had a lot in common: they both believed that furniture, as well as women, were better suited for display purposes only.

This was how deeply my mother had insinuated herself into my life. Like a serpent, her venomous criticism lingered long after she had departed. The bible says to honor thy mother and father but how many times can you turn the other cheek before you start feeling like a patsy? Why isn't it important to honor thy children, as well?

I found Mom in the kitchen. Her long black hair was pulled into her loose, trademarked chignon, secured with a jeweled clip. She was wearing a Chinese dress, real brocade, that made her skin glow. Wispy strands of hair fell into her face as she looked up from the sink, fixing on me the coal-black eyes that had made her the darling of the Dominican Republic in the 1970s, and my father fall madly in love with her.

With a surge of irritation, I resisted the urge to check my own hair. I wondered why she was so dressed up. Sometimes I suspected she did it to make me feel bad. "You're doing the dishes?"

"Rosalind is sick today."

Rosa was the maid. The only reason my mother knew her name was because she had to write the checks out every month. "You know she doesn't like being called that."

"Don't speak to me in that tone of voice, Christina Maria."

23

I backed down and said, "But it's *true, mamá*. It bothers her. It's what her ex-husband calls her." My voice sounded whiny to my own ears; I couldn't imagine what my mother made of it.

She sighed. "What have I told you about talking to the maid, Christina? It's fine to be polite, if you must, but she's a bit coarse. I don't want her influencing you. And besides, you know perfectly well how much I abhor nicknames. Not only are they *gauche*, they trivialize your God-given name. Rosa is very cheap-sounding, don't you think?"

"No." I knew a girl at school named Rosa. Her father owned a vineyard.

"Imagine," my mother said, with a grimace, "If we called you *Chris*."

I glared at her, opening the fridge. Why was she dragging me into this? "There are plenty of girls called Chris."

"And they are also probably lesbians, darling, which I am sure you do not want to be." The condescending smile slipped. "You're going to school in that, Christina?"

That was leggings, a blue knit dress, and flats I had bought on sale from Target for ten dollars. It was cold, so I'd put on a crocheted cap, which I'd secured in place with a couple of discreet bobby-pins. I thought it'd looked fine the other night when I'd laid it out. Standing here, in the pale, washed-out light of the kitchen, though, she made me feel hideous.

I set down the grapefruit I'd picked up. "There's no school on Fridays," I said. "I don't understand. This outfit was in a fashion spread in one of my magazines."

Annoyance flickered over her features at the comparison. When *mamá* was my age, she had been a model — good enough for the Dominican equivalent of *Seventeen Magazine*. Sometimes higher-end stores at the malls would hire her, too, for the glossy advertisements of their spring and fall sales. Now she was retired and designed clothes. We had the same eyes, the same cupid's bow mouth, the same dark hair. I was tall, too, and of swarthy complexion — just like her.

Strangers always said we looked alike but they were just being polite because that was were the similarities ended. Even in her forties, my mother was still far slimmer than I would ever be. She took my size — 5'11", 16 in juniors — as my personal attempt to spite her through self-destructive behavior, for the same reasons that other girls my age pierced their tongues, consumed alcohol, and dated men like tattooed Swiss Army knives. "If you lost that weight, you could be a model," she was always telling me. "You were so precious when you were younger. People were always telling me you looked like a porcelain doll. I called you my *muñequita*." Then she would sigh and shake her head. "When I was your age, I was a size four. *Four*, darling. And I was considered one of the heavier girls." She launched into this now.

I waited for the spiel to end, knowing that arguing would make things worse. I think she was mad at me because one of her friends had recently remarked that it was "a pity your daughter won't be able to wear your creations" with the same sort of sneering self-satisfaction women half her age had. The Lord also says love thy neighbor...but Mrs. Thompson lived all the way across town, so I didn't consider her my neighbor and felt free to loathe her at will. I couldn't imagine what my mother saw in her, or why she valued her opinion, but she did, and I was suffering all the more for it. When *mamá* finished bemoaning the embarrassment of my appearance, I said, "Why don't you just make your clothes *bigger*?"

This annoyed her, as I knew it would. "Because this is fashion. And with *big* models, you don't get to see the draping of the clothing to its full potential. All you see is the *girl*."

"Adopt a mannequin, then," I said icily.

"That's not the point. The point is, you've been gaining weight. Haven't you?"

I flushed. "No!"

"What have you been eating?" Her tone managed to achieve the perfect balance of sympathy, criticism, and moral superiority. In other words, she sounded like a preacher, which wasn't too far from the truth. My mother's religion was thinness; it was her false idol, her golden calf — and she was determined to convert me.

"What I eat is none of your business." I could feel the heat creeping down my neck and knew I looked like the very portrait of guilt. I wondered if she had noticed the empty bag of Doritos beneath my bed, with the bright red foil that was almost as incriminating as the blush staining my cheeks. The thought of her snooping around my room made me even angrier.

"Of course it's my business," her accent thickened, "I am your *mother*."

"Legally, I'm an adult. I can do whatever I want."

She let out her breath, all at once. It smudged her lipstick — something else for her to hold against me. "I just want you to be healthy. Is that such a terrible thing for a mother to want?"

What a joke, coming from a woman who worked for the fashion industry. Really. Starving yourself to fit into a size zero — why did that size even *exist*? Zero referred to the *absence* of something, but what did it mean in terms of a model's measurements? Her fat? Or her presence? How much could you cut away before the person herself vanished? It was hypocritical, that's what it was. I said as much, adding, "If you're so keen on me being healthy then you should have no problem accepting me for the way I am. *That's* what's healthy, Mom. Not being focused on all this freaky weight-

27

loss stuff."

"What do you want from me?" she demanded. "Permission to be as fat as you want? Fine. You have my permission" — with a dismissive wave, like Marie Antoinette asking the common people why they didn't just eat cake if they were out of bread — "Eat, then. Eat nothing but pizza and ice cream the whole time your father and I are gone this weekend. Will that make you happy, *puerquita*?"

Tears burned in my eyes. I picked up my bag and left the room before she could utter another scathing remark and before she could see me cry. Just before I slammed the door shut, hard enough to rattle the windows in their panes, I screamed, "I hate you!"

Mr. Next-door startled from watering his lawn and stared at me with an alarmed expression before retreating inside. A couple of dogs barked and howled back at the echo of my shout. I was humiliated. God, I hated this. I really did. Fighting with her. Each meal. Every day. It made me so sick, I wasn't even hungry anymore — so in that sense, I guess she won.

Chapter Two

Hunter

Michael:

Callaghan didn't make idle threats. While there was no immediate danger, I decided to make seeing Richardson my top priority; I needed to know what I had gotten myself into, taking on this assignment. Despite working here for the better part of a decade, he still didn't trust me. I wouldn't have been surprised if this was an attempt to put me in my place.

Well. I could play games, too. I took my sweet-ass time getting to his office. I bought a hot lunch from the canteen; submitted some paperwork I'd been saving for such an occasion; took a leak. When I arrived at the reception area, over two hours had passed. I was pleased; so pleased that I was able to mask my disappointment when his secretary informed me that he was "in a meeting" without even bothering to phone. This only served to confirm my suspicions that I was being screwed with. If he wasn't anticipating some form of misconduct, why was I being blacklisted? She smiled with too-white teeth. "Would you like me to take a message?"

"No. That's fine. I'll wait right here."

She eyed me as I sat down in one of the stiff-backed chairs. Chairs that were designed, I imagined, with the intent of making such visits as brief as possible. She opened and closed a drawer, the same one, over and over. "I'm not sure when he'll be getting out. Mr. Richardson did say to cancel all his afternoon appointments."

I bet he did. I also bet she had a gun in one of those drawers she kept fiddling with.

"I've got nothing but time." I pulled out the files Hennessy had given me, raising them in a silent toast, and set toward memorizing the data. From the corner of my eye, I monitored the watch on my wrist. The time was 11:06. I wondered how long it would take Richardson to cave, or whether he would force me to call his bluff. The secretary was watching me when I looked up. I smiled at her. I was betting it would take less than ten minutes. Maybe even five.

At 11:10 she said, proving me right, "Mr. Richardson will see you now."

The door shut behind me as I walked into the room.

Richardson was sitting at his desk — a much more ostentatious model, made of handcrafted mahogany, and every bit as expensive as the black leather seat accompanying it. The desk was the focus of the room and intended to intimidate.

"Mr. Boutilier" — a signet ring on one sausage-like finger caught the light as he set aside some files I doubted he'd been reading — "Now this *is* a surprise, isn't it?"

I sank into the chair across from him. "Meeting get out early?"

He ceased toying with the ring. "Nothing gets past you, I see."

"Your secretary didn't even bother to pick up the phone — or is she psychic?"

"I shall have to have a word with her about that, then, won't I?" He folded his hands in front of him. And not, I couldn't help noticing, answering my question. "What brings you to my office?"

"I think you know that already."

His eyes flickered. "You give me too much credit, Mr. Boutilier. I may be many things, but I am not psychic — unlike my secretary, it seems." He smiled. It disappeared when I didn't laugh. "No, I am afraid *you* will have to tell me what occasioned this visit."

"You assigned Callaghan as my back-up on the Parker job. I want to know why."

Richardson shook his head. "Mr. Callaghan is a very talented operative."

I snorted. He gave me a sharp look."Granted, he can be…shall we say, heavy-handed at times — "

"Sadistic."

" — but he always gets results. Something that cannot always be said for *you*, in spite of your finesse. I had hoped your respective strengths might compensate for your respective weaknesses." My expression must have been dark. He smiled again. "Do you disagree?"

"You know the answer to that question, too."

"I needed to assign someone who wouldn't be intimidated by you, Mr. Boutilier. Or your hubris. That is a short list. And of that list, even fewer are capable enough to meet my expectations. Mr. Callaghan was at the top of that list."

"It must have been a *very* short list, then."

"Yes. Almost as short as my patience with you, in fact." Richardson cocked his head. "I'm still not quite clear on what it is you want, Mr. Boutilier."

"I am tired of cleaning up after Ricky Morelli's mistakes. I'm tired of Morelli and Callaghan vying for power. I'm really tired of playing errand-boy — the next step, I imagine, is doing coffee runs and copying faxes." I slipped my hands into the pockets of my coat. "It's a waste of my ability and training, and a waste of your time and resources. I am *not* your secretary."

"The only thing you have in common with my secretary, Mr. Boutilier, is blonde hair."

Again, he looked at me expectantly. I raised an eyebrow and hardened my expression.

He sighed. "I *want* those spreadsheets, Mr. Boutilier. I will do everything that is in my power to get them back. You've raised some valid concerns about Morelli and Callaghan but they are not a priority for me right now. The weapons logs are. And if you value your job — and your life — as my senior operative you will not stand in my way in obtaining those spreadsheets. Is that quite clear?"

"Crystal." I stood up and walked closer to the desk. Under the overhead light his forehead was shiny with sweat. I rested my hands over the files, watching his face for any sign of weakness. One of his hands was out of sight, probably grasping a weapon of some kind. "Let me ask you this one last thing, sir."

I paused a heartbeat. He nodded.

"Do you even know what Callaghan does?"

"His job, I should imagine."

"I mean to *people*."

"Again, his methods may be unorthodox — "

"Why don't you say the words? Torture. Rape."

Mr. Richardson smiled. "You've become quite the human rights activist. Fine, then. Torture. Rape. I don't recall those methods being beneath you."

"I don't enjoy it," I snarled. "I don't do it for pleasure."

"So you say."

"He's a powder keg doused in petrol, sir, and you're holding the match. I've seen the things Callaghan does — and what he does, sir, he does for fun."

"I can hardly fault him for enjoying his job. It is distasteful, yes, but at least he has an outlet for his..." *Perversions?* "...unique talents." He glanced at his watch, then at me. "Is that all?"

"He's also liability to the company. He's violent. Antisocial — a psychiatric disorder that is, supposedly, untreatable. You can try to brush him under the rug, sir, but he is not going to go away, and he's interfering with my men's ability to get the job done. I've had to intervene to keep him from killing people on *our* side. His results are shit. The prisoners are so broken when he's through with him, they'd tell him whatever they thought he wanted to hear in order to make him stop. Not that it would work. He *destroys* people, and I'm pretty sure he'd run this agency into the ground if you let him. It may already be too late — he might have too much power, as is."

"That *will* be all, Mr. Boutilier. What you are implying now is treason and unless you have sufficient proof to back your claims, I suggest you keep such idle speculations to yourself. I have to question your motives in telling me this. Especially now. The timing is convenient." He straightened, causing his suit to stretch tight at the seams. "Too convenient."

"What are you implying?"

"There are some who say *you* are the — what was that phrase? Powder keg doused in petrol? — of this organization. Nearly all your allegations against Mr. Callaghan are applicable to you, Mr. Boutilier. Then there is the matter of these petty squabbles which, from what you tell me, you do little to discourage. You speak of abusing power — you, yourself, are not faultless."

"You think I want your job?"

"To be perfectly honest, Mr. Boutilier" — something hard pressed against my chest — "I'd rather not find out." I waited for darkness. "That is why I have asked Mr. Callaghan to do it for me." The pressure against my ribs disappeared. " Think of this as an incentive to find real proof." The gun was still in his hand, but it was no longer aimed in my direction. I couldn't imagine that was the incentive he was referring to. Even though it wasn't a joke, I almost did laugh this time.

"I think I'd prefer a pay raise."

"Be content with your life." Richardson tucked the gun back in its drawer; I noticed he didn't turn the safety back on. Was he losing it, or were his concerns valid? I was betting on a mixture of both. "Would you have allowed me to shoot you, Mr. Boutilier?"

"That depends, sir."

"On what?" He looked genuinely curious.

"Whether you intended to pull the trigger."

Christina:

My cell phone buzzed inside my black leather satchel. It was Renee. "Hello?"

"Where are you? Class is starting soon."

"I got into another fight with my mom."

She sighed. Or maybe it was static. "Again? Oh, Christina."

"She attacked my clothes."

It was definitely a sigh this time. "What were you wearing?"

"That outfit I showed you in Cosmo."

"What was wrong with it?"

"Apparently fat people are only allowed to wear sweatsuits," I muttered. "Tell Alvarez I'm going to be late. Tell him…I had a family emergency, or something."

"All right. But he's not going to believe me. See you when you get here." She hung up.

I ran.

Like any decent private school, Holy Trinity had a back story. It was built in the 1800s, as a mission. The original chapel remained at the heart of the heart of the school and was used for assemblies and graduation. Many people admired the sprawling stucco buildings—designed in imitation of the original Spanish Colonial Revival style — and we were reminded on a daily basis how lucky we were to attend a school with such a pristine and historical campus.

I would have been happy to go to an ordinary public school, like the rest of my friends from Lewis and Clark Middle School, but my parents pushed me to go to Holy Trinity because private school had status and prestige. That was important to my mom and dad.

Several female senators had gone to and graduated from Holy Trinity, as well as a number of female lawyers, doctors, and moderately successful business women.

I squeezed through the door of my Spanish class, out of breath from the run, trying to keep my expensive bag from hitting against the frame and getting scuffed. More scuffed. Señor Alvarez glanced up from the role sheet as I slunk into my seat. "Late again, Parker," he said. Across the aisle, Renee shot me an apologetic look. *I tried,* she mouthed.

"Sorry, sir," I mumbled, digging my Spanish workbook out of my backpack.

He rolled his eyes and some people giggled.

The uniforms were supposed to hide status, but everyone knew. These were teenage girls. My mother's name garnered prestige and a reputation, but since I didn't jibe with that reputation and wasn't the type of person to even want to, it didn't do me much good. My father was just a lowly programmer. And in a predominantly patriarchal society, it's your father's name that really counts.

"*Hoy, vamos a hablar sobre…*"

I tuned out. His accent got on my nerves. I already had a pretty firm grasp on the vocabulary, anyway. So what if I occasionally left off the odd accent mark?

"Señorita Parker, *¿Estás escuchándome?*"

I rattled off an answer to the question he hurled at me. He seemed disappointed when I got it right. I wished I was still taking programming, which I'd been taking at this same time block last semester. I'd always been interested in computers, even though I wasn't an expert user. Partly because it irritated my mother, mostly because I found technology fascinating. Programming was a second language, a secret code. You could manipulate the code to make it do anything you wanted. Holy Trinity offered an introductory course. It was object-oriented programming, the easiest. I'd wanted more. There were no accent marks. No conjugation. Just commands and numbers. Once you had the framework, you could manipulate the code in different ways.

My interest pleased my dad. Unlike my mother, who had threatened to faint dead away when I announced an interest in becoming an engineer ("why don't you just come right out and *say* you're a lesbian, Christina? That's what the world is going to think.") my dad was encouraging of any sort of intellectual pursuit, especially computers. He had once said that technology was like a skeleton key with which one could open many doors. The problem, he went on, was that many of these doors shouldn't be opened so you had to be careful when deciding how and when to exert that power.

I can still remember that conversation almost verbatim because it had made such a strong impact on me. We'd been in the kitchen. My parents were between business trips. Just one normal family, that was us. I was eating a Pop-Tart, ignoring the looks my mother was shooting me from across the room as she prepared sandwiches for lunch. I knew she wouldn't dare complain, not out loud. Not with my dad there. But at his words, she stilled.

"Why do you have to be careful? That wouldn't be your fault. It'd be a mistake."

"Rubens!"

Dad glanced at my mother. "Nothing, Sweet Pea," he said to me.

"I want to know." I put down the pastry and wiped my hands on my jeans. "It'll come in handy, in case I end up working with computers one day." I shot a defiant look at my mother.

Both my parents exchanged a long look. "Just because you can do something doesn't mean that you should," he said, choosing his words carefully. The fingers on his left hand drummed against the table as he sipped his morning coffee. "With great power comes great responsibility."

I was pretty sure he'd stolen that from a movie. "Dad, *please*. You work at a software firm. What harm could you possibly do?"

"Nothing in this world is without harm." He looked into my eyes. "Nothing. Promise me, Christina, that you will never open Pandora's Box."

"Um...sure, Dad. I won't open any weird boxes."

"That's enough." My mother's voice was quiet, but firm. "Christina. Put down that...*thing* and help me with the sandwiches."

Then Dad went silent. I watched him as I spread the pus-colored mayo "lite" on my mother's favorite revolting whole-grain bread. He said nothing else. That was three days ago and I was still replaying that moment in my head, trying to analyze those secret looks and unspoken exchanges. What had my dad been trying to say? That he had, in a burst of egotism, opened one of those that shouldn't have been opened? Or was it one of those normal parental caveats—don't have premarital sex, don't do drugs, blah, blah, blah? But if that was the case, why wouldn't my mother let him speak?

"Turn to *página catorce*," Alvarez said. "And we will correct the homework."

I had already finished my homework while Alvarez had been blathering on with the lesson. As I filled in the multitude of missing accent marks with red pen, my dad's final warning ringing in my ears. It had been so strange that I'd chalked it up to parental distress and said nothing more than "Um, sure." I wondered if there had been something more to his words than I thought. I stared down at my homework. Now it was full of cubes, all sizes, from different angles.

Promise me, Christina.

What was that even supposed to *mean*?

"Christina!"

I jumped when Alvarez's ice-blue eyes landed on me. "*Por favor, lee numéro cinco.*"

And, pushing such concerns from my mind, I did.

Michael:

I bought a one-way ticket to Barton, Oregon at the airport. With the assistance of a Brooks Brothers suit, I could play the role of the successful young entrepreneur just well enough. I bought an espresso and a copy of *The Wall Street Journal*. "Business trip," I explained to the attractive barista, who nodded in sympathy as she handed me my drink and my change.

It was early. Too early for a cross-country flight. Many of the shop lights were still extinguished, and I caught a glimpse of my reflection in the dark glass of a Mexican restaurant. I looked, I decided, taking a sip of the espresso, like a man with a plane to catch. Then I winced. The coffee was bitter and tasted cheap, but at least it made me alert. I drank half before tossing the cup. My baggage went on a conveyor belt to be checked. I slipped off my loafers and put them on top of my briefcase in one of the gray plastic bins.

"Can I see some ID?" the officer asked.

With a polite smile, I handed her my card. Edward Collins; 6'2",
blond hair, blue eyes. Twenty-seven-years-old. None of this was
strictly true.

She glanced at the picture, a cursory scan with no real interest,
and waved me through the metal detector; her eyes were already
beginning to focus on the British couple behind me.

Easy.

Once I was on the plane, I pulled out my laptop and accessed the
file I had hastily constructed on Rubens Parker during the wait in the
airport terminal. It was disguised as a company report. The words of
the real plan were typed in boldface font and needed to be strung
together for the message to be comprehensible.

Even though I could have recited it from memory, I skimmed
through the information the file contained. The man, Rubens Parker,
was a forty-six-year-old programmer possessing a high-ranking
position within the software engineering industry. His wife was
thirty-nine; an ex-model from the Dominican Republic. She spent
most of her free time designing clothing for her fashion line. They
had one child, an eighteen-year-old daughter who was attending a
reputable all-girls' school and on the fast track to a liberal arts
college like Reed, or Sarah Lawrence.

What might the parents pay to get their precious daughter back?
Taking hostages was messy but, if well-executed, the financial gain

alone could make it worthwhile. She seemed sheltered, soft. *If I were them*, I thought, *I would pay quite a lot.*

"Would you like anything to drink?"

I didn't lift my eyes from the laptop. "Perhaps later."

"We're going to take off soon," the attendant informed me. "You'll need to put that away."

I closed the computer obediently. "Do I have time to make a quick phone call?"

"Hurry." She repeated her initial offer to the people behind me, who took her up on it.

There were few other passengers in first class. Two men of Middle Eastern descent were discussing the stock market, and the businessman—the one who wanted the drink—and an elderly gentlewoman that looked British were both reading e-books on their Kindles. None of these people were particularly interesting but I kept an eye on them, regardless. The IMA had many enemies, with about a thousand different faces.

First class was expensive. But to the IMA, privacy was invaluable. I would not be bothered here. When I was certain that nobody was paying attention to me, I picked up the phone set provided in my seat and dialed the number I had committed to memory in the terminal.

"Hello, my name is Edward Collins. I'm new at Debutech. Yes, I quite enjoy it."

The person on the other line was eager to strike up a conversation on this slow Friday afternoon. I listened for about a minute and then got down to brass tacks. "Listen, one of my coworkers dropped a piece of personal mail in my briefcase by a mistake — a Rubens Parker. Yes. In the break room. I don't have his address, or I'd mail it myself. It looks urgent."

I paused.

"No, I'm afraid I can't bring it in. See, I'm on a flight as we speak. I'm visiting my kids in California. Yes, divorced. Tell you what, why don't you just give me his home address and I'll forward it to him myself?"

I listened, then nodded.

"I know. I figured this wasn't normal protocol, but the return address is smeared — must have been from last night's rain. Mailmen can be so careless. Otherwise I would have taken the initiative myself. No, it's no trouble." I typed out the address in the open file. "I understand. It'll just be our little secret. No, thank *you*."

Too easy.

Chapter Three

Quarry

Christina:

"Christina? Hey — wait up!"

Renee was galloping after me as fast as her schoolbooks would allow. I used to think her life was perfect before I learned how hard she worked to project that image of herself. She wasn't any more privileged than I and had told me things about herself that shocked me so deeply, I wouldn't believe her at first — not from somebody so strong, so flawless. I guess it just goes to show that we've all got something to hide. Like my mother pinching my stomach in an airport when I was fifteen, telling me how lucky I was that the airlines weren't charging extra for *that* kind of carry-on.

"Hi." I made room for her on the narrow sidewalk. There was barely enough room for us to walk side-by-side. "Thanks for trying to talk to Alvarez today, by the way."

"I'm sorry it didn't work. He said you had too many tardies. You were lucky he didn't mark you down for a cut."

"Speaking of which, I didn't see you in Stats. Did *you* cut?"

"As if. All members of the student council got to leave early so we could plan for the dance. We've already talked to St. John's and they're co-hosting." She flashed a quick smile. "Isn't that exciting? I feel like it's been years since I've laid eyes on a boy."

I loathed the St. John's boys. They hung out in front of Holy Trinity sometimes, hassling some of the younger girls as they walked home. Once a group of them had serenaded me with "Milkshake" until I'd fled to the nearest store. "How is that going?"

"Like a train wreck. We had to postpone it for a week because the stupid orchestra has practice and needs the gym for rehearsal before the *big concert*, and the school is too cheap to rent out someplace nice" — she threw up her hands — "and I *still* don't have a date."

She might have been on the student council but I held that she should have gone for drama since she had such a penchant for theatrics. "It's not the end of the world."

Renee eyed me intently. "You *are* going right?"

"Um, no." Her gaze got even more intent. "You know how horrible I look in a dress!"

"Christina — "

"Besides, I doubt that I'd be allowed to go. You know how old-fashioned my mother is." I raised my voice, adopting her thick accent, "You're wearing that? Will there be *boys* there, Christina? Boys don't marry girls who look like cheap French whores."

"I know, I know." Renee cut me off. "Then you say, No, mother. It's a *nun* party. It wasn't funny the first time, you know. Holy Trinity is just too close to being a parochial school."

Not close enough for my mother. In her view, there were three options for a woman. If you were beautiful, you got married. If you were ugly, you became a nun. If you were beautiful and stupid, or ugly and dishonorable, you became a whore. I think that was probably the only reason she was agreeing to let me go to college — she was hoping I'd get my "M.R.S. Degree."

"So are your elusive parents actually home?"

I grimaced, twisting my hair into a bun. "They shouldn't be. They were leaving this afternoon to go somewhere. Hawaii, I think. I wasn't listening." Had my mother even told me? "Anyway, they'll probably be gone by the time I get home."

"On a show?"

"Just leisure. And no, her dresses still cost upwards of a thousand dollars."

Renee sighed. "Your mom is so cool. I wish I had a fashion designer as a mom. Do you know how many girls would kill to wear one of her dresses to prom?"

"No you don't. It's a total pain. She's never home and I'm too fat to wear any of her clothes."

"You're *not* fat, Chris."

"Tell that to my mom. She's always saying to me, Size sixteen? How can you be a size sixteen? When I was your age, I was a size *four*. As if my self-esteem isn't low enough already."

"She's probably just worried....She shouldn't be saying those things to you, but I'm sure that's just because she cares for you. But you should still come to the dance. Don't you see? If you don't, you'll be letting her win because she'll have gotten to you. I'll help you find a dress, Christina — and you're going to look *great* in it."

"Maybe," I said unconvincingly.

"Hold that thought." Renee picked up her phone. "Hey, Dad. You're on your way? I'm with Christina right now on Anderson." She listened to whatever her dad was saying and gave me a funny look. "Huh. Interesting. Okay. Love you, too. See you soon. Bye."

"Interesting?" I raised an eyebrow, wondering what was up with the cloak and dagger stuff.

"What time did you say your parents were leaving?"

"Early. Around noon or one. Why?"

"That's weird. Because my dad said he'd just come back from Radio Shack. He said he saw *your* dad there."

"Really? Just now? In Barton?" She nodded.

That *was* weird. I didn't see why they would lie to me about their trip.

"Maybe they needed a security device," Renee suggested. "Or a new cell phone."

"Maybe." They had told me the plane was leaving this afternoon. Had they postponed the trip? If so, why? Last week, they had seemed quite anxious to leave. Or was I just being paranoid? This was the airport, after all. Flights got canceled and delayed all the time.

I still couldn't quash the anxiety that gnawed at my gut.

"Well, that's my ride." Renee waved as her dad pulled up to the curb in a gray Mercedes. "Do you want us to take you home?"

"I live just down there. It'd be out of your way." *And I could use the exercise.*

"Well...see you, then, I guess. Oh, and don't text me — I'm close to my plan's limit."

I waved and continued down the street to my house: a large, two-story mock Tudor. I entered through the side door, passing straight through the kitchen. Surprise, surprise, my parents weren't home. My kitten, Dollface, was, though, and ran up to greet me.

"Hi, Doll," I cooed, scratching him under the chin. He was a yellow tabby with a white tummy and white paws and had the privilege of being the most important boy in my life. This did not bode well for my future.

He purred, letting me pet him until he got bored with me and trotted off to his cat dish. Even I couldn't compete with chicken- and liver-flavored kitty kibble. Feeling hungry myself, I went to the fridge, surprised to see that there was a note waiting for me.

Christina — when you get home, call this number as soon as possible:

Cloak and Dagger by Nenia Campbell

Ten digits were listed below in my mother's feminine script.

I dumped my messenger bag on the linoleum and helped myself to a sandwich from the fridge. I wasn't concerned. My mother tended to overreact. Whereas my father was the stolid, logical one, my mother was the dramatic one who liked to pretend life was a giant *telenovela* where she had center stage. I consoled myself with the knowledge that if the problem was serious, my mother would have called my cell phone or left a message with the school.

No, I thought, pouring a few potato chips on my plate. Mom probably wanted to remind me to take my vitamin D, or not consume any high fructose corn syrup while she was gone. Besides, I had more pressing concerns. Like studying for my Spanish test on Monday. Later. I relocated to the living room and switched on the TV. My dad had left the news on from this morning. A blond woman with too much hairspray was saying, "...secret terrorist organization was discovered due to an unlucky hacker's computer exploits — "

I paused with my finger hovering over the channel button then surfed some more. None of the other channels yielded anything more promising. I settled for reruns of old cartoon shows. During the next commercial break, I took my plate to the kitchen. My eyes went to my mother's note. I should call her so she wouldn't jump the gun and do something drastic like phoning the police. I punched the number, twirling the cord around my finger. For somebody who used to be a professional model, my mother was incredibly lacking in poise.

The connection was terrible. Grainy. I thought I could hear somebody speaking amidst the static. "Christina, this is…warning… must get out…house…possible…danger." The voice went dead. I heard a beep. I redialed the number. Warning? Danger? If I listened to the message a second time, it might make more sense.

"The number you have dialed is no longer in service. Please hang up and try again."

I dialed again, with exaggerated slowness.

"The number you have dialed is no longer in service. Please hang up and try again."

The hand holding onto the phone fell to my side. Distantly, I was aware of the phone smacking against the wall. I had always been told not to believe everything I heard. I'd also been told that the mind can play tricks on you when you are afraid. Those two things in combination should have been enough to quell my fears but they weren't. Even if the call meant nothing, even if it was a *hoax*, I was terrified. I was home alone, getting strange calls from somebody who did not sound like my parents. I wanted reassurance from an adult that I was going to be fine.

But my parents weren't here. They were halfway around the world by now — unless Renee had been right, and they'd decided to take a detour. Wherever they were, it wasn't here, and there was nobody else I could….Wait. I backpedaled. That wasn't quite true. Renee. I could call Renee at home and ask if I could spend the night at her house. Her parents were well-versed in my mom and dad's erratic behavior. I was sure they wouldn't object to me staying the weekend. If necessary, my parents would compensate them for their time and resources.

I could still hear that disembodied voice in my head, chilling me to the bone. It had sounded like the person on the other end was saying that I must get out of the house as soon as possible because of the danger. That didn't make any sense to me, though — wouldn't it be safer to be *in* the house? *Not if somebody was already inside.* I brushed that thought aside, where it retreated to my unconscious and darkened my mood like a thundercloud. *Okay, that's it. I'm getting out of this house.*

Dollface mobbed me, rubbing his face against my ankle. "Not right now." I scooped him up, ignoring the indignant mew he uttered in protest. "I'm going away for a while. Out you go."

I could hear his paws scrabbling against the glass as he mewed to be let back inside the house. I shook my head at him and stumbled up the stairs. My messenger bag was lying on the floor near my bed. I dumped all the school crap onto my comforter, making room for a nightshirt and an extra set of clothes. I hesitated, then packed my Spanish book. No point in tempting fate.

A sudden creak made me jump. I picked up my cell phone from the nightstand and started to dial. My hands were trembling. The sooner I got this over with, the better I'd feel.

I waited as Renee's phone rang…and rang…and *rang*, before taking me to voice mail. "Hello, this is Renee. I'm not here right now but if you leave a message, I'll get back to you as soon as I can."

"Hi, Renee. This is Christina. I was just wondering — "

The only warning I got was a flash of black in the mirror over my dresser, as if one of the shadows in my bedroom had come to life. In the time that it took me to blink, he grabbed me and my cell phone, which had been in my hand, clattered to the floor. Disbelief gave way to utter terror and I inhaled reflexively for a scream that never got released.

A gloved hand had closed over my mouth. I could taste leather. "No," I screamed, "No, no, no — " before my words just dissolved into incomprehensible shrieking that not even the glove could mask. Something hard and cylindrical pressed against my temple.

"Be quiet. It's not in my interests to hurt you, but I will." The voice was sexless, emotionless, and lacked any discernible human characteristics, including mercy. Is your name Christina Parker? Nod yes or no."

I nodded, staring at my flowery mattress, which was starting to blur before my eyes.

"Are you alone?"

Yes, I was utterly and inescapably alone. Should this man know that? He'd already made it quite clear that laws meant nothing to him. He'd broken into my house and now he had a gun up to my head. What if he was going to rape me as well? What if he was going to *kill* me?

Please, God, let me get out of this and I swear, I'll start going to church again. I'll lose the twenty pounds my mother keep insisting on. Just don't let him hurt me. Please, please, *don't let him hurt me.*

I jumped, unable to hold in the cry that escaped my lips as my phone exploded into dozens of twisted metal shards that pelted against my leggings like shrapnel from a fallout, creating a stinging sensation I experienced through rubber skin.

"I don't miss twice." The small fragments crunched beneath his shoes as he shifted his weight. "Are you alone?"

I nodded my head, feeling as if I had signed my own death warrant. Perhaps I had.

"Good." There was a hot stinging pain, a flash of light, and then I blacked out.

Michael:

I caught her as she slumped forward, set the gun down on the floor, and pulled a silk, paisley tie out of my trouser pockets to bind her wrists behind her back. Then I adjusted the complimentary eye mask I'd received from the airline over her face. A thorough search of her school bag yielded nothing dangerous, though I removed the Spanish book. She wouldn't be needing it, in any case. Not where she was going.

The girl groaned. I eyed her, waiting for any sudden movements or surprise attacks. Nothing. She was out. I watched her a few minutes longer before turning to her dresser. It was littered with pictures and expensive baubles. Her family was well-off. *Too* well-off, even if her mother was a designer. I filed that away. Richardson would be interested to hear that, I imagined. I stuffed more clothing into her bag. Slung it over my shoulder. The girl was too heavy to carry with the bag; I settled for dragging her down the stairs.

Rubens Parker had a nice house. Low-key, with tasteful furnishings. He had done away with several thousand dollars, stealing from various companies by means of a special virus that deducted small increments of money from the payroll. The increments were small, mere fractions of a penny, but the totals added up over time. Fortunately, the IMA did all their transactions with cash, so this was not a problem for us. His hubris, however, was.

In the living room I opened my briefcase, revealing a small metal box with a black display panel. When I pressed a small button a series of digits appeared in red with a beep. I pressed the button again and the numbers began to count down from 15:00. Someone would hear the explosion. One of the neighbors probably had the number to the Parkers' hotel. When their daughter failed to show up for school on Monday they would think the girl had died in the blast. When they found out she was alive, in our possession, we would undoubtedly have their full cooperation. How much would they be willing to pay to save their lovely daughter?

Information was valuable. So was a child's life.

I hoisted the girl into the backseat of the company-issued black sedan. I had prepared for the occasion: I had jammed the locking mechanisms on each of the passenger doors and replaced all the windows with bulletproof glass. Not that I expected gunfire but one could never be too careful, and I didn't want her getting hold of a blunt object and smashing her way to freedom. There was a nasty bump forming where I'd pistol-whipped her but otherwise she was in perfect condition. Richardson wouldn't have my ass over one measly bruise; I'd gotten his quarry.

I pulled out my phone. *Subject acquired. Proceeding to step 2.*

When I was sure the message had been sent, and received the answering message — *Proceed* — I dropped the phone on the ground. Got into the car. Backed up. Made sure to crush the phone beneath the wheels. Another pained sound came from the backseat. I didn't envy the headache she was going to have when she regained consciousness. Or her thirst.

I bought a red sports drink at a gas station mart, which I paid for in cash. In the parking lot, I freed a white packet from my jeans. The packet contained a white powder, which I shook into her drink to keep it from settling. To my satisfaction, the opaque red liquid was viscous enough that it concealed the remnants of any powder that hadn't dissolved.

Perfect.

Twelve minutes later, I heard the scream of sirens in the distance. But try as they might, the only evidence the police would turn up was rubble and the crushed remains of a black cell phone.

Christina:

I woke up paralyzed. Had I gotten all tangled up in my sheets again? Then a violent burst of pain exploded from just beneath my ear and it all came flooding back — the strange man — the gun — my phone being blown apart. Over the sound of my racing heart I could make out the faint but unmistakable purr of a car's engine and somebody else's breathing. I thought I had a pretty good idea who that somebody else was.

An odd noise left my mouth as I twisted around, trying to free myself, trying to find out why I couldn't see. "Who's there?" I cried. "Where am I? What did you *do* to me?"

"There's no need for you to see where we're going."

The sound of that familiar voice made me jerk in place; it was the voice of the man who had held me at gunpoint in my bedroom and then knocked me unconscious. He was no longer speaking in a whisper, but it was definitely the same man. The implication of his words took a moment to sink in. "What do you mean? Where are you taking me?"

No response.

Why *was* I being kidnapped? My family wasn't powerful, or interesting. My father spent all day in front of computers deciphering, writing, and rearranging code. We had our flaws but we were good people, for the most part. There were no skeletons in our closets. I couldn't figure out what I had done to draw this dark man into my life, but his silence allowed me to jump to my own terrifying conclusions.

I'm not sure how long we drove before he stopped — it could have been hours, minutes. With the blindfold, I had no way of telling what time of day it was. I heard the car door slam and then my door opened. Something hard and plastic touched my lips. I jerked my head back, causing warm liquid to soak into the front of my dress. "What *is* that?"

"Gatorade. Drink it." His voice was hard and brooked no argument. I thought he might have a faint accent but if he did, he hid it well. That could be useful, if I got away.

That seemed like a pretty big if.

"I'm not thirsty."

"You'll be anything I damn well say you are." He pinched my nose until I was forced to open my mouth to breathe and poured in the drink. I gagged the cloyingly sweet liquid down. It certainly *tasted* like Gatorade but what if it was poisoned? Why would he go through the whole process of kidnapping me just to kill me?

"It isn't poisoned. One more sip."

I spat out the drink in the direction his voice had come from, hoping it would hit his face. He squeezed my jaw. His fingers were gloveless now, and the intimate contact filled me with disgust. "Now you listen to me. I don't think you know who you're dealing with."

I said a rude phrase to him in Spanish involving his mother and a goat. Pain flared up my cheek. "One of my men is stationed right outside your parents' hotel. He's waiting in a black sedan, wearing a Hawaiian shirt, sharpening a knife. All I have to do is give the word and you'll be an orphan."

I forgot how to breathe. "You're a monster." His hand left my face. I heard the unmistakable sound of someone punching in a phone number. My heart stuttered. "No — stop! Don't hurt them!"

My captor said nothing but, to my relief, he had ceased dialing. "I'll drink it…" I said. "Please…don't…"

The Gatorade was warm, as if he'd kept it in the car all day, and tasted of generic fruit. I swallowed it all with a grimace and the door slammed again. I felt the car shift from his weight as he got back behind the wheel. *This* was the man in charge of my fate. I couldn't remember ever feeling this scared and helpless. "Why are you doing this to me?" I said in a small voice. I don't think he heard me. Even if he had, he might not answer. He'd made it pretty clear how much — how little, I should say — he valued my input.

Time marched on. The steady rumble of the car's engine made me want to go to sleep. I closed my eyes, feeling the darkness around me grow even darker. The forced "nap" had left me feeling even weaker and less rested than before. I was so tired…like I might just drift away. How could I even sleep at a time like this, with so much adrenaline in my system?

Oh no.

My eyes snapped open. "What was in the Gatorade?"

He didn't respond. A tight feeling formed in my stomach. No way he didn't hear me this time. What was happening to me was his doing — because he'd do *something* if it wasn't. Right? Maybe not. He was inhuman. He had to be. Nobody alive could possibly be this cold.

"*What* was *in* the *Gatorade*?"

"If I wanted to kill you, you'd already be dead, darlin."

Darling?

Whatever he had put in it was potent because I could feel the need for rest overwhelming me, as if my whole body was fatigued. The roar of the car grew fainter and fainter, until, at last, it disappeared, and sleep swallowed me up like a black hole.

Chapter Four

Deal

I stared ahead, on the cusp of consciousness, wondering why my head felt like a detonated bomb, and why my mouth tasted like cotton. The last I could remember, that nameless, faceless man threatened me and my parents, and then forced me to drink a sports drink that I hadn't even wanted….

I breathed through my nose, struggling to remain calm. Drugged Gatorade. He had drugged the Gatorade, which I had been foolish enough to drink. And now…I was here, alone, in a darkened room that smelled like old garbage. At least he'd removed the blindfold. I twisted around in an effort to see my surroundings and nearly blacked out again. The throbbing behind my temples and eyes increased sevenfold. It was as excruciating as if someone were having at my brain with a rusty bone-saw. Whether this was due to injury or an aftereffect of the drug, I couldn't say. Slowly, *carefully*, I rotated my head until I could see behind me.

The only light came from a dirt-smeared window situated about six feet above the concrete floor. I was in some kind of alcove, and the light didn't reach me. My half of the room was in shadow. The walls hadn't been filled in with plaster, exposing a labyrinthine network of wooden framing, pipes, and fiberglass that reminded me of the boiler room in the *Nightmare on Elm Street* movie. My right wrist was handcuffed to one of the pipes. A dull ache in my shoulder suggested I had been in this position for some time.

Tears formed in my eyes. I felt them course down my cheeks and spatter my thigh through the leggings. I was being held captive by a man who didn't seem to care whether I lived or died. My head hurt. I thought I might throw up. I wanted to *go home*. "I want to go home," I said aloud, and I flinched at the sound of my own voice. I couldn't give into this panic.

Or I'd die.

A door opened, spilling a yellow rectangle of light over me. I shrank back against the wall, wishing I had the power to melt through it, and squeezed my watering eyes shut against the brightness. Footsteps were approaching, halting a few feet away. A shadow blocked out some of the light, and something hit the floor with a slap that made me jump. "I know you're awake."

Did he have cameras down here to watch me in my misery?

I cracked open an eye. By this point, most of the pain had subsided. I could make out his worn, black boots. My eyes moved upwards, taking in a body that was both powerful and intimidating. The thick black jacket he had been wearing earlier was gone, and so was the gun. He was wearing a white undershirt, yellowed in some places from sweat, and stonewashed jeans. He had no tattoos, no piercings, no distinguishing markings of any kind — except the mask. It covered the top half of his face, leaving only his mouth visible.

He was still looking at me. I lowered my eyes, studying what he had dropped at my feet. A manila envelope. The instructors at Holy Trinity used similar ones to store the attendance roster. *I doubt he's here because he wants to take roll.*

"Please. Where am I?"

Instead of answering, he dropped to his knees and opened the envelope. A permanent marker and a switchblade clattered to the floor. *A knife? He brought a knife? Is he going to kill me?*

Maybe he was just hoping to intimidate me. It was working. I winced at the painful dryness of my throat. At this point, I'd gladly take some Gatorade — drugged, or no.

"What are you going to do to me?"

"That depends entirely on you…and your parents."

"My parents? What do they have to do with this?"

"Everything." His voice was cold.

"I have no idea what you're talking about."

"Really." I could see him stacking what he knew against what he could tell me. "Let's start small." He dropped to one knee, so our faces were level. "What do your parents do for a living?"

His shoulders were quite broad and I could see the contours of his washboard abs beneath his grungy shirt. The man was fit — no, more than fit. Fit meant working out at the gym. He had a body adapted for thug work. So what was he? A government agent? A mafioso? A terrorist?

"Well?"

I still hadn't answered his question.

"My mother designs clothes," I snapped, because I had a feeling he knew this already. "And my dad has a cubicle job — he's nobody you know."

He hit me. The blow was open-handed, but it *stung*.

"Don't get cute with me."

"You hit me."

His face said he'd do it again. "Why did your parents jump on an international flight? Where did they go?"

I pressed my hand to my cheek. "What international flight?" I couldn't believe he hit me.

I hadn't forgotten about the gun — but guns were impersonal. An intermediary. It took a different kind of mentality to use your bare hands to hurt someone. One that might be worse.

"Our last record of them shows them leaving a plane in a Canadian airport."

"I don't know anything about that! I thought they were in Hawaii — that's what *you* said!"

We glared at each other — him, furious and impatient; me,

scared and defiant, with a growing sense of panic. The slap had knocked more than just pain into me. *Did he lie?*

"They must have been expecting an attack." Him speaking softly was scarier than him yelling. "Perhaps somebody told them we were coming. One of your neighbors. Or a friend with connections. It's the perfect cover. Plan a vacation. Change of plans at the last minute. And yet…one thread hangs loose. They leave you behind."

"Are you implying my parents used me as *bait*?"

"It *would* look suspicious, wouldn't it, pulling their daughter out of school? No, they had to leave you behind to maintain some semblance of normalcy. But they released the maid, the gardener… everyone but you. I don't need to imply anything, darlin. The message is loud and clear. They screwed you over; they threw you to the fucking wolves."

I pulled away from him. "Stop it! You're lying!"

He said nothing. He didn't need to; he'd already planted the seed of doubt. He just needed to be patient, let it take root.

"You're wrong," I said. "You have no idea what you're talking about. You don't even know them, you don't know what they're *like* — "

"I've seen their kind a thousand times before."

"But — "

"On *both* ends of the deal," he added.

Cloak and Dagger by Nenia Campbell

No. My mother and father would never do anything like that. He was just trying to put distance between us so I would be willing to betray them. Yes, that sounded about right. Well, it wasn't going to work. I wouldn't let him manipulate me.

"I've seen your kind before, too, Christina. You look like a good girl. Smart. I bet you follow all the rules. Well, follow mine and you'll be just…fine."

"Why do you need me? I thought you had a man outside their hotel." He shot me an impassive look. So he *had* lied. It was so obvious now. If he knew where they were, he would be there instead of here. My God, I was such an idiot. "I don't know where they are."

He regarded me through the holes in the mask. His eyes were green — acid green. Caustic. "I think you know more than you're letting on. And I suggest" — he grabbed my face, digging his fingers into the hollows of my jaw — "I *suggest* you cooperate."

"I told you I don't know where they are!" I tried to pull away. "Let go!"

"If you think being out of the country makes your parents safe, you're wrong. My organization does not have a specific jurisdiction. Your parents will not escape — and you are not doing yourself any favors by protecting them." He shoved me away.

Fresh tears burst from my eyes. My shoulder was on fire. "Why should I help you?"

"Because I will hurt you if you don't."

God help me, I believed him.

"I don't know where they are. I'm telling the truth. I can't help you — I *can't*!"

"That's where you're wrong."

"But I ju — "

"Do you know what a bargaining chip is?"

"What? No. No, no, *no*. My father would never negotiate with a killer. Never."

He picked up the knife, twirling it in his hand. The blade snapped out at me with a *click*. "Not even if his daughter's life was on the line?" I felt the flat side of the blade beneath my ear, raising a line of buckled skin. But not cutting.

Not yet.

"His very naïve, very *expendable* daughter's life?"

I tried to plead, to beg him not to hurt me, but the words lodged in my throat like barbed wire.

"I think he would, darlin."

He was right. I couldn't believe I had been so *stupid*. I pressed my lips tighter, trying not to tremble when his gloved hand dragged through my hair, pulling it free from the messy bun. My hair tumbled to my shoulders. He held up a strand in his fingers, examining it in the light.

"W-what are you doing?"

"Pretty color," he remarked. "Distinctive." Before I could blink he had hacked off three inches and slipped it into the empty baggie that had previously contained the knife.

Evidence. I thought desperately. "They might not believe it's mine."

He picked up the sharpie and began writing on the envelope. "I also have photographs."

Fumes from the marker filled the air, making my eyes sting. "I don't believe you."

He produced a crumpled sheet of paper and wrote on that as well. *Is that my ransom note?* My gut twisted around as I watched the letters span across the page. Did he really have photographs? When had he taken them? I hadn't seen a camera.

"What if you can't find my parents? What if they get away from you and your men?"

He didn't look up. "I have never failed before."

"But if *they* do?"

He lifted his eyes from what he was writing and looked at me. Then he left the room.

Michael:

Foolish girl, with her foolish questions. Did she have a death wish?

A red Toyota was stalling out front. Standing in front of the truck was a man dressed like a hiker. Faded jeans. Button-down shirt. Canvas backpack. But he wasn't a hiker, and I would have bet money that he was carrying at least two conceals. If not more.

"Hey. Nice mask."

He was also a smart-ass.

I held out the envelope. He turned it over in his bare hands, like a child with a fucking present on Christmas Eve. Jesus. He wasn't even wearing *gloves.* "You're gonna get that dirty."

He held out his clean hands with an affronted look.

For fuck's sake. "Fingerprints."

His face went red. Apparently he hadn't taken this into account. He slammed his backpack on the hood of the car and tugged out a pair of worn leather gloves. "See any quail?"

A message had just been sent to my cell with a series of phrases I had committed to memory before destroying the phone. He was asking, *Did you get the information we needed?* Communications always managed to come up with some cute little theme for their codes. This time around it was "nature." It should have been "I need to get fucking laid."

I glanced at the safe house. "No. I'll find some soon. I've been looking hard."

Torture wasn't my style. It was messy, and captives would blurt out any information they thought their interrogators wanted to hear, whether or not it was true. After two hours with Callaghan, a man might recall crimes that he never committed. I preferred a combination of scare tactics and mild physical assault. I tended to get better results with the *threat* of torture rather than the actual act itself.

The girl would be a difficult case. Not because I didn't think I could break her — I could, easily — but because she had to remain functional after I did it. When I took her to base, she would be evaluated by one of our psychologists to see if she was in a mental state where she could answer questions rationally. As frustrating as it was to proceed at this grueling pace, I had to respect the orders of my superiors. Even if I disagreed with them.

Especially if I disagreed with them.

The girl could use a good scare, though. She didn't appear to grasp the seriousness of her situation. I got the feeling she believed, on some basic level necessary for survival, that this was a nightmare she was going to wake up from. I needed to shatter that illusion.

"Maybe you're looking in the wrong place," the agent was saying.

I tore off my mask. "*You* don't question my methods. You just do as you're told. Is that clear?" His eyes widened in recognition. He bobbed his head. "Good."

"But…the quarry…Mr. Richardson will be wanting answers. What should I tell him?"

"You can tell your boss that he'll get his answers, but I need more time with this one."

He nodded quickly and got back behind the wheel. I watched him tear out of the clearing, filling the clean mountain air with the smell of burning rubber. I snorted, slipped the mask back in place, and started towards the safe house. For her sake, she had better start speaking — and soon. I wasn't sure I had the patience to wait much longer.

Christina:

Days passed without word from my parents.

Part of me took pleasure in the fact that they had managed to elude capture. But if my captor was as good as he claimed, we were all still in terrible danger. Especially me. I worried about them every day, but I worried about myself every *second*. After all, he already had me.

My captor had barely said one word to me since he had delivered his latest threat. It had been recent. Yesterday. Or the day before that. All the days blended together. My captor had come down to deliver my breakfast. He got too close, and I launched myself at him, digging my nails into his neck as hard as I could. He managed to pry me off, making me wish more than ever than I had both hands free. I went without breakfast that morning. Lunch brought a single glass of water. It was drugged. When I woke, he was there, setting my food down as if nothing had happened. There was a bandage on his throat. He reached into his pocket and showed me a fingernail clipping, with chipped red polish. "Next time," he said, "You lose a finger."

With the exception of bathroom breaks, which were few and far between, I remained chained up like a dog. I had the feeling that I smelled like one, too. A viscous membrane of grime surrounded me. When was the last time I had taken a shower? My hair was starting to feel wet, and when I ran my fingers through the matted strands they stuck up in clumps.

The bathroom contained a shower. The spigot was orange with rust, the tiles discolored by mildew, but I suspected it worked. My captor didn't have greasy hair. I planned my course of action accordingly, playing up the cooperative hostage bit to the point where he asked me, "What the hell are you up to?" I swallowed the question and shrugged, postponing my request until the next meal where I asked, in a suitably cowed voice, "Can I take a shower?"

"A shower?" He scoffed. "That why you've been so cooperative?"

I thought about denying it. No. With my luck, I'd anger him by lying and he would withhold showers as punishment. Then I'd be back to square one. "Please?"

He set the sandwich and the bottle of water down with a clatter. "This isn't a hotel."

"But I'm filthy," I protested. "I won't try to escape. Please. I just want to get clean. What if I get sick?" I tacked on, pouncing on his one weakness. He couldn't want me to fall ill if I was the bargaining chip. If something happened to me, he would lose that leeway with my parents. He couldn't afford that. Right? *Right?*

"No." He left the room. I sank into filthy despair.

Hours later, he returned with a key. I'd been crying and jumped when I heard him, swiping the tears from my eyes. He always managed to catch me with my head down. "Don't make me regret this." He unlocked the cuffs and yanked me along like a pull-toy. I barely noticed — or cared. All I could think about was the warm water and how good it would feel on my skin. And soap. *Soap.* Lovely white scented lather.

My happiness popped like a soap bubble. What was I thinking? I'd achieved nothing except making myself look even more pathetic and helpless than before. Worse, I'd shown him he could manipulate me. Jesus had been betrayed for thirty pieces of silver. I'd betrayed myself for *soap.* If he was even planning on giving me any. I wished I hadn't pleaded quite so hard now.

But I couldn't resist asking, greedily, "Do you have soap?"

"Yes. Mine. You can use some."

His? I said nothing.

The rest of the house was as shoddy as the basement. The carpet was burnt orange, the beige paint on the walls was cracked and peeling. All the windows were curtained, or so smeared it didn't matter. I wondered whether his intent was keeping me from seeing out, or others from seeing in. Both? Did that mean we were someplace where there were others around *to* see in?

We went past the living room. I caught a glimpse of cheap furniture through the rails of the staircase, a couple of bookshelves. There was a laptop on a desk but the screen was black. If he had a computer, we weren't completely removed from civilization. He had to plug that laptop in somewhere. And I'd seen him with a phone.

With that thought in mind, I allowed him to steer me to the bathroom. It was one of the worst rooms for wear. The counter was cheap fake marble that looked like plastic. The casing on the pipes certainly was. The floor was real ceramic but so chipped that the wood beneath was exposed in places. How could he stand to live like this? I pulled the shower curtain aside, checking for bugs or, God forbid, *rats*, and felt a stab of panic when he didn't leave.

"Um...you can go."

"Nice try," he said.

"You mean…you're staying?" I asked, appalled. "Here?"

"You hard of hearing?" He wasn't just trying to scare me, he was *serious*. He was really going to stand there and watch me while I showered. Even if the curtain was somewhat opaque, the thought of him being there while I was naked was terrifying. He read the look on my face and snorted. "Don't flatter yourself, darlin. You don't have anything I haven't seen before."

I started to cry. I couldn't help it. The tears just fell of their own accord.

"Would you rather go without a shower? 'Cause that is the only other option."

I swallowed hard and nodded, shaking loose the tears clinging to my chin.

"Oh, Jesus fucking Christ." I peered up through my wet eyelashes. He looked disgusted. "Just give me your goddamn clothes."

I clutched the hem of my dress. "W-what?"

"Your clothes. The fabric protecting your goddamn feminine modesty." He nodded toward a towel hanging on the metal rail. "Take them off, wrap yourself in that, and then give them to me. It isn't fucking rocket science."

Was it a trick? "

"Will you … leave first?"

"You have thirty seconds." He held up a finger. "*Ten* if I hear another word."

It wasn't until the door slammed behind him that I was able to breathe.

I disrobed as fast as I could. The dress was easy, the leggings were harder. I had a hard time rolling them off my thighs with my shaking hands. I had barely gotten the towel wrapped around me when the door burst open. My captor took the soiled clothes, exchanging them for a small square of soap. "Hurry it up," he said. Then he left, and the room plunged into silence.

The shower was wonderful. I didn't dare stay in there long enough for the water to heat up properly for fear he'd lose patience and barge in, but I'd never appreciated washing more. By the time I finished with my hair alone, I had almost no soap left. The dirt and stale sweat were scrubbed away. I was much cleaner than before. I wrapped myself in the towel again and opened the door. My captor was leaning against the opposite wall with a bundle of clothes under his arm. His posture was watchful but relaxed.

The stance of a predator at rest.

He straightened when he heard the squeak of the door hinges and clicked his tongue at the puddle of water at my feet. "Fucking water everywhere — go on, get dressed." He dropped the pile of clothes in my arms. They weren't the ones I'd left him with but I recognized some of them: a black shirt I'd worn the last time I went on a date, my third-best pair of *Lucky* jeans, my underwear —

"Where did you get these?"

"It's time to send your parents another picture."

"Did you steal these from my room? Did you go back to my *house*?"

"We need one where you look alive." He glanced over his shoulder. "Hurry up."

Chapter Five

Control

His treatment of me became increasingly unfeeling. He seemed disgusted by me. Disgusted and resentful, since he had no qualms about insulting me, tossing off a few casual threats, or even landing a few open-handed blows on my face and body for good measure.

Resisting, fighting back, hadn't worked. I couldn't seize control from him. Not by force.

I should have run when I had the chance, I thought. *Back at the house...I should have kicked him in the balls and found a phone to call the police. I should have done* something.

But I hadn't — because in the end, I had been too afraid.

Now, it was too late.

"Look at the camera, darlin. Show me that pretty face."

I hung my head. If he saw the rebellion in my eyes, he'd stomp out what resilience still remained. His flat affect was like a black hole; sucking away all emotions, leaving a void where the fear could take hold. It was tempting to sink into apathy, to lull myself with the thought that I no longer cared what happened. But that was a lie. I knew I wanted to live.

But time had become my enemy. I had both too much and too little. The more I tried not to think about its passing, the more it pressed down upon me, like an insufferable weight. I tried singing songs in my head. Then fairy tales. Then, when I had exhausted my repertoire, scriptures that had been drilled into me from both Sunday school and confessional. I soon stopped, though; they gave me no comfort. This dark, sunless place was out of even God's reach, and each word seemed to be echoed by the devil's own laughter.

His cell phone rang the day after he took the photographs, while he was bringing me water. He set the bottle on the ground, just out of reach, and took the call in another room. Usually these discourses lasted a couple minutes. He was gone for much longer than that.

The water bottle sweated beads of condensation. The need to drink surfaced. I didn't pay attention. For once the dryness in my mouth didn't seem to be caused by thirst. The calls *never* took this long. Something was wrong.

Over the pounding of my heartbeat, I heard the creak of his footsteps on the stairs. I turned towards the door. He glanced at me, then at the untouched bottle of water, which he nudged towards me with his boot. He wasn't talking — that was bad. He always froze over when he received a piece of news that displeased him. And then he took it out on me.

As he turned to leave, I said in a cracking voice, "Wait."

The grit beneath his soles crunched as he turned to face me.

"My parents." I took a sip of water, gagging on the mineral edge. "What about them?"

"We got them."

Those three words turned my blood to ice. I set the bottle aside, not noticing when it toppled, sending the precious water coursing away from me in shadowy rivulets. "You mean you captured them?"

"No. It's only a matter of time. The phone call came from somewhere near the Canadian border." He glanced down at me. "I suppose yesterday's photo shoot must have been convincing."

I flinched. "You're lying."

"What reason do I have to lie to you?"

Clearly, he was forgetting that he had lied to me already — several times — which was the reason I was currently chained to a pipe.

A horrible wailing pierced the air. It took a moment to realize it was coming from me. My parents were still alive, but it was unlikely I'd ever get to say goodbye. The last exchange I'd had with my mom had been a vicious argument, where I'd told her I hated her. My captor started to shimmer around the edges, blurring behind my tears. I made no move to stop them. My heart was breaking, and the jagged pieces were cutting me all up inside.

"Your tears won't do them any good."

"Why can't you just leave us alone?" I screamed.

The blurred form shook its head. "You are a stupid girl."

Yes, I was. Stupid to think he was capable of granting any kind of mercy.

"You're helping to pay off your parents' debt. Their greed is the reason you're here."

"Don't talk to me about greed, you bastard! You put a price-tag on my parents' lives! And you'd probably sell your own soul to make a cool million, too, you…you fucking hypocrite! At least my parents never killed anyone for money. You think you're so tough, so smart, so *right* just because you have a gun, but really, you're just a *cow* — "

In one stride he closed the distance between us and clamped his hand over my mouth. "Let's get one thing clear here, because your logic appears to have been clouded in the midst of your grief. You are talking about feelings. And *feelings* make you stupid. Yes, I have a gun. And if you continue to piss me off with your stupid sentimental bullshit, I am going to use that gun on you."

I spluttered and tried to pull free. He gave me a shake.

"I could care less how you feel about me, darlin. I only have to make sure you remain unscathed long enough for us to find your parents and use you as currency. After that, it doesn't matter what happens to you and all your bleeding-heart sentiments. You'll be a loose end. Maybe we'll let you live — or maybe, we'll just kill you. Welcome to my world. It's called Reality. Buy some property and settle down, 'cause you're gonna be here for a long fucking time."

He pulled away, wiping his hand on his pants.

I'd rather be a bleeding heart than have no heart at all.

As if he could read my mind, he added, "Don't think that your so-called status gives you license to sit here and insult me, making threats you don't have the ability to carry out. Like I said, you'll only end up pissing me off and trust me; you don't want that."

Something snapped then, as if the pain had roused some sleeping beast inside me.

"You're pathetic."

I'd said it under my breath but he'd heard me, because part of me had *wanted* him to hear me, and his eyes narrowed. "What was that? You have something you want to share with the rest of the class?" Part of my brain cried out that he was too close — that I was going to make him mad — that he was already mad — and that I shouldn't push my luck, just cash in my chips and stop *now*. But by then it was too late. Even if I wanted to, I couldn't reclaim my words.

My anger and grief were spiraling out of control and I was caught in the undertow.

"I said you're pathetic, you worm."

I paused for air.

(Don't say it.)

"You're lower than life."

Michael:

As any forest ranger will tell you, even the smallest spark is capable of culminating into a raging inferno under the proper circumstances. I had been insulted thousands of times, in a multitude of languages; it came with the job. But this girl was good at pushing my buttons — and there was a spark in her eyes, a little streak of defiance, that suggested she wasn't throwing words around. She was perceptive, selective; she *meant* them.

And she fucking pissed me off.

I straddled her hips, pinning her down to the basement floor. I waited until she tired herself out enough to calm down, then forced her to look me in the eye. She didn't like that. Too bad. "Take a long, hard look around you. You want to talk about pathetic? You're the one chained to the goddamn pipe."

I stopped, making sure she was still paying attention. She was.

"If you want that to change, as I imagine you do, I suggest you start cooperating with me and stop fucking fighting me at every goddamn turn. It *is* your own fault that you're here. Whether you believe that or not doesn't matter. What I want matters. And what I want is information."

"I'm not going to sell out my parents — and I already told you everything I know!"

She didn't seem to realize the contradiction in her words. Foolish girl.

"I have trouble believing that." I paused a beat. "You know anything about Greek mythology?" She went absolutely still beneath me. "Of course you have. Ever hear of something called Pandora's box?"

Terror lit up her entire face. She tried to play it off. She was a poor actor. "I took mythology in school."

"Your daddy was interested in Greek mythology, too. He sent us a little greeting card with a bit of Greek mythology. A greeting card that blew out some expensive and irreplaceable data. You know why, Christina? Because he saw something he didn't like. And if you don't start coming clean with me, I'm going to show you things that *you're* not gonna like."

I tightened my grip on her shoulders, which had started to quake.

"It's your choice, darlin. You can talk willingly, or" — I trailed my fingers down her jaw — "I can loosen your tongue a bit for you."

She headbutted me.

I dodged but her attack had other unexpected effects when her hips smacked up against mine, sending a burst of white-hot electricity pulsing through my bloodstream on collision.

"Cut that out."

She was beyond listening. She did it again, with more force this time. Had she actually connected with my skull, there would have been pain. Lots of it. I drew in an unsteady breath; it was like taking a hit. *She's a fucking kid. She's a hostage and she's a fucking* kid.

"Get the hell off me," she was shouting. "Get off of me, you filthy son of a — "

I slapped her, barely registering the squeal of pain. "Cut it out," I repeated, "Before you make me do something we'll both regret."

"Go to hell!" Her head knocked against mine. There was a brief, explosive pain as sudden and shocking as if I had been zapped by lightning, and I heard a growl in my throat. Okay, I was officially pissed. That fucking hurt. I turned to glare at her.

Her eyes had narrowed to blue slits. There was a flush in her dark skin, noticeable even in the half-light. I was suddenly painfully aware of her warmth, of the smell of my soap in her hair. For the first time, I noticed the girl cleaned up rather nicely. Too nicely for my peace of mind.

In fact…she was striking.

I leaned in closer, letting my hands fall on either side of her, caging her between my arms. How hadn't I noticed before? God, her *lips*. Her eyes widened, the pupils huge in the darkness. I let my gaze fall to her mouth. "I warned you," I said, very softly.

The IMA frowned on using hostages for what it called "recreational purposes" — something that, to this day, remains one of the best euphemisms for fucking that I've ever heard. Whatever you called it, it was unprofessional and distorted the relationship between captor and captive. This rule wouldn't have been a problem for me, except that it had been several months since I'd been this close to a woman and all that friction had gotten me hard.

Her expression changed, all the anger and hostility drained as if I'd yanked out an emotional plug, leaving only fear. Oh, part of her knew what I was thinking, in that uncanny way women have, and she didn't like it. At all. For the first time in her miserable little mind, I represented an imminent threat, not a distant one.

Well. She had asked for it.

Christina:

There are doors that shouldn't be opened. My father had opened one of these doors. Now, in spite of his warnings, I had gone and done the same.

I tried to slap him. He blocked the attack, pinned my arm down, and *bit* me. Hard. My head spun as the coppery taste of my own blood filled my mouth. While I was reeling from that he slipped off his shirt and began working on the buttons of mine. Nobody had ever hit me or hurt me in any other way — at least, not before *him* — and in previous conflicts, I'd been able to talk my way out. I had lived a sheltered life, free from violence.

That just made this more horrific. "What are you doing?"

"What do you think?" He ran his free hand through my hair, yanking it back from my face. I stilled when his lips touched my neck and the rough stubble around his mouth scraped at my skin. Terror replaced the blood flowing in my body. I wondered if he could feel my racing pulse. If he *enjoyed* my terror.

"Okay," I choked. "Okay, you win. I'll tell you anything… anything you want to know."

He lifted his head, and his nose brushed mine. "That's a load of bullshit, darlin."

"*Please*. Please. D-don't rape me. Please."

"I warned you." His hands were rough. "But now you have me all excited."

I curled my fingers into claws, aiming at the holes in his mask. He whipped his head to the side, so my nails raked against his cheek instead of gouging his eyes. An expression of mild surprise flickered across his face before he reverted to an emotion I was far more familiar with:

Anger.

I shivered at the raw hatred I saw there. The way he looked at me — as if he would happily kill me at that moment — was so terrifying that it took me a moment to realize *why* I could so his emotions so clearly. His mask had come off in my hand. With a startled scream I threw it aside as if it were skin I held in my fingers, not fabric. The mask fell to the stone floor without a sound as I looked upon my captor's face for the first time.

I had childishly convinced myself that the reason he hid his face was because he was either old or ugly, that his exterior matched his cruel interior. It had been foolish thinking — like I said, the thoughts of a child — but I was still surprised at being proved wrong.

He was startlingly young, with strong patrician features. His face was so warped with anger, it was impossible to discern his age. Twenties? Thirties? I stared at him in mute fascination, unable to take my eyes away even though I knew that the longer I stared, the more I incriminated myself. He was so...*normal*-looking. Nothing about him betrayed his stunning lack of regard for the human race. Not outwardly.

"That was a very stupid thing to do." He groped for me and squeezed hard. That broke the spell pretty quickly. I winced and looked away. "Now you'll never be able to leave this place alive."

"What? But — "

"*Shut up.*" His breathing was so labored, he could barely speak. He took a moment to compose himself. "Do you want your parents to die?"

"No," I whispered.

"Then do yourself a favor" — his callused hand slid down my stomach; I hated my stomach. I hated *him* — "and stop gambling with their lives. Understand?"

"Yes." My voice sounded small.

"I want to hear you say it."

"I...I understand," I sobbed.

"Good. Now shut up."

His mouth crashed down on mine, as if my sobs were something he could devour, and I realized he was right: I hadn't had any idea what he was capable of. I was beginning to find out. He fumbled with his belt. I heard the jangle of the buckle and closed my eyes.

I didn't want to watch anymore.

Please, God. Make it be over quickly.

His phone rang.

I held my breath.

Oh please, oh please, oh, please, please, please.

My captor swore. His weight lifted from me. He got to his feet in a fluid motion and left the room to answer his phone. I could hear his voice growing louder, instead of softer, as he climbed up the basement stairs — bad news. Just like him.

I waited until the rumble of his voice was out of earshot before refastening the buttons he'd undone. This simple task took me several minutes. *If the phone hadn't rang*, I kept thinking. *He would have done it. He would have raped me.*

A door slammed. Brisk footsteps came down the stairs. I stared at his shoes — black, scuffed-up combat boots — until his gloved fingers yanked my chin up, forcing me to look at him. He still wasn't wearing his mask but since he wasn't wearing his shirt, either, I was afraid that if my eyes dipped any lower he'd take it as a sign of submission or, worse, *encouragement.*

"When I get back we're going to resume this discussion, and you're going to tell me everything you know. There will be no further insults on your part — and you will *never* attack me again. Is that clear?"

"I hate you."

"You go ahead and do that, darlin. I don't care…as long as you keep your hands to yourself. But if you hit me, then I hit you back — twice as hard." He released my face, bending to pick his shirt up from the ground. As he pulled it over his head, he glanced at me. "The sooner you learn that, the easier it will be."

I didn't have a chance to ask him what he meant. I didn't see him again for hours, after crying myself into sleep, when I woke up exhausted, cold, and hungry, with a pressing urge to use the bathroom. My dreams had been consumed by nightmares but reality was worse. I couldn't escape from reality by waking up.

A door slammed inside the house. When he came down the steps, I wasn't sure whether to feel relieved or terrified. He had a bottle of alcohol, a roll of paper towels, a cell phone, and a small silver key. I knew what the key was for, but the purpose of the other objects was a mystery.

He dabbed the alcohol on the worst of my facial cuts, then unlocked my handcuff and did the ones on my wrist. He wasn't trying to be gentle, and I drew back from each painful burn until he tightened his grip and forced me to remain still. "You're going to make a phone call," he informed me, setting the alcohol aside. Out of my reach, I couldn't help noticing.

"I have to go to the bathroom."

The bathroom trip gave me some time to think, but only enough to make me realize how little I really knew. I suspected the call he wanted me to make was to my parents. Just thinking about speaking to them made my eyes tear up. I wouldn't be able to listen to my dad's voice without breaking down. I splashed some cold water on my face; it didn't help much. A familiar tightness was in my throat. Any moment now my captor would lose patience and give me the usual thirty second warning before busting the door.

"Hurry up," he said, right on cue.

We went to the living room instead of the basement. The orange carpet was even more hideous up close, mottled with a rainbow of stains. I looked at the desk: the laptop was gone. He wasn't taking any chances. "Sit." He pushed me onto the threadbare sofa and took the seat beside me. I scooted away, until I was pressed up against the arm. *The front door has to be around here somewhere.* I wanted to turn my head and look around but his posture was as rigid as a cobra poised to strike. If he got even the slightest impression I was planning on escaping, he'd hurt me.

Badly.

The phone he handed me was sleek and black and expensive-looking. I reached for it. He caught my wrist. His strong fingers were as constricting as any handcuffs. "I'll warn you once, and only once. Don't try anything cute like calling the police" — his hand tightened over mine — "If you do, what I'll do to you will make last night look like a tea party. Got that?"

"Yes," I whispered.

"Good. Here's the number…"

He reeled off a set of digits but I made no move to press the corresponding keys. It was like I'd been subjecting to a massive dose of Novocaine. His threat rang in my ears, and it was deafening. He shot me a fierce look, grabbed the phone, and punched in the numbers himself — so hard, I thought he'd break the phone in half.

"Remember what I said."

How can I forget?

I raised the phone to my ear. There was ringing. A man picked up on the second ring; it wasn't my dad. "Hello?" He had a smattering of an accent I couldn't place. "Who is this?"

My tongue felt like an arid desert.

"Hello?"

"Answer him," my captor hissed.

"Hi," I croaked. "This is…This is Christina — "

"What?" the man said. "Speak up, I can't hear you."

A bottle of water was thrust at me. I decided my captor wouldn't drug me while I was on the phone. I drained half of it in one gulp.

"I said, this is Christina *Parker*."

Voices murmured, conferring in the background. I started to wonder why my captor had made me call this number when I heard my mother's voice say, "Christina? Is that you? You are alive?"

"*Mamá*?" She sounded jaded and weary. Tears sprang in my eyes like clockwork. "Is Dad there?"

"Yes, he's here. He's fine. Are you? Where are you?"

The tears started to fall as concern for my parents' well-being was eclipsed by my own. "No, I'm not fine. Mom — *Mamá* — please, help me. Please. He's a monster."

"That's enough." He tried to grab the phone.

I clung on. "*Help*. He tried to — "

"I said, that's *enough*. Hello. Mrs. Parker-de-Silva, is it?" He leaned back against the couch, raking the hair out of his eyes as he kept them trained on me. "I'm the man who has your daughter. You've spoken to her. You've received photographic evidence that she is alive and well. And now — "

I heard her response. It was quite loud and didn't sound polite.

My captor shot me a menacing look. "She is lying. I haven't touched her."

"You son of a *bi* — "

Click.

He continued talking into the phone. Casually. Like he wasn't pointing a gun at me. "If you don't want that to change, I suggest you and your husband pull your heads out of your respective asses and get your act together. My employer is displeased with you two, and I am getting restless." He gestured for me to come closer.

I stared at the gun and stayed where I was.

"Come here," he demanded.

Mechanically, I shook my head.

He set the safety back on the gun and tucked it out of sight. *"Now."* I went. He handed me the phone and said, "I need you to repeat after me. Can you do that?"

"Can you do that?" I said obediently.

His hand closed around my wrist. *"Don't* toy with me."

"Christina?" My mother's disembodied voice floated from the receiver. I looked at the phone.

"Don't listen to her. Listen to me." He caught my other wrist. "Are you listening?"

I nodded.

"Say, 'Mom, I'm scared.'"

"*Mamá*, I'm scared."

"Me, too." She sounded faint.

"Now say, 'He wants the data that was stolen.'"

"He says he wants the data that was stolen."

An intake of breath.

"Mamá?"

No response. More whispering in the background.

"Did she hang up?"

I shook my head. He relaxed.

"Are you still there?" Her voice was a whisper, but she no longer sounded close to tears.

"I'm still here," I said, and waited.

My captor squeezed my wrist, which he still hadn't released, reminding me here was still here, too. "Tell them that if I don't get what I want from them by midnight tomorrow, I'll take what I want from you. Say it."

"Don't make me say that. Please. Not to my mother."

"*Say it.*"

"Please, no — "

He began to tug me closer with rough, painful jerks that made my shoulder ache.

"Let go!" I couldn't keep the terror out of my voice. "No!"
Ignoring me, he moved closer until I could taste his breath on my
tongue. I screamed. A bright exclamation came from the phone. I
stared at my captor's face and realized what he had been doing.
"You're *sick*."

"Say it."

I averted my eyes. "He says…he says if he doesn't get what he
wants by midnight tomorrow…he'll take what he wants from me," I
finished in a whisper.

My mother wailed. My captor took the phone from me, wincing
as Mamá let loose an ear-splitting curse. Good. I hoped he went deaf.

"Tomorrow, a colleague of mine will be waiting for you at the
Walk of Flags, in front of the Oregon State Capital. He won't be
alone. Others will be watching. So if you try to call the police he will
be gone and I will be informed."

I closed my eyes.

"See that you do, Mrs. Parker-de-Silva. I am not a patient man. I
might not make it to midnight."

I felt numb.

Drugged?

I no longer cared.

Chapter Six

Fever

Michael:

She stopped moving.

I reached for my gun, bracing myself for an attack. She slumped
against me. Unconscious. I reholstered the gun. She wasn't a good
liar; this seemed genuine. I reached out to take her pulse and her low
heartbeat confirmed this. Her skin was cool to the touch, a
characteristic symptom of shock. A fairly common response to high
levels of stress. Smelling salts were a quick means of reviving fainted
individuals. I had a ready supply upstairs but having Christina
unconscious simplified things. She had already provoked me once. I
did not want that to happen again.

I finished the negotiations with her mother, who was hurling
curses as if they were knives. The Dominican ex-model was a real
firebrand. It was easy to see where the girl got her attitude. Unlike
her daughter, Mrs. Parker-de-Silva seemed to be all talk. She was still
threatening me, even as I hung up the phone. Stupid woman. She
had better show up tomorrow for her daughter's sake. For both their
sakes. The two of them were wearing my nerves thin.

The girl was still unconscious. I took her pulse again; it was a
little slow but within the boundaries of normal. I picked her up and
carried her back down to the basement. I had no intention of letting

her remain in the living room, where escape would provide too much of a temptation. She was already starting to stir.

The girl groaned the moment she touched the cold stone floors. She didn't rouse. I decided to wait around until she regained consciousness...just in case there were complications. I pulled out my cell and started phoning the contacts who still owed me favors. All the numbers I needed had been committed to memory long ago. The best contacts valued secrecy — as did I. I wanted tomorrow to go off without a hitch. We had an image to preserve; my ass was on the line.

I called Kent first, a retired agent from the SIS. Retirement had been too quiet for him after three decades of work on the field. He had moved out of England, becoming a permanent expatriate, and turned to private investigation, offering his services to a small ring of exclusive contacts. I met him through one of our mutual clients and knew, from past experience, that his plans were always foolproof. "Everything ready?"

"Everything."

I had expected this answer but it still pleased me.

"Tomorrow, at the Walk of Flags — our man is going to be there?"

"I handpicked him myself."

"I trust your judgment."

"That means a lot, coming from you." Kent's voice was wry.

"We can't afford any screw-ups."

Kent hesitated. "There is one thing you should know…"

"What?"

"Your…quarry…made a phone call, shortly before you arrived on the scene."

I glanced at the girl, still collapsed at my feet. "I fail to see how that could be a problem. I destroyed her phone."

Kent coughed. "The problem is that the phone was recording a message up to the point you destroyed it. About a minute's worth. A case of poor timing if there ever was one," he added, in an attempt to be conciliatory.

The back of my neck prickled in alarm. "And the *problem*, Kent?"

"Her friend got the message. A girl named…let's see…Renee Patterson, if I'm not mistaken. She didn't like what she heard, so she called the police."

Shit. "What was on the message?"

"A rather desperate request, a scream, and a gunshot — in that order." Kent coughed. "Made the local papers. Everyone thought she was dead, killed in the blast. Now there's some speculation that she might still be alive."

I cursed, low in my throat, hoping Kent couldn't hear. If he could, he chose not to comment.

"Is this something that needs to be taken care of?"

"No. The girl knows nothing. I checked it out. Christina Parker was listed as missing by the police eight days ago. Her friend's phone call merely upped the amount of public interest, especially in her own county. I just wanted to point out that people are going to be looking for her — and you. If they haven't already started."

A thought occurred to me. "If the police report was eight days ago, why did her friend report the message now? It makes no sense to wait."

Kent laughed. "There's a perfectly innocent explanation for that. The girl ran up quite the extortionate phone bill. Her parents confiscated the mobile. She only just received it back. It's a dead end, Michael. One less detail to concern yourself with."

I pressed 'end' and stared at the phone before crushing it under my heel.

Christina:

The sound of crunching plastic woke me.

I stared at the plastic and metal fragments, then at his face. He didn't *look* angry, but I was beginning to suspect his moods were so unstable that there was actually a delay while his facial expressions caught up to his emotions. After all, he had just *destroyed* an expensive cell phone.

Cloak and Dagger by Nenia Campbell

He closed his eyes. I saw his chest rise and fall in quick succession. He reached into his jeans pocket just as nice as you please — and produced a brand new cell phone. I couldn't believe it. *He carries around spare cell phones in case he breaks one? Who is this guy?*

He punched in a number. "It's me. Yes. I just got off the phone with a contact — "

He never took his calls when I was in the same room. Never. Did that mean it didn't matter what I knew anymore? Was he going to kill me?

Maybe he thinks I'm still unconscious. Maybe he forgot I'm here.

No. I wasn't that lucky.

Was I?

"I don't care what he said. Finish the job now. That's a direct order." I found myself edging back from him, even though his anger wasn't directed at me. "Fine," he said. "You have three days until I come down there and finish the job for you. We do not tolerate traitors in this organization." He rammed the phone into his pocket and began scooping up the pieces of the broken phone.

I frowned suddenly, staring down at my wrist. *He didn't put the handcuff back on.*

"Hey. You awake over there?"

I sat up, keeping my hands in the shadows. "Hmm?"

"You fainted." He glanced at me, briefly, before turning his attention to the metal splinters.

"I did?" *Don't act too stupid. He'll get suspicious.*

His back was facing me, and I had a clear path to the stairs. I took a step towards them. If this was a trap, it was a poor one, riddled with potential loopholes. This man was not the type to overlook a loophole. That decided it for me. Not only had he neglected to cuff me, he'd also left the door open. I wasn't one to push my luck.

He was working at an efficient pace and still didn't turn around. There were a few chips to pick up and he was scooping them up, carefully, so he wouldn't cut himself on the sharp edges. The window of opportunity was closing. *He's almost finished!*

My first impulse was panic — but nothing draws attention faster than running away. Especially when running from someone accustomed to chasing people. Against every instinct, I continued at my slow pace. The stairs were about a foot away now. If I reached out, I'd just be able to touch the second step. I drew in a deep breath. *Please, don't turn around.*

He turned around.

"Where — "

He spotted me. The upper half of his body dropped into a lowered crouch. *No.* I bolted up the staircase, throwing all caution to the wind. He tossed the metal fragments aside. I heard the clang of the pan, the pieces as they scattered across the floor with a sound like sand. Then the pound of his boots against the squeaky basement steps.

He knew the house better than I did. He was stronger. I'd been banished to one section, kept on a minimal diet, and chained up to a wall — but I was desperate. I had to escape. Because I was fairly sure that if I didn't, he'd kill me. He wasn't speaking or issuing any threats. He didn't have to. The fact that he was running so fast said all that needed to be said.

He intended to catch me.

I went through the living room, to a kitchenette with only a fridge and a small stove. Outside the kitchenette was a small foyer and a watermarked door. I pitched myself at it, wrenching the handle in a choke hold. The door swung open and I fell off the porch, into an evergreen wonderland where golden sunlight dazzled my eyes. *So this is how Alice felt.*

Redwoods stretched as far as the eye could see. I caught a glimpse of mountains in the distance, still topped with virgin snow. Under other circumstances, I would have found such isolation beautiful, breathtaking, even, but now it chilled me to the bone. I was stranded here. With *him*. Nobody was around to save me.

Where is —

I caught the barest glimpse of movement before I went down.

He had caught up to me while I stalled, then tackled me from behind. My legs buckled under his weight and I fell, with him on top of me, getting a mouthful of pine needles and dead leaves. The air in my lungs was squeezed out as though from a tube of toothpaste.

No! Not when I was so close! I planted my hands on the mulchy ground and tried to push him off. My arms buckled, just as my legs had. I collapsed, promptly releasing any oxygen remaining in my lungs. He grabbed me by the shoulders and rolled me over so that I was on my back, facing the sky.

"I don't appreciate this."

I coughed, spitting out a dry leaf. "Please…" I gasped. "I can't…I can't *breathe*."

"You want to play rough? Fine. I can play rough." His hand dipped into the pocket of his jacket. I was expecting the gun, so when he pulled out a black case I was puzzled.

"What's that?" A note of hysteria wound its way through my voice.

He opened it at an angle so I could see what was inside: three hypodermic needles filled with a honey-colored liquid. He selected the one closest to him and flicked the glass to get the air bubbles out. "It'll knock the fight out of you for a couple hours."

I knocked the needle out of his hand. It smashed against a nearby rock. He hoisted himself higher, pinning my arms to my sides with his legs. Then he began unbuttoning my collar. "No!" My scream echoed through the trees and into the valleys, sending the birds nearby into a startled takeoff. I fought, thrashing my head, which earned me another backhanded slap.

"Shut up."

He yanked the shirt off my shoulder, plunging the needle into my upper arm. My fingers tore into the ground. "No." My voice was half-scream, half-cough. He depressed the syringe all the way before pulling the needle out; it hurt almost as much as going in had. He pulled away. I felt him take my pulse. "What was in that needle?"

"A sedative."

"A sedative?" I yelped. "What kind of a sedative?"

"A very powerful one," he said coldly. "Shut up."

"Sedative, like an opiate?"

"It's not like it's going to kill you."

His voice sounded dim, as if it were coming from the other end of a tunnel. I struggled to get to my feet. My legs felt disconnected from my brain. The trees were swimming in the sky. "I wouldn't do that if I were you." My captor reached out to steady me.

"Screw you." My words were slurring as if I were drunk. I shoved him unsteadily, managing four weaving steps through a landscape spangled by dots; I couldn't breathe. I stumbled, I fell, winking out of consciousness before my body could hit the mess of dead leaves below.

Michael:

I realized something was wrong right away. I got her into the house, jabbing her with an epi pen I kept in the kitchen. She gasped, and rolled over on her side to throw up. *Fuck.* Immediately, I dialed the number for my contact, Lionel Lott, one of the few doctors left who still made house calls — but only for important people.

He picked up on the first ring. "Hello?"

"I have a situation here."

I described the symptoms to Lionel. He didn't interrupt and waited until I had finished speaking before saying, in a calm voice, "Sounds like an allergic reaction. I'll be there as soon as I can. Do you have an epi pen?"

"Yes."

"Inject her with it."

"I did."

"Then put her somewhere cool to lower the fever. Keep the pen handy." He hung up.

I did as Lionel had advised, cursing the girl with every breath. This was supposed to be a simple job. She wasn't supposed to be this much of a problem. Her forehead was burning up. I slung her over my shoulder and carried her to the bathroom, where I stripped off her clothes. Her arm was swollen. Lionel hadn't sounded concerned so I assumed this was treatable. Richardson would be displeased if I allowed anything to happen to our only means of negotiation with the Parkers. I had been entrusted with this mission because I was the best; I could *not* fail.

With that thought in place I filled the tub with cold water and ice from the freezer before setting the girl in the bath. I sat on the lid of the toilet and glared at her. *This explains her fear of sedatives.* Forty-five minutes later I heard a knock at the door. I wiped my wet hands on my jeans. Keeping one free to reach for my gun, I said, "Who is it?"

"Lionel."

I could see the doctor through the peephole: a portly man with fair hair and a mustache about two hundred years out of style.

"Praise the Lord," I muttered, swinging open the door to let him in.

He took off his coat. "Let me see the patient."

"She's upstairs." I led the way. "In here."

I watched him examine Christina. "I couldn't have done a better job for her. Her fever is already starting to recede." Lionel glanced up at me. "It shouldn't go back up again, but if it does, call me. In the meantime, make sure she gets plenty of fluids — especially water — some aspirin…and maybe some Benadryl, if she can swallow, to help with the swelling. Keep her someplace comfortable and warm. For now, she should be out of the red."

I heaved the sigh of relief I'd been holding in. "Good to know."

"Would you mind telling me how this happened?"

My smile disappeared. "She was stung by a bee." he had undoubtedly seen the mark left by the needle, though he hadn't commented on it. Bee sting allergies, I imagined, looked similar — and with all that swelling, any minor differences would be erased. "I'm her bodyguard," I added. "Her parents will be displeased if she becomes ill on my watch."

Light glinted off his spectacles as he tilted his head up to look at me. "Young, isn't she?"

"She's eighteen, if that's what you're implying."

Lionel seemed surprised. "No, the thought never crossed my mind." I bet it hadn't. "I hold you in the highest professional regard." Lionel glanced at her, then back at me. "I only meant she seems a bit young to be running for her life, cloistered away like this. May I ask who she is?"

"No."

This was reasonable enough coming from a bodyguard, and he seemed to accept it. He tried to chat further but I was in no mood for idle pleasantries and couldn't answer most of the questions he asked. Eventually I escorted him back to the front door.

"You'll be compensated for your time."

He inclined his head. "It was a pleasure. I hope your little friend is all right."

I kept my face neutral. "I would appreciate it if you refrained from mentioning this incident. To anyone. You understand."

"Of course. The information I receive from all patients is strictly confidential."

"Good."

Like Kent, Lionel and I had been introduced by a mutual contact. Unlike Kent, however, he didn't know who I worked for. As far as he was concerned, I worked for the U.S. Government, "our side." I never corrected him. Sometimes, like now, I imagined he suspected he was wrong.

I watched him walk to his car, remaining stationed in the doorway until his Volvo was a distant, glittering speck on the horizon. Then I slammed the door.

Christina:

My dreams lacked clarity or continuity. I dreamed about being chased by a large predator: it always caught me just before I got away. I also dreamed I was back home, which was a cruel trick. Then there were brief moments of lucidity, where it was like reality was on the other side of a pair of thick, velvet curtains, and I was separated from the stage. After what felt like a hundred years the curtains parted and I woke with a start, gaping at the scenery. I was in a bedroom. In a bed. My arm throbbed, pulsing as if it were a separate living creature.

Is this another dream?

No. A pair of green eyes were watching me, far too intently to be anything but real. My captor was wearing a fitted gray shirt and black sweatpants, sitting so his body was angled towards mine. My leg was almost touching his back. I pulled it away. He was holding a bowl of water and a damp cloth, which he set aside. "Are you conscious?"

My memory of the events leading up to this moment were disconnected. I could recall running — him chasing me — the pine forest — the sedative. Each scene felt so surreal, like a half-forgotten nightmare. I tried to push myself up. The pain that followed changed my mind.

"What happened? What did you do to me?"

"You reacted violently to the sedative."

"What do you mean *violently*? What happened?"

"It almost killed you. You were out for three days."

The sedative. He must have used an opiate, like morphine or codeine. I was terribly allergic to opiates. "You didn't take me to a hospital?"

"No."

"Why?"

"Why do you think?"

I'd almost died. That explained the endless sea of sleep, the bizarre dreams. My feverish brain had been boiling in the stew of my thoughts. I wondered if he was telling the truth about how long I'd been out for, and why he'd bothered to move me. I could have crashed out in the basement and not known the difference until I woke up, encrusted in my own filth. "Where am I?"

"My room. I know a doctor. He suggested this might be more comfortable for you." There was an edge in his voice that suggested he considered such actions on my behalf frivolous.

I barely heard. I was studying my clothes. I had been wearing a plain white polo and jeans before but now I was wearing a long blue shirt several sizes too big — and nothing else. *He wouldn't have...not while I was unconscious and dying of fever. Even he can't be so soulless.*

My throat dried.

I was in his bedroom. Wearing his shirt.

And nothing else

He tried to make me drink some water. I balked at the feel of his hands on me. "Drink it," he said. "You're dehydrated. You need fluids."

I spat the mouthful in his face. He responded by sloshing the rest of the water into mine and stalking out. I lay there with water dripping down my face and neck, soaking into his shirt collar.

"If I don't get what I want from them by midnight tomorrow, I'll take what I want from you."

That had been two days ago.

I couldn't look him in the eye when he brought more food and drink several hours later. My stomach flip-flopped at the smell and sight of cheap lunch meat. "Are you going to throw up?"

Not if I didn't eat. I shook my head.

"Why aren't you eating?"

"I can't," I whispered.

"Is your jaw broken?"

"Did you rape me?"

He snorted. "That's what this is all about? Because you think I fucked you?"

The contempt stung more than his crude word for the act. "Did you?"

"We waited until midnight. *I* waited until midnight. My man went home early. There were no phone calls. Nothing. Your parents never showed."

What was he saying? That he had every right to rape me? I bit the inside of my cheek to keep from screaming at him. Because if that's what he honestly believed, he was far more callous than I had ever thought him capable of.

"If I hadn't gotten your clothes off and put you in that cold water, you would have died. You're lucky my contact makes house calls. And you're damn lucky that I'm bound by a contract to give a rat's ass whether you live or die: that I didn't just dump you in a river somewhere."

He leaned closer, and all but spat the words into my face. "No, I didn't rape you — and you owe me your goddamn life." He left, and I cried myself into another fever-driven sleep.

Chapter Seven

Killer

Michael:

The expense reports began to stack up. Keeping someone alive was a difficult task. I had a new-found respect for Lionel and those in his line of work. I had always considered my job challenging and yet death was nothing special. Not once you got past the details. We all died. I merely hastened the process — but not fast enough. Richardson started to ask questions. "You are beginning to cost me a fantastic sum of money, Mr. Boutilier, and I have yet to see any results. Do you have an update on our current status?"

"There were some complications."

"I don't want to hear that. I want answers. Results."

I went into town that day anyway to buy the girl and I new clothes and food. There I came across yet another unpleasant surprise — the streets were crawling with cops. I had chosen Nowhere, Oregon, deep in the Cascade Mountains, and I had been *found*.

Impossible.

The capital was nowhere near the Cascade Mountains. That was why I had chosen the Walk of Flags — to buy myself extra time. I knew the FBI liked to cast their net as wide as possible when dealing with criminals, but there was no reason why they should be spending so much of their time and resources looking here. *Unless they received a tip-off.*

I could call the IMA. They would deal with the police, throw out a false lead that would divert the FBI's attentions elsewhere. But Richardson would want another progress report and then I'd have no choice but to confess that my charge had fallen grievously ill. And if the leak had originated in one of the departments of my organization, as I suspected it did since all of my contacts — with the exception of Lionel and his sterling reputation — had as much to lose as I did by having me incarcerated, that would be a foolish move. Adding fuel to the pyre.

If I fled now, I would light up a thousand different radar screens. Moving the girl when she was so sick was foolhardy anyway. I would sweat it out. As soon as she was better, we would move. I already had another location in mind, close enough that it would be the last place anyone would suspect. I would not inform the IMA of the change. I would reroute communication so that it would appear as though I had never left. And then, once the job terminated, I would trim any loose ends, collect my paycheck, and forget the Parkers — and the IMA — ever existed.

If the cops did not follow me to the new location, I could conclude that the leak had originated from the IMA and take appropriate investigative action. If this wasn't the case, I could form one of two conclusions: (1) either one of my contracts *had* betrayed me or (2) the girl had somehow managed to communicate her whereabouts to somebody on the outside. Since neither of these scenarios were especially likely, my original suspicion remained the strongest.

Fan-fucking-tastic. I was a pariah.

Christina:

On my third day of consciousness, my temperature was still within the boundaries of a fever. A lower fever, but high enough to be concerned about. I'd thrown up several times already and each of those times he — my captor — would be outside the bathroom door, cursing.

Now that I had stood face-to-hooded-face with death, I knew for sure that I did not want to die. God had tested me, giving me the opportunity to lie down, stop fighting…and I hadn't taken it. I *wanted* to live, and I needed my captor to help me, much as I loathed being dependent on him. My one consolation was that if I did die, bad things would happen to him. He never said this expressly but I could see it in his face, written in the lines stress had carved there. Why else would he concern himself with me?

I was getting anxious, though. He hadn't mentioned my parents since I'd first awakened. My fever had left me so disoriented, I wasn't sure whether he had received any more calls. I wanted to ask what had happened since but didn't quite dare. My illness had left him in a black mood. I didn't want to provoke him, or remind him of his threat to my mother. All I could do was sleep.

The next thing I knew, my captor was shaking me awake. "Sit up."

I managed to throw a halfhearted glare in his direction. The back of his hand was cool against my forehead, and he pulled back as if he'd been burned. "You still have a fever." He said this like I had contracted one voluntarily for the sole purpose of pissing him off.

"I told you I was allergic to opiates," I said pathetically.

"No, you didn't."

"Well, you didn't exactly give me the *chance*."

There was a long, drawn out silence. No matter how sick I felt, I couldn't fall asleep knowing he was there. "Are you allergic to aspirin?"

"No…"

"Are you absolutely sure?"

"Yes…"

He left the room but only for a second. I heard the rattle of a pill jar. Aspirin. It was the cheap knock-off version, the kind you can buy for $4 at the store. He tipped two white pills in my hand, pushing a glass of tap water at me.

"I don't want any medicine."

"I don't care what you want. They're for your fever. Take them."

I let the pills fall to the floor.

His fingers closed around my wrist and he yanked me back up. I cried out in pain, trailing into a horrified squeak when he leaned forward until our noses touched. "You're in no state to go head-to-head with me," he said, shaking two more aspirins out of the jar. "Take the damn pills."

"They'll make me sick. My stomach hurts. I don't want them."

Why couldn't he leave me alone? I just wanted to sleep.

He pried open the fist I had made, grabbed the pills from my hand, and forced them into my mouth. I choked. He had my mouth covered with his hand so I couldn't spit them out. "Swallow. *Swallow*, you stupid girl. You're too weak for the Heimlich maneuver." I pointed to my throat and started gagging until he tipped the water glass to my mouth. "Fine. Drink."

The bitter taste of the aspirin merged with the water. I felt like I'd swallowed two pieces of jagged glass. My stomach lurched. I grabbed the water from it and knocked it all back, trying to get rid of the phantom pills I could still feel wedged in the back of my throat. My stomach felt bloated now. I imagined I could feel all the water I drank sloshing against the inside.

"I don't feel good."

He set the empty water glass on the nightstand. "You'll live."

No thanks to you.

He reminded me of the Rottweiler one of my mother's rich friends kept. The dog had been so well-trained, he never barked. Only growled — although if you were a burglar who had managed to get that close, it was probably over for you. The dog's yellow eyes were savage and followed you around the room. You could see him deciding whether or not to attack. At the slightest provocation he would. It was what he had been taught to do. "Go on and pet him, Christina," she used to say. "He won't bite. He knows you're friends." Dogs like that didn't have friends. They were *contained* until, one day, their switch was thrown and they turned on you. My mother's friend had named this dog Assassin. Azzie, for short.

"Assassin," I whispered, to myself. My captor looked at my sharply with a jerk of his head that reminded me disconcertingly of the dog. "You're…an assassin, aren't you?"

It all fit together — the hefty price-tags, the reclusive environment, the mysterious business contacts, all the cell phones, his unnatural physique. Everything.

"Who do you work for?" I pressed. "CIA? SIS? DGSE? Or are you a hired-gun?"

"Shut up, Christina." The warning in his voice was clear.

"You really are, aren't you?"

His lips thinned. A sign that I probably *should* shut up. But I couldn't. This was too horrifying. Somebody hated my family and I enough that they would send a hired professional to kill us? "Jesús, María y José — what did my dad *do*? Hack into the Pentagon?"

My captor left the room.

The aspirin did help, though I was loath to admit it. The next day my fever went down significantly. I didn't throw up the soup my captor brought. He said nothing, but his satisfaction was evident. I was better — he was in the clear. Lucky him.

There was no more talk about assassins and government agencies. I caught him watching me even more carefully now and wished I'd had the sense to keep my suspicions to myself. He had enough reasons to kill me; I didn't want to give him more. I tiptoed around him. Even though I knew I stank, I waited a few days before asking for a shower.

Like all the times before, he took my clothes and waited outside while I washed, allotting me a very short amount of time to get dressed. I jumped when he barged in, feeling the urge to cover myself even though I was fully dressed. "My pants d-don't fit. They're too short."

His eyes dropped to where my pants cut off, just above the ankle. I cleared my throat, face burning. "Next time...c-could I maybe have a razor?"

"No." He yanked me out of the bathroom.

"That *hurts*." What had I done to provoke him? Point out my hairy legs? "Where are we going?"

He didn't bother to respond. My imagination raced away from me. *Is this the part where I talk, or he kills me?* We stopped outside an ordinary-looking door — not his — and he kicked it open with the toe of his boot. I scanned the room anxiously. The floors were brown carpet that felt gross and dusty beneath my bare feet, and the gray wallpaper was peeling. *Probably laced with lead, too*. A mattress stood against the far wall, so stained and spotted with mildew that I tried not to think about what had transpired on it. On the mattress was a very thin blanket.

It didn't look like a torture chamber. It looked like a prison cell. There were even bars on the windows. He gave my arm an impatient tug that brought me stumbling to his side. "What is this place?" I asked, unable to keep the dread from my voice.

"Your new room."

He gave me a little push that sent me tumbling to the floor. Not much of a fall, but my body immediately started to throb. I got to my knees, putting both hands to my head to stop the spinning. I felt him laying me down on the mattress. *Oh, God, no. Disgusting*.

"I've waited long enough. Are you going to tell me what you know about Pandora?"

"Why did I get a new room?"

"Answer the question, Christina."

I hated the way he pronounced my name, staccato, emphasizing the first syllable like the boy's name, with a hard R that was almost a growl. Should I answer? He wouldn't have asked if he didn't have an ulterior motive behind it.

Promise me, Christina, that you will never open Pandora's box.

Where the two events linked? Did this have something to do with my dad?

My silence was making him mad. "Pandora," I said, stalling. "She was a beautiful woman created by the Greek gods to punish humans for taking the secret of fire from Mount Olympus."

He waved that aside. "Fairy tales."

"Well, yeah," I said slowly. "It's a creation myth, like Adam and Eve."

"What about her box?"

"It contained all the evils of mankind — jealousy, sickness, poverty. Everything. The box was sealed and Pandora was told never to open it" — *Promise me, Christina* — "but the gods had made her insatiably curious so she did, and then all the evils flooded out." I paused. "When she saw what she had done, she felt horrible and slammed the lid of the box back on, trapping hope, which was at the very bottom."

"Hope isn't an evil," my captor scoffed.

"Yes, it is. Hope is the worst evil of all."

That night, the telephone rang.

Morgan Freemason was dead.

As a colleague, I barely knew him. The IMA was huge and he worked in a different branch, only coming into contact with me when I began moving up the ranks, supervising a wider range of operations. Morgan had been on the Brownstone case — two married operatives from the IMA and their three small children. They had all been murdered, and so was he. Their killer was also an operative, a new recruit, but he'd been working for somebody else all along.

I deployed a team of my men. They had captured him — a man named Everett Blythe. He had attempted to flee just as the Parkers had. Unlike them, though, he had no loyal friends to provide him with plane tickets and secret identities. His boss had fled at the first hint of trouble. My men caught up with him in California, where he had been trying to rent a boat. I suspected his destination was the South Pacific. Lots of uncharted private islands down there. Great place for a mobster to hide. They apprehended Blythe at the docks and delivered him to a storage locker I had rented under an assumed name. When I arrived, he was trussed up to a chair; an oversized pig for the slaughter.

"*You,*" he said.

"Dismissed," I said to my men, who left without a word.

It was cold. The garage wasn't heated and it had snowed the night before, leaving the poorly-insulated metal walls chilled. My breath rose into the air in cloudy plumes. I flicked out my knife. "So you're the one who killed the Brownstones."

I expected denial. He surprised me. "They put a bust on a drug cartel for cocaine in South America. Ruined a big cocaine deal. The economy collapsed. An entire village in Colombia was destroyed in the fallout. Hundreds of people lost their lives. Several more were left to rot in prison."

"Spare me the noble bullshit," I said. "You don't care about any of that."

"And you do?" He clung to his bravado like a shield. "I've heard about you, Boutilier. About the sick shit you've done. Sounds like even you could give Callaghan a run for his money."

He was sweating through that fancy suit of his and his eyes were frightened. But not frightened enough to suggest he actually believed the crap coming out of his mouth. If he did, he wouldn't be insulting me — he'd be pissing himself, begging for mercy that would never arrive.

I did not go out of my way to find people's weaknesses for the sole purpose of exploiting them. If I did, it was out of necessity; it gave me no sexual gratification. "You betrayed us," I said, reigning in my anger at such fallacious comparisons. "You entered into a contract with the IMA knowing full well what the repercussions would be if that contract was terminated prematurely. You killed three highly respected operatives. I know money changed hands. That's a difficult request. And an expensive one. Not something you'd do for the hell of it."

"They were going to get killed anyway. If it wasn't me, it would have been someone else."

"And the children? Did they have to die, too?"

"Yes, they had to die, too," he said, speaking in a sing-song tone as he threw my own words back at me. "I was ordered to kill everyone in the house, or I wouldn't get paid. Don't tell me you have a soft spot for little brats?"

"How I feel about this is of little importance. If you don't talk, you will still die."

"A quick death is better than what they'll do to me if they find out I betrayed them."

"That's where you're wrong." I revealed the other implements I'd kept hidden in the pockets of my trench coat, letting him have a long, hard look at the steel tools. The crotch of his pants darkened and he began to struggle in earnest as I moved closer. "I don't recall saying I was going to kill you quickly." My voice was pitched low, but I know he heard me. Everett Blythe was a small man, but in the confines of the garage he screamed loud enough for five.

Christina:

His car pulled up in front of the house early in the evening. I peered through the bars of the window trying to get an idea of the mood he'd be in and gasped aloud at the state of his appearance. Dirtied black boots, jeans, and a trench coat, which he pulled off as I watched, balling it up and locking it in the trunk. When he stepped out of the redwoods' skeletal shadows and into the dying light, I saw that his shirt was smeared with what could only be dried blood.

He looked around to make sure the coast was clear and then he looked up — and saw me. I gasped again, louder this time, and covered my mouth with both hands. *Oh no.* I ducked down and leaned back against the wall beneath the window ledge. If there had been any lingering doubts in my mind about what he was, they were gone.

Murderer.

I heard him coming up the stairs and stumbled to my feet, wishing I had somewhere to run as the door slammed open. "Spying is never a good idea, darlin. Not with me."

"I didn't mean to — I was just — "

127

"What? Enjoying the view?" He peeled off the bloody shirt. I averted my eyes.

"*Murderer.*"

"What did you think assassins did, you foolish girl?"

I ignored the barb. "Who was it? Who did you kill?"

I could feel him gauging me as he folded his shirt into a neat square, avoiding the bloody spots. "No one you know," he said at last.

And I was relieved. Somebody had died and I was *relieved* because it hadn't been my parents.

I was a horrible person.

"Another innocent family?"

"A traitor."

My mind spun with all the definitions "traitor" could encompass in this world I could never hope to grasp; this world where the lines between "good" and "evil" were so blurred that it was impossible to see where one started and the other ended.

"What did you do to them?"

He glanced at me. I took a step backwards, whimpering when he matched me step for step. "Why do you want to know that?" My back hit the wall and he hedged me into the corner, barring my escape with his arms. "You get off on hearing about that kind of shit?"

"N-n-no…" I was too scared to meet his eyes but was too scared. He smelled like sweat and blood and musk: a monstrous fuse of man and animal. I stared at my feet. "I-I just — "

"It's none of your goddamn business."

"Was this because of any information I gave you? Did I help you kill them?"

He paused a long time, then scoffed, "This had nothing to do with you."

Nothing to do with me. I repeated those words to myself, like a chant. An absolution. *Not my fault.*

"The man I killed was directly responsible for the death of a very young family because of a petty grievance he'd nursed for the better part of a decade. He was a drug-dealer and a gangster, descended from a very long line of drug-dealers and gangsters, and he happened to be a particularly nasty and greedy one. Does that make you feel better?" His voice was sarcastic. "Does that make me the hero in your deluded little fantasy world?"

"No." I still wouldn't meet his eyes. "I still think you're sick."

My captor grabbed me, digging his gloved fingers into my cheeks. His *bloody* gloved fingers. "I'm an assassin. I'm whatever the job necessitates."

I could smell the blood; it smelled like old, dirty pennies. "Then you're a whore."

"I'm a mercenary."

"What's the difference?" I spat. "You sell your body for money and you have no morals."

His other hand slammed against the wall, making me jump. His fist left cracks in the plaster. "You're a naïve and foolish child to provoke me."

"What do you want from me? My approval? I thought you didn't care what I thought."

His eyes dropped, briefly, before flickering back to my face. Something changed. I saw him grow colder before my eyes. He laughed and it was joyless: a sharp, brittle sound. A mockery of real laughter. Then the heat of his body vanished, cold air rushing to fill his place. The door slammed. He'd left the room, taking his mangled, bloody shirt with him, leaving his previous insult ringing in my ears. A few minutes later, I heard the shower run.

Cloak and Dagger by Nenia Campbell

Chapter Eight

Sabotage

Michael:

The cold water stabbed at my skin like dozens of tiny needles. I
braced my arms against the tiled wall, letting the spray run down
my back, over my hips, to pool at my feet. When I couldn't stand it
anymore I shut off the water, swiping the drips from my face with
the heel of my hand. Though my skin now felt shrink-wrapped, the
mountain water had done nothing to cool my temper. Just thinking
about my charge's attitude made me burn with rage and other, more
troubling sensations.

What do you want from me?

Everything.

I wanted everything. And I had been so close to slamming her
against the wall and taking it. Tangling my hands in her hair and
tasting her. I could still remember the sweetness of her mouth, of the
tender, yielding skin of her throat. When she insulted me, she made
me feel vindicated; it was a rush — psychological *and* sexual — and I
sought it out, provoking her, intimidating her, plunging us both
deeper into the vicious cycle. It was unprofessional. I knew I should
call the IMA, tell them to have Callaghan take over the case. In one
with this uncertain of an outcome, forging relations with the hostage
was catastrophic. But I couldn't — the case was *mine*.

131

She was mine.

I stepped into my jeans. A black strap over my chest kept my gun holstered to my hip, where it would be in easy reach in a pinch. I adjusted the strap and pulled on my shirt, doing up all but the last three buttons. My knife got tucked into my boot; it was the weapon I resorted to when all else failed. I grabbed my watch and gloves off the counter, forgoing the bulletproof vest for now. It was effective but hampering; the lead lining was heavy.

I dialed Kent's number as I pulled on my gloves, keeping the phone pinned at my shoulder. "It's me." The leather creaked when I made a fist.

"Michael? How was Oregon?"

"A total no-show." I filled a glass with water. "Both subjects fled the scene."

"Parenting's gone downhill since I was a lad," Kent said dryly.

I shook my head. "What kind of parent in their right mind would leave their daughter with a man like me? She's too sheltered; did they think she could possibly survive?"

Kent — wisely, I thought — affected thoughtful silence.

"I want your assessment on this case."

"By when?"

I unlocked the cupboard and took out a jar of pills. Slipped the key back into my billfold. Shook out the maximum dose and crushed them with the bottom of the water glass, grinding the pills against the counter until they were reduced to a fine powder. "I'm going back to the agency this week. They're expecting a full report. I already submitted the debriefing — now I have to deliver the bad news again. In person."

"Hard luck."

"Luck is irrelevant." I scraped the powder into my palm and sprinkled it into the water. Then frowned down at my gloves. The fingers were caked in whitish residue. "I need this done as soon as possible. My charge has healed and the window is about to close." I wiped my hands on my jeans. "Look, the reason I called is that I need you to come down here tomorrow and help me sort out some of the particulars."

"...Particulars?"

"I think there's a leak — a big one." I stirred the water with a spoon. "One of the local mountain towns was crawling with cops. I didn't stay long enough to hear who they were looking for, but I suspect it might be yours truly."

There was another pause, longer than the first. "What do you want me to do about it?"

That was why I liked him — straight and to the point.

"I have a list people who would stand to benefit from my disappearance. I'd like you to check them out...see what you can dig up." I dropped the spoon in the sink and covered the water with plastic wrap, securing it with a rubber band. "Something has changed. I don't like it."

"You're being very cautious."

"With good cause."

He sighed. "I'll see what I can do."

"I appreciate that." I put the glass in the fridge and leaned against the door. "How much is this going to cost me?"

"For you, Michael? Five hundred."

"Thousand?"

Kent laughed. "Five hundred *dollars*."

Five hundred dollars. Most mercenaries would have demanded ten times that amount — at least. An agent as sophisticated and efficient as Kent could easily charge twenty times more than that. I peeled the gloves off my now-sweaty hands and rubbed my eyes. "Quite the bargain."

"Hardly. If you die, Old Boy, I lose one of my best customers. This is self-preservation."

Christina:

At some point the water shut off. The ensuing pause filled the cabin with an imposing silence. I thought he might have left until I heard a door slam downstairs. It sounded like he was still angry.

Calling him a whore had been a bad move on my part. I was regretting it more with every passing second.

He slammed around down there for a while and then I heard his footsteps coming back up the stairs. The door swung open: he stood in the doorway, his face devoid of expression. I flicked my eyes over him nervously. In his hands was a glass of water. Without saying a word, he set the glass on the ground. Water dripped from his wet hair with the gesture, soaking into the carpet.

I stared at the water glass, frosted with cold. I had insulted him, made him furious…and he was bringing me ice water? My brain drew the logical conclusion. *Would this man poison me?* Thirsty as I was, I made no move to take it.

"Have you had enough time to cool down?"

I didn't meet his eyes. "I thought you killed my parents."

"I know. And I think you owe me an apology."

His face was composed, but there was a tightness to his jaw that hadn't been quite so prominent before. "Excuse me?"

"I have tolerated your childish insults long enough." His voice was like velvet — velvet that cloaked a poisoned blade. "I have been patient with your stunning lack of respect" — I must have made a noise because he added, viciously — "and I am not a patient man by nature. But my patience, or what's left of it, is wearing thin. You do not appear to grasp the severity of your situation."

"No, I don't understand. You think my life needs to be even more miserable?"

"I think *you* need to learn your place, and quickly. I have held back before because I was bound by a contract." He exhaled through his nose, turning his piercing eyes on me. "Now that contract is almost null and void. Professionalism will no longer protect you from harm. This is your final warning. Any more displays of petty defiance, and I'll make you regret it."

I swallowed — hard.

"Now…" He folded his arms. "Don't you have something to say to me?"

I met his green eyes with poise and trembled at what I saw. His face was ashen with fury; he looked inhuman. My composure was fracturing. At any second, I would fly apart.

I spat an apology at him, wishing it was grit and broken glass instead. Which probably would have satisfied him, except I added, "Did I hurt your feelings, you bastard?"

He gave me a rough shove that sent me sprawling forward, so I was nose-to-nose with the carpet. Something sharp dug into my throat. "Your parents have fled, leaving you with little value. My boss no longer cares what happens to you. I don't think you get what that means. I can do anything I want to you, and nobody will care."

The world seemed to halt. I could feel was his breath on my

neck.

He gave me another rough shove. I turned around in time to see him sheathe the knife. "I suggest you exercise more caution when speaking to me." The door slammed closed. I heard the lock click. Then through the wood, I heard him say, "Else I might take it upon myself to find a new use for that pretty mouth of yours."

I heard the car pull away. I threw the water glass at the wall. It smashed satisfyingly, sending water and glass flying everywhere. I threw myself against the door, pounding until my hands were red and sore. Cursing and screaming at him, at my parents, at God — at anybody whose name I thought to invoke. I screamed until my throat was raw, until I was too exhausted to do more than collapse on the mattress and burst into tears. Soon, I ran out of those, too. I lay there in the darkness, watching the sky grow dark as it filled up with black clouds that swallowed up the stars. A heavy rain began to fall. I was still listening to it as I fell asleep.

Michael:

Kent suggested we meet in a place called *The Mountain View Bar and Grill*. I followed the directions from his e-mail, using the odometer for reference. I nearly missed one of the narrow turn-offs, which ran in the shade of the densely-packed trees.

Mountain View Bar and Grill was an old, run-down building made out of dark brown wood. The sign was hand-painted with the intention of looking rustic. I had never heard of Mountain View before but suspected it was either an old mining town or an old lumber town that had tried being a tourist trap and dismally failed.

The inside of the bar was no better. The wooden furnishings were worn from many years of water damage and rough handling. The faint, musky smell of mildew and old beer hung in the air like smog, merging with the piney scent of the mountains. An old jukebox was playing "Wild Horses" by the Rolling Stones, and a small group of men sat nearby with quarters at the ready, dominating the music as they watched closed-captioning football on ESPN.

Kent was at the bar. Normally a fan of tweeds, he was dressed in a red-and-black-checked hunting shirt and a pair of hiking boots. He had traded his usual pipe for a pack of Camels. There was already a beer in front of him. He was staring down at a notebook.

I sat down on the stool next to him. A bartender materialized and asked me if I wanted anything to drink. Kent sat up a little straighter, pretending to notice me for the first time. "Get him a beer on me," he said, in a dead-on American accent.

"No thanks," I said, before the bartender could comply.

Kent waited until the bartender was out of earshot before saying, "One beer won't hurt, Michael. You look a little tense."

I bristled. "That's because the situation has gotten more complicated. I can't afford to be caught drinking on the job. It's imperative that I do what any situation asks of me." And I wasn't sure what I might do to my hostage with alcohol in my blood.

Kent shook his head. "Aren't you afraid that you're becoming too good?"

The jukebox switched to "Before He Cheats" by Carrie Underwood. "I'm afraid I don't understand what you're asking."

Kent blew a smoke ring. "I'm talking about your job. It's all fine and dandy when you always get your man — but people are beginning to wonder: who's going to get *you*?"

"I pay my loyalty where it is due."

"That doesn't matter. You're too strong. That scares them."

I motioned towards the notebook. "What's this?"

"This is a list of people who wouldn't mind seeing you disappear." He rifled through it, showing me the pages. The notebook was full, and he had used both sides. Some of the names were highlighted.

"Yellow are the people who wish you harm but don't have the means to carry it out themselves. Orange are people who have the means but haven't attempted it yet. Pink are people who have, at some point or another, attempted to sabotage you — but failed."

There were people from the IMA in there. Several bore pink

slashes. Callaghan and Morelli, included, but that was no surprise. I pushed the notebook away. "I appreciate the effort."

Kent drained his beer and flagged down the bartender for another. "That's not all. I investigated your run-in with the cops; they received a tip-off." The bartender placed another beer in front of Kent, who gave him an effusively slurred thanks. Kent winked at me, swallowing down another mouthful of beer. "A command like that would have been issued from someone pretty high up on the chain, don't you think?"

Richardson.

I was in trouble.

Christina:

I lay on the mattress with the blanket wrapped around me, trying not to move. My stomach had taken on a dull, achy edge. All my captor had left for me was that single glass of water, which I had thrown against the wall. He'd never taken it upon himself to starve me before. *Maybe I really am becoming disposable.*

I listened to the house settle, trying not to focus on my thirst or my stomach's loud rumbling. The rumbling got louder — and it wasn't coming from me. Voices in the house. People *talking*. I recognized one of the voices: it was my captor. I pressed my ear against the floor but couldn't make out anything they were saying through the carpet. I could only hear the inflections in their voices. The conversation they were having didn't appear pleasant.

A floorboard in the hall creaked. "…has the motive but…too cowardly…himself."

That had been the unfamiliar voice. It was deeper than my captor's, punctuated by phlegmy hacks and coughs. He sounded British.

"He's always been spineless." My captor. His cold tenor was unmistakable. Even through the solid oak doors, his voice carried easily. He must have been angry if he was speaking so loudly.

"What…your boss?"

"The IMA is like a pack of wolves — nobody will challenge the leader unless he shows weakness. Richardson has taken special care to make it appear he has none. I have heard him describe me as ruthless. He thinks I want to ascend to power."

"No. There are too many people who are loyal to him, and would not appreciate the shift in power. It's not worth the trouble or the time. I'd rather watch Callaghan and Morelli fight for it."

"And *I* would rather see you leading them, Michael, than see Callaghan in power. That man is insane. There are stories about him that chill the blood — "

Michael? Is that his name? It didn't suit him at all.

"All of them most likely true."

"Seizing control now, while you still have the chance, might help your situation."

My captor — Michael — said something in response, but they must have gone to a room that was farther away because their conversation became indecipherable again. I wondered about the people they were discussing. Were they like him? Unfeeling and immoral? I guessed yes. He — Michael — had referred to them as a pack of wolves, and he was not exactly model citizen.

I sat there, mulling that over, and the voices got close again. "… escaped from state lines."

"How did that happen?" The British voice again. "Last I heard, they were on the east coast."

"They had friends on the outside."

"Who?"

"I'm not sure, but I think the man I got yesterday was a red herring. A ruse."

"The man who killed the Brownstones?" A cough. "How?"

"I think they bribed someone they knew on the inside. That's why they never showed, I bet. Blythe was going to bite it anyway — someone just rushed him along. I don't doubt that he *was* working for the mafia, and that *that* was the reason for his murders, but I also don't think it was coincidence that he chose to show up on the west coast. I suspect somebody waved money at him. The Japanese man I interrogated has been taken in for questioning since he worked with Rubens before...and I suspect I might be next."

"The two events could be unrelated — unless you think you're being set up for a fall?"

"I've considered that, too. I'm trying to examine every angle. Not an easy task when I've got the whole world breathing down my neck. My agency keeps telling me that the time for bargaining is over. They think we need to show Rubens we're not just fucking around."

Rubens? Are they talking about my dad?

"Oh? And what stunningly insightful conclusion did the IMA reach?"

"That I use the girl as an example. I said, 'Are you suggesting torture?' And Richardson said, 'I am willing to use whatever means necessary to solve this problem. Use your own judgment.'" There was a pause and my captor — Michael — added darkly, "*My* judgment. Seems rather ironic, doesn't it, since that's exactly what's being called into question here. Of course, he suggested that if I didn't feel up to it, I could always send her to Callaghan..."

My head was starting to spin as I tried to absorb all this information. I didn't want to listen anymore, but I had to; I now knew that my life depended on it. As if picking up on my thoughts, the British voice said, "Is it safe to talk here? I noticed the walls are rather thin…"

"I already checked. There aren't any wires or bugs. We're alone, except for the girl."

"Does she know what the IMA has plans?"

"She doesn't know anything."

I do now.

I had crept closer until my cheek was pressed against the peeling white surface of the door.

"How long have you had her?"

"Nearly five weeks." The door knob clicked as a key was inserted. I fell back as if it had grown painfully hot. My eyes shifted around the room looking for a weapon, but my captor had thoughtfully cleared it of anything remotely hard. *Hold on, there's the broken glass.* I snatched one of the sparkling pieces and held my breath.

"She should still be out. I gave her enough sleeping pills to knock out a bear."

That bastard. My hand tightened around the shard and I gasped as the sharp edges sliced open my palm. *Shit.* I had no time to get back on the mattress, the door was opening. I collapsed in place as it swung open. Two sets of footsteps entered the room. The stench of cigarette smoke and beer filled the air, burning my nose and searing my lungs.

"Odd place to fall asleep," the British voice said.

My captor didn't respond. I was prodded in the side with a boot. I continued to play dead, trying not to jerk when he bent closer. Gloved fingers brushed against the band of exposed skin where my shirt had ridden up. It took all my willpower not to yank down the hem.

When he touched my throat next, searching for my pulse, his fingers were bare. I tensed involuntarily and the hand was replaced by a knife. "She's not asleep; she's awake."

Would he know I'd been eavesdropping? He was crouching over me, wearing the plaid shirt and jeans from that afternoon and looked furious.

The other man wasn't wearing a mask, surprisingly, and looked about seventy. He had large, startled eyes, like an owl. "The sleeping pills didn't work?"

"She broke the damn glass." Michael had just spied the glittering shards, lit up from the light in the hall. "Bet you think you're clever, don't you?"

I lashed out with my piece of glass. Michael tore it out of my hand with the leather-clad fingers of his other hand and slammed both my wrists over my head. "You little saboteur. You'll stop at nothing to piss me off, won't you? I should have known."

"It was an accident," I said weakly.

He pressed down harder. "I'm sure it was."

I looked at the man, wondering if *he* was going to help me, but he was turned away, facing the window and whistling "Before She Cheats" as he watched the drizzle.

"Stop looking at him. He won't help you. Look at *me*."

Shaking, I did.

"Tell me everything you heard. Don't leave anything out — or I'll start using this." He held up the knife.

It occurred to me that my captor — Michael — might be harsher when his business associates were watching. He wouldn't want to risk looking soft in front of them, and he had already declared that he was short on patience with me. Would using me in an act of male posturing take a toll on his conscience? An iron hand clenched my stomach. "I didn't hear anything."

The knife nicked just beneath my ear. "Don't fucking lie to me, Christina."

I couldn't reveal what I really knew — he'd kill me. Or send me away to that horrible man to be tortured. "You put sleeping pills in my water," I wept.

His eyes searched my face. "What else?"

I shook my head, squeezing my eyes shut. "There was nothing else!"

He drew the knife across my skin, down my throat, and I cried harder. "You're afraid. I know you heard something you didn't like."

"I'm afraid because you've got a *knife*."

"Kent."

The old man turned around, halting in the middle of "My Baby Shot Me Down." He glanced at me. I thought I thought a flash of sympathy on his face. "Yes?"

"Please leave." Michael's eyes never left mine. "I need to deal with my hostage. Alone."

My blood turned to ice. "What are you going to do to me?"

The man — Kent — headed for the door. "I'll keep in touch."

"What are you going to do?" I repeated in a higher voice.

He kept staring at me. It wasn't exactly hatred on his face, but something similar. "Whatever I want." Like a man possessed, he leaned closer, letting the knife fall to the floor with a clatter. I could smell the alcohol in his pores. *Is he drunk?* "Let's start with your mouth."

"No!" I choked. "Michael, don't — *please!*"

He froze, looking down at me with a curious expression. And then I realized my mistake; I had called him by his name. Which I wasn't supposed to know. The front door slammed. Michael didn't even glance in the direction of the hallway. Neither did I. Nothing else existed; he was the center of my universe. I was just one hapless planet orbiting far too closely around a lethal sun. "The game you decided to play is a very dangerous one."

I raised my eyes to his, just in time to see his fist connect with my temple. A constellation of stars filled my vision, shimmering and white, before being absorbed into an endless black hole.

Chapter Nine
Wildfire

Christina:

My arms were stiff and bound behind my back with hemp rope. I sat up with a groan, stretching to see out the window. I caught glimpses of trees, interspersed with brief flashes of the mountains. My captor — I mean, Michael — was driving. I turned my neck, which hurt for some reason, and hissed, "You punched me."

He didn't respond.

It was strange having a name to attach to the face of my nightmares. Maybe it suited him better than I'd thought. Michael was the angel of death — and war. "You — "

"I heard. I punched you." His eyes studied me in the rear view mirror for a moment before returning to the road.

"Are you trying to scare me? Is that why you're doing this? Am I supposed to beg?"

He laughed, low in his throat. "Oh, you have *no* idea, darlin."

The hairs on my arms prickled. "You can't heart me," I said. "I'm your bargaining chip."

"Not anymore."

"My parents *will* come." I couldn't muster up any conviction, though. Even I didn't really believe it anymore. "They love me."

"All the more reason they should have protected you. And yet they ran. Your parents won't get any sympathy from me. My organization wants you dead. You aren't so useful anymore, even as a bargaining chip. They think you know too much. And you do." He paused. "You should be more concerned about yourself at the moment."

"Where are you taking me?"

"My agency."

We're going to the place where they want to torture me? I opened my mouth, then closed it, remembering that was another piece of information I wasn't supposed to have. "Why? Why are we going there?"

Michael didn't seem to hear me. He was staring at the road with a fixed intensity. I stopped asking questions. We stopped at another desolate-looking building farther down the mountain, overlooking the foothills. I wondered how many sites there were like this; places that existed for the sole purpose of holding people captive. These derelict homes were nothing like the steel-doored mansions I saw in so many spy movies at home. They looked like what they were: prisons; places where you could leave and forget someone.

He had to drag me out of the car. I screamed and kicked at him, prompting him to say, "You can be conscious or unconscious when I take you through that door. You choose."

I stopped thrashing.

After he cut the ropes around my wrists and cleaned the resulting wounds, I was instructed to take a shower. *Instructed.* I took no solace from the soap or warm water or even the razor he had procured for me. I was badly frightened. He was acting strange. I wrapped myself tightly in the towel before leaving the bathroom, dreading what would happen next.

As usual, he was waiting outside with the clouds. New ones I hadn't seen before. When I reached out to take them, he pulled me up against him. Not as violently he had in the past, but it still wasn't gentle even if it didn't quite hurt. I didn't think he was capable of gentleness. His face was so twisted, so distorted by ill-concealed emotion, that he seemed to be in pain.

"Don't give me that innocent look."

"I'm not — "

There was a sharp pain as his nose hit mine. "You're not what? You're not giving me a look? Let me tell you something, darlin. You can't look at a man like that and expect him not to notice. You've succeeded in making me look like a fool, and gotten me into a real shit storm. You've *fucked* me, darlin." He moved closer. "It's only fair that I return the favor."

"Don't do it," I pleaded.

When he spoke, his lips brushed mine. "You wouldn't be able to stop me."

"That's an excuse, not a reason," I said, trembling.

"This is the *least* you can do for me," he added, with such venom that I jumped. "How's that for a reason?"

"I don't owe you anything!" I lifted my knee in a sharp upwards jab. He knocked my leg aside with a growl, pressing me against the wall. *Not like this.* I squeezed my eyes shut when his mouth touched my throat. *No, no, no. Not like this.* "No," I gasped. "I won't *let* you, you bastard. I *won't.* I said *no.*"

Michael ignored me, moving lower. The room spun. I could feel the towel slipping. I began to cry — loud, hitching sobs. If he was going to do this to me, he was going to get to experience the whole of it; I wasn't going to hide any of my misery, fear, or disgust.

It took me a moment to realize he was no longer touching me. "Jesus Christ. What are you — " His face was a torrent of conflict as he looked at me, as if really seeing me for the first time. I stumbled away from him and my knees buckled; if he hadn't caught me, I would have collapsed to the floor. He drew in an uneven breath and cursed, pushing me away from him.

What is he doing?

He shoved the bundle of clothes at me. "Get the fuck out of here. Out. *Now.*"

I grabbed the clothes, trying not to touch him, and ran for the first empty room I saw. I glanced back, a lump in my throat, half-expecting him to chase me. No. He was still leaning against the wall. Doubled over. One hand was digging into his forehead, driving the bone-white knuckles of his clenched fist into his skull. I'd seen enough.

I closed the door behind me, breathing hard. *Oh my God*, I thought. *What was that?*

After a while, the lock clicked. The house was submersed in silence.

Sniffling, I drew my knees to my chest, burying my face in the fabric of my skirt. This time, I hadn't provoked him. I hadn't done anything wrong. There was no reason for his actions other than sheer spite and his own sadistic enjoyment. *But then why did he stop? Is he trying to scare me?* Well, it worked. I was scared.

The house remained silent, empty, as the shadows chased each other on the floor. I doubted Michael was going to hold himself accountable for the situation — he never did — which left only one other person to take the blame. He would blame me, as he always did, and use my behavior as an excuse to further justify his own actions.

I would never be safe around him.

The door downstairs creaked open. Footsteps started up the staircase. I stood up. They sounded...aimless. Michael knew the building well. This person, on the other hand, seemed unsure about where they were going. Lost. My feelings of unease intensified when my door rattled, but did not open. Michael had locked it himself. That meant somebody else was in the house. *Maybe it's a hiker — or a policeman!*

The footsteps were receding, moving farther down the hall. *No!* I began pounding on the door. "Help me! If you can hear me — help me, please!"

I thought they moved closer again, but there was no response. I stopped my pounding, realizing for the first time that the trespasser might be a burglar or some other criminal. If it was a burglar, he (or she) could very well have a gun. I hoped he might not hurt me if he found out I was trapped here against my will, and had no qualms about him taking what he wanted from the house. I'd have just as much to lose by ratting him out. If I explained that, he might even be willing to take me into town. Burglars weren't necessarily bad people, right? They were just desperate.

Well, so was I.

I began hitting the door again. "I'm being held hostage! Please! Help me! You can take whatever you want from the house — just please, *please* help me!"

More silence met my plea but the footsteps were definitely coming from right outside the door. A series of clicking sounds and mechanical whirs emanated from the other side. My heart was pounding quite furiously, nearly blocking out the sounds. *Please, God. Let me come out of this safely.*

The noises stopped. The door swung open with a shriek five seconds later, confirming my suspicions: the man in the doorway was not Michael.

This man was tall — taller than my captor, even, though not as broad in the shoulders — and a little older. Late twenties or mid-thirties. He was wearing a white shirt tucked into black slacks, carefully creased. I didn't notice any of this until much later, though, because in his hands was a far more prominent accessory: a gun. And it was aimed at me.

I should have felt hysterical but mostly I just felt numb. My horror was dull and distant. It wasn't that I wanted to die, because I didn't, just that being held at gunpoint wasn't much worse than anything else that had happened to me so far. How sad.

"I'm unarmed," I squeaked, raising my hands to show they were empty. "Don't shoot!"

His eyes, the color of slate, studied me a moment before he set to examining the room. "Are you alone?" He had a soft accent I couldn't place. It sounded British, but I knew it wasn't — the cadences were different from the way that other man, Kent, had spoken.

What is he doing here? He had a strange, foreign accent, he had found — and then broken into — the safe house, and he had a gun. He wasn't a hiker or a cop. I was pretty sure he wasn't a burglar, either. The equipment he had used to break down the door seemed pretty sophisticated. Like, government-issue sophisticated. Those thoughts propelled me into motion.

"Who are you?" I demanded. "And what — "

There was a muted *click* and I froze.

"That was the safety." *As if I don't know that.* "Make another move, and I'll shoot."

Swallowing, I lowered my arms back down to my sides and stayed where I was. He walked farther into the room, appearing to wander aimlessly, but his steps brought him closer until he was standing only a foot away. His eyes were even fiercer up close, like a hawk's. And at some point in the past, I noticed, somebody had broken his nose.

"I believe I asked you a direct question."

"Yes," I said. "I am alone." *Is he one of them?*

He smiled. It wasn't reassuring. "Is your name Christina Parker?"

I was instantly on my guard. "Maybe."

"You certainly look like her." He fished into his pockets, producing a picture I had trouble recognizing at first. My senior photo. My face was fuller, my color less pallid, but it was me. I almost reached for it but stopped myself just in time. "Strong resemblance," he said, glancing first at me and then at the photograph. "Wouldn't you say?"

"Who *are* you?" I repeated.

"I'm detective Timothy O' Rourke."

Detective? Like a private investigator? Did my parents send him?

"You are Christina Parker, yes?"

I hesitated. "Yes…"

"Good." He winked at me. "Won't be needing this, then." He lowered the gun, turned the safety back on, and tucked it back into his holster. "Your parents hired me to find you and rescue you," he added, making my deadening heart flutter with renewed hope.

"You mean…they're still free?"

"Aye. Somewhere safe. But I'd rather not say where. Just in case — " His fingers grazed my cheek, touching the bruise Michael had left when he'd hit me. It sent waves of pain rippling down my face and I shied away. "That's a nice shiner you've got there. Who gave it to you?"

"My captor," I said flatly.

He raised an eyebrow. "Captor?"

"I've been kidnapped and he's holding me hostage here."

"Does your captor have a name?"

It stuck me that if he had asked me this yesterday, I wouldn't have known the answer. "Michael."

"Michael Boutilier?"

The French surname made me blink in surprise — Michael certainly hadn't *looked* French. "I don't know," I said honestly. "He was careful around me."

"Not careful enough, I daresay." The detective's voice held a hint of a smirk, though when I looked at him his face was impassive.

He took me by the arm, leading me down the stairs. I felt a surge of relief so strong it was dizzying. *Michael won't be able to hurt me or threaten me anymore. It's almost over.*

"Michael Boutilier is a very powerful man."

"I'll bet," I murmured. I would have agreed with him if he'd said the sky was yellow.

"Aye," Timothy said. "Murder, arson, kidnapping, robbery. He was a criminal long before he joined the IMA. Prominent member of a Cajun gang in Lafayette during his teen years. Louisiana still hasn't lifted the bounty on him." He stopped, and said in a tone I couldn't quite read, "You're lucky to be alive, lass."

"What's the IMA?"

"Integrated Military Affairs. It's not affiliated with the U.S. military or any other department of the U.S. Government, although they know it exists. You didn't hear that from me, though."

"*Who* are they?"

"Mercenaries, Christina Parker. Powerful mercenaries, trained like soldiers."

Timothy stopped walking. There were splinters of wood scattering the floor of the hallway. He must have broken the door down. "Right. You don't have any shoes on. I'll carry you."

"That won't be necessary."

"Don't be ridiculous. You'll get splinters."

The detective swung me up, in spite of my protests, forcing me to cling to him like a monkey as he stepped over the sharp pieces of wood. My breath caught as I surveyed the landscape. I could see hazy mountains in the background, closer than they had been before, and the vibrant green of the hills below us; they were dotted with yellow wildflowers.

It was beautiful, but wild and unaccommodating.

"Lovely, isn't it?" the detective murmured. "So isolated. Takes your breath clean away."

It was as if he'd read my mind. Timothy was far more perceptive than I'd initially thought. Stronger, too. His lanky, awkward frame belied a formidable strength. "How did you find me? I'm still not clear on that."

"They have multiple bases around this area. It was a matter of hit-or-miss."

"Hit-or-miss?"

"We had no way of knowing *which* base he'd take you to. Ah, here we are." He stopped at a black, unmarked sedan.

Just like the one Michael drives. "Is that your car?" I tried to clear my head.

"No, it's the agency's." He set me down to open the door.

The interior was spotless. I saw a bottle of iced tea in the cup holder. Lemon flavor. I couldn't see this man anything so sweet; it seemed like a prop. *Stop it. You're being paranoid.*

"Nice, hmm? Gets the job done."

Granted, if he did belong to a detective agency they'd be able to afford nice cars. Of course, they'd want them to be conspicuous, and it stood to reason that investigative agencies might buy their cars in bulk from the same dealership. *But still…*

Timothy held open the door for me. I swallowed. "Um, I'm sorry, but I'd like to see a badge before I get into the car with you."

"Smart girl," he remarked. "I was afraid you wouldn't ask. Here."

He handed me his billfold. I opened it carefully, tracing the gold ridges of the crest with my finger. His ID was in there. I looked at the photo and then at his face to make sure they matched up. He looked a little younger in the photo but couldn't be faulted for that; it was him.

"Sorry," I said again, handing the wallet back.

"Don't be, Christina. It's not every girl who would get into a strange car with a strange man."

I smiled, feeling foolish and uncomfortable. Timothy slammed the door behind me and got in on the driver's side. I was initially glad he hadn't put me in the passenger's seat since it meant I wouldn't be obligated to converse with him, but the backseat conjured up unpleasant memories of being a prisoner, bound and gagged, treated like baggage.

The car lapsed into silence. Though the heater was on, the air seemed to grow colder. After a few minutes, he turned on the radio. A slow, moody rock song came through the speakers. It was pretty old, from the late eighties — before I was born.

"Are you Irish?" I tried to take my mind off the dark synthesizers and unsettling lyrics.

His eyes regarded me in the rear view mirror. "How could you tell?"

"Partly the name. O' Rourke. Mostly, though, it's your accent."

Against the song's dark melody, my voice sounded falsely bright.

Timothy scanned a deserted mountain pass and made a right turn. "You've a good ear."

"Where are you from originally?"

"Kildare."

"What brought you all the way to the United States?"

"You shouldn't ask so many questions, Christina Parker. Don't you know that old saying? Curiosity killed the cat."

I smiled nervously. "Well, I guess it's good I'm not a cat, huh?"

His laughter made me want to leap out of the car. I stopped trying to talk to him and looked out the window instead. Tall evergreens towered over the car, throwing it into shadow. A river ran parallel to the road, slipping in and out of sight through the trees like a winding blue ribbon. *We really are in the middle of nowhere.*

I wanted to cry when we finally came upon a weathered sign informing us that we were just twenty miles from the nearest town. "Hale," I said reverently. Just the name sounded comforting. "Do you think they'll have a police station?"

"Probably," he said thoughtfully.

We passed more trees. The river ended. I watched one minute tick by on the dashboard clock. Then ten. Fifteen. Half an hour. *We should have arrived at Hale by now.* The trees were growing thicker. It looked like we were getting farther from civilization, not closer.

The car jolted; the road was no longer paved, but dirt. I leaned forward, gripping the armrest of the seat in front. "I think you missed the turnoff."

I know."

He did? "Weren't we going to Hale?"

"No. We're going to my agency. I need you to fill out a statement."

"Where is your agency?" I no longer cared if I sounded suspicious. This detective with the sharp eyes and broken nose had me on edge. He'd purposely led me to believe we were going into town and I wanted to know why. "Is it in the middle of the woods?"

"You'll know when we get there," was his cryptic response.

It *was* in the middle of the woods. The building's facade was a dark gray stone, granite maybe, surrounded by a steel gate ringed with barbed wire. Two men in green uniforms were standing guard. Both wore sunglasses, though the building threw them both in shadow. Timothy reached into his shirt pocket and flashed a pass. They waved him through.

I couldn't help but notice that Timothy had kept his pass facing away from me.

It's nothing.

It didn't feel like nothing.

"What is this place?" I whispered, feeling goosebumps erupt up and down my arms. It seemed wrong to have all this in a mountain forest. "It doesn't look like a detective agency."

Timothy turned around, smiling brightly. "It isn't."

"What?" I thought I'd misheard him.

He reached for my hand. I thought it was a smarmy attempt to comfort me — until the handcuff snapped around my wrist. *Shit.* I lunged for the door, already knowing it was going to be locked. Timothy reached around the seat and fixed the other cuff to the door handle.

A malicious smile twisted his lips. "This isn't a detective agency, and my name isn't Timothy O' Rourke."

"I figured that out when you wouldn't show me the other badge," I lied.

"Smart lass." He grabbed for me. I jerked my leg away, crawling as close to the door as I could. "Too smart. I thought you might not come with me, but I'm *so* glad you did. What is that charming saying you Yanks have? Like a lamb to the slaughter?"

"Don't condescend to me, you lying bastard. What's your real name?"

"Adrian Callaghan," he said, slipping out of the car.

What have I gotten myself into? I'd been better off with Michael.

The other passenger door opened. I lashed out with my foot. "Stay away!"

He raised an eyebrow at my reaction. "Did Michael mention me to you?"

"In passing," I snarled. "It didn't sound like he thought very highly of you."

"But I'm very good at what I do," he said, in the same tone you would use to console a child. "I suppose you could say that I get a... certain pleasure out of my work."

I screamed.

"Nobody will come." He gave me a devastating smile and got out of the car again. A few seconds later the door I was leaning against opened. I tumbled out of the car, still attached to the door by my wrist. My head banged against the metal ridge at the bottom and I bit my tongue. I could taste blood in my mouth when I sat up.

"You can imagine my disappointment when your parents escaped."

"It must have been *crushing*."

"Oh, believe me; it was. But I feel so much better knowing that I'll have you in their stead, my bonnie lass." He pulled out a dishrag. Fumes rose from the terrycloth, sickeningly sweet. He forced the rag against my mouth and nose. I clawed at his hand, scratching, hitting, punching.

Adrian pressed down harder. "Hmm...you're a feisty one."

My chest felt like it was going to implode. I wouldn't be able to hold my breath much longer. He knew it. I knew it. I squeezed my eyes shut, trying to summon the strength for a final desperate attack — and he *punched* me in the stomach. I inhaled sharply, and got a lungful of the noxious fumes. Right before I lost consciousness, I heard him laugh. Felt him lean in and whisper, "I'll be looking forward to breaking you."

I opened my eyes.

I was tied to a swiveling computer chair with my hands bound behind my back. In the middle of what appeared to be a large conference room. In front of me was a large desk. A man was seated at the desk, his fingers steepled at his mouth: olive skin, black hair in tight curls, a face like a toad. I started, wondering how long he'd been watching me —and why.

"How kind of you to join us."

I looked pointedly around the otherwise empty room. "Us?"

"Mr. Callaghan will be accompanying us. I believe you've met."

I struggled to look over my shoulder. He was leaning against the wall, arms cushioning his head. His smile grew when our eyes met. I looked away. "What do you want?"

"Only your cooperation, Miss Parker."

"That's all?"

"You'd be surprised. But Mr. Callaghan over there can be quite persuasive."

Don't you dare look over there. "I don't know my parents' whereabouts."

"I believe you. But I never said anything about wanting information on your parents." *He doesn't? Wait, what?* "I'm actually more curious as to why you're still alive."

"I was taken hostage."

"Ah, but Mr. Boutilier was ordered to kill you when your parents escaped." I hated to think how my expression must have looked. "You didn't know?"

I once read that surprise is the most difficult emotion to fake. I hoped to God that was true, and that I looked like I was playing the part. "No."

"Do you have any idea why he might have gone against this direct order, Miss Parker?"

"No."

"I see." He leaned back. "Mr. Callaghan? Any thoughts?"

I heard him step away from the wall. "She knows more than she's letting on."

"Really," the boss said calmly.

Adrian pulled the collar of my blouse aside — *oh my god he's right behind me* — and said, "Look at her neck, sir. She didn't do that to herself."

The boss leaned forward, causing the dimples at his wrists to deepen. "He's right, Miss Parker. Care to explain yourself?"

"I don't understand." The healing knife scars? Any hostage might walk away with marks like that. They proved nothing.

"Minor hematoma," Adrian clarified. "Hickey, in the

167

vernacular."

My whole body went rigid. *Oh, God.*

"Thank you, Mr. Callaghan. I'll repeat the question: Do you have any idea why Mr. Boutilier might have kept you alive? Do not lie to me this time, Miss Parker."

I started to cry. I'd thought I was escaping at last; I'd traded one circle of hell for another.

"Crocodile tears will not help your situation."

"Fine! He tried to *rape* me, you bastards. Happy now? Oh, and for your information — *these are real tears!*"

The two men exchanged a look.

"She isn't the type he usually goes for. And Michael has been known to defy my commands in the past simply because he can. There is a possibility, however remote, that she is telling the truth."

"She's already lied once." Adrian glanced at me. "Give me an hour with her. I'll make sure she'll tell you anything you want to know."

"No!"

"That's enough." The boss rubbed his temples. "Take here to one of the holding cells. I'll deal with her later — do *not* harm her."

Holding cell apparently meant "white padded room." A security camera in the corner recorded our progress as Adrian dragged me inside. There was no furniture, not even a bed. Off to the side, hidden from the view of the camera and door, was an alcove with a toilet and sink.

Adrian drew a knife from his pocket. I took a step back. "Your boss said not to harm me."

"Don't you want to be untied?"

"I'd rather take my chances with the rope."

He laughed and pushed me up against one of the soft walls as he started sawing through the fibers. I stared at the wall and tried not to think about what else that knife had cut. "Is this how you treat all your guests?"

"You could say you're being given preferential treatment."

The ropes fell away. I rubbed my wrists, repressing the urge to scratch the sores. "I'd hate to see how many pieces your regulars are in then."

Adrian tucked the knife back into whatever secret pocket he'd produced it from. "In a few more minutes, they'd be on their knees, telling me anything I wanted to know." The implicit meaning in his words was not lost on me.

"You're trying to scare me."

"I don't have to try. I know you're already scared. That was a good show you put on, by the way. I thought the tears were a particularly nice touch."

"Leave me alone."

He took a step closer instead. "He makes you feel so weak, doesn't he?"

"Who? I don't know who you're talking about."

"Oh, I think you do. Why do you provoke him, Christina Parker, knowing the result will never change? Unless you changed…" He swung out his arm in a lazy grab. I stumbled trying to get away from him. "I can see why he would want you. You're just his type — female and alive."

"You're a bastard," I hissed.

His cold laughter stayed with me long after he'd left.

Chapter Ten

Pressure

Michael:

Driving relaxed me. It was mindless, automatic, and required just enough concentration to keep my mind from wandering. It usually worked. Not today. The mountain silence bothered me. I didn't need *peace*. I needed a violent way to release this pent-up energy in my veins.

I switched on the radio. Loud music pulsed through the car, keeping time with the throbbing in my head. I tore the top off a bottle of aspirin and chewed two of the bitter pills.

Bad enough that my boss was showing me an astonishing lack of respect; somehow the deprecation had trickled down to my hostage. I didn't see how she could keep it up under circumstances where men much tougher than her had crumbled.

I'd only intended to intimidate her a little. That was why I'd used the knife — that, and I felt I had, inexplicably, been too easy on her. She sobbed every night in her room but still didn't look upon me with real fear — and hadn't, not since the night when I forced myself on her. I didn't intend to make that mistake again. Not when I found myself enjoying *that* more than I should have. There were bridges I did not want to cross; taking sexual satisfaction from a woman's pain was not something I wanted to indulge in. I'd tried brutish violence.

171

But when she walked out of the bathroom in that white towel, solemn and wide-eyed and innocent as a goddamn child, something inside me just snapped.

I wanted her — and knowing I couldn't have her made her fucking irresistible. Being aware of the cognitive processes behind the attraction made it no easier to bear. She wasn't worth the trouble. This was going to get me killed. My goddamn body just wouldn't get the fucking message.

I'd received another call from the IMA. Not from an office grunt this time, but my actual boss. He wanted an update, which I had given to him, glossing over the unnecessary details. "And the virus, Mr. Boutilier?"

"She knows nothing. The only thing she could tell me was a story behind its origin." Because I felt like irritating him, I told him the story.

"How delightfully amusing, while simultaneously being a complete waste of my time." He paused and said heavily. "You may as well know, her parents jumped again."

Off a cliff? No. I wasn't that lucky. "Where?"

"We're not sure. I have agents on it. We suspect the Dominican Republic."

If they were in South America, they'd be taken to Target Island upon capture. Rubens Parker would be subject to all kinds of unpleasant means of persuasion until he disclosed the nature of the virus and what he had done with the information he had stolen.

"Really wearing out their travel passes, aren't they?" I said dryly.

"Do not joke, Mr. Boutilier. This whole ordeal is severely trying my patience. I do not want to waste any more resources on this mission. I have already spent a fortune on air fare and paying off the local authorities — all to no avail. The girl has revealed nothing of use, and her parents appear not to care about their child at all. In any case, they are not leaping to the bait as I had hoped they would," he concluded.

"What are you proposing, sir?"

"I want you to neutralize the girl."

I pulled up at a gas station. The tank was running empty, and the nearest IMA building was still a good twenty miles away. I filled up the tank, reparked the car, and then went into the store, mindful of the security cameras over the doorway. My sweatshirt hood was up, hiding my hair and casting my face in shadow.

The inside was pretty empty. The female cashier was flirting with a local. Two guys in leather motorcycle jackets were perusing the dirty magazines with a cop giving them the eye while he munched on a bagel. Nobody appeared to notice me.

I had neglected to notify the IMA that I had changed my base of operations. Surprise, surprise. No cops. That cinched it for me. Kent had dug up some disturbing information on some of my colleagues that suggested a mutiny was in the works, and the IMA had screwed us over before. Contract killers were not exactly known for their outstanding sense of loyalty but I never imagined that when the time came to select a scapegoat, I would be the top choice.

I picked up a six-pack of energy drinks and brought it up to the counter. The cashier turned away from her man to ring up the purchase. "Is that all?" Her tone suggested it had damn well better be.

"No," I said. "I would also like" — I eyed the selection of doughnuts behind the sneeze-guard and remembered I hadn't fed the girl yet. The cashier shuffled impatiently as I dallied — "some of those," I finished. "One old-fashioned, one jelly-filled."

"I need to see some ID. For the energy drinks."

I handed her the one for Edward Collins. She studied it longer than necessary while her boyfriend chuckled and made snide comments. Nobody would think I was under eighteen. Even the suspicious cop in the back would laugh at such an accusation. I glanced at him just in case, but the cashier hadn't attracted his attention; he was keeping his eyes on the bike gang, who were starting to get rowdy as they picked out their desired brands of cigarettes.

The cashier glanced in that direction, too, handing me back my

ID without another glance. Probably deciding I was just another scruffy lowlife. "Your total is twelve-fifty. Here's your change." Her body was twisting itself around to maneuver around the checkout counter, so she could go and assist the cop in dealing with the trouble brewing.

I didn't pull down the hood of the sweatshirt until I reached my car. I pulled out of the lot with the doughnuts and energy drinks in the front seat. Neutralize her. *Kill* her. Buying the doughnuts seemed foolish now. She would undoubtedly see it as a last meal.

Fuck. I beat the steering wheel. Another driver honked back angrily. I gave them the finger. Kent had been right; the IMA would be far better off if *I* was leading them. I knew what my first order of business would be: have Callaghan executed for treason, and make the use of hostages an absolute last priority. They were too much fucking trouble.

My phone chose that moment to ring. Caller ID was blocked. *Shit.* I toyed with the idea of letting it go directly to voice mail, then pulled off to the side of the road like the pussy I was. "Michael."

"Hello, Mr. Boutilier."

"Hello, sir," I said, with forced civility. "What do you need?"

"I need you to report to the nearest IMA base immediately," he said, just as pleasantly. "I don't know where you are, Mr. Boutilier — all I know is that you are not at your assigned location, which means you are AWOL. If you do not touch base within two hours, we will consider your intentions hostile and hunt you down."

"Unfortunately, sir, my assigned location was infiltrated by the local police. I have moved to a new location, which I will report as soon as I have made progress with the subject. Sir."

"...You mean base one-two-eight?"

Lucky guess. I let myself betray no reaction. "I repeat, sir — "

"Drop the act, Mr. Boutilier. I already know that you have been using base one-two-eight without permission. That would be trespassing. But no matter, I already sent Mr. Callaghan to pick up Miss Parker. As of this instant, she is no longer in your charge."

She's with Callaghan? "Why would you do that, sir?"

"Mr. Callaghan was assigned as your backup, Mr. Boutilier, in the event that something like this transpired."

The bastard must have been thrilled — one more thing he could lord over me.

"She arrived in remarkable condition," Richardson was saying. "Not a scratch. I find that very strange considering that I distinctly recall ordering you to kill her."

He was pretending he knew more than he did. Standard intimidation techniques. It was used to make subjects feel as if they had no choice but to confess. I found it annoying and offensive that he was attempting to use such basic methods on me.

"I felt it would be an irreparable mistake." I only just remembered to add "sir" at the end. "The decision seemed rash. I waited — in case you changed your mind. Killing a hostage is easy. *Unkilling* them is difficult enough that nobody's mastered it yet."

"I pay you to follow orders. Not to feel."

"Her parents are already skittish. Killing her would send them running to the other side of the globe with their tails between their legs."

"Their daughter was withholding information."

"She knew nothing, sir. I was very thorough with her."

"Yes...I'm sure you were, Mr. Boutilier." Richardson let that hang. "You also disobeyed a direct order."

"With all due respect, that direct order was horse shit."

"You have always had a penchant for insubordination, Mr. Boutilier. A quirk which I have tolerated until now because of your ability to get the job done. This time, your reckless disregard for the rules has compromised not just yourself, but me, and the entire agency.

"We are going to have the girl interrogated. Provided her answers match yours, you have nothing to fear. You have two hours — one hour, fifty minutes now — to report to the nearest IMA base. If you do not, we will consider your intentions hostile and I will send a team of men to take you down. We will not tolerate subversiveness, Mr. Boutilier. Not even from you."

The phone went dead.

Christina:

The boss came in while I was eating lunch, picking charcoal from a brownie the soggy, TV-dinner-style tray. He was accompanied by a nasty-looking guard displaying an equally nasty-looking weapon. I gritted my teeth and concentrated on the meal, trying not to look at either of them. It was difficult — particularly since they made no effort not to look at *me*.

"I apologize if I offended you earlier, Miss Parker." I glanced at him. The obsequious chagrin on his face was almost as horrible as Adrian's cruel smile.

At least I knew what Adrian's intentions *were*. I had no idea at all what the boss's investment in the matter was. I *thought* I had, but he said he wasn't interested in my parents anymore. Instead he'd asked me all kinds of questions about *Michael*.

"I have spoken to Mr. Boutilier. He has informed me that he is on his way."

I was about to ask who Mr. Boutilier was. Then remembered that Adrian had addressed my captor as *Michael Boutilier*. Michael was coming? Here? *It all comes back to Michael. Michael, Michael,* Michael.

"I suggest you speak freely while that opportunity is still

available to you, Miss Parker."

"I already told you everything I know."

He regarded me with dark eyes. "And you have no questions?"

"Okay," I said, looking up. "Where are my parents?"

The look in his eyes said I'd failed some kind of test. "Fleeing the country, if Mr. Boutilier's testimony is any indication."

There he was, dragging Michael's name into this again. "Good."

He sighed. "Not good for you, I'm afraid, Miss Parker."

"My name is *Christina*." The guard touched the butt of his gun as I swayed to my feet. "What do you want from me? Why are you asking me these questions? Why are you hurting us?"

"You feel strongly about this."

"You're messing with my life and the lives of the people I care about. Why wouldn't I?"

"Mr. Callaghan seems to be under the impression you're keeping secrets from us."

I'd been in the process of raising the brownie to my mouth. "I already told you everything I know."

"He believes Mr. Boutilier may have revealed inside information to you."

"Why?" I asked. "He had no motive."

It seemed like all of the questions he had asked were leading up to this moment, that he had been building up to some horrifying conclusion. I was right. "Perhaps you gave him a motive."

"He kidnapped me, threatened my family, threatened *me*. You can't possibly be implying that I would — " Images rushed through my head. Horrible images, rousing the darkest fears in my subconscious. I shook myself, trying to dissolve them. "No. *No*. I wouldn't. Never."

But the boss was nodding, as if he'd expecting this. "That's how it starts, I'm afraid."

"How *what* starts?"

"Have you ever heard of Stockholm syndrome, Miss Parker?"

"You can't be serious." I took a step forward and the guard reached for his gun.

"Careful, Miss Parker," the boss cautioned.

"Are you crazy?" I demanded. "How many levels of sick do you have to be to think that I would ever feel anything for that bastard other than hate?" I found myself closing the distance before I was aware of what my right arm was doing. I felt possessed by some demonic spirit, the weight of my anger was so great. "Do you know what he tried to do to me? *Do* you?"

I hadn't even realized I'd slapped him until the guard tackled me to the floor. The 250-something pounds of muscle slammed all the air out of my lungs, bruising a few ribs to boot. He pinned my throat with his bulky forearm, preventing any oxygen from making it back inside my lungs.

"That was very unwise."

His voice sounded far away. Red and black spots danced before my eyes, standing out in stark relief against the white padding. Then suddenly, I could breathe. My throat ached, my head was buoyant, and my eyes felt like they might just burst, but I could *breathe*.

"If you ever assault me again, physically or otherwise, I will let Mr. Callaghan have his way with you." The boss gave me a hard look that belied his fake tan and round paunch. "I suggest you learn your place — and quickly. Is that clear?"

I nodded.

"As I was saying, Stockholm syndrome is not an uncommon disorder, especially in isolated cases like these, when the captor is a member of the opposite sex. Stockholm syndrome, Miss Parker, is about power. Mr. Boutilier had power over your life and undoubtedly informed you of that. Perhaps he showed you some small gesture of kindness, established rapport — something that made you believe he was showing you favor?"

I found myself remembering the razor, the new clothes, and the way his face looked when he shoved me away in the hall — almost *tortured* — but no, that meant nothing. Only that he had the tattered remains of a conscience. That he wasn't as bad as Adrian. Not yet.

But he had also forced himself on me, *hit* me, and cut me with a

181

knife.

The boss was confusing guilt, a normal, healthy, *human* emotion with something more. Something sinister and warped.

"Did Adrian tell you I was perfectly willing to turn him in?"

"Denial is a powerful thing. It can lead one to… overcompensate."

"I spent every day thinking of escape — or, at the very least, survival. Michael showed me little kindness. I was lucky if I received food and water. He made no attempt to establish *rapport.* Living under his regime of terror was a nightmare. You're sick in the head if you believe otherwise."

The guard decided to intervene at this point. I heard the snap of handcuffs and shot the boss a glare.

"Miss Parker," he said, in a voice that reminded me of slimy, crawly things. "Perhaps *your* head is the one that needs to be examined."

I cursed at him. The boss stood there, accepting the abuse, waiting for me to calm down enough so he could deliver more of his own. Whereas my blows were glancing and superficial, his cut straight to the bone.

When I had run out of curses and fallen into a seething, livid silence, he said, "Are you ready to be reasonable, Miss Parker?"

"He almost killed me."

"And yet he didn't, Miss Parker, and you stand before me as the very picture of perfect health. My operative would never defy a direct order unless it was in his interests to do so." He didn't have to say what these were; his gaze said everything.

"How closely do you actually watch him?" I snapped. "Did you ever stop to think that he might be working for somebody else? That maybe he didn't feel like listening to you?"

Both the guard and the boss froze over. I'd hit the nail on their head — and hearing their own suspicions voiced by such an unlikely candidate had taken them by such surprise that even they, with all their training, had let down their guard. For a few seconds, at least. Both their faces became indecipherable masks. "We will have to see what Mr. Boutilier says."

He might as well have pushed me into the ocean with cement shoes and told me to swim.

Michael:

I pulled up to the base, flashing my ID at the guard. The green light flashed and he waved me through. That was a good sign. I locked up the car, glancing around at the too-silent trees, before making my way to the base entrance. There were no lights outside because those could potentially be spotted by passing planes at night.

The man who'd built this base had designed the exterior based on his experience in Vietnam. He'd been impressed by the way the Vietcong had used the thick foliage of the jungle environment to their advantage, which was why he'd chosen the middle of the woods as a location. There were many traps located around the outside. Some I knew about, some I didn't; I always stayed on the path. Of the few prisoners that had managed to escape, none had survived.

I dialed Richardson's number to tell him to call off the dogs. He wasn't picking up. *Great.* I shoved the phone in my back pocket. *Looks like we're doing this the old-fashioned way.*

The most innovative and brilliant detail of the base's camouflage was the garden on the roof. The granite walls dipped down, forming a basin several feet deep at the top of the building, rather like an earth-filled swimming pool. Pine trees and natural forms of ground cover had been planted there. Combined with the granite, extracted from the quarries in the Cascade Mountains, the base was invisible from the air.

I continued down the path. Then I paused. A soft sound, almost too soft to hear, echoed briefly in the clearing. A footstep, just a beat too slow. I bent and pretended to tie my shoe, looking around for any sign of my pursuer. Nothing. Gritting my teeth, I walked the rest of the way, aware of the footsteps ghosting mine. I didn't glance behind me or slow my pace again.

Someone was following me. But why? When I got through the door, there was another unpleasant surprise. A security checkpoint. Two guards, a man and a woman, regarded me through their shaded visors. *This is new.*

"Someone was tailing me outside," I informed the woman.

I thought I saw her eyes flicker behind the tinted frames. "Michael Boutilier?"

"Yes." I didn't bother to hide my impatience. "Why am I being treated like suspicious personnel? My card was cleared."

A scuffling sound drew my attention away from the female guard long enough to glance over my shoulder. Another guard was now standing in front of the door. Blocking it.

"And you must be the welcoming committee."

A harsh sound escaped the man. It might have been a laugh. I turned towards him since he was the only one who'd given me a reaction. "What the hell is going on?"

The woman said, "Disarm, and put your hands against the wall."

So Richardson hadn't been making idle threats. "I was under the impression that I had two hours to reach the base and file a report. I want to speak to Richardson."

"He will see you."

"Good." I moved to get by her but she intercepted me.

"After you disarm."

I tossed my issued gun into the plastic tub the man kicked at me. The woman sighed at her partner. "Eric?"

He shoved me into the wall, yanking my arms behind my back. The woman frisked me methodically, taking, in addition to my gun, a Swiss Army knife, a lock-picking kit, the keys to my car, my cell phone, and the knife I kept in my boot. I turned around, breathing hard, and glared at the three of them. "My *car* keys?"

"These items will be inventoried. They will be returned to you on your way out."

"I see no reason why I should be forced to endure such a humiliating breach of protocol."

"We have our orders," Eric said.

"So do I." I took a step forward, gratified when they all backed away. "Step aside."

Cloak and Dagger by Nenia Campbell

Chapter Eleven

Terror

Christina:

I ate though I wasn't hungry. I needed my strength. I was going
to see my captor again. The man who had made these past couple
months' worth of hell. I tried to tell myself I could do this. That I was
a strong young woman and — oh, who was I kidding? He terrified
me, and now he was returning at the worst possible time to damn
me. His boss already believed I had Stockholm syndrome. Now my
word was completely dependent on his testimony, and there was no
doubt in my mind that his arrival would lead to an even closer
inspection of all my behavior.

In fact, I was beginning to suspect that the IMA wasn't ever
going to let me go, in spite of their assurances that I wouldn't be
harmed if I cooperated. Not after they had brought me to one of
their top-secret bases. I might have been young, but wasn't *stupid*.
They knew I could point out faces and names. The FBI would want
to talk to me and perhaps the CIA. I would be interviewed. My
release, if it happened, would be widely televised — the IMA had
become a liability, just as Michael had, by letting me see their true
face.

I finished the juice, pushing the empty carton away from me.
The air conditioner, regulated by a thermostat I could not see,

switched on and I shivered, wishing I was wearing something more substantial. The temperature in the cell was always about ten degrees too cold.

I scooted into a corner, pressing myself into the padded wall. It was only mildly warmer than the center of the floor. I looked up at the blank ceiling. The empty white room had bothered me from the beginning and now I knew why: it looked like the solitary confinement rooms in insane asylums. The padded walls, the absence of stimuli, the buzzing silence — the similarities were chilling. I fought to stay alert, but my eyelids were heavy. Almost like lead.

I was so tired…it was easier just not to move.

And the nightmares began.

I dreamed about gunshots in the middle of a dark forest where redwoods pierced the sky like black lances. The tops of the trees climbed higher and higher until the sky fell away, and the trees became the iron bars of a prison cell. I dreamed about concrete mansions and endless hallways where a faceless man chased me, slowly closing in. In a flash I was no longer the hunted — I was the hunter: cold-hearted and intent. No matter how badly I wanted to, I couldn't keep my finger from pulling the trigger of the gun I held. Something slammed into my back, blazing with heat, and just as abruptly I found myself on the floor, swimming in my own blood, looking into the piercing green eyes of my killer.

With a gasp, I shot up. The door to the cell was sliding open. I stared at the guard with a dazed, bewildered expression. "Get up," he ordered.

"Why?" I asked. Oops. I should have asked where. *Why* sounded a mite too confrontational. Clearly the guard thought so, too, because he snapped a pair of steel manacles around my wrists and did not answer my question. I grimaced into the padding of the wall. Several of the more sensitive sores reopened as the sharp edges of the metal rings chafed my flesh, forming identical bracelets of pain. "You're hurting me," I said. "My wrists are bleeding — they'll get infected!"

The guard muttered something surly and dragged me to my feet. I watched him type a long passcode into the access panel. With a whoosh of air, the steel doors slid open and we were in the hallway. We were the only ones, and the heels of the guard's boots echoed like gunshots. The hallway seemed to extend infinitely in both directions and all the doors were identical — solid steel, and airtight.

Even though I'd been distracted by the discovery that my "savior" was a sadistic madman, I didn't remember the building looking this big from the outside. Were we underground? Or did the walls just *look* deceptively huge? I couldn't even figure out how the guard was managing to navigate until I heard him under his breath. *Counting. Counting the* doors. That crushed my hopes of escape. Even if I somehow managed to break free from my cell, I still wouldn't be able to find myself out unless I memorized the floor plan.

It was ingenious; it was *insane* — and I hated them for it.

We stopped outside a door. Door number twenty-six of this hallway, from the guard's count. He pushed in the access code, his fingers stumbling in his haste. "Get in," he said, articulating the command with a push.

Get up, get in, get bent.

The guard gave me another shove and I stumbled forward, yelling as the floor came rushing up to meet my face. I had just enough time to think about how much it was going to hurt having my face smash against the stone tiles before the guard caught me by the chain links of my handcuffs. I stared at my scared reflection in the polished floor as the guard set me back on my knees.

Still shaken from the vertiginous fall, I looked around the room. Three of the walls were eggshell white but the one nearest to me was an opaque black glass that shone as smoothly as polished obsidian. If I looked closely, I could see the faint outlines of a room on the other side. *One way glass?* I moved closer and the guard yanked me back.

Was I being watched? "What's going on?" I yelped.

"Be quiet," he said edgily.

There was a slow revving noise, like an engine starting, and the ground beneath my feet *rumbled*. I felt it *move*. I jumped again, looking around with wild eyes, recounting all the high-tech traps I had seen in James Bond movies. One of the eggshell walls was parting to reveal a large TV screen. Confused, but still afraid, I watched the screen snap on to an analog channel. Then it flickered again and a man appeared on the screen. He was middle-aged with brown hair that was going gray, a drab suit, and easily forgettable features. He was also tied to a chair.

I squinted. The man's eyes shifted towards something off-screen. His face widened in a silent O of horror as another man walked on-screen. Michael. He was wearing a tight gray t-shirt, jeans, and a trench coat. I caught a flash of silver in his left hand, his switchblade. I saw the man's mouth move as Michael listened, his face impassive as he flicked the blade in and out. He must not have liked what he was hearing because he produced several sharp, gleaming objects from his pocket and started towards the other man. I looked away when the crotch of the bound man's pants darkened to black. *There but for the grace of God go I.*

This was the traitor that Michael had killed the day before I was brought here. The one who had killed a family. A family who had worked for the IMA. This man's blood had been on Michael's clothes. He looked like he should be teaching college students World History.

And if *this* man was capable of committing such atrocities, what sins had the family been guilty of to incur his wrath?

I shivered again. In the flickering lights of the garage, with his coat flaring out, Michael looked like a ferocious angel of death about to deliver his final judgment.

"I thought I'd spare you the audio."

Adrian.

He was propped against the door, holding a small remote, clearly delighting in my reaction. I hadn't even heard him come in. *How long has he been standing there?*

Adrian pressed a button and the TV disappeared. I looked around for the guard to find he had vanished. His edgy impatience now made sense. He knew who he was delivering me to, and didn't want to stick around to watch the show. My mouth wanted to curve into a scream. I couldn't let it; once I started, I wasn't sure I'd be able to stop.

He slipped the remote into his pocket. "Alone at last."

My lungs constricted. "Why did you show me that?"

Adrian didn't answer but his weight shifted towards me. I edged back. "Is that why I'm here? To watch your sick home videos?"

"No," he said, stooping down. Even kneeling, he was almost a full head taller than me. "That's not why you're here." He prodded my wrist. "This looks painful."

"That's because it *i* — ahhh!" I jerked away from him, gasping like a stuck pig. Something warm and liquid trickled down my wrist. *Blood. My blood.* I saw drops of it on the floor, gleaming under the lights like small garnets. *He ripped open one of the sores.*

"Oh dear," he said. "Are you going to faint?"

I'd landed in an even more vulnerable position. My fear was so thick it seemed to shimmer before my dizzy eyes like a desert mirage. He crawled closer, like a spider, looming over me. "You *are* going to faint." His glee at this was evident.

Panic exploded as I thought of all the unpleasant things he could do to me while I was unconscious. But even conscious, I was helpless without the use of my hands. I was trapped — and he knew it. I could only watch as he tilted his head to get a better look at me, like a painter studying a canvas. He was calculating how — and *where* — to hurt me next.

"I'm not going to faint," I said, without much conviction.

"Not yet," he agreed, his accented voice still pleasant. A genteel sadist.

"Your boss said not to hurt me."

"Not yet," he repeated, in that soft, seductive voice. "Poor Christina. So alone...so terrified."

Cloak and Dagger by Nenia Campbell

"No!" I gritted my teeth, grateful he couldn't see how tightly my fists were clenched behind my back. "I'm not afraid of you!"

"I said I was going to break you. And I will." His voice dropped, so low that I had to strain to hear him. I didn't want to, but for some reason I couldn't seem to shut him out. "My boss doesn't believe your amusing little tirades. And Michael won't save you, either. That boy only cares about his own worthless hide." He grinned suddenly: an artist inspired. "You couldn't stop him, could you? Well. When the time comes, you won't be able to stop me, either..."

I froze as he leaned closer. His fingers tilted my face upward for inspection. It took every fragment of control I had not to look away from his scrutiny or scream at his touch; I had a feeling that to do so would mean the end of me. "No," he mused. "I don't think you are going to be as entertaining as I thought." He smiled again, tucking some strands of hair behind my ear. "We'll just have to make do with what we have, won't we?"

He opened his mouth to unleash more poison and a series of beeps filled the air. Without moving back from me, he took the call. The world halted on its axis as he listened intently to whatever was being said to him, toying with the strand of hair that had caught his interest. When he hung up, he sighed. "Speak of the devil," he said, with mock regret.

"What?" I mouthed the word, unable to vocalize it. My head was still full of his sinister promises, the unpleasant feel of his fingers, the sickening knowledge that I had just escaped a fate too horrible for words alone to describe.

"Never mind." Adrian slipped the phone into his pocket. "Come on," he said, as I stumbled upright. "Michael, the prodigal son, has arrived home at last." He flashed his teeth; it wasn't a smile.

Michael had been the nameless man of my nightmares so long, I still felt my adrenaline kick-start every time I saw him — like a Pavlovian experiment gone wrong. Most of the fear I had for Michael was being canceled out by an overwhelming terror of Adrian Callaghan. There was something very *wrong* with him.

His hand was on my shoulder, steering me. My wrist throbbed behind my back, too sore to be gripped; we both knew the consideration on his part was a farce. I could still feel that phantom tearing sensation, and the white-hot agony that had followed in its wake. The expression on his face…it had been like a shark that smelled blood.

He looked down at me curiously. "Something wrong?"

I didn't answer, and felt his hand brush the back of my neck. I jumped, hissing like a cat and heard him chuckle, quietly satisfied.

It was a long walk. He had ample time to make me squirm. My nerves were shot to pieces when we arrived at our destination.

This room was big, the size of a classroom, with white walls —

195

no opaque one-way windows this time — and navy blue carpeting. A large oak table sat in the center, surrounded by a number of chairs. A waste considering that the only other people in the room were the boss, his purple-scarred escort, Michael, and a couple of guards flanking the doorway with their weapons in easy reach.

Adrian pushed me into one of the chairs farthest from the door. With my arms behind my back the way they were, I was in constant danger of slipping off the edge of my seat. The boss laughed at my discomfort. "You can remove her handcuffs, Mr. Callaghan. She's not going anywhere."

Adrian knelt down, close — much too close — to my leg. The handcuffs loosened and slipped away. Without a word, he settled into a seat one down from me, setting the handcuffs on the table with a clatter. I was sitting across from Michael. I could feel his eyes boring holes into me like acid. I sneaked a look at him through the screen of my lashes.

He was wearing plainclothes and looked absolutely furious; jaw tight, military-straight posture, the muscles in his arms as taut as the bowstring on a crossbow. I immediately thought of that video, which was odd because in the parking garage he had showed no emotion at all.

"Is everyone present? Excellent." The boss shuffled some papers noisily. "Then we can proceed. I heard you had some trouble with the security checkpoint, Mr. Boutilier."

Michael's scowl intensified.

"Perhaps you will be pleased to hear that the answers you gave me are consistent with those of Miss Parker." His eyes flicked towards me, before going back to the waspish Michael across the table. "I apologize. I had not realized the nature of the situation. Perhaps your judgment was not as erroneous as I thought."

Adrian coughed.

"Thank you," Michael grated. He shot a menacing look at Adrian, who continued smiling.

"Regarding the girl's case: after much thought, I have reached a decision that should satisfy those who were entertaining…certain doubts."

He definitely looked at Michael when he said that.

"We will give her parents an ultimatum. They will have seventy-two hours to turn themselves in, or face the consequences. Mr. Boutilier, I hereby release you from your previous assignment. You will be replaced by your backup, Adrian Callaghan. *You* will fly to Michigan with one of our other operatives. I have already booked you a flight; the plane departs tomorrow."

Michigan? Why Michigan? Are my parents there? I thought they had fled the country. But Michael nodded, looking as though he had expected nothing less. "Yes, sir."

"What consequences?" I broke in. Everyone in the room looked at me when I said, in a loud voice, "What are you going to do to my parents?"

The boss raised an eyebrow. "Nothing."

I stared at him disbelievingly. "Nothing?"

"If you parents fail to meet our demands, we will do nothing — to them. They are too flighty, and I grow weary of this perpetual game of hide-and-seek. But I am afraid that you, Miss Parker, are an entirely different matter…"

Adrian drew a finger across his throat.

"I'll need a map of the location," Michael said.

If my parents don't cooperate, the IMA is going to kill me?

Adrian glanced away from me, letting his hand fall to the arm of his chair as he lifted his body higher. "You're letting the traitor go?"

"Mr. Boutilier passed all the lie detector tests with flying colors, and allowed our physicians to administer a truth serum" — he gave Adrian a meaningful look — "and I believe him. The girl will remain here. Under guard. Keep her in the holding cell but, again, do not harm her." This time Adrian received the stare weighted with disapproval. He dropped into an aggressive slouch.

"Coimhead fearg fhear na foighde," he said, pushing in his chair and walking out of the room. The guards made no move to intercept him as he passed, and his words rang in the silence. They had been in a

language I had never heard before — and it certainly hadn't been Latin-based. Gaelic, maybe. There was no misinterpreting the anger in his voice.

The boss frowned and tugged at his collar. "Mr. Sheffield, I'm putting you down as Callaghan's backup." This was addressed to one of the guards at the door. He nodded his assent, though he didn't look pleased. "Mr. Boutilier, would you take the girl back to her cell, since Mr. Callaghan has decided to leave prematurely?"

Michael nodded, getting up from his seat as well.

"Wonderful." He clapped his hands. "Everyone — dismissed."

I cried out when Michael took my by the wrist. Adrian had taken the handcuffs with him when he left — it figured that sicko would have his own personal pair — and Michael's fingers made direct contact sores. "What is it?"

"My wrists hurt."

There was a pause, presumably as he glanced at my wounds, and his hand relocated to my shoulder. His grip was surprisingly loose. I suspected I might even be able to tear out of it with a sharp lunge, but that would be fruitless — I had nowhere to run and he was faster. The only thing I'd accomplish would be getting myself a different escort and another pair of wretched handcuffs.

I could sense his mounting agitation; it was obvious, from the restraint in his hold. I assumed it had something to do with me and some unknown *faux pas* I committed in the conference room. When he said, "What happened to your wrists?" I was thrown.

"Why do you care?"

"If my subordinates are out there delivering their own brand of rough justice without my permission, I have the right to know. Answer the question."

"It wasn't a guard. They brought me to Adrian and — " I closed my mouth, remembering who I was talking to. What if Michael told Adrian what I said? Hell, he'd been about to send me to the man himself, back at the safe house.

"Who did?" Michael's grip tightened on my shoulder. "Tell me what happened."

"No."

"Tell me."

I had never heard such concentrated rage in such a short sentence; it was like being slapped in the face. I leaned away from him, shutting my eyes to close him out. But I couldn't turn off the pictures in my head as easily, and that pressure was bringing back too many memories.

—Except now, Adrian had joined the slide-show, too.

"Stop it," I gasped, when he shook me. "It's your fault."

"Why is it my fault?"

I pressed my lips together.

"Look, darlin. Callaghan is going to tear you apart. He will get inside your head and destroy you from the inside-out. You are completely" — he drew in a deep breath — "and I mean *completely* out of your league here."

"Why do you care?" I repeated adamantly. "*You* won't help me."

"Insurrection in the hallways?" an amused voice observed. "Michael, you know better."

"I'm taking the girl back to her cell — step aside."

I took a step back so Michael was standing between us. I hoped neither of them noticed. Adrian's eyes weren't focused on me, so I don't think *he* did. "I *am* sorry. I didn't realize you were already preoccupied," he murmured. "Don't let me keep you."

I saw a tendon in Michael's throat jump. "What do you want?"

"Answers." When Michael hesitated, Adrian sad, "I've been assigned as your replacement. I just have a few questions about her case. Nothing more." He looked at us both through hooded eyes, and I immediately distrusted him.

"Make it quick."

Adrian looked at me meaningfully and said nothing.

"Oh, for fuck's sake — " Michael took two steps closer. *"What?"*

Adrian bent his head to whisper in Michel's ear. I couldn't see his face, but the muscles in his shoulders bunched up. Whatever Adrian had asked him, he didn't seem to like it. "No?" Adrian asked, and laughed. "Oh, *good.*"

Michael punched Adrian in the face.

The movement was so fast, I barely saw it coming. Adrian must have, quick as he was, but he took it anyway. He reached into his slacks, pulled out a handkerchief, and began dabbing at the blood trickling from his nose.

"Oh my God," I said.

"Get out," Michael said. "I can break your nose again — and I *will* if I hear any more rumors about you playing judge, jury, and executioner with my hostages in my absence again."

The color drained from my face as Adrian slowly turned to look at me. "I know the truth," he said, folding the bloodied handkerchief into his pocket. "And no amount of lie detectors in the world will keep you safe from that. Either of you."

"Get *out,*" Michael roared.

Still laughing, Adrian went.

Michael:

Callaghan was literally insane. Not just desensitized; he was a card-carrying psychopath. I'd heard that, at some point, he had been forcibly hospitalized, but that was mere speculation. I wasn't sure I believed it, anyway. Most crazies I knew got better with medication. Callaghan clearly hadn't. I watched him walk away thinking that if *anybody* in this building should have their weapons confiscated, it was him. His mocking words were still in my ears.

Had her, yet?

The girl lurched in my periphery. With a final glance to make sure Callaghan had actually left, I walked towards her. Slowly. It had better not be another one of the escape plans she seemed able to conjure up so indefatigably. This was neither the time nor place to pull such stunts. "What the hell are you doing?"

"I can't stand the sight of blood."

"Are you going to faint?"

She went whiter. "No."

"Are you sure?"

She opened her eyes. "I...think so."

I could feel Christina staring at me as I guided her down the hallway. She wasn't stupid. She must have known that Adrian had said something to bother me. I knew she wanted to ask what that something was. It was none of her concern. She should know that by now.

"Why did you tell him that?"

I glanced down at her. "Tell who what?"

"The part about the rumors you heard about him playing judge, jury, and executioner. Why did you tell Adrian that? Now he'll know I told you what he did."

Of course. It all came down to self-preservation in the end. "He won't care. If anything, it pleased him. He likes to know when he's gotten to people," I said grimly. "And besides, what I said had nothing to do with you. There's bad blood there."

"But that's not what *he'll* think! You mentioned hostages!"

She was probably right. I shrugged. "I don't like torture. It's not effective and I don't need him undermining me. That's all. If you — either of you — choose to interpret that in a different way, that's your problem. Not mine."

I could tell she didn't like being grouped with Callaghan. I tightened my grip on her shoulder, warning her not to say anything else. We were close to her cell. I hurried along, wanting to get this over with. She was too insightful. Too nosy. She had to cut that out if she wanted to live.

As if further proof of this was needed, she asked, "What did Adrian say to you?"

"It was a private conversation that's none of your concern."

She stopped walking. I pushed her and her feet slipped and slid on the floor, but our progress was hindered. And I knew from experience she was difficult to carry for extended periods of time. "What?"

"I…think it is. My concern. I want to know what's going on."

I snorted. "Trust me. You don't."

"I *do.*"

I had started pushing her again but at her insistence, I stopped. Her eyes were wide, earnest, afraid. She was a little fool. I shoved her into the security cameras' blind spot. "Even if you do want to know, I am not going to tell you. You're too reckless and emotional."

"As opposed to having no emotions at all?"

"I almost forgot how irritating you are. You still haven't learned your place."

"Your boss said the thing."

I didn't want to contemplate the kinds of things she must have said to draw such a remark.

"Did you ever stop to consider that he might be right? Maybe whatever Callaghan has in store for you is going to do you a world of good, because someone needs to take the piss out of you. Now I am going to take you to your room" — I ignored the silent tears streaking down her cheeks — "And you are not going to say another word to me."

"They put a cap on my *life.*"

"No talking."

Anger was beginning to assert itself in her voice. "You knew this was going to happen."

I hadn't actually, but it didn't surprise me. The IMA were notorious for their ruthlessness. A little collateral damage was nothing. They had done worse, much worse. All things considered, Christina had been extraordinarily lucky so far. I shrugged.

"Were you going to wait until you slept with me before you killed me?"

The idiot. She was hopeless. The hall was still clear, though a bug might have picked up the audio. I dragged her down the hall, into another blind spot. "Are you *trying* to get yourself killed? If they think I told you something confidential, you are dead. Why do you think they're bothering with this spiel about Stockholm syndrome? It's not because they care about you, darlin — Callaghan is proof of that. No. They think I screwed up. Big time. This is all strictly standard procedure. It's a way to make people feel a confession is the only choice, the only way out."

Her eyes widened. "What kind of confession?"

I hesitated. "Do you still want to know the truth? Because once I tell you, you can't *unknow* it."

She nodded furiously. I had to give her credit; she had guts. I made sure the coast was clear for a final time and whispered, "They plan to kill us both."

Cloak and Dagger by Nenia Campbell

Chapter Twelve

Jeopardy

Christina:

I stared at him stupidly. I had been expecting something far more fantastic and complex. One of those intricate conspiracies that served as the plot line for so many action movies — not hostile takeovers and knowing too much! But this could be worse…because it was such a mundane explanation, there was no doubt in my mind it was also true.

It took me a moment to find my voice, lodged somewhere in the back of my throat. "You? Why?"

"The story they've been kicking around the office is that I'm a traitor; that I allowed myself to become seduced by my hostage and gave you some information I shouldn't have in a moment of… weakness. Information that you leaked, which allowed your parents to escape. It's scandalous enough that most people will probably believe it. Or want to."

"And the truth?" I managed.

"I'm a senior agent: old enough to be taken seriously, young enough to look like a threat. I have many enemies within this organization. When I relocated without notifying my superiors in advance, it looked a lot like insubordination. I don't screw up very often. I imagine they probably leaped on this opportunity like a pack of rabid dogs."

"But they're sending you on a mission to Michigan," I protested, still trying to make sense of this. "Why would they do that if they didn't still trust you?"

The look he gave me was full of scorn. "Do you know where Lake Angelus is?"

"It's a wealthy suburban town in Michigan. And there's a lake, of course," I said haughtily. "It's the type of place we'd go on vacation."

"Which is exactly why your parents wouldn't go there. They aren't that stupid." He had a point, though I begrudged him for being so snide about it. "I'll tell you what *is* there," he continued. "A team of highly-trained agents being paid to neutralize — I mean, kill — me if necessary."

"How do you know all this?"

"I have informants." He paused. "And if you cooperate with me, I can get you out."

"You're offering to help me?" *It has to be a trap.*

"The IMA has been fucking around with me for years" — his vehement tone made me flinch — "so I've been expecting something like this for quite some time. Counting on it, even. And what better way to get back at them than stealing one of their hostages right out from underneath their noses? It'll make fools of them, and they take pride on being foolproof." His eyes met mine. "Keep in mind that this is revenge, and nothing else. If you get in my way, I will kill you."

I could accept that if it meant getting out of here alive. "What do I have to do?"

"Be my eyes and ears while I go to Lake Angelus."

"You know it's a trap and you're still going?"

"I've never turned down a mission before. It would look unseemly. Besides," he added, "Sometimes it's better to" — his eyes narrowed — "run."

Sometimes it's better to run? "What?"

"Just do it. Run."

"Wh — "

"*Now.*"

I did. He tackled me, and we both went crashing to the floor. I gasped loudly and felt tears jump to my eyes. My knees had hit the floor pretty hard, and I could feel a dozen new bruises forming all over my body.

"What's going on here?" an irritated but unfamiliar voice demanded.

A man in a uniform and carrying a rifle was glaring down at us. Beside him were two other men, one in uniform and one in plainclothes. The man who wasn't in uniform was quite young, maybe only a couple years older than Michael, with dark skin, curly black hair, and five o' clock shadow that was just beginning to turn into a beard. He was standing stiffly with his arms behind his back. His attractive, fox-like face was grave.

As I looked at him, our eyes met and he gave me a somber nod. I took in his tattered clothes, disheveled appearance, and bleeding lip, and realized that he must be another prisoner. He had to be. The stiff posture was undoubtedly due to injury, maybe from torture, and I just bet his hands were cuffed like mine.

"She ran," Michael said, diverting my attention. "I pursued."

"Where are her handcuffs?"

"Somebody took them. But that doesn't matter. I have her under control now. I will see to it that she is returned to her cell and properly confined."

The guard, who appeared to be the leader of this small party, nodded and the three men continued in the opposite direction. Michael yanked me to my feet and let out his breath. "Jesus," he muttered. "That was close."

We continued to my cell. I couldn't forget that young prisoner. The haunted look in his dark eyes hinted at unspeakable horrors. As soon as I figured we were far enough away, I whispered, "Who was that?"

Michael's face closed off. "As long as you're here, you still have a fighting chance. Just remember this: once they move you to one of our internment bases, it's over."

Michael:

The IMA had many enemies, and some were considered too dangerous for ordinary imprisonment. We had two special high-security prisons similar to Guantanamo Bay for such individuals. One was in Russia and called Ground Zero, or GZ for short. The other was off the coast of Mexico, called Target Island. If the IMA ever officially turned on me, they would send me there.

I recognized the man in the hallway because I had been assigned as his bounty hunter. He'd been a double agent, working for a left-wing quasi-terrorist organization called the *Bureau du Nuit*, or Night Bureau,. They were a group of radicals who wanted political recognition. They regarded us as hypocrites and occasionally tried to thwart our missions. Until recently, they had never been successful.

Pierre Dupont was a very proud, very determined man. 27-years-old. Intelligent, crafty. One of their leaders. The BN was unique in the sense that those in power actually performed their own dirty work. It was why they considered themselves superior to the rest of us: socialism at its best. It also made them easy targets. Pierre would be taken to one of our high-security internment bases. He would be tortured and then, ultimately, executed.

The girl didn't realize how much danger she was in. That *both* of us were in.

Christina:

I was so full of adrenaline I thought I might burst. I couldn't sleep. I couldn't eat. It had been easier to believe my situation was completely hopeless than to believe I had a microscopically small chance at escape. *Hope really is the worst evil of all,* I thought wretchedly.

I curled up in a ball on the floor. When the door opened, I couldn't bring myself to sit up. *Probably the guard again, threatening to inject my food into me intravenously if I don't eat it. Maybe if I act pathetic, they'll assume I'm too weak to be defiant and leave me alone.* "I ate *most* of it," I mumbled. "Please...let me sleep."

"Oh dear," an unfamiliar voice said. "You *are* in bad shape."

A woman's voice? I cracked open an eye. There was a pretty red-haired woman standing over me. I blinked. She didn't go away. *Well, that's a good sign.*

"Hello," she said, nicely enough for someone who was probably a murderer.

I hadn't seen many women since my arrival. This particular woman was wearing a pencil skirt and a blouse that looked exactly like the one I'd been drooling over in a magazine last month...when fitting in and test scores had been the worst of my problems....

A sob rose in my chest. I morphed it into a whimper.

Her face creased in concern. She approached with a guard on her heels. "Don't cry."

Was this a trick? A good cop/bad cop routine? "I'm not crying. Who are you?"

"I'm here to help you," she said, neatly sidestepping the question.

A bubble expanded inside my chest. "Can you get me out of here?" I asked eagerly.

She laughed at that, but not unkindly. "I'm afraid not. They haven't been treating you very nicely," she said, examining me closely. "Your clothes…and your hair" — her eyes fell on my wrists — "Oh, dear."

I yanked my hands away from her. This pretty, well-kept woman was making me feel even more drab and scroungy than I had felt before. Worse, she was a painful reminder of just how good a set-up I'd had back home.

"Are you here to torture me?"

"No. I was told to let you take a shower."

"That's all?"

"Well…" She looked confused. "And give you new clothes, of course."

I didn't care about new clothes. I wanted to believe *one* person in this place didn't want to see me bleed.

"Think about how nice it will feel," she said encouragingly.

Even if it's a trap, at least I'll die clean.

"You can call me A," she told me in the hallway.

I looked over my shoulder. The guard was following at a discreet distance. Discreet meaning close enough to overhear everything I said in the conversation but not so close he was breathing down my neck. "A? And what do you do here, A?" *Lead the office in a cheery rendition of the alphabet song?*

"I have a desk job," she said, either not hearing or choosing to ignore my suspicion. "Research. Graduated from Smith *magna cum laude.*"

"No offense," I said. "But you don't exactly look like an agent."

"I suppose that's a compliment considering the way most people here dress. But I can only wear these around the office, because otherwise, people might stare."

I stared at her.

"My friends think that I work for a bank," she explained. "Part of my cover story. A new Versace dress might raise unseemly questions regarding the annual income of an alleged banker."

Is she for real? "Have you ever killed anyone?"

"Goodness, no!"

The locker room was exactly like the one at Holy Trinity, except that each locker had an access panel instead of a flimsy combination lock, and probably contained more than unwashed gym clothes and body lotion. "The showers are this way," she said, gently but firmly steering me away from the lockers. The guard didn't come in but I suspected he was right outside the door.

A was right. The water did feel good, though the soap and hot water stung my wrists. The water pressure at the safe houses had sucked — here, I was able to get almost as clean as I had been before getting kidnapped. It was heavenly.

Why was A being so nice to me? Was this supposed to be a happy send-off before I died? And had she *really* never killed anyone, or was that a lie?

I rinsed my hair a final time and changed into the clothes A had hung over the door. They looked expensive. The quality was superior to what Michael brought me. I pulled on the pristine white sweater and blue jeans, searched fruitlessly for shoes, and walked out of the stall feeling cheated.

A was sitting on the long wooden bench with a first aid kit. "Let's have a look at your arms." She pulled out strips of gauze and a bottle of peroxide.

"No shoes," I said.

"Afraid not." A wrapped up the minor cuts on my left wrist. The ones on the right were worse. "These are nasty things, aren't they?"

She tried to sound upbeat, but she was frowning at the long gash —
the one Adrian had torn. "Who did this to you?"

It was still red and angry-looking, like a screaming mouth, and
puffy with infection. *It doesn't look as bad in my cell.* "Most of them are
from the handcuffs. But Adrian — "

"Adrian?" Her hazel eyes burned with anger. "Adrian
Callaghan? They sent *you* to *him*?"

"Um…" *I shouldn't have said that. For all I know, she could be a
plant.* "Is it bad?"

"Not good, but not terrible, either." She drizzled peroxide over
the cut. I dug my fingers into my thigh to keep from crying out. "Just
deep."

Inwardly, I heaved a sigh of relief. Subject changed.

"That's the best I can do for now." She capped the peroxide. "I'll
check on it in a few days."

"Can I ask you one more question?"

She started packing up. "That depends on what you ask."

"Why are you helping me?"

She paused. "All Mr. Boutilier said was that you were in bad
shape. He was right, although he neglected to inform me just *how*
bad."

I was speechless.

Cloak and Dagger by Nenia Campbell

Michael:

A gentle, lacustrine breeze ruffled my hair through the open window of the van. Lake Angelus was full of large residences and small specialty stores geared towards the elite. With the average annual income hovering around a cozy $112,000, they could certainly afford it. This was a *scenic* little town, too. Big valley filled in with a large blue lake, with the surrounding tree-dappled hills reflected in the placid surface. Whitewashed cottage houses. Very WASP-y.

My partner, Miles Trevelyan, was too busy staring at the houses to notice the surroundings. "Wow," he whistled. "Look at the size of that place." he shook his head, slowly, so I would catch the significance of whatever he was going to say next. "It pisses me off how some people can choose to live like this."

I'd never cared much for Miles. I found his jocular personality overbearing, and his interactions with Richardson bordered on insidious. Usually an office grunt, he had undoubtedly bounced around like a puppy when he found out he had been marked down for one of the coveted field assignments. I wondered how thrilled he'd be if he realized the reason he'd been chosen in the first place was precisely because of how expendable he was.

The IMA would not suffer a serious loss if, say, Miles somehow got caught in the crossfire. *Assuming they use guns.* "Are you saying that you, as a mercenary, feel you are less driven by money?" I asked absently.

Miles rolled his eyes. "Nah. But one-percent of the people in this world hold ninety-nine percent of the world's wealth. It's just something to think about."

I was thinking I had seen that printed on an ad somewhere.

I parked the van in front of one of the larger houses. It matched the address I'd committed to memory in the debriefing room. Richardson rented our van under an assumed name and had it painted with the logo of a prominent local cable company. I'd made a point of checking the van out. It was clean. No detonator. Just a couple bugs. All the parts were operating normally; nothing was rigged to blow. Clearly, I was intended to survive the journey. That meant they intended to off me in the house. It was two and half stories, with a watered lawn. There was even a new champagne-colored Porche parked in front of the house. The IMA had gone through a lot of effort to make this plausible. In spite of myself, my heart began to pound. *They must really want me dead.*

"Nervous?" Miles asked, looking down at my hands.

I unclenched them from the wheel. "You wish, rookie."

Miles rolled his eyes again and pulled out a pair of binoculars. "Place looks secure. No guards, though."

"That's because they're idiots," I said with grave finality, "Who have been lulled into a false sense of security by a series of lucky escapes and close calls. Their mistake." I was pleased. That sounded like something I might say under ordinary circumstances.

Miles stared at me. "Here's something I don't get. What's the point of being out here if Richardson is going to give them the ultimatum?"

"Seeing as how they didn't come when we had their daughter, I hardly believe that they are going to come to us of their own volition." I slung my arm out the window. "Don't ask me any more questions until we get inside."

"Can I ask you something first?"

"Is it pertinent to the mission?"

"There's a rumor going around the office that you slept with your hostage."

"Disregard it."

"Is it true?"

"Give me those." I tugged on the binoculars. Unfortunately, they were still looped Miles's neck. He made a strangled sound: an improvement over what normally came out of his mouth.

"Something's moving in there," he rasped.

I eyed the house. "Where? Which room?"

"The one on the left. Kitchen, maybe."

"remember what I told you." I released the binoculars. They

smacked harmlessly against Miles's chest. "Corners are your friends — and your enemies. Check both sides before ascending a staircase or entering a doorway and, most importantly, stay off my tail."

I suspected the shot would come from behind. It was doubtful the shooter would care about a little collateral damage, provided he got his quarry. I opened the door, gun drawn, and checked both hallways before pushing it wide open.

The hallway was empty.

"All right, it's clear. Miles — *Miles?*"

He had vanished.

One less thing to worry about.

I moved down the hall, about to turn right. Something socked me in the back. It took me a few moments to feel the pain, hot and burning, like a ball of fire in my chest. I clutched at the front of my uniform and my gloves came back coated in blood. My blood.

What the fuck —

I turned around. The last thing I saw was a scared-looking Miles holding a gun in his trembling hands. I started for him and he fired again.

Everything went dark.

Cloak and Dagger by Nenia Campbell

Chapter Thirteen

Sickness

54 hours left.

I was instantly wary when the doors opened and a guard entered the room. "What's going on?" It was just the one, but his expression was dark.

"They want to question you," was his only comment.

Again?

I was getting used to the labyrinthine hallways. They were still intimidating, but less impressive. The guard led me up a flight of stairs, which lent support to my initial theory that part of the building was underground. The upper floor was less prison-like and more office-like. I had never liked change, and under these circumstances it seemed especially bad. Why was I being questioned again? Had somebody overheard my conversation in the hall with Michael?

The guard opened a plain wooden door that didn't have an access panel; we just went right in. With its tacky wallpaper, the heavy-duty sink, and the cot backed up against the corner, the room looked *just* like a doctor's office. There were other furnishings as well, these more out of place: a student desk — the kind with a table attached — and odd equipment hooked to a monitor.

The interrogator looked up as we came in. He wore a bland

221

smile on a face like a withered apple. I would have placed him in his mid-sixties but it was hard to pinpoint his exact age; he could have been ten years younger or older. He was wearing a suit, a pair of wire-rimmed glasses, and had a goatee that looked like a tuft of white cotton candy. For some reason, he also looked vaguely familiar. The thought that I might know somebody here was so distressing it took me a moment to realize he reminded me of a picture of Freud I had seen in my psychology textbook. *Ah, that's why.* I was relieved. God, he gave me the creeps.

"Sit." The guard forced me into the stiff-backed chair of the desk. He unlocked one of my handcuffs and refastened it to the bar that connected the seat of the desk to the table.

"You must be Christina," Freud said, smiling pleasantly.

I didn't deny it. I didn't agree, either. I said nothing.

His smile faded. He placed the monitor on the counter beside me. "Do you know what a polygraph is?"

A lie detector? I shrugged. Clearly he'd never heard of CSI.

"It's more commonly known as a lie detector. It measures various physiological responses, such as your pulse, blood pressure, respiration, skin conductance, and so on, after establishing a baseline." As he spoke, he placed two black loops around my ring and index fingers. That wasn't so bad. Then came a blood pressure cuff, which was uncomfortable, and two metal bars around my chest, which was weird.

"Your name is Christina?" he said, looking at the monitor. "Yes, or no?"

"...Yes."

He nodded. "Let's start off simply. Why don't you tell me about yourself, your school life, your hobbies..."

Why was *that* important? "I don't know."

"Withholding information will only make your situation worse." His frown deepened, causing an eruption of wrinkles around his mouth and forehead. "You can cooperate with me, young lady, or I can let Mr. Callaghan pry the answers out of you. It's your choice."

Freud seemed to accept that. He kept the next question simple. "Where do you attend school?"

"Holy Trinity."

"Is that a Catholic school?"

"Yes."

"Are you Catholic?"

"My mother is."

"Are *you* Catholic?"

I sighed. "No."

"Do you believe in God?"

"Yes."

"Any idea where you want to go to college?"

"No." *Not anymore.*

"What are your grades like?"

I wondered if I should lie. Maybe if he thought I was stupid, he'd ask me stupid questions. These were getting a little too personal. *But they could look that up.* "They fluctuate from year to year."

"What is your collective GPA for *this* year?"

"Not as high as I'd like it to be."

Freud steepled his fingers in front of his mouth. "What about your parents?"

"I don't know. They haven't been in school for a while."

A searing pain tore through my scalp. The guard had hit me with his gun. The tears that stung my eyes came unexpectedly. "Don't be a smart-ass," the guard snarled.

"Don't be so rough with her!" Freud chastised the guard. He turned back towards me, pulling out a hanky to dab at his sweating bald head. "How would you describe your *relationship* with your parents?"

Well, let's see. My mother had positively medieval views about women. She was terrified of getting old, and so she tried to relive her modeling days vicariously through me. My father was never around and when he was, he was more like a distant relative, rather than the close confidante I thought a father *should* be.

"It was great, until I got kidnapped."

"Your parents still haven't gotten back to us. Don't you find that odd?"

"Maybe they're scared," I suggested.

"That doesn't seem very responsible."

"My parents *aren't* very responsible."

Freud jotted something down in a little black notebook. "But you just said you had, and I quote, a 'great' relationship with them."

"You can have a great relationship with someone even if they aren't responsible."

"Even if those someones are your parents?"

I shrugged and closed my eyes. "You tell me."

"Your father is a computer programmer. What does he do at work?"

"He bakes bread," I said in a flat voice. "What do you think he does?"

The guard approached again, and Freud held him back. "Can you be a bit more specific?"

"No."

"Did Michael Boutilier ever talk to you about the IMA?"

"No." *Not intentionally.*

"Did he ever attempt to bargain with you?"

I told myself this was just the "story they were kicking around the office" that Michael had warned me about. The hallway had been completely empty when we'd talked, and he was too proud to incriminate himself. There was no way we could have been overheard.

…Right?

"No."

"Did you ever have sexual relations with Michael Boutilier, at his behest or yours?"

"No!"

"Take her back," Freud said, after a long pause. "We have enough for one day."

Michael:

Breathed in and heard a bubbling sound. Felt liquid in my chest. Tried to move. Couldn't. Restrained by something. Too dark to see what. Ground was vibrating. Tried to sit up. Last memory was Miles — with a gun. Miles — betraying me. Couldn't believe I'd overlooked him. Had seemed so incompetent. Didn't matter now. Needed to move. Arms were bound behind back. Felt like handcuffs. Shoulders ached, so had probably been unconscious for a while. If was going to die, would have done so already. Relief. Been through worse. Much worse. Would heal if got proper treatment in time.

If.

Needed to figure out where I was. Why I had been left behind.

Probably thought was dying or dead, if just left like *this*. Arrogant to leave operative to die if death not certain. Or just very, very stupid. *Miles*, I thought again. Shifted weight to abdomen to bend waist. To sit up.

Agony.

Gasped. Sounded like cheap carnival whistle. Moving definitely bad idea. Ribs felt like they were being sawed apart by rusted metal implement. With dull edges. Shirt was damp with sweat and blood. Could smell blood everywhere. Knew it was mine from way shirt was plastered to skin. "Fuck," I whispered raggedly, and heard bubbling sound again. Blood — in lungs. Jerked and knee hit something hard. "Fuck," I said again, louder.

"Did you hear something?"

Froze. Voices faint, but close.

"Don't be so paranoid, Trevelyan. We got him."

Trevelyan — Miles. And somebody else. Sounded familiar but not very.

"I heard something move around back there."

"It's just your imagination."

Long pause.

Was I...in the trunk of a car? Felt like coffin. No wonder couldn't move. Thought of most trunks, how small they were. Wondered what contortions they had performed on body to get to fit in such small dimensions. Muscles cramping. Suspected was folded up like origami crane.

Heard trunk pop open. Suddenly light. Kept eyes shut. Pretended to be unconscious. Was not hard. Wanted to be unconscious. Wouldn't be so painful that way.

"What the — the fucker's still breathing?"

Wanted to laugh. Lungs scalded like fire. Felt like heavy weight was pressing down on chest. Coughed instead. Tasted blood in mouth, salty and metallic. Spat out blood. Bubbling in chest diminished. Maybe lungs weren't pierced after all.

"I told you I heard a thump!"

"Well, if you had shot him point-blank like I'd told you to, that wouldn't be a problem."

Recognized voice now. Was Sheffield—Callaghan's backup. Son of a bitch.

"Never mind. Throw his body in the lake. He won't be breathing for long."

Was surrounded by water…and freezing. Couldn't move hands. Couldn't swim. Couldn't breathe.

Fuck.

Christina:

49 hours left.

Cloak and Dagger by Nenia Campbell

"Rise and shine, Christina Parker."

My eyes snapped open to meet a familiar pair of mocking gray ones. I blinked rapildy, praying the nightmare in front of me would vanish.

He didn't.

No! It's a dream, he's not real, he's not —

He reached out for me, just missing my chin. I felt the displaced air swoosh in front of my face. I shrieked, scrambling away by kicking my feet as hard as I could against the floor.

Adrian raised an eyebrow, letting his arm fall to his side. "You don't look happy to see me."

I searched in vain for the guard. "Get out!"

"*You* don't order me around." He didn't say it in a threatening way, as Michael would. He said it in an amused way, in the same tone as if the command has come from, say, a child. He rose from his crouch. "I saw the results of your polygraph."

I pushed myself to my feet. His eyes tracked me. How had he seen the results already? I'd only taken the test hours ago. Then I remembered — Adrian was the backup on Michael's previous assignment. Me. Adrian was in charge of *me*. Freud hadn't been threatening me with Adrian for the fun of it; he was threatening to send me back to my new captor if I didn't cooperate, who would then use his own preferred means of extracting information.

I'm in trouble.

"Figured it out, have you?"

Big trouble. "Stay away from me."

A slow smile wound its way across his face. He took a few brisk steps towards me. I matched him step for step, curling my hands into fists.

"I said, stay *away* from me."

"You're a liar, Christina," he purred.

I veered to the right to avoid his idle grab for my arm. "I didn't lie."

"According to the test, you did." He faked to the right and laughed when I nearly fell trying to avoid him, just barely managing to evade his lunge to the left. *My God, he's fast.* His feint attacks were exhausting to avoid, his footwork perfectly choreographed. I could feel myself getting tired at an alarming rate. Adrian stopped several feet away from me, giving me a heartbeat to catch my breath as he stopped to think. "Several times, actually. Why would you do that, I wonder?"

My back hit the wall.

"Maybe you *wanted* to be alone with me."

I leaped away from the wall, shooting a nervous look at him. I couldn't let myself get cornered. Adrian seemed to enjoy the sound of his own voice. Maybe I could hold out long enough, keep him talking, and A — or a guard, or Michael — would intervene.

"I didn't *lie!*"

"Oh, don't apologize to me." He laughed quietly. "*I* don't mind."

I bet he doesn't. God, he was sick.

"Or maybe," he continued, looking at me thoughtfully, "you're protecting someone."

"I'm not protecting anyone," I snapped, glaring at him.

His smile widened. I saw he had been expecting this response. "Not even yourself?"

In that instant, I knew three things: (1) he was playing with me, like a cat with an enfeebled mouse, and perfectly willing to draw this out as long as I was, which meant that (2) no guards were going to come — or he believed no guards were going to come, which pretty much amounted to the same thing, and (3) he had clearly done this before many, many times because the fluidity of his speech and the quickness of his responses were so synced up that it was as though he were reading aloud from a script.

Adrian lunged. I screamed as I bounced off the wall. Not from pain — the soft padding absorbed most of the blow — but from sheer terror. His hands hit the wall on either side of me, boxing me in. His eyes drifted leisurely down my body but there was nothing sexual about that look. "Are you afraid?" he whispered, bending his head towards mine.

"No." *Oh, yes.*

He sighed. "So stubborn."

I punched him. He caught my fist before it could reach his face, spinning me around like a dancer and then, when I had gathered enough momentum, let go. I hit the ground with a thud. The padding absorbed most of the impact again, but this time it actually hurt. For several seconds I was stunned and barely managed to dodge the blow he'd been aiming at my unprotected side. His shoe clipped me — had it connected, it would have bruised my kidneys, or worse.

I got to my feet but was exhausted and shaking too badly from fear to be stable. He had military training: I could barely get through gym class. I leaned against the wall for support, willing my knees not to buckle out from under me as I frantically hobbled away.

When he socked me in the stomach all the wind was pummeled out of me. He punched me again, lower — just above the groin — and there was a sharp ache that made me feel, for an instant, like I desperately had to go to the bathroom. The floor hit my knees. I barely noticed. I was too intent on hugging my aching midsection, as if I could hold the pain in with my arms alone.

It was a painful reminder that if I wanted to trade punches against the men in the IMA, they would always win.

"Look at that," he taunted, "Already on your knees."

I told him he could go fornicate with himself in the crudest way possible, borrowing one of Michael's favorite words. For my efforts, I received another blow. I doubled over, in the fetal position. I didn't even bother trying to get up this time.

Adrian leaned over me. His shirt was a stark white. I had a sudden vision of how my blood would look spattered across the fabric, like a grisly Jackson Pollock painting.

He nudged me in the side with his foot. "If only you could see yourself...how pathetic you look. I could kill you with just a few more blows." He ground his shoe into my side a little harder and my sob became a scream. "Maybe only two."

"You'll *pay*," I gasped.

"To whom? Michael? Did you really believe *he* could protect you?"

He's using the past tense. I struggled to sit up. White-hot pain lanced through my stomach, arcing through my ribs, my bladder, and both my sides. Like some ghastly compass rose. *Pain in all directions.* "I don't...know...what you're talking about."

"Oh, I think you do — "

He saw me trying to get up and swiped my legs from beneath me.

Wham.

Back on the floor.

" — I know all about your deal with him."

If I tried to speak, I was going to throw up.

"But he's sleeping with the fishes, Christina; I doubt he'll wake up any time soon."

"He's...dead?" A bubble of blood burst from my lips.

"Out like a candle," he agreed.

I'd wanted Michael dead so many times. After he'd tried to rape me, I'd fantasized about killing him myself. Now I'd gotten my wish and he'd been replaced by an even greater evil. And with Michael died my only hope for escape. I turned on Adrian, my anger and disappointment providing me with the energy to shout, "You sick, twisted *fu* — "

He kicked me again, casually, and I broke off in a strangled yelp. Blood drizzled out of my mouth, spraying the floor with crimson. Adrian hadn't been exaggerating. A few more of those *love-taps* would probably kill me. The harder blows, definitely. Easily.

This wasn't pain anymore. This went beyond pain. This was *hell*.

"Get up."

"I can't...you bastard..."

"No?" He dropped to his knees beside me, his features arranged in mock solemnity. "Well, that's what you get for trying to play with the big lads, my bonnie lass." He traced my lower lip. I braced myself for the pain that was sure to follow because he was like a sadistic King Midas, turning everything he touched into pain.

But he didn't hurt me. Just wiped the blood from my mouth almost...tenderly. No. That wasn't the right word. His face wasn't sympathetic or repenting; he looked rapt, almost fascinated. When he finally withdrew, his fingers were coated in my blood.

"It's a pity he's dead."

Michael? Was he talking about Michael? "Why...pity?"

"Because." He raised his eyes to my face as he licked my blood from his fingers. "I rather hoped he'd be around to watch this."

Chapter Fourteen

Nightmare

Michael:

"That was cutting it close, even for you."

Kent was frowning down at me. If I tried, I could hear water slapping against a solid surface. We must have been aboard Kent's houseboat. I was lying on the dining room table, cleared to make room for me. "Sometimes...you need to take a few risks." I examined the blood-stained bandages covering my torso. Nothing vital appeared missing.

"This was more than a risk, Michael. This was reckless. You could have died."

Scoffing, I tried to sit up and gasped. "Oh, *fuck* me."

Kent gave me a look that plainly said, *I told you so.* "The bullet went through your kevlar. There was some internal damage."

I slid my legs over the side of the table and tilted my head. There wasn't as much blood as I'd initially thought, though Kent had cleaned me up a bit. My bullet-proof vest had absorbed most of the bullet's impact. "Was it deep?" I probed at the wound and winced. It hurt, but not too badly.

"Nothing a first aid kit and some skulduggery couldn't fix. Did you know they'd be using propellants?"

No, I hadn't. I'd been caught completely off-guard. It was the mistake of a rank amateur but — Miles? His hands had been shaking so hard, only luck and the fact that I had been standing stock-still must have allowed the bullet to meet its mark. If I had been in motion…

But dwelling on the past did nothing for my present situation. It would not speed up my recovery, it would not undo my error. The fact that Richardson had enlisted *Miles* to be my assassin instead of somebody more qualified was downright insulting, as he undoubtedly intended it to be. My death would be made both a mockery, and a warning.

Which reminded me. I was operating on a strict time frame. In just two days, Christina would die — and I'd be forced to await another chance to fuck them over. By then, news of my death would have already been released. I had to act *now*, while there was still secrecy. This botched assassination attempt had left me with an even greater thirst for retribution, and I was not to be denied.

Kent watched me get up. "Where are you going?"

"I need to get to the Cascade Mountains."

"You just took a bullet. If you go back like this, they *will* kill you. Wait a few weeks. Get your strength back. *Then* worry about getting revenge."

"I don't have a few weeks." I pulled on a shirt he'd laid out for me. "Get me on the first flight heading back to Oregon."

Kent shook his head mournfully but picked up his phone. "Your funeral, Old Boy."

Christina:

48 hours left.

"I'll be back," he breathed into my ear. "Don't go anywhere." And then he laughed.

My fingers clenched. Every move I made elicited pain so strong, it was like being stabbed all over by a red-hot iron. Everything ached. The effect was strangely neutralizing, as if the sheer abundance of agony had driven my brain into automatic shutdown. I closed my eyes and tried to focus on breathing. *In. Out. In. Out.* Each breath was a slash to my lungs.

The worst part was, despite giving the fight — if I was being perfectly honest, it was more of a slaughter — my all, I had barely hurt him. All of this damage, all the bruises and blood, had taken minutes to inflict. And he had walked away with nary a scratch.

In. Out. Since when did breathing hurt so much?

Adrian could have killed me. He didn't, but I was under no false illusions as to why. He wanted to save me for later, the same way animal predators will drag their half-eaten meal into a tree. His expression had been so alien, so *bestial*, that I hadn't been able to recognize it for what it was. I'd never seen that look on a human face before.

It was a primal lust for drawing blood and inflicting pain. A gratification from the former that bordered on sexual. His face, as he had licked my blood from his fingers, had been that of a man caught in the throes of passion. What was he going to do to me now? What was *left* to do?

Footsteps echoed in the hallway, coming closer. I turned my head towards the door, the muscles in my neck straining with the movement. Was it one of the guards? Or was it Adrian, back to finish the cruel game he'd started, coming back to his tree to devour what remained?

I heard the beeping of the access panel from the other side. The door whooshed open. A horrible silence ensued. I counted three and a half ragged breaths. The voice, when it finally came, was measured but concerned. "Oh my sainted Jesus — Christina?"

A.

I saw her shimmering form through my tears. She was wearing an aubergine dress suit with matching heels. A white silk scarf draped around her throat. She dropped to her knees beside me, an angel wearing purple, her fingers gently rolling up the hem of my sweater. The sweater *she* had given me, hopelessly ruined now. Her hands were cool to the touch, painstakingly gentle.

"Mr. Callaghan," she spat, her soft voice discordant for the first time since I'd heard her speak. Her mouth was a thin, tight line as she pulled her hand back, which I didn't want her to do at all — I needed her touch to make sure I was still alive. A wish I regretted, when her finger pressed against a bruise too hard. A's face softened, becoming lovely again, as I recoiled, and she said, "I'm sorry! Are you in a lot of pain?"

No, I'm just lying here because I feel like it.

My laugh came out as a hacking rasp that quickly became a soundless cry. I managed to nod. It hurt too much to talk.

"You're hemorrhaging. That's why this is black." Her finger hovered over one of the darkest bruises but she did not touch me this time. I nodded faintly. I wasn't sure exactly what that meant, though I remembered hearing it before on *ER* and I knew it wasn't a good thing.

"I can't move you by myself, and it isn't safe to. We'll have to wait."

Wait for what? Who? Adrian was going to come back.

A fine mist of sweat formed on my forehead. The fabric of my sweater felt wet and sticky on my back and under my arms. A placed her hand on my forehead, smoothing back my hair the way my mother used to when I was younger. "Why did he do this to you?"

I tried to think past the pain that veiled my thoughts. "He said I lied...on my polygraph." The last syllable came out as a choke. Spit hit the ground beside me; it was veined with blood. I looked away. "But...he also said...he wanted to break me." My chest hitched, sending ripples of pain down my body: a facsimile of a bitter laugh, or the beginnings of a sob. Beyond the agony, I didn't know what I was feeling. Nor did I care, particularly. "He got what he wanted... I'm definitely broken."

I watched her watch me. Under this light, her hazel eyes looked green — as green as *his*, though considerably less cold. *As green as his* were. He was dead now. One less thing in the universe to concern myself with.

Did you lie? seemed to hover in the air like a ghost between us, making the air grow cold. To tell the truth, I was no longer sure whether I had or not. It didn't seem to matter; it certainly hadn't to Adrian.

Finally, A nodded. She pulled down my sweater, allowing me a modicum of dignity. She was trying to be gentle, but the drag of soft fabric scorched my skin like flame. My wince alerted her, made her ask, "Are you in a lot of pain?"

"Yes, goddammit!" My own voice had become a stranger's.

Unfazed, A reached into her handbag and pulled out a black case. My skin shrank in recognition. I'd seen one of those before. I flinched when she pulled out one of the needles, and then flinched from my own flinching. "No."

She frowned at me. "This will help you relax."

"I'm allergic."

"To opiates. I know. This is different."

The needle slid beneath the skin of my forearm. The room seemed to tilt. "You'll have to be hospitalized," she was saying. "If this isn't operated on right away, you could die."

Hope buoyed me to consciousness. If they were taking me somewhere public, like a hospital, questions would be asked. Somebody might recognize me. Milk cartons bearing pictures of my face were probably circulating around school cafeterias. *Have you seen this girl?*

I was just beginning to fantasize about the bust, the police having just received an anonymous tip-off from a hospital intern with a heart of gold who was too noble and good to accept the IMA's hush money. The reunion with my family. Seeing Adrian sentenced to a life in prison without parole.

"We have a fully functional operating room on the premises," A added.

The dream shattered, like brittle glass, the pieces scattering even as I reached out with the desperation of a beggar grasping at dropped coins in a busy street. I shook my head.

Misunderstanding, she said, "He's a very nice man. Very skilled. He got his medical degree from John Hopkins. He works on the field agents who are injured while on assignment. You'll receive better treatment than at most hospitals."

That's not the point. I'll still be a prisoner.

"You can't have it both ways."

It was as if she'd read my thoughts. No, she was just saying that I couldn't get better without moving. She thought I was concerned about the pain. She was right, either way. I *couldn't* have it both ways. I never have. My life has always been full of tough choices, ever getting harder.

"Does this mean…they don't want to kill me?"

She looked at me for a long time — for so long that I wondered how the answer could be anything but "no". Slowly, she shook her head. "Yes. At least, not yet. If he truly wanted you dead, he would have ordered Adrian to finish you."

Those grim words hung between us until the sedative took effect. I was out —

(*like a candle*)

On the edge of a lake surrounded by trees, under overcast skies the color of concrete. Curls of mist rose from the still surface, though I didn't feel cold. The water seemed to stretch out forever but I could make out the lines of houses through the sheer curtain of vapor. It looked like it might rain.

I wasn't alone.

Michael was leaning against one of the trees, sharpening a knife against a wet-stone. That's when I realized I had to be dreaming. That, or I had died — and this was hell. Michael took no notice of me, but I knew instinctively that he was aware of my presence. The scraping noises stopped, and he looked up at me with his strange eyes: perfectly green and cold, like two pieces of bottle glass set in his haggard face. They perfectly mirrored the stormy sky above.

"What are you doing here?"

I took a step back, loose racks grating against my sneakers. "What are *you* doing here? You're…dead — aren't you?"

Michael looked up from his knife. "Do I look dead?"

I could see the muscles in his bare arms working as he continued to sharpen the blade. There were numerous scars crisscrossing his torso, of different shapes and textures. Some had nearly faded away into his tan skin, and others stood out in relief. He looked so untouchable. I was suddenly terrified — *more* terrified.

One of the scares was more pronounced than the others: a gaping rictus, still red and fleshy, just above his left nipple and only half-healed. It looked so *painful*. He stopped sharpening his knife and followed my gaze. "That one hurt the most."

"How did you get it?"

Michael moved like a panther, so fast I wouldn't have been able to dodge even if I'd tried. I was knocked from my feet to the ground, the air crushed out of my lungs on impact. With it, went my ability to scream. I was painfully aware of his body pressed against mine, cold and hard, like stone. He leaned in. "I was weak."

He pressed my hand to his chest, splaying my fingers over the scarred, opalescent skin, just over where his heart should have been. *No heartbeat.* I tried to yank my hand bank. He held on tightly — tighter, when I tried to pull away. His mouth covered mine, and he tasted cold and dead and salty, like raw fish.

"You see?" he said. "I feel nothing now."

I screamed, scrabbling at his heartless chest.

Michael seemed to hesitate. His hand, the one holding the knife, was halfway beneath my shirt. The tip of the blade pressed into my skin and I shivered. His skin felt slack and loose, peeling away where my fingers had gouged, revealing the carmine muscles and pallid bone beneath. He *was* dead; he was a corpse.

The blade was warm in contrast, and that seemed wrong somehow, almost obscene: as if the metal was alive — an extension of him and his wrath.

"If you want to survive against us, you have to be cold like us."

I didn't even have time to scream as the knife pierced my skin, past the protective shield of my ribcage, deep into the recesses of my heart.

Michael:

Compared to the humidity of the east coast, Oregon was far cooler. I pulled on my black coat as I left the PDX Airport and popped some of the pain relievers Kent had procured for me, dry. My chest was aching in the cold like a son of a bitch. But I could still fire a gun. Even with the bullet wound, I was a formidable adversary.

— Oh, *Christ.*

I nearly reached for the bottle of pills again. Stopped myself. At least the pain would keep me alert. I didn't want to arrive at the IMA's doorstep doped out of my mind, and I'd well exceeded the advised dosage.

I was aware of the eyes on me as I hurried through the terminals with my single carry-on item. Some people stared at me curiously, others avoided me entirely. Perhaps they could read the death warrant in my eyes. More likely, it was the fact I kept hacking up blood. In either case, I was attracting far too much attention. I quickened my pace, and my chest tightened.

Outside the airport, the roar of the departing planes was deafening. I scanned the curb, looking for a sign with the name "Coleman." That had been Kent's suggestion. Even though I had "died" the IMA may have released my fake name to the public in an obituary. It would not be good for Edward Collins to be seen walking around, back from the dead. Coleman was just close enough to Collins that there was no chance of my forgetting it.

There was no Coleman sign. My driver hadn't arrived yet. I cracked open the can of orange juice from the flight and glanced down at my watch. I had forty hours.

Christina:

Forty hours left.

I shot up and immediately regretted it as pain lit up and down my sides like lights on a jukebox. I fell back against the cot, clasping my hands over my stomach as though in prayer. *A dios.* My heart — my poor, wonderful heart — was hammering in my ears. *Just a nightmare.*

Not all of it. Michael was still dead. And I was an invalid. A must have brought me to the hospital. I didn't remember arriving here. I didn't remember anything except pain. I was sore beyond description, but now it was the dulled ache of healing wounds as opposed to the sharp, raw stabbing of fresh bruises and open, stinging cuts. I was wearing a loose shirt and beneath it I could feel the ridges of what proved to be neat bandages, wrapped with the precision of a surgeon.

That's when I saw him. He was sitting down in a chair behind me, on the edge of my periphery — why I hadn't seen him on my initial, cursory inspection — and he was toying with something small and metallic hanging from a chain at his neck. At my gasp of startled horror, he looked up.

"Oh, good," he said. "You're awake. I said I'd be back, didn't I?"

I opened my mouth to scream. He crossed the room quickly, clapping one of his hands over my mouth. "I wouldn't do that." I wanted to bite his hand, and *would* have if not for the distinct possibility that he would take it as an invitation to "play" — and I wouldn't survive round two.

Against the instincts to attack, scream, and hold on for dear life, I made myself to relax. Adrian raised his hand up and off my mouth. The fabric of his shirt lifted with that movement, revealing a gun holstered at his hip. He hadn't wanted me to scream, so that might mean nobody knew he was here. I tasted blood; I'd bitten right through the skin of my lower lip.

Adrian noticed me staring at his gun.

"The lesser known instrument of the surgical world." He drew it. "Generally used as a last resort, of course." The detachment in his voice, plus the fact that nobody had rushed in at the sight of his drawn weapon, was terrifying. His smile grew as he slipped the gun back into its holster. "So, beneath the skin of the lion beats the heart of a rabbit, hmm?"

"And what are *you*?" I had meant to sound brave, but my voice cracked mid-syllable. He smiled accordingly, adjusting his shirt so the gun was hidden from sight.

"I'm very good at what I do."

I braced myself for the attack — a blow to my stomach, a quick, backhanded slap. He leaned in and deliberately licked away the bead of blood clinging to my lip. His breath was hot, metallic, and sweet. Like molten copper. Like blood. I snapped at his tongue and he pulled away.

"You *are* a pretty little thing, aren't you?"

I said nothing.

"But pretty things are so easily broken." My hand looked so fragile in his, when he caught it. "Here's what's going to happen," he said reasonably, running his thumb over my pulse. "First, you're going to tell me everything. Then you're going to beg me for your life. And perhaps, if you're very, *very* convincing, I might even let you live."

"Screw you."

His fingers tightened, past discomfort, to the threshold of pain and then beyond that, too. "No," he said, still civil. "I don't think so."

He's going to do it. He's going to break my wrist. I could kick him. I wasn't sure how much it would hurt, but if I aimed right, it might

249

get him off me. *And then what? You're incapacitated.* I didn't care. I'd deal with that when — and if — the time came.

I poised to strike, cocking my leg back beneath the sheets. A crack resounded in the room. I stared in amazement as Adrian Callaghan collapsed on top of me — unconscious.

Chapter Fifteen

Rendezvous

Christina:

Panic overrode logic. I flailed, trying to get him off. I didn't care
that he was unconscious. I just wanted his body away from mine.
There was a sickeningly sweet powdery smell, like talc, clinging to
his clothes and skin, which made me feel like vomiting.

Adrian was a big man, but I was desperate. I felt him start to
slide and then give way. He hit the floor with a heavy thud that
made the medical equipment in the cupboards rattle. A groan
escaped him. I did the sensible thing: I opened my mouth again to
scream.

A soft, feminine hand covered my mouth before the sound could
escape. I began to thrash again — that was how Adrian had reacted,
too, which meant that *this* person also wasn't supposed to be here. A
voice as feminine as the hand whispered, "No. *Please*. You must be
quiet. Trust me."

A looked as though she'd aged ten years since I'd seen her last.
The expression on her face was horribly familiar: I'd seen it every
time I looked in a mirror. Sheer terror.

My eyes shifted from the collapsed Adrian to her disheveled
appearance and back again. Had *she* been the one to knock him
unconscious? Her tweed dress was rumpled and askew, revealing

the lace-edged slip beneath. She looked like she had been in a scuffle. Her handbag dangled limply from her hand. Its contents had spilled out on the floor. Adrian had been felled by a Coach bag. If I hadn't been so sickeningly relieved, I might have laughed.

"Listen to me," she said, in rushed, clipped tones. Her mouth was locked in a grimace, and her lipstick had bled onto her perfect teeth. "We don't have much time. I can get you out, but you must do exactly as I say. Do you understand? Nod once."

"What — "

She shook her head, motioning to the security camera. *Right.* She had angled herself in such a way that her face wouldn't be visible to the lens. Could the people watching the cameras read lips? Probably. After all, these were the same people that forced their guards to memorize the floor plan in order to navigate.

"Do you understand?" she repeated, her eyes urgent, pleading.

I brought my head down in the heaviest of nods.

A tugged me out of bed — rougher than before, but I suppose she had to keep up with appearances. I was relieved I wasn't wearing one of those flimsy hospital gowns. It was humiliating enough, being dragged around *without* having your butt visible.

"Follow me."

Easier said than done. My sides ached with each step. The tide of endorphins helped some. I hardly dared believe I was going to be released from this place — alive. Unless…was this a trick of some kind? To test me? With a shaking hand, A punched in the access code. Her fear didn't seem feigned, but Adrian had managed to fool me, too. Good acting seemed to be a prerequisite.

I edged carefully around Adrian's fallen form. His chest rose and fell, and I begrudged him each breath. I suppressed the urge to stamp on his throat and end his life then and there, hurrying after A. The doors slid open and I could barely keep up with her. A's white, open-toed sandals clicked noisily on the floor and I wondered why, if she was so eager to remain unseen, she was wearing such *loud* shoes. Then I saw the logo on the back of the heel and rolled my eyes.

Prada. "Where are we going?"

"Out."

Out? Out of this hallway? Or out-out? "Where?" I persisted.

"I can't tell you right now." She glanced around nervously. "We're in serious danger."

She's only just figured that out now? I almost laughed, but my throat was too dry. I could feel the pain returning now that I was coming down from my high; neurotransmitters could only go so far. "I know," I whispered back. "You knocked Adrian Callaghan unconscious. When he wakes up, he's going to come after us and… there will be trouble."

"No, not just us — we *all* are." She spread her arm in a broad half-circle, as if to encompass the entire building of the IMA.

I was gasping now. My stitches felt about ready to pop. "Why?"

"Because Michael Boutilier is alive."

Michael:

It didn't occur to the two grunts the IMA had posted as guards to be on the lookout for one of their own. I'd suspected as much. My killing would be strictly on a need-to-know basis for the next few days, allowing for an adequate amount of time to pass for Richardson to "discover" the "horrible news." After all, he wouldn't want to leave his people with the impression that they could get bumped off before retirement — not with a mutiny already in the works.

The guards nodded me through. The clearance light flashed green. That meant I hadn't been declared dead yet. Good. I went through the door, keeping my head down. Nobody had stopped me but I doubted that my luck would stay this good. I had to assume that somebody had already seen me, recognized me, and made a phone call to the powers that be.

A piercing siren tore through the silence of level one. A light, surrounded by a cage of wires, suddenly started to flash. My hand tightened around my Glock 22, and I ran down the stairs, trying to ignore the fireball in my chest.

Showtime.

Christina:

"Adrian told me he was dead."

"That's what we thought, too." She shook her head, causing her red hair to fan out as she hustled me down the hallway. "He was growing too powerful, too ruthless, and had many enemies. When I heard he planned to take over the IMA..." She shuddered, as if the thought of a Michael-run IMA was too horrible to bear. "We were so relieved when we got a report saying that he might have drowned. I thought it was the end to all our problems. But he's alive. I don't know how, but he managed to survive — and he's coming *here*."

My dream came back to me with frightening clarity. But what — I'd overheard Michael telling Kent he had no intention of taking over the IMA. He *knew* that he had many enemies, and that too many people would resent him for precisely the reasons A had just laid out. He'd also mentioned that he wasn't the only one hankering for a little power. Two other men wanted to lead the IMA, and one of them was Adrian. Did that mean A thought an Adrian-run IMA was better than a Michael-run one? I couldn't see that. Michael wasn't a *sadist*.

But again, this was stuff I wasn't supposed to know. I didn't know where A stood in the midst of this. Not enough to regale her with all the forbidden information I had managed to acquire. "You weren't afraid of Michael before."

"Of course I was!"

"But you didn't act like it — he told you to help me, and you did."

"He was under our control then. Now he's like a grenade without a ring. He could do *anything*." I had a feeling that wasn't the whole story behind why she was afraid. And the plural pronouns confused me. Was A protecting someone? Or was she referring to the IMA as a whole? A piercing alarm cut loose, splicing both my eardrums and my thoughts.

We both jumped.

"If that's true, why are you helping me?" I had to raise my voice to be heard.

"I have a daughter about your age." She paused, adding swiftly. "I don't want to see you die. This is no place for a child." We were outside the locker rooms. She handed me a long navy skirt and another white blouse. "You'll stand out too much dressed the way you are now. This way, you can pass as a secretary. Executive assistant. Just change — quickly!"

I tried to find the words that would simultaneously thank her for everything *and* wish her the best of luck with her own problems because I suspected she had many, but in the end all I could do was nod awkwardly and duck past the doors before the two of us were spotted.

Michael:

The guards had come out of nowhere. I'd already incapacitated several and killed just as many. I'd salvaged a helmet and two AK-47s. Assault rifles were powerful but made too much noise. I was going to have to use them if the Glock ran out of ammunition. Running footsteps down the corridor snagged my attention, turning it from thoughts of artillery. I dropped into a defensive stance, ready to shoot on-sight.

No guards.

It was — I couldn't believe my luck — Christina, accompanied by Richardson's little whore. How had Christina persuaded that bitch to help her escape? I stared, edgy, sore, and shocked as they conferred briefly. I couldn't hear what they were saying over the alarm, but I could guess. A shoved a handful of clothes at the girl, who disappeared into the locker room. A muttered something under her breath, turning down a different hall.

I considered following her and asking her what the hell she was thinking, turning against Richardson like that — dis she believe she was more exempt from insubordination because she was sleeping with him? That he'd let her off with a fucking spanking? The sound of more footsteps swiftly changed my mind.

I dove into the locker room after the girl.

Christina:

39 hours left.

I got dressed in the privacy of one of the shower stalls. The light in here was good; it gave me a more intimate glimpse of my injuries than I would have liked. The mottled bruises and thick, black thread that laced through my skin like the stitching on a rag doll, made me want to retch. I tried to focus solely on the clothes.

The scream sounded as I was zipping up my skirt. It echoed shrilly off the yellow tiles. I paused a beat before slipping on the flats. Was it coming from the locker room? I could swear it was. Slowly, I pushed open the stall door, stepping out as my eyes restlessly swept the aisles of lockers. Nothing.

I made my way to the door that led back to the corridor. As I moved closer, I could make out voices — one male, one female. I cracked open the door and peeped out. Adrian had A pinned against the wall by her throat. "I can make you speak, or you can talk freely. Where are Michael and the girl? This organization does not tolerate traitors."

I looked at A to see what she was making of this. She just looked scared. So A's vagueness *had* been because she was protecting someone. She knew what had happened to Michael, so that meant... she was probably connected to someone directly responsible for killing him. She probably thought Michael was going to come after her for revenge.

Adrian must have been in on it, too. He had encountered Michael and I in the hallway, that one time. He'd whispered something that Michael wouldn't repeat. All his thinly veiled threats, his baseless interest in me — which was looking less baseless by the minute. His premature certainty of Michael's death. Suddenly, the situation began to make sense.

"I'm not a traitor," A protested. "I was doing what was best — "

"For whom? The IMA? All evidence points to the contrary. Releasing hostages, stealing company property — "

She flushed angrily. "The clothes are *mine* — and Michael might have killed the girl."

"She'd have made a pretty little trap then, wouldn't she? Why are you protecting her, A? I know you set her free. The door showed no sign of being forced, so I know Michael didn't do it, and we all know Richardson gives you unlimited access to the codes..."

I started forward and a hand clamped over my mouth for the third time that day. "Don't move."

Michael? I went so still I could feel the rise and fall of his chest against my back. *Oh God.*

"I'm not here to hurt you," he said in a strange, muffled voice. "But you have to keep your goddamn mouth shut."

I nodded. He released me. I wasted no time in backing up and increasing the space between us. The muffling was caused by a riot helmet that covered all of his face in hard black plastic, except for the transparent visor. He was wearing black pants tucked into heavy black boots and, over a long-sleeved shirt, a ribbed vest that was probably bulletproof.

He looked as terrifying as I remembered, and very much alive.

I tried to scramble around him but he was standing between me and my escape. My heart echoed the sounds of his hands hitting the metal lockers. "Hold it." He was looking at the outlines of my bandages through my shirt. "Callaghan's been playing with you."

I tried to keep myself from looking at the door — and failed.

"And you're still alive? Interesting." He let his hand fall away. "Did you find anything useful?"

"A and Adrian were both in on your death. And A might be close to one of the key people"d — his tawny eyebrows lifted — "but if she is," I added ferociously, "You have to promise not to hurt her, because I'm sure she didn't mean it."

"Oh, she means it, Christina. She's just as cruel as the rest of us."

"She isn't! She helped me when nobody else would! She kept

Adrian from killing me!"

Michael sighed and rubbed his eyes. There were dark circles around them that hadn't been there before. He made a forwarding motion with his hand.

"Your death wasn't accidental."

"Impressive."

Sarcasm? I couldn't tell. In the silence that followed, I heard A cry out again. I turned in that direction and again, Michael blocked my path.

"Leave her."

"I can't. He's killing her, don't you see? She *helped* me, and he's killing her!"

"Callaghan can't hurt her. Not as long as she's fucking his boss. You are a different matter. If he's attacked you once, he will do it again — especially if he left you alive."

"A is *sleeping* with Mr. Richardson?"

"That's one way of putting it. I doubt they do much sleeping."

I colored. "Her daughter…"

"It's his."

"I don't believe you."

"She's not as innocent as she looks. I'm surprised she bothered to help you at all."

"What does she see in him?"

"Power. Money." I might have imagined the pause. "Sex."

"That's disgusting."

"You asked. Don't ask things you don't want to know the answers to. I don't have time to argue. Can you walk?"

"Yes."

"Not fast enough." He swung me over his shoulder so I was draped around his neck like a mink coat. I was too tired and too surprised to fight him. It wasn't a good idea, anyway. Not when I was six feet above the ground. His face said the subject was non-negotiable, anyway, and his threat about not getting in his way was still clear in my mind.

A tremor coursed through his body. He stumbled. I probably wouldn't have noticed if I hadn't been on his shoulders, but I was and I had. "Put me down," I said hastily. "I can walk."

"You're in worse condition than I am."

"Then why are you helping me?"

Michael opened his mouth to respond and I heard gunshots. He set me down on the bench. I watched him draw a large gun.

"He *killed* her."

"Stay here. Don't make a sound."

On the edge of the bench, my hands were white. The sirens were still going off. I could see one of the alarms near the ceiling, flashing like a police car. Michael made his way towards the door and one of

---

the spinning red beams turned his hair and skin flaming red. He opened the door slowly at first, then threw it wide open. I caught a glimpse of the sterile white hallway. He pointed the gun at me, giving it a downward shake, motioning for me to stay where I was, and slipped out the door as silently as a shadow.

I counted the seconds — he was gone for less than thirty. When he returned, there was a rigidity to his face I didn't like; it made him disconcertingly similar to the Michael-corpse from my dream. I wanted to ask him what he'd seen but didn't quite dare.

"Sit down," he said brusquely.

"What happened to getting out of here?"

"Change of plans. Sit down."

"What do you mean, change of plans? What's going on?"

Michael fired the gun. "Sit *down*."

I sat down.

"There is a rift going through this organization. Roughtly half are satisfied with the way things are now. The other half thinks we've gone soft. They want to turn the IMA into a freelance mafia. The main advocate of that is Callaghan. The other is a man named Morelli but he's not the one to worry about — and that's not what's important. What *is* important is that, right now, they are united by *one* thing and that is their mutual desire to see us both dead."

"You're only one man," I said.

"Two." I stared at him, not understanding. "Including you. You're in this with me."

I nodded, thinking I could escape the moment he was gone. Screw his plan. I wasn't going to get myself killed because of him. He wanted to go play Rambo, fine — he could do it by himself. I was going to look for A.

Something cold snapped around my wrist. Michael snapped the other cuff to one of the wooden legs bolting the bench down to the floor. "What the *hell*?"

He dropped the key into his pocket. "I need you. I can't have you running off."

Was I that transparent? "They're going to find me here!"

"Then you had better be really quiet."

He was going to leave me here as bait so he could get away. I couldn't believe it. "Bastard. I should have known I couldn't trust you."

"You shouldn't trust me. But trust me on this: I *am* coming back."

The alarm was still going off.

"*Say* it."

"You're coming back."

Michael glanced at the doorway. "That's right, darlin. You'll hardly know I'm gone."

And then he was.

Chapter Sixteen

Valiance

I noticed, and didn't enjoy the feeling of helplessness. I tugged on the handcuff. Stainless steel — it wasn't going to break. The bench was a different matter. The wooden peg wiggled when I pulled. Not a lot, but enough to show a weakness in the design. *Enough to work it free?* I jostled the peg back and forth. It got looser. Finally, it fell out with a hollow clatter that made me start guiltily, half-expecting Michael to burst through the door with a face fit to kill.

But no, I was free. Better yet, I had one-upped the man who used to baffle me with his thoroughness. I felt like Houdini, only better. I shoved the dangling handcuff up my sleeve. Provided nobody got a good look at me, it wouldn't be noticed. I hoped.

Except for the incessant alarm, there was silence. I waited thirty seconds before opening the door and scanning the hallway. Empty. Almost empty. There was a uniformed man lying on the floor, facing away from me. Was he unconscious? Or dead? I stepped closer, surveying him frowningly. His posture was relaxed, his eyes closed — then I saw the other half of his face. Or what remained behind the liquid mess that dripped into the ragged caverns where his features had been. I bent down, trying to keep whatever I'd last eaten from rising back up.

Someone had been shot here, only mere feet away from where

I'd been hiding in the locker room. Shot in the *face*. I remembered the gunshots — Michael's expression. Was *this* the sight that had greeted him, that had made his face look so grim? Nice to know he was still capable of being shocked. There hadn't been a scream, at least. Maybe it had been painless.

What if this happened to my parents? What if they're locked up in a bunker somewhere, being tortured by a man like Adrian?

I looked down the hallway, avoiding the dead man. I'd never been through these corridors on my own. I always had an escort before and the size of the place made an impression on me all over gain, now that I was alone. The alarm made me less shy about trying the doors than I might have been, but all of them were locked.

Of course.

The alarm cut off mid-shriek, plunging the corridors into a deathly silence. Who had shut it off? And why? Had they caught Michael? Apart from A, he was the closest thing I had to an ally in this place.

In the sudden absence of sound, my breathing and the soft scuff of my feet on the polished floor sounded so loud, I almost wished the alarm would come back on. Without that blaring sound to mask me, I would have to be twice as careful about making noise.

There was another gunshot, farther off. I could barely make it out for what it was. I quickly headed in an alternate direction, farther from the gunfire, towards a series of darkened rooms with large glass windows. I could see the faint glow of computer monitors inside. They looked like laboratories. I tried one of the metal doors but these also required access codes and no one had been hasty enough to leave them unlocked. Or maybe they locked automatically in the case of an emergency. I rapped the windows — the glass was thick, the kind used in pressurized tanks. They wouldn't shatter. Another dead end.

I headed back into the main hallway. Somebody crashed into me. Another uniformed guard. Young. His dark eyes were wide with fright, his hand clapped over his side as though favoring an injury. I held my handcuffed arm behind me, just in case, but his eyes barely skimmed over me as he mumbled an apology and broke into a sprint. I wondered if he would have done anything, even if he had noticed that I'd escaped. Somehow I didn't think so. He'd seemed desperate…almost panicked. As if the devil himself was after him.

He'd dropped a badge. The cord that had held it around his neck was broken. Snapped. Like someone had pulled it too hard. *Miles Trevelyan*. Didn't know him. Shrugging, I tossed it back on the floor. Never would, either. But I saw somebody I *did* know.

Adrian.

I dove back into the small corridor with the laboratories, pressing myself up against the shadows and praying he wouldn't see me. I could hear him running. His breath was a little pushed; it sounded like he had been running for a while. Had he been chasing the guard? Or was somebody else chasing both of them? There was another gunshot, closer this time. Adrian glanced over his shoulder and headed into my corridor.

His gray eyes widened in surprise. "Well, well — I was looking for you."

He was? I tried to hide the handcuff.

"All dressed up with nowhere to go. I'm impressed you still have the energy to escape." I watched his eyes flicker to the hallway. He was definitely the chased. For once. But when he looked back at me, his smile was full of assurance. "Maybe I was too easy on you."

I should have stayed in the locker room.

There was another blast. "Oh, Michael."

"What?"

"The rifleman. He didn't even bother attaching a silencer to that handgun of his — and he's got two assault rifles to boot. Setting off alarms left and right. He must want to be caught." I almost mentioned the other two gunshots, then thought better of it. Adrian didn't need to know. With any luck, they'd shoot him next.

"Michael is in big trouble," he informed me.

I took a step back. "Isn't he always?"

"Mm-hmm. You know him well. A little too well. But this time, he has outdone himself. Not only has he failed at being dead — and *staying* dead — he bribed a technician here to wipe the database clean and then ran off with the back-up disk."

"Too bad." I took another step back. "What was on it?"

"Everything. An entire library obliterated in a matter of seconds. The little fool didn't even realize what he'd agreed to until I interrogated him. Then he did, but it was too little, too late..."

The sneer was wiped from my face as I grasped what he was alluding to. Before I could come up with a response, he leaned over me, sliding his hands down the wall until they were level with my face. "That reminds me — where did we leave off?"

I looked at the hallway, hoping to see...anyone.

"Everyone evacuated." He found my desperation hilarious. "In a matter of minutes, special forces will be coming in to take Michael down. Until then, we're alone."

Stall him. "He was chasing you, wasn't he? He was going to kill you."

"Oh, Michael and I go way back, Christina. I taught him *everything* he knows."

"Y-you did?" *Everything?*

"Nobody else wanted him. He had a foul mouth, and a criminal record to boot. But I *like* a challenge. He requested a transfer after a year. I suppose I can be a little much for people. They tend to prefer me in small doses — or not at all, if they can help it." He flashed his teeth. "They usually can't."

"Because you're a sick fuck who tortures people!"

He wagged his finger at me. "You make it sound so *simple*. It isn't. Not at all. Torture covers a broad spectrum. The two main subgroups are physiological and psychological, but these can be divided into the subcategories of spiritual, emotional, physical, and sexual. Everyone has at least one weakness in at least one of these areas that can be exploited. Finding it only requires patience, and a suspension of societal norms.

"Tell me," he continued. "Why is it that this gets me no results" — he dug the heel of his hand into one of my stitched-up sides — "but *this* does?" I waited, trying not to breathe, as I braced myself for the pain to follow. His breath tickled my face unpleasantly. Too late, I realized what he meant to do.

It wasn't a kiss, because that implied at least some form of emotion was involved — hatred, love, lust. This had none of these things. It was a passionless attempt to hurt me. He was *assaulting* my mouth — and it was working. I was revolted by everything. The smell of him, like the dry, crumbly sweetness of baby powder. The girlish softness of his lips. The way his breath tasted of *mint*. It was worse than I could have imagined, and I did the worst thing possible.

Cloak and Dagger by Nenia Campbell

I screamed.

He gave me a cold, knowing smile. I was shaking so hard, it took a moment for my larynx to work. "Your boss — "

"Will do absolutely nothing. Michael pushed him over the edge. Derailed his conscience. Richardson wants information — by any means necessary. I take care of the rest."

"This is hypocrisy."

"Wrong again," he said cheerfully. "I'm only following orders. I can't be faulted for *enjoying* my orders — not by him, anyway," he added, as I began to launch another protest. "And yes, while you are, admittedly, quite fun to play with and I do *so* enjoy the time we spend together, if Richardson changed his mind and told me to slit your pretty throat...I'd do it."

I believed him.

"You were worth quite a bit of money alive. Rewards were posted galore. Michael could have turned you in and kept that money for himself if he wanted to sabotage us. The authorities mightn't have killed him — not if he told them what they wanted to know. He could've pleaded for a lesser sentence by putting away some of his old mates. But he didn't. You were with him for over a month, Christina Parker. Do you honestly expect me, or anyone else for that matter, to believe that he let you live without" — he lowered his eyes meaningfully — "a bit of *bargaining* on your part?"

"It's the *truth*."

"We'll see if your tune stays the same once I get you singing." He loosened my collar. "Just like a wee bird." I raised my leg and kneed him in the groin. I heard him retch. It was the most satisfying sound I'd ever heard in my life.

I turned to run. A metallic click stopped me dead.

Adrian was still half bent over, clutching his abdomen and looking like he might be sick, but he was smiling. *Smiling*.

"No," I whispered. "Shit — "

"Oh, yes." He caressed my face with the muzzle of the gun. "Now, what say you and I go someplace a little…quieter?"

"You'll do no such thing. Drop your weapon."

Michael had one of his guns drawn. He looked hot, sweaty, and fatigued. The dampness on his clothes suggested blood, though it was impossible to tell whether it was his. When I encountered him in the locker room, he'd already been injured.

Michael gave me a look that suggested there would be hell to pay later — if there *was* a later. "Drop the gun, Callaghan. Now."

"Whatever you say, Michael." The gun fell to the floor with a clatter.

I heard him step forward to pick it up. "Hands against the wall." He directed with the big rifle. "I have a clear shot at your head."

Adrian moved as if to obey. The crinkle of his heavily-starched shirt was the only warning I got as he grabbed me, whirling around so I was pressed against him, back to front, with his knife at my throat. I remembered what he had told me, only moments before.

"Don't come any closer, or she dies."

"I'll shoot you both."

"What?"

"You won't. I know you're empty. If you weren't, you would've killed me when my back was turned." He paused, adjusting the knife with the neatest flick of his wrist, and I felt something warm trickle down my throat. "And we both know you don't really want to kill her."

Less than half an inch deeper, and he'd slice into my jugular vein.

Michael held his stance — and the bluff — for a moment longer, then tossed the assault rifles aside, producing another handgun that had been tucked out of sight at the hip. Sweat trickled down my face, down my neck, making the cut sting. "Let her go. You want me."

"Not quite, Michael, my boy. Not quite."

Without warning, he pushed me. Michael caught me by the collar, tearing the back of my blouse. He stopped my fall, though my knees still hit the tile hard enough that I felt the shock of it in my bones. "Get behind me," he said under his breath.

His next words were cut off by the alarm. It had started up again. He didn't jump, as I had, but it was enough of a distraction that he almost missed the flash of silver headed towards his chest. "Look out!" I gave him a hard shove, and he twisted around to fight me off so the knife plunged into his left shoulder, instead of his heart. The gun went off as his fingers contracted spasmodically. By now it was no longer aimed anywhere near Adrian, and the bullet took out one of the ceiling lamps with a loud bang, sending down a shower of sparks and broken glass.

I covered my face and head as Michael began to curse at the top of his lungs. The knife was small, but at least two inches of it were embedded in his skin. The sight of it, standing straight up like that, was unnatural. Michael moaned, his fingers digging into the flesh of his shoulder.

"Are you…all right?"

"No," he hissed, switching the gun to his right hand. Another litany of curses escaped him. One of the doors nearby opened and a man in black uniform burst out. Michael fired, but the bullets didn't pass through the heavy-looking material. Not at such far range. But there was a gap between helmet and visor, so the guard could speak and breathe unimpeded even without removing his protective gear. Michael dropped to his knees, angled upward, and fired. A spray of blood hit both visor and floor. The man collapsed.

Cloak and Dagger by Nenia Campbell

Michael glanced over at me. I saw a lot in that gaze; it scared me.

He bent over the man, examining the uniform. He examined the guard's gun, turning it over in his hands, testing the weight, looking at the ammunition. "It's a stun gun." That didn't sound as bad as a real gun, but his tone made me wonder. In the guard's other hand was a small, black device. Michael's face darkened. "He called for backup."

Several other doors opened with identical whooshes of air as all the access panels were activated at once. Men in black body armor poured into the small hallway. Gunfire erupted, pounding at my brain like a jackhammer. I wondered if I would go deaf. I wondered if I'd live long enough to find out.

Michael grabbed the fallen guard's riot shield. "Stay behind me!"

I ducked behind him — and the shield — and felt a tiny prick in my arm. I met the smooth, tinted visor of the man who had shot me and fell to my knees.

Michael tore open a pack of bullets with his teeth, loaded the magazine of his handgun, and fired off another round into the writhing sea of guards. He was holding the shield in his bad arm. Drops of his own blood spattered the tiles at his feet as his old wounds oozed and bled through their wrappings. The only sign of his pain was the sweat on his face and the tremors that wracked his body with every hit of the recoil. A dart whizzed by. He pulled his torso back and fired at the shooter. The man dropped, and another stepped forward to fill his place.

Then — Michael was hit. He cursed as the dart embedded itself in his shoulder and he dropped the shield. With a grim expression, he continued shooting until one of the darts spiraled into his exposed chest, sending him stumbling backwards through a slippery trail of blood. He collapsed, was handcuffed, and then taken away. One of the guards approached me, next —

And the scene faded to black.

Cloak and Dagger by Nenia Campbell

Chapter Seventeen

Bound

Christina:

29 hours left.

The floor, the ceilings, my clothes — even the air — were all different.

I sat up, taking in my surroundings. Gone were the padded floors and walls of the containment cell. Gone was the stale underground air, riddled with the intolerable chill of the AC. I was in an open room with no furniture and smooth, curved walls that made me feel as if I were on the inside of a large metal egg. The air tasted salty, reminiscent of the sea. There were no windows to check, but I suspected we wear near the ocean. Or on it. A mechanical hum hinted at an engine.

Somebody — I hoped it was a woman — had changed me into black sweatpants and a white t-shirt. I couldn't understand why I kept getting white clothes. They hadn't maintained their color long. Maybe it had to do with transparency, and being able to hide foreign objects in the folds of your clothes. Or maybe the IMA just bought all of the supplies for their prisoners in bulk and the cheapest t-shirts happened to be white.

My right wrist was handcuffed to Michael, who was either asleep or unconscious. His breathing sounded labored, so I opted for

277

the latter. The guards had really nailed him with those darts. Assuming they all contained the same amounts of tranquilizer, he'd easily received five times the does that I had.

Michael was also wearing sweatpants. No shoes. White strips of bandages were wrapped around his bare left shoulder, where somebody had removed Adrian's knife. There was another set of bandages, also on the left side of his body, scant inches away from his heart and stained blood. I knew he'd been injured, but had no idea how *badly*. He didn't have many scars, though — not like the Michael from my dream. There were a couple, mostly on his arms, but the nastiest was just above the waistband of his pants.

It was easy to see why the IMA wanted him dead. I'd watched him take out something like twenty armored guards with a bullet wound and a bad arm. He had a body like Action Man with muscles so defined, they looked like they could cut glass.

I realized I was staring and turned away. My left arm was puffy from the sedative. Not an opiate, or I'd be ill — or dead. Somebody wanted me alive. Wanted *both* of us alive.

Why?

The door opened. A guard walked in. He threw a wary glance at Michael before setting down a food tray and two water bottles without caps. I tried to stop him. He threw off my arm. "Wait — where are you taking us?"

Cloak and Dagger by Nenia Campbell

The door slammed shut behind him.

I couldn't move with Michael holding me down like a deadweight, so I remained where I was, picking at the fruit the guard had brought. *Why did they handcuff me to Michael? If they think we're accomplices, wouldn't they lock us in separate rooms?*

Michael was still out cold.

I'd never been so afraid or uncertain.

I must have blacked out. I woke to the chain tugging my wrist. Michael was stretching. Pain tore over his face as he clenched his healing shoulder. His eyes opened, meeting mine. I saw them widen in shock. "What — " He looked around. "What is this?"

"A handcuff," I said. "Good morning, sunshine."

I saw his fingers whiten as he gripped the bandages and glared at me. Maybe I was being a bitch — he deserved it. *He* was the one chained up like an animal. *His* life had been thrown into uncertainty. The hunter had become the hunted. "Does it hurt?" I asked, nodding at the bandages.

"More than you can fucking imagine that."

"I doubt that." Even operating at half-capacity, he was far stronger than I.

"Are you afraid, Christina?"

"Are *you*?"

"Fear is a useful emotion," he pointed out. "It makes the body alert."

"You didn't answer my question."

He sighed. "Yes. I'm afraid."

If *he* was afraid, where did that leave me? "Why? What are they going to do to us?"

"I'm fairly sure we're on a stealth boat. They have cloaking devices invisible to most forms of radar." He leaned back on his elbows, the strain in his face obvious even to me. "They're either taking us to their base in the Ukraine, or the one in Mexico."

"What's the difference?"

"Temperature."

A whirring noise drew my attention skyward. Two of the panels in the wall parted to reveal a flat screen — rather like the one Adrian had used to make me watch the snuff film. The screen flickered, revealing an office replete with a desk and a potted banana plant. A man walked onscreen and sat behind the desk.

Richardson smiled pleasantly. "Good afternoon, Miss Parker. And Mr. Boutilier — back from the dead."

"No thanks to you."

I looked at Michael. He shrugged.

"Is the food to your liking?"

I'd barely tasted it.

"Don't waste our time with your pleasantries. We know this isn't a fucking cruise."

"Still sore, Mr. Boutilier? Remind me, how many men did it take to bring you down?"

"Ten."

"You took out some of my best men."

"They couldn't have been that good if I could take them out with a bad arm."

The smile disappeared from Richardson's face. "You could have gone far, Mr. Boutilier. I have yet to see your equal in the training field. You will be difficult to replace."

Michael shifted uncomfortably. I remembered how badly Adrian had hurt me. I had tried to hide my suffering and failed. There is a point at which you can no longer keep everything inside and all the agony bleeds outwards like an open wound. It had to be costing him a lot not to let a single ounce of that excruciating pain show in front of his boss.

"Where are you taking us?" I asked.

"Base ten."

"Where is that?"

Richardson smiled. "Mexico."

The interment base Michael was telling me about?

"We call it Target Island," said Michael.

"Do you plan on giving us the backup disk, Mr. Boutilier?"

"No."

"What about telling us how you escaped from the lake?"

"No."

"I know you had help, Mr. Boutilier. Even you aren't strong enough to break solid steel."

Michael said nothing.

Richardson sighed. "One way or another, we *will* get the information we want." He glanced at me. "It is a pity, Miss Parker, that you allowed yourself to become enmeshed in the situation."

"I didn't allow myself to get *enmeshed* in anything!"

"Mr. Callaghan has provided me with information that points to the contrary. I did not know the nature of your business dealings was quite so…intimate."

"Go fuck off," Michael snapped.

"I am not speaking to you, Mr. Boutilier. You may be interested to know that we have finally made contact with your parents."

"You…have?"

"They have agreed to meet us. But now, I am afraid the deal is off. You simply know too much. We cannot allow you to live. My dearest sympathies. You will arrive at your destination in approximately twelve hours. Enjoy the remainder of your journey — and your life."

Cloak and Dagger by Nenia Campbell

Michael:

A month ago, if somebody had told me I was going to end up branded as a traitor handcuffed to my hostage on a boat headed towards Target Island, I would have shot them in the face for such insolent slander. That was before I woke up, shackled like a common prisoner. All my weapons were gone. All my old clothes were gone, too. Operatives were skilled at weapons concealment. I wasn't surprised that they had taken my shirt or my shoes. I was lucky they hadn't left me fucking naked.

The room were were in was too large and too oddly-shaped to be anything but the lower level of a boat. I could feel the engine's vibrations. Probably a stealth boat. The curved, smooth chamber was about the size of an ordinary room. There was no furniture, which was only to be expected. Furniture could be made into weapons. A couple pillows were strewn about. Somebody had come in while I was asleep and set down a plastic tray of food and water. Fresh fruit, raw vegetables, sandwiches, even pastries. I didn't understand why they took the bottle caps and left the food — if swallowed whole, a carrot could be just as much of a hazard.

I looked around again, frowning. Considering the conditions most prisoners traveled in, this bordered on ludicrous. Left to wallow in their own filth, the trip itself was a prelude for the unimaginable horrors to come. Richardson's pitiful attempt at

283

bribery was laughable. He thought he could buy my compliance with a bit of food and some *pillows*? He really was a fool.

I leaned back again, not in the mood for eating. Richardson's long-winded speech had left me with a sour taste in the back of my throat. I was exhausted. It was like I hadn't slept in years. My chest was aching again and my pain-killers had been confiscated with my pants. The last reserve of my energy had gone into that final stand-off against the guards in B-1.

How much information did that bastard have in his possession? Too much, clearly, if he had known somebody helped me in Michigan, though that could just be fancy guesswork. A keen sense of insight had always kept him from being a total pushover. I wished there was a way for me to contact Kent, to warn him.

Christina sat as far from me as humanly possible, putting tension on the chain and my shoulder by proxy. The chain hadn't slackened once during my thoughts. I thought she might be asleep, but when I turned to check she was staring at me. Even now, en route to Target Island, she was still afraid of *me*.

I found it ironic that I hadn't been able to instill the proper terror when it had actually mattered, and now that it didn't, and she actually needed my help — and I, hers — she was skittish, mistrustful, and afraid. I took a long drink of water. Irony was a bitch.

She was in sweatpants nearly identical to mine and a white t-shirt. I wondered absently why they hadn't just dispensed with it altogether, and given this dying man a sight for sore eyes. I felt my lips curl into a bitter smile. "What is running through your head Christina?"

Christina:

26 hours left.

I didn't understand — why would Michael destroy the disk? If Richardson was telling the truth, and the only reason the IMA was keeping us alive was to learn its location, then any bargaining power we had was as hopelessly crushed as those tiny pieces of silicon. What did he think the IMA was going to say when they found out? That's okay, accidents happen? *That* was what was running through my head.

Luckily, a guard came in with more water before I had to respond. A different guard than before, younger. I thought that because of his age, he might be more amenable to asking questions. I asked how much time was left before we docked. He snorted and muttered something sarcastic under his breath as he unceremoniously set the bottles on the floor.

"They won't answer any of your questions."

I grabbed one of the carrots and took a huge bite. Not because I was hungry but because I needed something for my jaw to work on, else I was going to grind my teeth into a fine, powdery dust. If my mother was here, she would be pleased. She had always tried to find a way to transition me to snacking on carrots. The answer had been under her nose all along: all she had needed to do was threaten me with untimely death.

When I looked up, Michael was watching me again. "You never answered my question."

"Dieting," I answered. "I think the prisoner look is going to be the new heroin chic. What about you? What's on yours?"

He just looked at me.

Michael had been a different man since his attempted assassination. It wasn't that he had stopped being dangerous, because he *was*, but that he had become dangerous in a different way. Fire instead of ice. Explosive instead of contained. Mercurial instead of predictable. I found myself looking at him sometimes and wondering what he was going to do next.

"Your father is good with computers," he said suddenly.

I nodded, taking another bite of carrot. *Where is he going with this?*

He paused only a beat. "Did you know he was a famous computer hacker?"

The carrot I was chewing lodged in my throat. Carrot flecks

speckled the floor as I coughed, *"What?"*

"He sent a virus to one of our computers, causing an entire network to shut down. It was an accident — or so we believed at first. He was taking his little experiment for a test drive. Seeing what it could do. When he broke through our security system, he didn't realize what he was getting himself into. But I imagine he figured it out when he deciphered our encrypted weapons placement orders describing a list of powerful artillery recently bought and sold — artillery not available to the general public."

My father? A hacker?

It made sense why *Mamá* had gotten so upset over Dad's telling me about the "forbidden doors." That must have been after he'd already broken through the IMA's security system. The allusion to Pandora's box had been a reference to his hacking, and perhaps even directly to his foray into the IMA computer mainframe itself.

"So…that's why…all this?" I moved my free hand into a swoop.

"No. We could have bought his silence. But he turned what he had found into the police."

Dad had known all along — and he hadn't told me. Why? To keep me safe? That had worked really well. To protect my image of him as a father? The betrayal hurt worse than the knowledge of his double life. I stared at the wall. "If he turned it into the police, why haven't they launched an investigation?"

"Infiltration."

"So, in other words, you have agents who pose as policemen."

Half his mouth twitched. "Something like that."

Well I had fallen for Adrian's act hook, line and sinker, until he dropped the charade. If he hadn't been so keen on lording my mistake over me, letting me stew in my own fear, he probably could have kept me fooled right up to the point where they slapped the handcuffs on me and slammed me in a cell. Could Adrian have fooled an entire police force? Probably, if he wanted to. I was sure the IMA had plenty of operatives who would feel even more comfortable in that role.

An onslaught of questions were tumbling into awareness. "Why was I kidnapped?"

"The message referred to a 'curious girl.' We thought that girl might be you, that you might have something to do with the virus's code, or the stolen spreadsheets."

"Well, I'm *not.*"

"I realized that. So we decided to try blackmail. Hold you for ransom."

"Fat lot of good that did you." I drew in a shaky breath. "I wish *you* hadn't told me this." By which I'd meant, *I wish my* parents *had been the ones to tell me this.*

But Michael took my words at face value. "I thought you'd be grateful to know."

Grateful. "All it's done is make me realize that my life sucks more than I thought."

"Oh? The IMA may enjoy playing judge, jury, and executioner, but even *they* need proof."

"They do have proof," I said. "You said so yourself. It's on the —
"

The database? Which he had wiped clean?

"The disk showed a digital footprint of the pages he accessed. Without the disk, they have no proof, as well as a couple other terabytes of information, including some on you and me, that I'm sure will be missed. I told that idiot technician Richardson wanted the computers backed up. Richardson hadn't let the lower-ranked operatives of the IMA know that I was dead. I was enough of a superior that he had no reason to doubt me. Then I re-released your father's virus into the system. Unchecked, it tore the computers apart from the inside-out."

"You could have used it as a bargaining chip!"

"They would have killed me, anyway. You, too, in spite of what you may think. Even if your parents had agreed to the ransom, and met up with my man at the Walk of Flags. The moment you saw my face, you were screwed. Only difference between then and now is that the IMA will be just as screwed as we are."

I paused, remembering something Adrian had told me. I hadn't paid it much thought at the time, focused as I'd been on escape, but now it made me wonder. "Is it true you were in a gang before you joined the IMA?"

Michael had closed his eyes but cracked one open to regard me in a steely squint. "Where the hell did you hear that from?"

"Adrian."

He laughed sourly. "I should have known."

"Well, were you?"

"Yes," he said. Both eyes closed now. "I was."

"You don't have any tattoos."

Another unpleasant laugh. "That you can see."

He was goading me, daring me to ask. "Why did you join a gang? It didn't seem to make you happy."

"What the fuck are you? A therapist?"

"No...I..." I'd overstepped myself. I'd forgotten who I was talking to. I wished I could take my words back. "I was just curious."

"You think that's the root of all my problems? That if I hadn't joined a gang, I'd be a sweet, upstanding young thing like you? I grew up in the slums of backwoods Louisiana where there were two choices: join the gang or get the shit kicked out of you. At least if you joined the gang, you got some petty cash. Don't attach any of your pathetic childish fantasies to me just because I saved your father. For once, our wants coincided. You think I put my ass on the line for you for the hell of it? Because I thought it was the right thing to do?"

The hostile barrage of words spoke at a long-harbored resentment that had been left to kindle. What reason did he have to hate me? He had ruined *my* life — what would possess him to even hint that I had done the same to him? "If you really feel that way, then why didn't you let Adrian finish me?"

He leaned towards me. "Perhaps I *should* have."

"But you didn't."

"No. I didn't. I came back." His hand cupped my face. "For you." I flinched, but his fingers were, for once, oddly gentle. "My mistake." His lips covered against mine, and his free hand closed around my wrist. He nudged me backwards —

And dizzily, I fell into darkness.

Michael:

Something was wrong. I don't know how I made myself stop, but I did. Her breathing had slowed. "Christina?" Speaking was an effort. No response. I lifted her eyelid. The pupil was dilated. Then I looked at her half-drained water bottle.

Drugs.

The water.

The *goddamn* water.

I could already feel the effects of it. A heavy lethargy. A feeling of being disconnected. A cold sweat had broken out over my body despite the fact that the room was not that hot. I pictured Richardson watching these scene, as relayed by whatever bug he'd installed in here, and imagined him laughing. *Revenge is a dish best served cold*, he would say.

I should have known he would take it literally.

Christina:

I wanted to throw up when I saw the guards' sleazy grins. Just like the St. John's boys, only worse because these were *men*, and there was something much more lascivious in their expressions. Much more...adult. Almost pornographic.

"Rough night?" they said to Michael.

They ignored me. *After all,* I'm *only a* girl.

Michael looked exhausted. The shadows beneath his eyes had darkened, and his chin and cheeks were covered in golden bristles. He squinted into the dimming sunlight, blinking excessively, and then glared at the guards through slitted eyes.

What is that supposed to mean?

I couldn't remember anything beyond waking up on the boat and discovering we weren't in Oregon anymore. I distantly remembered talking to Michael about...something.

Cloak and Dagger by Nenia Campbell

What? What had Michael done to me?

Two armed guards escorted us off the boat with their weapons
drawn. A warning sign near the beach said *PRIVATE PROPERTY;*
TRESPASSERS WILL BE PROSECUTED. I walked purposely slow,
drinking everything in as I searched for a way to escape — until the
guard jabbed his gun into the base of my spine to hurry me along.

The dirt was a soft dark brown that felt like sludge and smelled
like sewage. Beyond the sunken path was a dense subtropical jungle.
Birds chirped in the bushes. Periodically, I would hear a rustle from
the undergrowth as something scampered away from our footsteps.
It seemed like it would be easy — painfully so — to slip away. There
had to be a second, hidden line of defense. Mines, maybe. Otherwise
more people would escape, and Michael had said that once you were
taken to an internment base, that was the end.

I stumbled over a rock half-buried in the muck. Michael caught
me. I tried to push him away — I didn't want his hands on me, not
after what we...*he*...might have done — but he caught my wrist to
restrain me. Probably thinking I was going to make a run for the
foliage and get us both killed. *He's always treating me like some idiotic*
damsel in distress. I yanked my arm out of his grip with more violence
than necessary and lost my balance. I fell, dragging him down with
me, and we landed in an ungraceful heap, inches deep in the foul
mud, at the nearest guard's feet. All my injuries awakened like

hungry lions and I screamed —

Only to hear slow laughter.

Mr. Richardson was standing at the edge of the path. Somehow he'd managed to find a dry patch of land to stand on. Adrian was at his side. He was still dressed to impress in spite of the swampy heat, but I was pleased to see him suffering for it. Richardson, in contrast, looked far more casual. He had traded in his suit for Bermuda shorts and a Hawaiian shirt. *All that's missing is a flowery lei.*

"Welcome to Target Island. In Spanish, the translation is closer to Target-Shooting Island, but that's a bit of a mouthful," Mr. Richardson spoke as if he were just a tour guide relaying the history of a wonderful tropical paradise. "This is where we bring our operatives to…retire."

Adrian clicked his tongue making a sound similar to a gun's safety being turned off.

Mr. Richardson gave him a glare and us a rueful smile. But his eyes were unrepentant. "Consider yourself lucky, Michael. Most people have to wait until they're sixty-five for that particular pleasure."

"What did you drug the water with? Rohypnol?" Michael demanded.

"Rohypnol," Mr. Richardson agreed. I inhaled sharply and he turned towards me. "I know what you are thinking, Miss Parker.

And no, you would not have done anything that you hadn't subconsciously wanted to do." He smiled simperingly. "Perhaps there is hope for you yet, Mr. Boutilier."

I felt like sobbing — and *throwing* things. I started forward and so did the guards but Michael, being cuffed to me, got to me first. He grabbed my arm again, holding me back. As he struggled to keep me, and my temper, under control ("his mouth has always been like his ass" — this whispered remark interspersed with a furious look at his ex-boss — "the most unbelievable shit comes out of it") a small, traitorous voice whispered, *Would it have been so awful?*

Mamá had always made it clear she believed girls who got raped deserved it. I hadn't done any of the things she said "bad" girls did, though. I didn't parade myself around in sluttish clothes and make untoward advances. But *Mamá* had been wrong about everything else so far, so maybe she'd been wrong about that, too. Maybe it didn't matter whether you were bad *or* good, prudish *or* wanton: maybe just being female was enough, for some men. Maybe, like so much else, it was only about control. *But then why do I feel so guilty?*

"Don't touch me," I said to Michael, who dropped his hand.

Mr. Richardson was watching us. "You don't remember what happened, Miss Parker?"

"*No.*"

"Pity," he said. "It was…rather touching."

I felt Michael stiffen. "What did you do?"

"I don't remember."

"What do you *think* you did?"

"I don't fucking *know*."

He sounded just helpless enough that I believed him.

Adrian, apparently disliking being ignored, said, "Your orders, sir?"

"Ah, yes. Escort the two lovebirds to Node Six, Mr. Callaghan. Get them cleaned up and so to it that they receive food and a change of clothes — I won't have them stinking up the cells as they are."

Adrian did not look pleased by the prospect. *Fastidious bastard.* "Separate rooms?" he asked, glancing at me.

Oh God, no.

"No." Richardson turned to face us. "Leave them together and double the guard. The girl is weak and slow. If he attempts to escape, she will drag him down; and he won't leave without her."

Chapter Eighteen

Release

Christina:

12 hours left.

"Dismissed. Get them out of my sight." Behind the casual dismissal, the careful authority, the fury in Mr. Richardson's voice was like a giant splinter shredding through his words. I vaguely remembered what Michael had confessed to me — the ship was bugged. Had the confession been for his boss's benefit? If it had been, Michael's ploy worked: Mr. Richardson was pissed. "Now," he added savagely, prompting the guards into immediate action.

Michael and I were separated. My handcuff was unlocked and I was thrown into a new pair. Oh, boy. The guard grabbed me by the shoulder and marched me away from the beach. It was a long walk. By now, the sun was a distant memory. The stars shone overhead, clearer than I had ever seen them before. In the distance, I could hear the hiss of the ocean waves. The sludge beneath my feet soaked into the fabric of my sweatpants, weighing them down until it felt like I was dragging a pair of smelly sandbags around my ankles. Soon, I was shivering.

I knew we were close when the muddy ground yielded to cement walkways. All the buildings were postmodern behemoths shaped from steel and shatterproof glass, twisted into asymmetrical shapes. The futuristic monoliths were at odds with the deep navy of the Pacific Ocean, just barely visible from where we were now, and the thickets of palm trees. I remembered the dense jungle that surrounded the beaches and realized now why the guards hadn't been concerned about escape: there were watch towers posted around in even intervals. Each tower contained two armed guards. My heart sank. Target Island wasn't that big, but the base itself took up a significant portion of the land. Escape from here would be nigh impossible.

Node Six turned out to be a large L-shaped building. A large metal six stood in front of it, and I could see a five further down. The automatic doors parted with a woosh of air. We were in an office, except guards were posted at every door. A few people looked up from their computers, then lowered their eyes again. *Sympathy or boredom?* Neither was reassuring.

I stumbled beside the guard, no longer able to keep pace with his military-precise steps. My injuries were aching from the long and arduous walk. My feet were blistered with splinters. I was cold and wet and exhausted. "Are we almost there?"

"Shut up," the guard said, with such viciousness I balked.

By the time we reached the showers, I was ready to collapse. The moment the guard released me, I did. He looked like he was considering hoisting me to my feet but I suppose he decided it was less effort to let me lie there on the floor while we waited. I closed my eyes and wheezed.

Footsteps approached. Red shoes and black boots appeared in front of me, about eye-level from my current position. *A?* I looked up hopefully. It wasn't A. It was another woman I'd never seen before. A dark and curly-haired woman with wide black eyes and red lipstick that looked much cheaper than anything I'd ever seen A wear. Her white sundress was a tight fit on her curvy body and had a plunging neckline. When she bent to my level, I saw more than I wanted. *A native?* I wondered if she spoke Spanish.

"Tan joven y tan viejo," she said. So old and yet, so young. Even if she wasn't a native, her Spanish was perfect.

It occurred to me that I ought to pretend I couldn't understand her, that I might overhear the guards say something in Spanish if they assumed I didn't speak it. But the guard beside her gave no indication that he'd understood a word she said. If he *did* speak it, his bluff was much better than mine would be. If the guards here *were* stupid enough to converse about their secret plans *in Spanish* in front of *me*, my shock would probably give me away.

Plus, Latinos have this assumption that anybody who looks Latino can speak Spanish. One of my classmates at Holy Trinity, a Native American, gets approached by random Hispanic people all the time in airports, grocery stores, and buses. Even though I'm half-white, I still definitely look *Latina*.

"¿Usted habla Español? Por favor, ayúdame." Just to make sure she understood how desperate I was, I used the most respectful form of address; the kind you use when you want to be really polite or formal, or acknowledge rank.

The woman shook her head and said in English, "I am sorry."

"Por favor."

"You'll speak *English*," the guard said, punctuating his gruff command with a jab from his gun. "Nothing else." I don't think he meant to do it so hard but the pain was exquisite. I found myself on my knees, guarding the bruise he'd assaulted.

The woman gave the guard a dirty look and helped me to my feet. I lurched off-balance, hitting a wall of dizziness and nausea. With my tired legs unable to support me, I sent both of us toppling to the ground like felled dominoes. The guard fixed us with a look that conveyed his scorn of all things female. "Are you sure you're going to be able to handle her alone?"

"Yes, I am certain." Her voice was beautiful, even when angry, and her English was quite good. She had a delicate accent that was clearly cultured. "Wait outside."

The bathrooms were a step down from the base in Oregon. There were no lockers. Everything was in shades of gray, as if the architect had been trying to make the place look as gloomy and miserable as possible. To my horror, the showers had no stalls. Just spigots suspended from the ceiling with a drain in the floor to catch the runoff. "No stalls?" I croaked.

"I promise I will not look."

Seeing my indecision prompted her to give me a towel and a sunny smile. I was not won over so easily. What did she think this place was? Some kind of resort?

"What's your name?"

"B."

Bee? Or B? "What happened to A?"

B avoided my eyes and would not respond.

The water of the shower was warm, but it couldn't melt the layer of ice beneath my skin that was like the permafrost of the tundra. I was terrified. Yes, I'd survived a lot longer than I would have thought possible, but I was running out of time and ideas. In a matter of hours, Richardson would give my parents his ultimatum and they would die, not knowing they had given their lives up in vain.

And what had happened to A? Adrian had accused her of being a traitor, saying, *You wouldn't want to end up like Michael*. Richardson appeared to take what Adrian said to heart now. What if his testimony had gotten A killed? Was B the replacement? Was Richardson working his way through the alphabet? An alphabet of soft, feminine women with beautiful voices and an irrepressible urge to shop? *God, he's just as sick as Adrian.*

I shut off the water and wrapped myself in the towel. B handed me some underthings, sweatpants, and another white t-shirt nearly identical to the one I'd been wearing before. I pulled the shirt down as far as it would go, which wasn't all that far, and tugged on the pants while staring at B's turned back. "Are there any cameras in here?"

She shook her head.

"Microphones?"

She nodded. "Please. At least tell me…are my parents here?"

Another nod.

I drew in a sharp breath. Maybe she hadn't understood the question. *How couldn't she? Even if her English weren't perfect, which it is, parents is a cognate; it sounds exactly like* parientes. "Are you sure? Rubens and Liliana Parker? They're both here?"

She nodded. In the mirror I saw pity flash across her face.

"No! You're monsters! *Monsters!* I hate you all!" B tried to shush me, and I lunged at her. I didn't need her pity, her superficial concern. She was like the priests who read the last rites to a prisoner on death row; she was only here to make sure I died without a fuss.

It was futile struggle on my part. All I achieved was alienating the one person who had treated me even remotely decently, and a sharp jab from the guard, who had rushed in at the first sign of trouble. I was half-dragged, half-carried back from the showers. He pitched me into my cell like a bowling ball. I ran to the door, rattling the bars until my arms were sore, screaming until my voice was hoarse. When I ran out of energy, I let my head fall forward, until my face was pressed against the bars. The rush of AC was like ice against my tear-streaked skin.

"They got your parents," a familiar voice behind me commented.

My hands tightened around the rods. "You shut up."

I heard the cot creak. Michael was sitting up now. His hair was wet, as mine was, and I guessed he had received a new pair of sweatpants as well. The guards had made certain improvements: both his hands were now cuffed together behind his back and there was a cut on his cheek, bleeding freely, which hadn't been there before.

"I had a little altercation with the guards."

"What did you do?"

"They underestimated me. I doubt it will happen again."

I turned back around and stared into the hallway. There were four guards now. One of them was staring directly at me.

"Christina? Come here."

"What do you want?"

"Come *here*."

"You can't make me. You don't even have the use of your hands."

Michael smiled. It was not a nice smile. "A minor setback. Come here."

Oh, *fine*. I closed the distance and said, "What?"

"I need you to get something sharp. A paperclip or a nail or…" He snapped his fingers. "A hairpin. B should be able to give you one."

A hair pin? "Why?" Oh. I got it. He wanted me to unlock his handcuffs. He was still trying to escape. Still trying to get his stupid revenge, even at my expense. I was nothing more than a tool to him. "Great idea," I hissed. "Why don't I just ask them for a key, as well as a pardon?"

"Now, now. Seducing your guards is exactly what got you here in the first place, darlin."

I turned away from him. "Fuck you, then." I'd just lost my parents to the IMA. I was never going to turn twenty-one. I felt emptier than I ever had in my whole entire life, which was about to end. All of my dreams, my hopes — shot down prematurely. I was really tired of being written off as collateral damage. "I hope you rot."

"You aren't doing your parents any favors by remaining locked up."

"Do *not* talk to me about my parents," I hissed.

"You need me."

"Stop *saying* that."

"Remember it, and I won't have to remind you. You know nothing about this business or this complex. Even if you somehow managed to escape, you wouldn't get far before you were apprehended by a guard and killed." His words cut into me like lances. "You're here precisely because of that naivete and inexperience."

"No," I said. "I am here because of *you*."

Michael:

That had not gone well.

I cursed myself and my temper. Attacking the guard hadn't been wise, but I was pissed and they'd given me the opportunity. By now, word had spread amongst the guards in Node Six that the ex-IMA prisoner wasn't as incapacitated as he looked at a glance. They would be doubly cautious now.

I watched Christina sit in her corner. If only Richardson hadn't opened his trap about the effects of the goddamn Rohypnol. I should have known that my rant would anger him, that he would seize any opportunity to put me in my place. I wasn't going to let him do that.

Was *she*?

She hadn't let that stop her when *I* was holding her captive.

I wondered if she ever stepped out of that fucking fantasy land of hers long enough to realize how much danger she was in. Her reaction was typical of delusional people forced to confront their denial. They give up in an attempt to convince themselves they don't care what's happening. Some might call that "acceptance." I call it sticking your head in the fucking sand like an ostrich.

"So that's it? You're just going to give up."

"So?"

"So nothing. It's your life."

She shook her head. I caught the strong, fruity scent of whatever she'd washed her hair with. "Not anymore. How long...do we have?""

Her voice was hard. Superficially so. She wanted to trust me, in spite of her misgivings.

"Our execution is scheduled for around ten am. Twelve hours from now."

"That's only half a day," she said, sounding stunned. "I didn't think..."

I didn't give her a chance to finish the thought. I was being manipulative, using tactics that I'd learned in my second year of training. I didn't want to die; I suspected that, deep down, she didn't, either. "If you want to die, you won't have to wait that long. But if you want to be screwed that badly, I can think of a much pleasanter way to do it — you could ask *me*."

I could feel her eyes on me as I rolled back to face the wall.

I allowed myself the privilege of a smile, knowing she was hooked.

Christina:

10 hours left.

B returned to the cell, accompanied by one of the guards. A Spanish-speaking one, this time. "*¿Está durmiendo?*" she asked, glancing at Michael.

"*Pienso.*" I honestly couldn't tell.

The guard relaxed a hair. B smiled. "*¿Hay algo que tú necesitas?*"

"*Una horquilla, por favor.*" I held up a strand of my frizzy hair.

The guard looked like he thought I was a very vain and foolish girl. B reached into her red leather purse and handed me several of her own tortoise-shell bobby pins. I made a show of smiling and using one to pin back my bangs. I was so afraid the guard would see through my display and confiscate the pins, but he turned on his heel with B trotting after him as obediently as a dog. Neither looked back.

"Michael?" I turned towards him, eager to spread the news of my victory. Even to him. He still hadn't opened his eyes. He really was asleep? I grabbed his shoulder and shook him gently, screaming in surprise when he kicked my feet from beneath me.

In the next instant, he was sitting upright, breathing hard, and looking down at me with eyes that looked too white in the dimness. "Jesus. I could have killed you. What the fuck were you doing, getting so close to me?"

"You weren't answering," I protested, still scared. What Michael had said before about the uselessness of his hands being a minor setback no longer seemed like an idle threat. The kick had heart, its delivery subconscious. I had no doubt he could do much worse.

Michael groaned and flopped back against the mattress. "What did you want?"

"I got the pins."

He didn't congratulate me or even thank me. "Are there any guards outside the cells?"

I checked. "Six."

"Good. Being in large numbers makes them overconfident. How many are actually watching us?"

I looked again. "Two."

Michael released his breath through his teeth. "All right. Get on top of me."

"Um…what?"

"I need you to unlock my cuffs. You won't be able to do it from the floor."

"You didn't tell me I'd have to do that!"

"What, did you think they would just magically unlock themselves?"

You're doing this to save your life. You're doing this to save your parents' lives.

I knelt astride him, feeling incredibly uncomfortable. "*There.* Now what?"

"Reach around me. Can you feel the handcuffs?"

"No."

"Then you have to move closer." He leaned up a little, as if doing a sit-up, causing the muscles in his abdomen to flex. "That should help."

I think I'm close enough. I bowed my head so I wouldn't have to look at him. I thought I could feel the hole in the handcuffs where the key was supposed to go. I bit my lip and fumbled with the pin in my sweaty fingers — and Michael leaned up to kiss me.

I pulled back with a cry, snapping the pin. The two halves fell to the floor with a *tink.* "Nice," he said flatly. "You broke the goddamn pin."

I covered my mouth with a shaking hand. "You — "

"If I fooled *you*, I must have been fooling the guards, who, I might add, are now *all* watching us — thanks to you."

"It wasn't my fault! You tried to…and the guards — you might have warned me!"

"You've been warned. Was that the only hair pin?"

"I have extras." I slipped the one from my hair.

"This will be more difficult with the guards watching. We'll have to give them their money's worth."

"What do you mean, give them their money's worth? What are you going to do?"

"Don't waste any more pins. We might need them later. Reach behind me."

"What are you going to do?"

"Just reach behind me."

An uncomfortable sense of *déjà vu* wrapped around me like a thick fog when he kissed me. I tried to concentrate on the cold still of his handcuffs but the feeling wouldn't leave. *Why is this so familiar?* My left thumb brushed against the small keyhole again. I pushed the key into it.

"Did you find it?"

"Yes."

"Good," he whispered. "Now, slide the pin between the notches and the ratchet."

"I am," I hissed, even though I had no idea what a ratchet was.

"Push it," he said impatiently.

"I *am*."

"At an angle?"

"It won't go in that way."

Michael leaned up, forcing me to grab onto his shoulder to keep from falling off. "Then push harder, darlin, and *make it* go in that way."

He was making me nervous with his shouted commands. What if I broke the pin again? What if the guards heard and caught on? "It's slipping," I said. "Stop moving, I can't — "

"Harder."

One of the guards made a sound of disgust and pointedly looked away. I froze, yanking my hands away from him, just in time to hear a soft snap. I got to my feet as quickly as my injuries would allow.

Michael smiled at me. It was a fierce smile, purely triumphant, and made me wonder if setting him free had been such a good idea.

"Was it as good for you as it was for me?"

Chapter Nineteen

Cataclysm

Michael:

I woke from my light doze to tingling arms. I discreetly shook them to get the blood circulating again. No one would see. The cell was dark. There were no windows so it was impossible to tell what time it was, though I suspected it was around one or two in the morning.

In several hours, we would die by firing squad.

I bit the inside of my cheek, scanning the room for anything that could be used as a weapon. The cell was empty, cleared of anything even remotely dangerous. Even during meals, a guard was present at all times, standing sentry at the door to make sure the dishes were returned.

Hmm. I might have a plan.

I got up, keeping my movements slow for the sake of the guards, and prodded Christina in the side with my foot. She rolled over, guarding, and muttered something intelligible.

I applied a little more pressure this time. She stirred and looked at me blearily. "What?"

"Bathroom," I said, jerking my head in that direction. "Now."

She shook her head and started to curl back up on the floor.

I nearly grabbed her by the shoulders. Caught myself just in time. "Do you want to get out of here?" I said instead. "If you do, then don't breathe a word. Just follow me."

I started purposefully for the bathroom without looking back over my shoulder to see if she was following. I heard her stumble to her feet. *Good.* The bathroom, which I had examined earlier on the pretense of using it for its intended use, was one of the few areas that didn't have cameras. Pointless expense in a cell, when all other areas are monitored and you can easily time the prisoner's comings and goings.

I wasn't worried about being inconspicuous — not after our earlier display. The guards would assume I wanted one last screw before I died, and that was exactly what I wanted them to think.

Christina leaned against the sink, rubbing her eyes. "What?"

I clapped a hand over her mouth. "There may not be any cameras in this room but that doesn't mean it's not bugged. So be *quiet.*" I waited until she had nodded. "We have a couple hours before the guards take us to Node Seven — that's the island's shooting range, namesake, and the end of the line, as far as we're concerned. But I have a plan. If you do as I say, you have a chance at survival. A *chance,* mind you, and a small one at that: there's no guarantee that either of us are going to live. Understand?"

Christina nodded again. Good. She was a fast learner.

I whispered the details into her ear, repeating the most

important ones several times. My superiors had always said that three was the magic number — I'd always suspected it was their attempt at excusing away the fact that they were senile old bastards that couldn't help repeating themselves, but it seemed to work, regardless.

She nodded in all the right places without saying anything, absentmindedly pulling down the hem of her shirt. Which, I noticed, pulled the fabric taut over her breasts. There was some pink in her cheeks, too. Quite a bit different from the sickly pallor I remembered from her basement days. In fact …she looked very fuckable.

The guards must have thought so, too, because I saw them nudge each other and snicker as we came out of the bathroom together. *I should start charging some goddamn admission.* How could she be so oblivious? She hadn't caught on about the lock-picking display either — not until the end. Where the hell had she gotten her education? A parochial school? Remembering the name of it — Sacred Heart, or something like that — I suspected that might not be too far from the truth. And here I thought Catholic schoolgirls were supposed to be kinky.

"Isn't it the girl who's supposed to be tied up, Boutilier?"

Guffaws all around.

I smiled tightly and lay back down. *Let's see how much you're laughing three hours from now.*

Cloak and Dagger by Nenia Campbell

Christina:

5 hours left.

I woke to the sound of the cell door opening.

My body was already nervous, edgy, and high on adrenaline. I saw Michael move in the corner of my eye. He was watching the food-bearing guard the same way a cat fixates on a person with a can opener. The guard eyed him with wariness that bordered on outright alarm.

"Stay back."

I grabbed the tray, letting the food slide to the floor with a loud crash. I was starving and sad to see it go but Michael said that with the amount of running we'd be doing, I'd most likely throw up anything that went into my stomach. The guard's head whipped towards me as I raised the tray over my head, leaving Michael free to land a hand punch to his throat. The guard made a garbled sound, a little like Donald Duck, and crumpled to the floor, whereupon Michael promptly seized his handguns.

The guards in the hallway started to fire the moment I seized the tray. Warning shots — or so I thought, until a bullet whizzed dangerously close to my leg. I held the metal tray in front of me, trying to shield my head and torso.

"Fuck!"

A bullet missed Michael's arm by less than a millimeter, near enough to draw blood. We squeezed out of the cell door as the guards closed in. It was 5am. The guards were exhausted. According to Michael, the day shift relieved the night shift at 6am. After almost twelve hours of surveillance, the guards would be crippled with exhaustion; their hits would not be as accurate as they would have been at, say, 6pm, when they were refreshed, awake, and alert.

Or so Michael had said. Their shots seemed plenty accurate to me.

Over the sound of the gunfire and Michael's own shouted commands, I could just make out the static from the guards' walkie-talkies. "The prisoners in cell 6-34-899 have escaped. They are armed. I repeat, *they are armed*."

"The hell should I know?" another guard was saying. "All I know is, he don't got them on anymore and he has a goddamn guys!"

"Give me that tray," Michael said.

I reluctantly handed it to him. He grabbed my arm and yanked me into a small alcove I hadn't noticed, leaning around the corner to fire off some rounds of his own. Bullets slammed against the tray, denting the metal. "Useless," Michael growled, tossing it aside. It hit the floor with a metallic clang. "This way."

He twisted open a door, urging me inside with the hand

wielding the pistol. I found myself in a dark hallway with two sets of staircases: one led into a dim corridor, the other had a sign that said simply *TO ROOF.* I headed for the lower set and Michael shook his head, grabbing me by the back of the shirt and said, "Roof."

A loud siren cut through the air.

"What if you're wrong?"

He shoved me up the stairs. I tried not to think about what his silence meant.

"Do you think A is here?"

"Probably. Richardson doesn't tolerate disloyalty from anyone, especially not from one of his whores. The moment she helped you, she signed her own death warrant. I don't know what she was thinking…" He trailed off, looking at me thoughtfully.

"Don't call her a whore! She saved my life — "

"Or just bought you more time. I warned you once not to underestimate her. A may not curse or parade herself around with her tits spilling out like B, but she still slept with him for money — and she had a child with him out of wedlock. Both things make her a whore in my book."

Him and my mother both. "It's *my* fault she's here!"

Michael shrugged, though how he managed to find the energy to do so as he ran was a mystery. "She chose to help you. Unless you held a gun to her head and forcibly made her choose, you have no culpability in the matter."

"We have to save her — and my parents."

"No."

"But — "

"They're going to triple the guards on each of those cells now that we've escaped. It's going to be a nightmare. We won't last five minutes. No."

"Then I'll save them!"

"Alone?" he scoffed. "Unarmed? You might as well have me shoot you right now."

"I won't leave without my parents," I said stoutly. "Or without A. I wouldn't be able to live with myself, knowing that I had the chance to save them and didn't take it."

"I've got news for you, Christina. You aren't calling the fucking shots."

"Please."

Michael pushed open the door to the roof, ignoring me.

"*Please.*" I touched his shoulder and he swung around like I'd hit him. "I'm begging you."

"That's not begging. That's commanding with a please in front of it."

"But I — "

"It's going to be difficult enough getting the both of us alive

Cloak and Dagger by Nenia Campbell

without *company*."

I blinked back tears. "But I have to! Don't you see that? I *have* to — it'd kill me not to. I won't be able to look at myself in the mirror. I'd think, *There's the girl who murdered her parents*. For the rest of my life." Just the thought of all those years stretching before me, and the endless guilt, was unbearable. "I have to *try*."

"Your parents left you for dead. You should return the favor."

"I can't do that," I whispered. "I *love* them. With all my heart."

"Then you're even more foolish than I thought."

"You're a mercenary, right? You'll do anything for the right price."

Michael set his jaw and said nothing.

"Well, I'll do anything, when we get out of this — anything you want." He looked at me then and I said, "I'm sure my parents would pay you. Money, a pardon, whatever you want. My mother has some friends in the Dominican Republic who work for the government. They could probably hook you up with citizenship if I asked" — more like begged — "and obviously, I would never reveal your identity or your whereabouts to anyone."

He closed his eyes. "Anything I want," he repeated. "Really."

"Yes."

When his eyes opened, he looked angry. "I suppose if you've learned anything, it's how to drive a hard bargain. Well, the only way that could even *possibly* work is if the generator — "

"What?"

"They'll be sending the guards to your parents' cells and A's. They probably won't be guarding the generator. If we can get there and shut down the power it'll create total chaos. Prisoners escaping, lights not workers, the works. Maybe buy us an hour of time to find their cells."

I felt a swell of hope. "It'll work?"

"It's a shot in the dark. Which, incidentally, is what we'll be getting if we don't *move*." He gave me a push. "Just remember, you owe me."

"I know," I said equably.

"No, I really don't think you do."

Michael:

Except for the door and the ventilation duct, the roof was completely empty. Too open. I searched for the fire escape. It was exactly where I remembered. I hurried the girl towards it just as the roof door swung back with a heavy bang and two guards began firing. They were alone, which meant that the IMA was searching the buildings for us and these two had gotten lucky.

Or unlucky.

"They're on the roof. Requesting backup on the — " I shot him in the face and then his partner, in the back, who was smarter and had tried to run. Not fast enough.

Christina froze on the fire escape. She was staring at me. "What are you waiting for? An RSVP? Go!" My gun hadn't been fitted with a silencer. The sound of the shooting, combined with the guard's alarm, was sure to bring company.

I suspected that the guards, when they did come, would expect us to bolt for the beach where the boats were docked. They would head us off accordingly. The generator happened to be conveniently located in the opposite direction, in the jungle, which would buy us a few extra minutes. Maybe more, if we were lucky. I wasn't counting on too much luck at this point.

I tucked the gun into the waistband of my sweatpants. "Stay low. There are watchtowers all around here."

"I know. I saw them as they were taking me to my cell."

A bolt of pain arced down my left arm. I'd forgotten about my injuries and fired at the guards instinctively with my dominant hand. "You are running up *such* a tab," I muttered, wincing.

"I told you before, my parents will compensate you for your — "

"No, they will not. Because they can't give me what I want. Only you can."

Her eyes grew to the size of dinner plates. "M-me?"

I don't know what made those words come out of my mouth.

The bargain she had made was downright reasonable. Citizenship in a foreign country. A new identity. Money. Kent had received such an offer from one of his more generous friends; Kent wasn't the name he was born with, as he'd told me once in that sly way of his. I had never developed a close enough relationship with any of my contacts that I had ever hoped for the same; I'd certainly never expected to receive such an offer from a *hostage*.

Ex-hostage.

What was I doing? It was madness.

Say, "They won't listen to me. They'll listen to you. I need your word. It's easy to promise things you, personally, can't deliver." The words were on the tip of my tongue but I couldn't bring myself to say them. "You," I confirmed.

"But that wasn't — "

I heard the snap of twigs before I heard the guards and before she could finish her sentence. I covered her mouth before she could utter a startled scream, dragging her into one of the bushes. She was shaking her head, trying to dislodge my hand. I tightened my hold, pressing her into the soft ground as I tried to burrow us both deeper — and soundlessly — into the foliage. The beam of a flashlight swung by in a lazy arc, missing us both by inches.

"Hear something?" the guard asked.

"Probably just a wild animal. Johnson said they were headed

towards the beach."

God, I love being right.

Christina was trembling when they left. Relieved, I thought. Or shocked by what I'd said.

Until she kissed me.

It was awkward and inexperienced and slobbery. She didn't even know how to *kiss*. That should have turned me off. It didn't. The way my body reacted, she might as well have jammed her tongue down my throat and her hand down my pants. I shoved her away before she could realize what a depraved man I was. "What the hell was that?"

Her blush was visible even in darkness. "You said…I thought…"

"You thought I wanted what?" When she didn't respond, at least not right away, I went on, "*You?* How conceited."

"But you said — "

"Only you could give me what I wanted. Right. I never said what."

Her face darkened further. She ducked her head, but I caught her before she could turn away. "Hold on. I never said I wasn't interested. But what kind of fool would I be if I turned down a fresh start for…you? You're pretty, darlin, but you're no Helen of Troy. Let's say I take you up on the money and the free citizenship. That covers you and your parents — since you helped me out a bit, I'll give you a twofer on that — but what about A? Without Richardson, she's broke. I don't risk my life for gratitude."

"So you *do* want — "

"I don't like A. She's a blood-sucking vampire and the world would be a much better place if she died. Asking me to save her is a mighty big sacrifice on my part. If you want me to do that, you have to show me you're serious." She'd refuse. Any *normal* woman would refuse.

"OK," she whispered. "A deal's a deal."

Fuck.

Christina:

Not even the imminent danger of the guards could take my mind off the feel of his chapped lips and his hard body against mine, burning with a promise I had unwittingly sealed.

"We're almost there. Keep quiet — there might be guards."

Maybe he *had* done a lot for me. I didn't think I should have to *pay* him to fix the lives he had torn asunder. I thought I'd been generous. I was going to have a time of it convincing my parents to give him the things I'd promised. I knew I *could* do it, because I had learned at great cost just how much they valued their own lives.

Clearly, Michael didn't think so. All that crap about "sacrifices" and "sweetening the deal" was just that — crap. Nobody should have to pay like that. No amount of rationalization or bribery could convince me otherwise. I wasn't B. I wasn't even A. I didn't find the IMA or their lifestyles attractive. They were high profile, full of flash, but all their relationships were superficial, from what I'd seen. I suspected the ruthlessness they exhibited in the workplace carried over to their personal lives. Nobody could be so callous and remain untouched. He would hurt me, I knew it. if not physically, then emotionally.

But as long as he got what he wanted, he wouldn't care.

Michael stopped walking. I nearly crashed into him. We were standing in front of a metal building that looked like a glorified garden shed. A red and white sign was slapped on the front: *DANGER: HIGH VOLTAGE.* "This is it?"

"No guards," Michael said. A startled but pleased laugh escaped him. "*Fils de putain.*"

He was right. There weren't *any* men standing guard. There wasn't even an alarm. The door had a lock but obviously it hadn't been changed recently because the access code Michael entered opened the steel door.

"That doesn't seem wise," I said. "An electric code to the generator? How are you supposed to get inside if the power fails? And was that French?"

He gave me a sharp look. "Wait outside. Quietly."

The lights of Target Island's main facility twinkled through the trees like stars, blurred by the fog and the tears in my eyes. Then, as if by magic, all those small spheres of light were swallowed up by darkness with a faint hum. Michael ran out of the generator room, letting loose a hushed *whoop*. "Now we ro-day the hell out of here."

A silence had settled over the island. I could no longer hear the peal of the alarm in the distance, and even the sounds of the crickets chirping in the bushes seemed to have stopped.

"Your parents are probably in Node Three or Four."

"How do you figure?"

"Prisoners are ranked according to how big a threat they are, with those in Node One being comparatively harmless to those in Node Six being a dangerous liability."

We had been in Node Six. Not just Michael. Both of us. *I* was a dangerous liability?

I was aware of Michael watching me, measuring my response. I turned away. *Stop looking at me.*

"Why so quiet, darlin? This about what I said earlier? Do you think I'm asking too much?"

I shrugged, privately alarmed. He could read me far better than I liked. It was disturbing. But not surprising, considering I had been with him for the better part of two months. Longer than my longest relationship. *Oh, God.* "Leave me alone."

"One night and I'm out of your life forever? Sounds like a pretty good deal to me."

"Why?"

"*Mais*, for starters I think your parents deserve to die for their displays of cowardice. Because A is a gold-digging Jezebel who knowingly fucked my boss despite knowing full well who he was and what he did just because he gave her some pretty clothes to play dress-up in around the office. I certainly don't feel like doing them any fucking favors. You owe me a favor, you're attractive enough, and you won't be in tears if I leave first thing in the morning."

Oh, there would definitely be tears. Probably well before he left.

"Is that all I am? Some kind of down payment to you?"

He caught the disgust in my voice. "You're pitching an awful lot of fuss for something that hardly matters. I really don't think I repulse you as much as you let on."

"You'll get your money," I said coldly. "I'll make sure of it. But this doesn't mean I'm attracted to you. As far as I'm concerned, it will have never happened."

He got angry, then. Angrier than I had ever seen him.

"And why is that? You going to run out and get baptized the moment I'm through with you? Is that it? Become a born-again-fucking-virgin?"

"No. It's because I know that this is God's way of testing me. To see if I'm strong enough to see what I *know* is His way through the end. And that is rescuing my parents *and* A."

Michael shook his head and turned away without another word.

At least *I* still had my conscience.

Chapter Twenty

Ultimatum

Christina:

Node Three was dead quiet; when Michael cut the power, he'd also shut down the alarm. He suggested we try Node Three, first, since my dad wasn't much of a danger to anyone without a computer in front of him. That sounded reasonable enough to me.

Like Node Six, there were long rows of cells. Most of them were empty. Given the island's name, I wasn't sure whether this was a good thing or a bad thing. Some of the cells had shadowed forms in them, curled up into various shapes of hopelessness.

I recognized two of those shapes.

Breaking away from Michael, I ran up to the bars. "Mom? Dad?"

The bigger of the two shapes looked up. "Christina?" Dad did a double-take. "Christina! What the hell are you doing here?"

"I got captured."

Dad looked completely shell-shocked. "They told us they let you go."

"They lied," I said flatly, tugging on the door. "They were going to execute me this morning but we escaped." The access panel had been disabled, but I had forgotten about the additional manual lock because our cell had been open when we escaped. I gave the door another fierce, pointless tug and my dad gave me an awkward hug through the bars. *Daddy,* I thought, with a childish need I thought I'd left behind in grade school.

"Oh, Sweet Pea," Dad said softly, as I began to cry all the tears I'd bottled up from when I'd thought they were dead. He patted my hair, hesitantly at first, as if I were an animal he thought might run away. "I was afraid I'd never get to hug my little girl again."

"Why didn't you *rescue* me?"

"We wanted to, Sweet Pea. But your mother didn't think it was safe. She was afraid it would only put you in more danger."

I took a step back from the metal door. That didn't sound like my mother. She had never concerned herself with my safety, only my obedience. Until recently, I'd thought they were interchangeable. "Dad, they were going to torture me! How could I possibly be in more danger than that?"

"We didn't know," he was saying. "We had no way of contacting you. We only knew what they told us, and even then, we couldn't be sure of the truth — "

"Christina." My mother's voice. Her dark eyes assessed me through the bars. Hooded, as though she had been sleeping. She raised her eyebrows. Even in prison, the arches were still perfect. "Is that you? I barely recognized you; you've lost so much weight."

"Nice to see you, too, Mom."

"Is that all you have to say to me, after all this time? "'Nice to see you?'"

"You abandoned me. What am I supposed to say?"

"Think of this from your father's and my perspectives. When that organization began sending us threatening telephone calls, we didn't have time to think. They didn't mention you at all. Why bring you to their attention? Our staying in that house would only put you in danger."

Bullshit. "But that *isn't* what happened. They *did* know. And you left me there — like a sitting duck. Plus, there was that message. The one on the machine. You had to have known."

"Message?" Dad looked confused.

"She's talking about a warning I had the detective leave her, just in case." My mother looked annoyed at having to explain herself so much. "You're completely missing the point, Christina. Listen — "

"No! You listen. You don't know what's happened to me over the last couple weeks. What I've sacrificed by coming here. While you and Dad were running around and fleeing the country, I was almost killed. Yet whenever people pressed me for information about you, I lied, like a good little girl. I said nothing. I risked *everything* — because I thought you would save me. But you didn't." I drew in a deep breath. "Now — what have you really done for me? And complimenting me on my *prison* weight loss or giving me one pathetic warning don't count."

"We turned ourselves in to save you, you ungrateful child. Isn't that why you're free?"

"Liliana, Christina, do we have to talk about this now?" my father pleaded. His eyes were restless, searching the darkened corridors for guards. It was plain to see he thought our argument was going to attract unwanted attention. "Christina, your mother really did try her best to keep you alive, but I really think we should focus on getting out of here. We can work out the details later, go to family counseling, anything you think is necessary" — my mother muttered something sarcastic — "But for now, I think — "

"It doesn't really matter what you think," Michael said, in a voice like steel. I felt him come up behind me. "The only reason this girl is alive is *me*."

"Michael, no — " I cut off as he wrapped his arms around my waist.

"Let me handle this."

"That voice! I recognize that voice," my mother growled. "It's the *hijo de puta* who kidnapped Christina."

"I think you owe your daughter some answers. I'm interested in hearing them myself, actually."

What the hell is he doing?

"You think you — *you* — of all people have a right to tell me how to do my job?" my mother squawked. "I'm not telling you a thing! Get away from my daughter, or I will scream for the guards!"

"Liliana, no!" Dad cried. "Are you crazy?"

"You do that and they'll kill us all." I felt the mean laughter as it vibrated through his throat. "Come on, Mrs. Parker-de-Silva. For once, in your miserable fucking life, think about somebody besides yourself — because I'm not letting you out of this cell until you do."

Dad sighed. He knew Mom's rages too well. "Hear him out. We don't have much choice. Looks like we'll have to deal with this sooner, rather than later." To me, he said, apologetically, "The call came so suddenly, we didn't know what to do. Adults panic, just like children. Maybe worse than children, because we have the ability to do so much more harm. You were in school. We didn't want to pull you out and drive you into a panic. We had no way of knowing that they knew anything about you. I suppose we made some bad decisions. I'm sorry, Sweet Pea. If I could do the whole thing again, I'd do it differently. I really would."

He was crying. I'd never seen my dad cry before. Coulda, woulda, shoulda — why hadn't he made the right choice when it really mattered? Why hack at all?

Michael seemed to be thinking the same thing. "Your wife left her at my mercy. I am curious. Did you think I was bluffing? Or were you simply not concerned? I have difficulty believing any real mother would willingly allow her child to be raped."

The irony of that statement. I wanted to throw up.

"Liliana — what the fuck is he talking about?"

Mom looked Michael straight in the eye. "He demands no money. Instead he makes cheap threats to sound like a bigger man. What kind of man trades information for a girl, instead of asking for something sensible?"

"Mother!"

"You stupid bitch," Michael said softly.

"What do you want from us?" My dad still looked sick.

"I am here to help you at her request." He nodded at me. "If you follow my instructions, you have a chance at survival."

Mom looked hopeful, then angry. "I told you to get your hands off her."

"I have kept her alive," he said in a chilling voice. "Which is a lot more than you can say for yourself, leaving her with a man like me."

"Don't talk to my wife like that."

Michael turned towards me. "I've had enough. Give me on of the hair pins."

I handed him one. Ignoring my father, Michael jimmied the manual lock while checking over his shoulder for guards. The door slid open after a few terse seconds. "Get out," Michael said. "Quickly. Use the door on the left."

"We came in through the right."

"Which is exactly why you should take the door on the left."

"It's a trap," my mother said. "He's trying to kill us, as before."

"I'm not so sure it is." Dad gave me another hug. "I am so, so sorry, Sweet Pea. Thank you for saving us. You're my little Guardian Angel." It was a sad hug, an apologetic hug, and it made me feel... nothing. I was numb. Dad shot my mother a furious look, so full of disgust that she actually balked; Mom never balked at anything.

She recovered quickly enough. "Coming Christina?"

"No."

"What? You want to stay with him?"

"No. I am going to save the woman who helped me when nobody else would. And I'm sorry to say this, Mom — because I still love you — but that person wasn't you. I wish that weren't true, but it is." She flinched. I felt bad for a moment, until I remembered all those nights I had spent cold, alone, and unhappy — because of her. My heart hardened...just a little. "Get out of here," I added. "That's what you really want. I'll just slow you down. Just as I always have."

She looked stunned. "I feel like I don't know you anymore."

"You never did," I replied, just as coolly. "You were always too busy thinking about who you would *like* me to be that you never thought to ask who I actually was."

Mom shook her head. Even now, she couldn't deal with anything that contrasted against her world views. Catholic guilt made children in perpetual debt to their parents for a gift that was immeasurable and holy and impossible to repay: life. My sudden rebellion was not because of any fault of hers, in her eyes, but through some failure of mine.

"You look different. Act different." She scowled at Michael, clenching her hands into fists. "What did you do to my daughter, *puto*?"

Michael turned on his heel. "Are you addressing me?"

"Yes, I am talking to you…you…*mamagüevazo.*"

I flinched. "*Mamá.*"

She'd just used one of the most profane insults particular to Domincans. Her tone left little need for a translator, and Michael narrowed his eyes accordingly.

"You rob my daughter of her innocence, turning her into a whore no decent christian man will want — and then brainwash her? To turn her against me, her own mother? Who bore her from her own *womb*? You monster! When will you be satisfied? You — "

He backhanded her across the face. "Shut the fuck up."

She pressed a hand against her cheek. "What?"

"Shut the fuck up," he repeated, "And get out of here — or I'll kill you myself."

Mamá looked at him. Then at me. Then she ran. I closed my eyes and turned away.

"Come on." Michael gripped my wrist. "We don't have much time."

I swiped at my cheek with the heel of my hand. "Just a moment."

"Your mother is a vain woman. Too accustomed to getting her own way. She's not worth a moment of my time. Or yours."

Words could be as cruel as knives, though. Her old modeling photographs were on the mantle, above the fireplace. One of my friends once told me it was like a shrine, but I hadn't understood — until now. I used to look at them and hate myself, wondering what was wrong with me that I didn't look like that. Now I realized belatedly there *was* no problem with me. The problem was with her. She didn't like herself, but she liked me even less for not surpassing her own personal standards. Even if I *had*, that still wouldn't have been enough. She liked lording her superiority over people. I could be the most successful model in the world and I suspected she would still consider me inferior to her own talents and abilities, resenting me for what she undoubtedly would consider a "lucky break."

The truth had been staring me in the face this entire time, and I'd been too blind to see. My parents weren't perfect people. I knew that, obviously, but hadn't really understood the implications. I'd been taught never to question; that my parents were on a level of

337

authority surpassed only by God. But my parents weren't divine. Not hardly. They were people, fallible, with weaknesses and flaws. My mother, with her unfulfilled hopes and cripplingly low self-esteem — what kind of woman attacks her daughter for passing remarks one of her catty friends makes? I'd completely internalized the insults. Now they made me think. Was my mother *really* ashamed of me? Or was she ashamed of herself and looking for a scapegoat?

I understood, but that didn't mean I liked it or that it hurt any less. My parents' flaws had caused them to disappoint me when I needed them most. I still loved them; I wasn't sure if I could ever forgive them. Just the look on my mother's face when she looked in my eyes and shamelessly called me a whore. "She wants nothing to do with me," I said sadly.

"You cut right to the core of her. Of course she wants nothing to do with you. You made her look inside herself and see how self-centered she is. Nobody appreciates being disillusioned. But you're alive. Your parents are alive. The cowardice gene appears to have passed you over. You ask me, you've got a lot to be grateful for."

Grateful. Yeah, right.

"You don't think so?"

"I found out my parents value their lives over my own today," I said. "It *kind of* sucks."

"You think you're the only person this happened to? I've seen many people take a fatalistic approach to danger — to hell with everyone else. If people are meant to live, they'll live. If not, more room for the rest of us. There's a reason that kind of mindset prevails, darlin. Attachments make people vulnerable; they can be used as a weapon against you. Because when you think about it, it's pretty fucking counter-intuitive for survival to be thinking, 'What if that bullet hits *her*?' instead of 'What if that bullet hits *me*?'"

I didn't know what to say. It was a surprisingly profound statement, especially coming from him. Emotions had seemed to be a foreign language to Michael: one he refused to learn. He'd said countless times he considered them a fatal weakness. And yet, what he just said implied insight into the minds of others. Insight, sympathy, and maybe even a bit of regret.

Maybe that was wishful thinking, on my part. I was one of those fatally flawed people who actually had emotions, with a tendency to romanticize to boot — but somehow, I didn't think so. I opened my mouth to issue some Hallmark sentiment of my own but was drowned out by gunfire.

Michael:

With a feeling akin to gratitude, I whipped around and returned fire. By now, my eyes had gotten adjusted to the darkness. I saw

339

several guards drop. A savage joy filled me each time I felled one of the fuckers. I nearly forgot about the girl standing beside me. Her face was drawn, turned away from the carnage. I gritted my teeth. Readjusted my aim.

Click.

Empty.

A sign from God, the girl would say, given her hatred of violence. The guards had started to advance the moment they realized I was out of ammo — and that had been my last viable gun. I was starting to reach my limit and I suspected Christina had reached hers long ago. She stumbled along beside me. I practically had to drag her.

"Where do you think A is?"

I tried to hide my annoyance. "Probably Node Five."

"Why so high a number? She never killed anyone."

"You don't need to kill people to be dangerous. Sometimes just knowing things is enough."

If A was in Node Five, the place would be swarming with guards. Not just the regular kinds, which were bad enough, but the special ops guys. The ones with the bulletproof armor and riot shields.

"I don't remember this many doors being open before," said Christina.

She was right. All of the office doors were hanging ajar. With no manual locks, there was nothing to keep them from opening.

"There they are!"

A bullet shot past my neck.

"In here." I darted into one of the laboratories. The equipment was far too expensive for the guards to risk more careless shots. Glass instruments and electronic equipment and wires were strewn about, organized into haphazard piles awaiting assembly or experimentation.

If this place led where I thought it led then…yes, we'd be close to weapons storage. That door hadn't had a manual lock back when I'd worked here all those years ago, but they could have upped the ante on security since then. I forced myself to stay focused. The guards were coming through the doors, edging around the tables. They wouldn't shoot unless it was point-blank. They wanted us trapped in here. But the easternmost door wasn't blocked yet.

"Get ready to run in three seconds," I whispered. "Two…one…"

"Wha — "

I tightened my grip around her wrist and darted around the tables, keeping low. A single shot went off, followed by a smash and a curse. One flight of stairs and two corridors later, we were in the weapons storage room. *Am I good or what?* I gave the door a push, holding my breath. Would it open?

It did.

During my first week on the job, I'd been assigned as a researcher. Richardson had sent me on a business trip to Target Island to see what an internment base looked like, as well as to stock and itemize all the hand-held weapons used by the IMA. As most young men do when dangerous weapons are thrown into the mix, I'd all but drooled. The IMA imported weapons from all over the world. Spectre M4 submachine guns, grenade launchers, TT33s and AK-47s were just a couple of the nasty toys that the IMA just had lying around, gathering dust. There was also a wide assortment of knives, bulletproof armor, and emergency equipment like flares, smoke balls, and tinned rations.

I strapped one of the kevlar vests over my chest and grabbed one of the handguns, a Firestar, feeling like a kid in a goddamn candy store. Handguns were the weapons I used most often, and the ones I was most comfortable with, though I snagged a mine launcher and its detonator and a couple knives to be safe. The vest had pockets for auxiliary weapons and I placed these latter in the corresponding compartments.

In a small bin in the corner I found some fingerless gloves. I flexed my fingers and the leather squeaked satisfyingly. After spending literally hundreds of hours in this room, I knew it like the back of my hand. This was my element. I turned my head, and caught Christina looking at me strangely. "Yes?" I raised an eyebrow as I strapped the detonator around my wrist, beneath the gloves, where it would remain concealed from sight. "See something you like?"

She shrugged and looked back at the shelves of guns.

I helped myself to a couple smoke balls. A diversion could come in handy if — *when* — they fixed the generator. They were probably working on it even now .Then they would be back with reinforcements. That girl was going to need protection. Inside or outside, her white shirt made her a walking target. She might as well have been a flag of surrender.

"Come here," I said. She turned away from the grenade launchers with a guilty start. The first vest I found for her was too big. I managed to find a smaller size. She jumped when I fastened the belt around her waist. I wanted to roll my eyes. "It needs to be tight. Trust me, you don't want this gaping open on you."

"It's heavy," she whined, tugging at the straps. "Is it supposed to be this tight?"

"It's heavy because it's lined with lead. To keep you from getting fucking shot." I tested the straps, tightening and loosening as I saw fit, before pulling back and studying the overall effect. Very sexy. *No. There's no time for that.* I clicked my tongue in impatience. "You need a gun."

"I don't want one."

"Too bad."

I got her one of the TT33s, a small silver handgun with a kick. I suspected she would find it less intimidating because of its size. "Be careful with this," I warned her. "None of these have been fitted with silencers. It may look harmless but it isn't a toy. It makes a lot of noise when fired and you can kill somebody with it."

She stared at the gun as if expecting it to come alive and bite her.

"Have you ever fired a gun before?" I queried, already knowing what the answer would be.

"No."

"Do you want to learn?"

"No."

"Let me rephrase that, then. You're going to learn." I grabbed her hands, trapping beneath mine in such a way that her finger was on the trigger. I showed her how to take aim. "Sometimes it helps to close one eye. This is the safety. Always treat a gun as if it's loaded. Keep it on at all times…unless you're firing, of course." I raised her arms, aiming at an imaginary target. "Relax your shoulders."

"Won't the guards hear the noise? You just said — "

"By the time they get here, we'll be long gone. This is more important. Relax your shoulders." She remained tense, as if the slightest movement would snap her right in half. I tried to press her arms down so she wasn't all hunched up and her hand tightened around the gun. She squeezed the trigger and the gun went off, startling us both. My vest absorbed most of the shock from the recoil, but it didn't do shit for the shock circulating elsewhere.

"Christ," I muttered. "Hopefully you won't need it."

Her vest wasn't the only thing feeling a little too tight.

Christina:

Node Five was bigger than Node Three, which suggested the IMA considered the vast majority of its enemies dangerous. The inside was as silent as a grave. Our breathing sounded impossibly loud in the darkness, almost obscene.

"Stop that gasping," Michael hissed. "You're not in a porno, for fuck's sake."

He *would* know. I tried breathing through my nose but that didn't work; I didn't get enough air that way, and it made my chest start to ache.

When I turned my head to the side, Michael had his gun out and drawn. He was looking around, scanning the cells, a worried line between his eyebrows. "Something's wrong."

"What?"

He compressed his lips and gave a slight shake of his head. He didn't know yet. His eyes, however, were restless. Vigilant. "I know what it is," he said a moment later. "All the cells — "

"Yeah?"

"They're empty."

Something collided with my chest, sending me back against the bars of one of the cells. It was like being punched. Something clattered to the hard floors. A bullet, spent. If I hadn't been wearing the vest, I'd be *dead*.

"They evacuated the prisoners." Michael's words dissolved into an outraged cry when a bullet clipped his shoulder. "I *knew* something like this was going to happen — "

More gunfire. It was like thunder in my ears, shaking the bones of my skull. I couldn't question his judgment this time. We both knew we were only here because I'd asked to be; a request that seemed noble at the time but was growing more foolish with each passing second. Was A really worth it? I'd already gotten my parents.

Michael shouted something incomprehensible. My injuries awakened from their dormancy, screaming reminders of their presence when he tackled me. "You moron," he was yelling, "You almost took a bullet in the head."

He shoved me through one of the doors, slamming it behind us. I could hear the footsteps of the guards storming past the door. I stared at it, numb, feeling his breath stir my hair. *It's pretty fucking*

counter-intuitive for survival to be thinking, 'What if that bullet hits her?'
Instead of, 'What if that bullet hits me?'"

He had jumped into crossfire to protect me.

"...standing there, like a deer in the goddamn headlights..."

The signs had been there all along. I'd just been too obtuse to see them.

"...*maudit*. No sense whatsoever — "

"You...saved me," I said. "You...actually care."

"Christina." He sounded genuinely angry. "Shut up."

Shutting up would be a good idea. But my mouth wouldn't obey. "Why don't you act like it? The way you treat me, nobody would ever — "

"Because it doesn't change a thing."

"It does," I said. "More than ever."

"Not to me."

"It does to me."

"I don't think you understand. I saved you because you're useful to me." He decreased the distance between us. "In more ways than one. That's all."

"No," I whispered. "You're lying."

"Want me to prove it?"

"Not now."

"When?"

My heart stopped. "What?"

"When?"

A shiver snaked through my spine. I looked desperately at the door; the hallway had fallen silent. "I…I don't know when. I can't think…not more than a couple minutes in advance. I'm tired. Just not…not in this *place*. People have died here."

"We won't." Coming from him, it sounded more like a threat than reassurance.

"Please."

He looked at me a moment longer and nodded shortly. *Not here.*

Static crackled through the intercom. A familiar voice rang through the building. "Mr. Boutilier and Miss Parker, we have the building surrounded."

I froze, every muscle in my body tightening.

"It's a bluff," said Michael, though he didn't sound certain.

"Exit the building with your hands up. You have five minutes before we begin to execute one prisoner for each minute past the deadline."

A familiar cry.

"Starting with A."

Michael:

Richardson had made his point clear. He held all of the cards, even the trumps. We had knocked out the electricity but that was by no means the only power we had to worry about. Not even close. Christina stared at the loudspeaker, wide-eyed. "Do they really have us surrounded?"

"Probably," I said, "He has the whole complex at his disposal."

We still had a chance at survival. Richardson didn't know where we were, as evidenced by the fact that the guards weren't bursting down the door. He wouldn't have bothered with threats at all if he through he could get the drop on us.

I had a plan. Risky, but I didn't have much choice.

I left the building, followed by Christina. Because they would be expecting it, I fired off a few seemingly careless shots — at the roof, where there were snipers, at the guards — until I was tackled and the weapon was removed. The guards didn't look at the gun too closely. I was glad. If they had, they might have realized it wasn't an ordinary gun, and that my shots hadn't been all that careless.

Christina screamed. She must have been apprehended, her weapon also confiscated. And then I turned my head and realized who was doing the confiscating. "Aw," Adrian said, cupping the girl's face with the hand holding the gun. "It's so easy to get people to cooperate when they care about each other."

I got two steps in before I was restrained by the guards.

Slow clapping broke the silence. Richardson was standing nine meters away, holding a struggling A at gunpoint. That was cold, even for him. "Congratulations, Mr. Boutilier: you have managed to waste approximately six hours of my time and destroy several thousand dollars' worth of irreplaceable equipment. I hope you're pleased with yourself."

"As punch," I said. That earned me a clip from one of the guards.

"I always knew that you would someday betray me," Richardson continued. "I hoped to be rid of you before that happened. I never imagined, however, that when you did pull such a stunt, my own whore would be among you. I was always under the impression you two didn't like each other. Points for ingenuity, Mr. Boutilier, but then again, you always did manage to exceed expectations."

"Whore?" A repeated, outraged. "*Whore?* Is that all you have to say to me you son of a — "

"Ah, ah, ah. Don't make me gag you, my dear." He gave the woman a poisonous smile.

She spat in his face. I didn't know she had it in her.

Richardson was unimpressed. "Gag her." He foisted her upon the nearest guard, dabbing the spit from his face with a handkerchief. "As for you, Mr. Boutilier, you have two options. Choice one — die where you stand."

"And the second?"

He was interrupted by a bright exclamation from A, who was trying to kick the guard with the gag. Richardson shot her an annoyed look before turning to face me. "I would hate to kill one of my best soldiers. You may live, provided that you prove your loyalty to this agency and to me" — he nodded to the girl — "by killing Miss Parker."

Chapter Twenty-One

Motive

Christina:

Adrian smiled. For one hideous second I was paralyzed by my fear, like a mouse locked in the hypnotic eyes of a serpent. His smile didn't quite reach his eyes, though — it never had, which had been one of the first things that alerted me to his true nature. They were almost blue in the sunlight, as cold and hard as ice. There was no mistaking the boundless killing drive that lurked behind them, like a demon peering though the windows of its mortal prison.

I remembered the gun a split second before he reached me. I whipped it out of the vest pocket, hooking my finger around the trigger. "Stay away."

"That's a dangerous toy, Christina Parker."

I heard several gunshots. My heart leaped as I caught a glimpse of Michael in my periphery. To my utter disbelief, all of his shots *missed*. Only one bullet came even remotely close to hitting anyone and it rebounded off the rooftop of Node Five, causing the snipers to break rank.

"Poor marksmanship," Adrian scoffed. "He's usually quite good. Hard to distract. I wonder what's gotten into him."

"I'll shoot you," I bit out, tightening my grip on the gun.

"Do it."

I stared at him incredulously. Did he want to die? He reached out for my wrist, intent on restraining me and seizing the weapon. The answer seemed to be "yes." I saw, as if watching somebody else, my finger tighten involuntarily on the trigger.

Click.

With a growing feeling of dread, I pulled it again.

Click.

A soft, derisive laugh burned my ears. He wrenched the gun out of my sweaty, shaking hand. "Works better without the safety on," was his only comment as he unloaded the clip and tossed it aside. I stared at those discarded bullets. Adrian had *goaded* me into firing at him. And I had let him get to me…eagerly, even. If the safety hadn't been on, I would have killed him.

I couldn't remember what the bible said about self-defense.

"Poor Christina," he said. "You should see your face."

He moved before I had time to register his words. I screamed, stumbling away from him, glancing over my shoulder as I did so. There was nowhere to run. Michael had already been handcuffed by the guards. We had been running all morning. I was exhausted. There was no way I was going to win. Adrian knew it, too. Because he laughed again, and that laugh tore through my defenses and caused my anger to reach its breaking point.

With a growl, I launched myself at him. I managed to lunge a clumsy punch at his face. But I was running on empty and adrenaline was no match for a soldier in riot gear. He caught me by the wrist, twisting that arm behind my back. When I tugged my arm the pain increased tenfold and I gasped wretchedly.

Michael looked at me, his expression black. He managed exactly two steps.

"Aw," Adrian said. His cold fingers slid beneath my throat, and I felt the textured surface of the gun against my skin, still warm from my palms. "It's so easy to get people to cooperate when they care about each other."

I forced myself to stay silent.

Slow clapping filled the clearing. Mr. Richardson, in addition to his usual entourage of guards. A was with him. At gunpoint. I let out a wordless cry of rage. Adrian bent my arm back a little more. "Don't be *rude*, Christina — it's not polite to interrupt."

"Congratulations, Mr. Boutilier," Mr. Richardson said, in a voice that conveyed his irritation and his triumph perfectly. "You have managed to waste approximately six hours of my time and destroy several thousand dollars' worth of irreplaceable equipment. I hope you're pleased with yourself."

"As punch."

Adrian chuckled. "It's not polite to show up to your own execution, either, is it?"

"I always knew that you would someday betray me," Richrdson continued. "I hoped to be rid of you before that happened — but I *never* imagined that when you did pull such a stunt, my own whore would be among you. I was always under the impressions that you two didn't like each other. Points for ingenuity, Mr. Boutilier, but then again, you always *did* manage to exceed expectations."

"Did he exceed your expectations, too, Christina?"

"Stop *talking* to me!"

"Mhmm. Soon you'll wish the *only* thing I ever did was talk to you."

Ignore him.

"The boss has a surprise for you, Christina."

Don't give him what he wants.

"I helped him pick it out, just for you."

I stared ahead resolutely, not letting myself think about what Adrian might have picked out as a surprise for me. Panic was already pecking at me from the inside like a small, frantic bird.

"As for you, Mr. Boutilier, you have two options. Choice one — die where you stand."

"And the second?"

"This is the good part," Adrian whispered.

I twisted my head away.

"I would hate to kill one of my best soldiers. You may lie,

provided that you prove your loyalty to the agency and to me" — he nodded at me — "by killing Miss Parker."

"That's the *surprise*," Adrian said.

Mr. Richardson pushed past A, now gagged and looking both livid and frightened, and made his way over to me. I backed up automatically and bumped into Adrian's chest. Loathing merged with my fear and I had to choke back a suddenly overwhelming urge to puke all over his shoes.

"Hello, Miss Parker."

Adrian gave me a nudge.

I said nothing.

"I would say I feel some regret for what is about to happen to you, being young as you are, but I don't. You two have sabotaged an entire mission, destroyed precious equipment, freed two potentially dangerous prisoners, and wreaked havoc over entire base…" I fixed him with a flat look of hatred. He went on, "For which you will pay with your life. However, you have managed to earn my respect — your determination *is* nothing short of remarkable."

"Lucky *me*."

"Quite so." My sarcasm appeared to fly over his head. "And that is why your death will be painless. Such is my generosity."

Adrian's hands locked around both my wrists as I took a step forward and told him what he could do with his generosity.

356

"*Well*. It appears that you have spent entirely too much time around our operative, Miss Parker. You're beginning to sound like him."

"Screw you."

He held my gaze a moment longer. "The vest she is wearing is bulletproof, as well as company property. Kindly remove it, Mr. Callaghan."

Adrian had to let go of one of my arms to comply with his boss's order. I braced myself for that moment, swinging around — scratching, kicking, clawing, going for his soulless eyes. I heard Adrian choke and latched on with the grim determination that comes with imminent death. One of the guards cracked me over the head with the butt of his rifle. Bright flashes of light erupted before my eyes. I relinquished my grip on his throat with a gasp, dropping to my knees.

"I'll get you for that," he said, ripping the vest off with unnecessary force, his voice burning like hot oil in my ears. "And I'm going to enjoy it." My heart was slamming against my ribcage, as if trying to break free from my chest before the bad things started happening.

Satisfied, Mr. Richardson turned around. "Your decision, Mr. Boutilier? Quickly — I am a busy man and you have had considerable time to think over your choice."

Michael spoke the three words that made my breath come to a stuttering halt.

"I'll do it."

Michael:

Richardson had been the head of the IMA for a long time. His expression suggested that he had seen it all, and none of it had impressed him. I focused all my attention on his face as my words sank in. Though I could not be sure, I suspected he was satisfied, suspicious, and wary.

"No tricks, Mr. Boutilier?"

I shrugged.

He continued to study me. I did not shrink under his scrutiny. Standard intimidation techniques would not work on me; I had long since become immune. "You will use one of my guns," he said at last. "You understand of course."

Of course.

"Release him." This order was directed to the guard holding my left arm. "Let's see what he does."

Lefty was not as easily convinced. "Are you *sure* that's a good idea, sir?"

"He's right, sir," Righty echoed. "WE've been chasing this bastard all morning. He ran us all over the island. Now that we've finally caught him, you want to give him a *gun*?"

If they were trying to dissuade him, they were doing a poor job of it. Richardson did not like being chastised by subordinates, especially not publicly. "We have confiscated all of his other weapons. If he can bring himself to shoot the young woman he seems to place so much value on then he will have proved his loyalty to me, and may therefore live. If not…"

Richardson glanced back at me, clearly looking for some kind of response. He got none.

"If not, you may deal with him accordingly — if the snipers don't get to him first."

Seeing they had no choice, the guards unlocked my cuffs but didn't release me. Not yet. I straightened to my full height as Richardson approached. He was not a tall man — in fact, he was several inches well below the national average — though he gave no indication that he found my stature intimidating. He had a gun, I didn't.

Overconfidence didn't become him.

"One wrong move," he said, just loudly enough to be overheard by the guards. "And they will not hesitate. You will die in more agony than you ever believed possible."

Richardson snapped his fingers without breaking eye contact. "Hernandez," he said, speaking to Lefty. "Give me your gun." The guard stepped forward and handed over the aforementioned firearm. "One wrong move," Richardson repeated, pressing the weapon into my hands. "And there will be no more chances for you, Mr. Boutilier. I do not find you nearly as amusing as Miss Parker, and your death will be neither quick nor painless. Do you understand?"

"Perfectly."

I bit the inside of my cheek and turned to face the girl. Her stiff posture betrayed her fear and she grew even more rigid as I approached. That front of hers was crumbling. I knew, from experience, that the overt brightness of her eyes was a sign she was close to tears.

"Get away from her," I said to Callaghan.

"Whatever you say, Michael." He backed away with a mocking bow.

Christina's legs were poised to run. She took several large steps backwards until Callaghan moved to intercept her. She came to an abrupt stop. "What are you doing?"

"Exactly what it looks like. You know what the problem with being a saint is?" I had to force myself to press the barrel against her chest. Hard, to be convincing. Hard enough to make her wince. "You have to die first."

"You coward." She spat in my face. "I hope you burn in the

deepest, darkest circle of he — "

I punched the button of the detonator around my wrist.

The ground beneath us rumbled as Node Five burst into flames. My "aimless" shots hadn't been quite as aimless as they'd chosen to think. The gun — which had been the mine launcher —shot highly explosive mines instead of bullets, and all those shots had been strategic. Remembering Richardson's warning. I pressed the watch again and the snipers screamed as their lofty range suddenly caught fire. Five shots. Five large explosions.

Target Island was going up in flames.

Christina:

Time seemed to stop when I heard the gunshots. Two, in quick succession. No pain came. I wondered if the bullet really was that quick, that painless — whether I'd already died. I did feel strange. Not completely without sensation, but it seemed…minimized. A strange sour taste was in my mouth, thick and peppered with small motes that stuck to the back of my dried-out throat. When I reached out to steady myself, soft, wet earth sifted through my fingers.

"Get up."

A familiar voice cut through the fog, as harsh and grating as sandpaper, and I stared up at the tall figure looming above me from my seat on the ground. My brow furrowed. If Michael was here, I wasn't in Heaven. Which meant (1) either he had been killed, too, and we were *both* in Hell, or (2) we were both…alive.

A hand circled my wrist, tangible and much too tight. Somehow I was on my feet, running, with a hot, dry heat pressing in on all directions. I quickly realized we were *not* in Hell, though we might as well have been. Node Five was a raging inferno and the fire was spreading rapidly, bridging across the dried palm leaves on the ground, already cresting towards Node Six as I watched.

"I'm alive," I said, and this surprised me. I could still feel the phantom barrel pressing against my chest, digging into my heart. Just thinking about that made me feel cold all over. I had seriously believed he was going to kill me. Maybe he had been. Nobody could sound that cold and detached on command, right? Not unless they meant it. And what about those two gunshots?

"Neither of us will be alive for very long unless you *move*. Faster."

He didn't need to tell me twice.

"How…?" I croaked. Smoke stung my eyes, burned my nostrils. I was having trouble breathing, even though we both ran with ducked heads. The sour taste of it clotted my throat.

"Mine launcher. They weren't expecting that. Probably too busy gloating over my bad aim."

"But…I heard gunshots."

"Gun*shot*. Just one, at the smoke balls, to buy us time. I didn't pull a gun on you."

"There were definitely two," I said, "One right after the other."

He cut me off with a sharp jerk. "Then you imagined it. You blacked out there, for a moment. Probably heard the same shot twice. Come on." We were running towards the beach. I could tell by the smell of salt, which grew overwhelming as earth yielded to mud and then wood. We were on the dock, which was slicked with water that had been sluiced across the splintered slats by rough winds. "Get on that boat."

That boat was bigger than a motor boat, and conspicuous. Not just because of the color, which was jet black, but because of the size. It looked expensive, too. Did he think the IMA wouldn't notice if we took it out for a joy ride?

"Don't stare at me," he said. "Get on the boat."

Reluctantly, I stretched out a leg to make a short jump. I collapsed the moment my feet hit the deck. My legs simply ceased functioning and gave out from under my weight. After running for so long, on so little, getting up was out of the question.

I could hear Michael hot-wiring the engine, cursing with every mistake, knowing each second of delay was a second closer to being captured by the guards. This time, there would be no mercy. I was pretty sure they would just shoot both of us on sight.

And then the motor revved to life and I was sinking into an oblivion of nothingness.

Michael:

I steered for about an hour and a half before I felt comfortable enough to set the boat on cruise control. I had to make sure I wasn't sending us into circles. It was difficult enough to steer in the open ocean and I didn't have time to search for a compass.

I stretched, causing my stiff and tired muscles to groan in protest, and saw Christina passed out on the deck. Her face looked troubled, even in sleep, and I found myself recalling — as if against my will — the expression on her face when I turned the gun on her. That look of betrayal.

I stared at the thousands of miles of flat Pacific Ocean that awaited me. Exhaustion was setting in as all of the functions that had been shunted off to one side suddenly clamored for my attention. The slate gray water was already starting to blur before my eyes. Whether I wanted to or not, I was going to have to stop somewhere — and soon.

And risk drifting ashore on Target Island?

I slapped myself. All that smoke wouldn't go unnoticed, even in such a remote location. Some plane would eventually fly over the area, see the smoke, and phone in the Coast Guard. I didn't want to be anywhere near Target Island when that happened. *Stay awake, couillon.*

I scooped the girl up from where she'd passed out and set her down on a cot below deck. It was a risk leaving the boat on cruise control unattended — we might hit a rock — but I didn't want any surprises when the girl regained consciousness. When I returned to my seat, a weight lifted from my chest at her absence.

The radio, which had emitted nothing but white noise since I'd turned it on, suddenly crackled to life in a burst of static. I jerked upright in my seat. Glanced at the radio, surprised, then wary. For several more seconds, there was just more static and indecipherable background noise. Then I heard a voice say, quite clearly, "Hello, Michael."

I froze. What did Callaghan want? How did he know I was here? *He's bluffing.*

"Don't bother pretending you're not there. All the boats are fitted with GPS navigators. Or did you forget?"

I ducked under the seat and saw, to my disgust, the small, blinking chip. Mocking me. I got to my feet, looked around. Spotted the propeller wrench hanging on the back wall where it would be in easy reach for repairs and set about prying the chip free. It didn't work well — the wrench was too blunt.

Come on.

I clenched my teeth and pulled — hard. The locator chip fell to the ground. I pitched it into the water with a splash.

"Oh," Callaghan taunted, "Destroying the chip won't help you. I already know where you are."

"What the fuck do you want?" I demanded, nearly ripping the speaker off the cord.

"Temper, temper."

"Don't you fucking tell me — " I drew in a deep breath, counted to five. "Put Richardson on."

"I'm afraid I can't do that."

"Why *not*?"

"He's dead."

"What?"

"Dead, Michael. Worm fodder. Which would make the new head of the IMA…me. What an amazing coincidence, wouldn't you say?"

My fingers tightened on the receiver. Callaghan could be lying. He'd always been a liar, and a convincing one, at that, but I doubted whether even Adrian could sound so smug — unless this was true. I steeled myself for the worst. "How did that happen?"

"Easily. He was far too busy staying two steps ahead of you that he never once thought of looking behind him. Where I was waiting. I'm a patient man, Michael. I can wait a long time. I have to say, it was pathetic how quickly he turned against you. Noble Michael.

Patron saint of chivalry. What was it you said to the girl? Problem with being a saint is that you have to die first?"

I growled.

"Richardson never did care for that temper of yours, though. And you were young, strong, uppity. He was terrified of rebellion and you were the prime candidate."

"Obviously, I wasn't."

Adrian chuckled. "Quite."

I recalled Christina telling me that she had heard two gunshots. At the time, it hadn't made sense. But now I remembered Adrian taking the guard's gun after I'd thrown it aside…I had never gotten it back. I'd used a different gun to set off the smoke, which I'd stolen from one of the guards felled in one of the blasts. Which led to one undeniable conclusion. "You shot him."

"Of course. You made it easy for me with your little fireworks display. Nobody heard a thing."

"And A?"

"Also dead," he said lazily.

"What do you want?" I repeated, taking the boat off cruise control and picking up speed. "You could have sent a chopper by now, if you really wanted to detain us."

"Us?" Callaghan laughed again, and I realized my mistake. "The girl's with you? I wondered where she went. Don't worry. I'm far, *far* too busy to bother hunting you down. Right now."

"I don't understand." But I thought I might. I was hoping I was wrong through.

"Michael, Michael. Richardson said it himself — he had yet to see your equal on the training field. Killing you would hardly benefit my purpose. I want to the rebuild the IMA, not tear it apart. You were an integral part. Killing you would be like destroying the keystone of a bridge."

"You enjoy destroying things."

"Not always. Sometimes, I also like to create."

Chaos, maybe. "Your seizing power is going to start a full-fledged war. The IMA will fall apart from the inside and then you'll have pure anarchy. It's going to be a fucking mob."

"Let me worry about that," he said sharply. "Regain your strength, Michael. Play with your pretty hostage. Just stay out of my way."

"You wanted that," I said, pressing my face into my gloved hand. "All that power." Richardson was but, but Callaghan was infinitely worse. "You *wanted* a mob."

"We were already criminal. By gradually infiltrating various civil offices, we can also gain power and extend our influence at a fantastic rate. Richardson was not the man for that job — he wanted to keep the organization small because he felt discomfited by the idea of such a large organization. Wanted to keep his contacts close and small, like an Old Boys' Club. The fool. He was holding us back, costing us valuable funds, which was precisely why he had to die. Because he was so pathetically weak.

"You don't care about money," I heard myself saying.

"No," Callaghan conceded. "I don't...but the operatives do. Let's be honest, Michael; they may not like me, but if I keep them satisfied, they'll do anything I say. Anything. I can be *very* persuasive."

I frowned. Was that a thinly-veiled threat, or was the bastard gloating? Knowing Callaghan, it could be either — or both. I was quiet for a long time. Finally, I said, "Why are you telling me this?"

"I'd hoped that, one day, I might persuade you to join me."

I snorted. "Play Godfather all you want. I'm not joining. Fuck you."

"Oh, no, I don't think so," he said amiably. "But young Christina Parker on the other hand.... She *is* a pretty thing, isn't she? I might take her for myself. I could even call her C." He paused. "So quiet, Michael. Don't tell me that I've gotten to you already? I have, haven't I? Ha. You're still the same rag-tag ruffian you were seven years ago. The only thing that's changed is your French patois."

I swore. The bastard laughed.

"Same old temper, though. Consider my offer, Michael, or I'll consider the girl. *Slán.*"

The radio went dead in my hands.

Cloak and Dagger by Nenia Campbell

Chapter Twenty-Two

Friction

Michael:

Life on the streets had doled out a healthy sense of reality to me. Fear was one of the first emotions I'd ever learned. Working for the IMA only served to reinforce that crucial guiding principle: kill, or be killed. Fear supported this principle, it kept me alert.

Terror, on the other hand, was new. Terror could get me killed.

The boat was low on fuel. I drove the boat inland until I reached a small port town. There were no signs that I could see. We could have been anywhere. I wasn't sure if we had even left Mexico, yet, though from the look of the locals, I suspected we had.

A new problem occurred to me: I had no shirt, no shoes, and no money.

I went below deck to see if I could salvage anything. The girl was still asleep. Her chest rose and fell in concert with each inhalation and the troubled expression had left her face. She looked peaceful. I remembered Callaghan's threat; it made me wonder how peaceful she'd look if she knew what that bastard had planned for her.

No. I wouldn't think about Christina. I'd come down here to search for clothes and money. There had to be some around here. Field agents got roughed up — it was part of the job.

I found a pair of boat shoes more or less in my size lodged behind some life preservers in the supply closet along with a number of dried goods, bottled waters, and two emergency flares. *Good to know, but not particularly helpful at the moment.* I slipped on the shoes, hoping I could find some petty cash to buy fresh food. The dry stuff would come in handy in case we encountered a real emergency.

Since the Phantoms were used by field agents, they were well-equipped for a myriad of situations. They should also contain an emergency supply of international money from countries like Europe, Canada, Mexico, and the United Kingdom. Hopefully it hadn't been depleted by the last operative using it.

Sure enough, there was a small fire safe in the back of the closet. I found the key hidden under the driver's seat. Some of the money was missing, but there was still plenty. I emptied the safe of all the U.S. dollars, stuffing the bills into the pockets of my sweatpants.

There was a small retail store within walking distance. Racks of cheap swimwear and Hawaiian shirts were being sold outside. It was off-season for beachwear so they weren't getting much foot-traffic. I glanced around out of habit and caught a couple people looking my way. Since that was probably because I looked like a vagrant, I decided not to be concerned. Ignoring the stares but still on guard, I selected a couple shirts and pants that would allow me to move around freely in case Callaghan decided to be a bastard and send a couple of his goons out to cause me strife. At this point, I wasn't ruling that out as a possibility. The man wanted to see me burn.

Regain your strength, Michael. Play with your pretty hostage. Just stay out of my way.

He'd been quick enough to frame me and even quicker to get me out of the picture. What was he hoping to gain by keeping me around?

I turned back to the clearance racks and got some jeans in the girl's size, as well as a number of tops in neutral colors like gray and black. I intended to stay out of public places as much as possible but we would have to make runs for fuel and food. I did not want to stand out. Callaghan was no fool. Sooner or later he would send spies. Probably sooner.

"Can I wear this out of the store?" I held up one of the gray shirts.

The cashier was a woman, with eyebrows so thin they looked drawn on. She arched one: a reddish-brown too dark to match her blonde hair. "Certainly. Let me just remove the tags for you."

"Thanks." I pulled it on while she rang up the rest of my purchases.

"For your girlfriend?" she asked casually, glancing at the

lingerie.

"Not exactly," I muttered.

"Oh?"

Something in her voice made me look at her twice. She wasn't as old as I'd initially thought, because of all that makeup. Rather than the late thirties I'd estimated, she was a great deal younger. Late- to mid-twenties, maybe. Blonde. Thin. The type of woman I always went home with. My libido stirred. I knew, without a doubt, this woman would come with me if I gave the word. She wouldn't flinch if I came near. She wouldn't cry if I propositioned her. If the overt way she was sizing me up was any indication, I could probably even get her to do me in one of the changing rooms. *Probably a scratcher, too*, I thought, staring at her red nails. I'm not sure what it is about red nail polish.

"I love your accent," she purred. "Are you a Southern boy?"

"Louisiana. Yes."

She tapped her nails on the counter, *click, click, click*, as she waited for the receipt to print out. Smiling at me, she said, in a meaningful voice, "Is there anything I can do for you? Anything at all?"

Images immediately popped into my head of all the things she could do for me. I knew I had to get away, quickly, because I was deprived enough to take her up on it. "No, thanks, keep the change."

Cloak and Dagger by Nenia Campbell

I didn't want to think about what would happen if my fingers brushed against hers. I knew what would happen. It'd happened a hundred times before, always ending in the same way. Waking up with a woman in my bed who I'd slept with but had no real interest in as a person. The joke was always on me, because they never looked as good in the morning as they had the night before with alcohol in me and makeup on them. And even though they always came across as tough as nails in the bedroom, scratching and biting, they always cried when I made them leave.

They wanted to change me. They didn't seem to realize that I couldn't be change. Or I'd thought I couldn't. I'd never turned down a free fuck before. Forcing a smile, I left the store with my blood pounding in my temples and the cashier's disbelieving eyes boring into my back. Wondering what was wrong with me. That was the million dollar question, wasn't it? I didn't know what was wrong with myself. I'd spent so many years looking at a stranger in the mirror that I didn't recognize who I was anymore. And now, for the first time, the image was starting to clear. Surprise, surprise — I didn't like what I saw.

Christina:

I sat up, shielding my eyes from the light. I half-expected to see the iron bars or the blank, white walls from the containment cell.

Instead I saw glorious sunshine flooding in through the open window. I was free — free from the IMA. Against all odds, I had escaped.

I had the perverse desire to jump up and cheer. Instead I stood up and promptly bumped my head on the low ceiling. "Ow!" I muttered. With a curse, I climbed the small set of stairs leading up to the deck. A rush of ocean air assailed me. I blinked at the pungent saltiness of it.

Michael was driving, his back towards me, wearing jeans and a fitted gray shirt I couldn't remember seeing before. I sat down in the seat beside him and said, "Hey."

"You're awake."

"Barely. I was beginning to think I'd never be able to get up again." I looked around at the endless expanse of ocean. "Where are we?"

"About twenty miles off the coast of Southern California." He tossed a carton at me. "Eat."

It was a sandwich. Egg and cress. Still cold. I didn't hesitate; I hadn't eaten for almost two days. I ripped into the carton and tore at the bread with my teeth, not caring that I probably looked like a wild dog with my matted hair and filthy clothes. I savored each mouthful, pausing only long enough between gulps to ask, "Where did you get this?"

"I picked up some things. Don't eat so fast, you'll get sick."

I had to tear myself away from the lovely food again. "When?"

"About two hours ago." He paused. "You were asleep."

Something in his voice — something almost accusatory — put me on edge. I swallowed the final mouthful of sandwich. "Where are we going?"

"Seattle."

"Seattle?"

"That's what I said."

"Seattle, *Washington*?"

He didn't bother to respond. Just looked at me in that unnerving way of his. "Get dressed," he said at last, turning back towards the ocean. "You're a mess."

I looked down at my once-white shirt, now ripped and stained and smeared with dirt and blood. "Are there clothes on the boat?"

"There are now."

"Wow…thanks."

He turned away. "Don't thank me."

"The sheets — "

"I'll rinse them all in salt water. The clothes are already clean. I went to a laundromat."

Giving him a look — wasn't he just Miss Suzy Homemaker all of a sudden — I went back down below deck and saw a bag bearing the logo of a fairly prominent store. I sifted through it, frowning. Two pairs of jeans, one light and one dark. A sweatshirt. A sweater. Some t-shirts. Some tank tops. Flannel pajama pants. No pastels, everything strictly monochrome. Cheerful guy. The bra was, disturbingly, the right size. And the underwear he'd picked out made the heat rush to my face because they were all a bit lacier than the white cotton I'd usually wear.

I got dressed, tugging on the jeans — Jesus, I couldn't remember the last time I'd been able to squeeze into a size 12. Not since… Freshman year, at least. I picked out the sweater because it was cold on deck and looked decent enough.

When I climbed back up the stairs, Michael had the boat set on cruise control. He was sitting sideways with his legs resting on the seat I'd just vacated. One of his arms was dangling over the back of the chair and he was drinking some orange juice.

"Why are we going to Seattle?" I asked. "I live in Oregon."

"Because I need to locate your cowardly parents."

He held out the bottle of juice to me, which I refused. I folded my arms over my chest and tried my best to look outraged. "You didn't answer my question."

"We can't live on the boat. We have a limited amount of both money and food. Neither you nor I have any form of identification and the IMA is still presumably looking for us."

"You blew them up!"

"Callaghan survived. I'm not sure how. The man is like a fucking cockroach."

I fell back against the passenger seat. "Oh, God."

"I phoned one of my contacts. They're going to meet me in Washington, hook us up, so we're going there. I rented my apartment there under an assumed name that the IMA don't have on file. Callaghan won't find us."

His apartment? We were going to his apartment?

"That a problem?" he asked, taking an indolent swig from the juice.

"No." I had to force the word out.

"It's safe, if that's what you're worried about." *Not with you there, it isn't.* He set the half-empty bottle down. "They don't know about my lease. And it's under an assumed name, as I said. The worst is over. You can relax a bit."

"How can you say that with Adrian still alive?" I threw up my arms. "He's twice as dangerous as Mr. Richardson ever was."

"Because you can't live on adrenaline twenty-four seven." His eyes dropped. My shirt had ridden up again. I moved to pull it down and he caught my wrists. I had unconsciously walked closer while shouting at him, bringing me within arm's reach.

"Let go."

"I have news for you, darlin. You're on a boat. In the middle of nowhere." He gave me a tug so I tumbled into his lap, and promptly leaned over me to cut the engine. "You're not going anywhere." I could feel his heartbeat — it was pounding, almost as hard as mine.

Something corkscrewed in my chest. He put my hands around his neck. I didn't stop him. He put his hands around my waist. I didn't stop him, either. Gentle, deliberately, he began to caress my skin with small, firm strokes, without looking away. "Ça c'est bon," he whispered.

"Was that…French?" I asked desperately.

"Mm-hmm." His lips pressed against mine. His mouth tasted like orange juice. One of his hands moved to my hair, tangling in the lank and greasy stands. I stank — we both stank, despite the new clothes — and his hair looked just as unwashed as mine. "Ça c'est très bien." I pulled my hand away from his neck and pushed his face away.

"I can't — "

"Christina — don't do this to me." From him, it was an order, not a plea.

"I'm not doing anything to you."

"Believe me, cher," he said. "You're doing plenty." He grabbed my hand, placing it on the inside of his thigh.

I made a face. "Cut it out." Ignoring me, he continued guiding my hand upwards, placing it over a hard bulge in the denim of his jeans. "What are you doing?"

"That," he said, curling my hand around it, "Is your fault." Keeping his hand over mine, he leaned forward to kiss me again.

"No, it's not," I whispered.

"Oh no?" That made him grin, a slow, sinful smile. "I'm flattered."

"And I didn't know…it would be like this." *Why can't I breathe?*

His eyes widened a little, in surprise. "What are you talking about?"

"You" — all the words evaporated from my mouth — "and me."

"Like what? This?" he repeated, giving my hand another squeeze and barking out a laugh when I winced. "You really did go to a fucking parochial school, didn't you. *Pauve ti bete*. What did you think you'd agreed to? A kiss and a walk on the beach?"

I said nothing.

"I'm a man, darlin."

"You're a bastard, is what you are."

"That may be. But tell me something. What is it about this that's bothering you? Are you afraid that you might actually…enjoy it?"

I pulled away from him then, landing on the floor. Pain licked at my elbows. I ignored it, scrambling away before he could reach me. "As if I would. You stink, anyway."

"So do you." The setting sun threw his face into shadow. "Get out of here, then. Get. Take a shower. We'll settle this later."

Michael:

I couldn't sleep.

At first I chalked up my insomnia to the cold and tugged on the jacket I'd purchased in the store. Then I'd gotten too hot and stripped off both coat and t-shirt. The ocean wind was mercilessly cold against my damp, bare skin and still I sweated. As I stared at the black water, lit only by the full moon overhead, keyed up far more than any man should be at four o' clock in the morning, I had to admit to myself that I had a problem. A problem currently asleep below deck, completely oblivious to my torment.

No. Not completely oblivious. She knew what I wanted from her; I had made myself explicitly clear. She hoped that if she didn't acknowledge it, I'd forget. It was the mentality of a child hiding from monsters under the bedsheets: If I can't see it, it doesn't exist.

Well, I hadn't forgotten.

I paced around the small deck restlessly, trying to walk off the energy buzzing around in my bloodstream. Exercise wasn't what I needed. I needed something else.

Someone else.

I found her lying on the cot, wrapped up in the blanket. Fast asleep. Or pretending to be. She shivered as I climbed down the steps, as if picking up on my dark mood, and pulled the blanket more tightly around herself. Her black hair fanned out around her face in a dark nimbus, tangled and unbrushed. She was sleeping on her side, curled up to make herself as small as possible so the blanket would cover more of her body. I was pleased that it didn't. I wanted that pleasure for myself.

I reclined beside her, careful not to disturb her, and pulled her against me. She was soft and warm. When she squirmed, I felt the shuddering movement in a thousand places. For several moments, my healing wounds throbbed from tension as I fought to remain still.

Being a contract killer ate into my personal life. Though I tried to keep the two separate, and succeeded within reason, such black-and-white distinction was impossible when I was on-call twenty-four/seven. I never had much time for sex; on the odd occasions I *did*, it was usually quick and impersonal. Personal relationships were a liability.

I slid my hand into the folds of the blanket, cupping the curve of her breast through the thin fabric of her shirt. Her heart fluttered against my palm. *Thank you, God.* I stroked her through the thin fabric, stirring the peach-fuzz on her neck with my breathing. There was a hot, liquid weight pressing down hard on my lower belly, shooting fire into my groin. I was like a dam about to burst. I wanted to stop the dreams. Stop *thinking* about her. I suspected sex wouldn't do that. I suspected I was attempting to rationalize something that would just make it worse: that it would fuck me up even more than I already was, and her, too — but I wanted it anyway.

I wanted *her* anyway.

"Christina."

No response.

I leaned closer, shaking her bare shoulders. She bumped her head and hugged the sheet to her chest. "What are you doing in here?" she demanded, in a gasping voice I would have called seductive from any other woman. The fact that it wasn't intentional made it doubly provocative.

What would my name sound like, breathed like that?

And then I knew I was in trouble.

Christina:

Michael was leaning over me, inches away from my face. Shirtless, leonine, cast in shadow: he bore sinister resemblance to a panther. I stared at him, but when I blinked, he didn't go away. "What are you doing here?" I repeated groggily. "What do you want?"

He laughed. Slow, breathy laughter that made the hair on my

arms stand up. "You."

"What?"

"You heard me."

"W-were you watching me sleep?"

"Sleep?" The smile on his face disappeared. He looked at me unblinkingly, his hands sliding down my arms. And I found myself remembering his erratic behavior on deck. He no longer smelled like prison; he had washed his body and his hair and I thought I caught a dash of cologne. "How could you possibly sleep?"

"I was tired…" I swallowed again. "Aren't you?"

"No." He moved closer. "And it's all your fault."

If he moved any closer, our lips would touch. His words from earlier — *all your fault* — echoed in my ears. I pressed myself against the pillows. "What did I do this time?"

"It's what you didn't do that's the problem." His mouth brushed my ear, the words buzzing straight into my brain. "I want you."

"But — "

Michael leaned in and caught my lower lip between his teeth. "Now," he added. As if that was all the explanation he needed, he slid his hand under my shirt.

I grabbed his wrist, feeling heat race up my throat as his fingers splayed defiantly over my stomach. "I'm *tired*," I said piteously.

He managed to bring his hand up a little higher. "You slept all day long." He nipped at my lip again, flicking his tongue against the corner of my mouth. "*Ça va*. Nap time is over."

His voice was deep, his accent more pronounced than I'd ever heard it. My grip faltered, and he started tracing slow concentric circles against my prickling skin. A spark of something that wasn't quite pain arced through my body as he began sucking at my throat. "Don't," I pleaded.

"Your skin is so soft."

"*Michael.*"

He glanced at me, a challenge inscribed upon his face, before lowering his head and kissing everywhere he exposed as he tugged my shirt off. The stubble around his mouth chafed, but in a way that made heat pool in my stomach. In a way that made me forget how to breathe.

I twisted my fingers in his hair, trying to pull his head back. He grunted and flicked his tongue against a very sensitive spot. I squeaked and his eyes lifted to regard me, pale even in the moonlight.

His lips curved, and his tongue traveled over my skin a second time, then a third, longer each venture, but always halting just before — before…something. He laughed when I jerked beneath him. "You want me to stop?" When I didn't respond, he blew on my still-damp skin, watching my face. I choked on the dryness of my own mouth.

I began to struggle in earnest. I raised my knee, hoping to hit him in the stomach or groin. He rotated his hips to avoid the blow and pinned me against the thin mattress, settling between my legs. The directness of his gaze made color crawl up my neck. I didn't understand how he could be so unselfconscious when I was so painfully aware of how vulnerable I was.

"You promised," he said, speaking in a normal voice now, though he sounded a little out of breath. "The only rule you set was that it couldn't be on Target Island."

I was breathing just as hard, to my shame. "All this for something that won't mean anything to you?"

He tugged at my pants. "I never said this meant nothing to me."

"Of course it does." I was sobbing now. "You just want to sleep with me. You think I'm trash — nothing."

"If all I wanted was a quick fuck with some cheap whore, I would have gone home with the blonde," he snarled, angry again. Blonde? What blonde? What nonsense was he talking about?

I stared at him. He glowered at me and tried to kiss me again. Then he said, "Stop that."

"Stop what?" I steeled myself for the inevitable.

"That *look*. I know what you're doing, what you're thinking. The prayers. The crying. The goddamn" — he made a harsh, grating sound in the back of his throat and his hands hit the mattress on

387

either side of me — "*you*. Why do you do this to me?"

I shook my head wordlessly, pulling the blanket up to my chin.

"Do you think I enjoy watching you cringe? You think I couldn't get other girls, prettier than you, who wouldn't fight me? Who wouldn't act like I'm fucking torturing them? Who wouldn't pray to their fucking gods for deliverance like I'm some kind of devil?"

I blinked back fresh tears and said viciously, "Then why *don't* you?"

"Because I don't *want* them. For reasons I can't quite comprehend, I want *you*." He expelled a breath and said, in a quieter voice. "I want you. Only you — here and now." His lips brushed against my ear, my racing pulse. "Just kiss me, darlin. *C'est tout.* I'll do the rest. And I'll be…careful. Just don't fight me."

"Just kiss you," I repeated shakily. He nodded.

I closed my eyes, drew in a deep breath, and closed what little distance remained between us. He was as still as a statue, even as my trembling lips found his. He opened his mouth. I leaned in to seal our lips together. He made a low hum of approval in his throat that I felt all the way in his chest. Then he seized control with a deep kiss that had my head tipping back, until we were both lying flush against the cot, breathing as if we were about to drown.

"Good girl," he whispered.

I felt him slide off the blanket, which he tossed unceremoniously on the floor. Felt him tug off my pants. Felt his hips as he leaned back over me, solid and corded with muscle. A whimper escaped me. There was a crinkling sound. He closed his eyes and gasped. I felt him moving my legs. *What is he doing?* I opened my mouth to protest and something swiftly changed my mind.

"Oh — "

"Shh."

"*Ow.*"

"Just relax, darlin."

"*Aah.* Hurts," I cried. "Hurting me."

"I know." His hand was around my wrist, and he squeezed. Whether in warning or comfort, I wasn't sure. I tried to find the words to ask him to stop but was choked off by a hitched gasp. The first thrust brought tears to my eyes. The second made me scream.

"Oh, *fuck* you're ti — ah...I mean..." He darted a look at me, guilty and slightly surprised, as if he had forgotten I was there. Then he grunted, recapturing my mouth, and pushed harder. There was a slow, sharp tremor of pain that seemed to last a lifetime, like my skin was being forced to adjust to something unnatural.

"Worst part's over," he panted. "That's...as bad as it gets. I promise."

I sobbed quietly. *It still hurts.* He settled into a slower rhythm and the pain lessened, just as he had promised. The burning died down to a dull, tolerable ache. This was interspersed with little nips and licks that made my body break into a fresh sweat. He was making me feel what he wanted me to feel…and it was not quite as unpleasant as I would have liked.

"Enough. You got what you wanted."

"Not yet." His breathing sounded labored. "Don't cry…*mon…cher*."

I couldn't help it.

"You feel…so…good."

There was a final flash of pain, one thrust that felt deeper than all the others. He shuddered and collapsed on top of me with an explosive gasp. For a while, we just lay there. I stared at the ceiling, waiting for it all to be over as his chest heaved against mine. I was horribly embarrassed.

Gradually, his breathing quieted. I was aware of him looking at me, searchingly. He sighed again, stirring my bangs. "Oh, Christina." He gave me a quick kiss, a proper one on the mouth this time, before pulling back to look at me. "That wasn't so awful, was it?"

"Yes, it was."

Michael blinked. "What?"

"It was humiliating, and painful, and *empty*."

He returned my stare evenly for several seconds. "I'm sorry."

"I don't want to talk about it."

"Your call." He rolled off the cot. Tugged on his pants. There was no hint of insecurity in any of his gestures or movements. He was the picture of male confidence. He bent to get his shirt, revealing the smooth curve of his back. He hesitated, then flung it at me. "Put that on, though. You're shivering."

I started to cry again.

Michael shook his head. I barely noticed him as he finished getting dressed. All I saw, though the blur my vision had become, was the shirt. Because I had realized something horrible: the shirt and now had something in common: we both *belonged* to Michael.

Chapter Twenty-Three

Scars

Christina:

I stirred awake with the notion that something was irrevocably wrong. It wasn't a sudden epiphany, but an unpleasant suspicion that nagged at me as I slept, burrowing like a drill bit into my brain. There had been dreams about…something I couldn't — and didn't want to — remember. I could feel it building up, all those unpleasant emotions and fragmented memories threatening to break the surface.

My eyes opened, cleared of sleep, and widened in horror as I took in the dark cabins and musty furnishes. Then I *did* remember — everything.

Michael.

I was lying with my back to him. One of his arms draped carelessly over my waist, keeping me pressed against his chest. The warmth of his skin burned through my — *his* — shirt like the glowing heat of a furnace. Each one of his soft breaths tickled my neck. I shivered, unable to ward off the images that came like a flock of vultures to pick off what remained of my heart. The shame as memories popped up, unbidden, paralyzing me with recollections of what he had done to me, what I had *let* him do to me, and the fact I could have said no —

But hadn't.

Michael stirred again and the mattress creaked under our combined weight. When I turned his eyes were open and he was propped up on one muscled forearm, watching me. I nearly hit my head on the low ceiling when I saw him smile. It was a proprietary smile, cool and assessing, and it *did* something to me.

"Hmm." His eyes disappeared briefly, opening at half-mast. "Morning."

I'd seen him pretend to sleep too many times to fall for that. "You might have said something."

"How do you feel?"

"Like I have to take a hot shower."

He nodded. His face contained the studious intent of a predator. And then I realized that I would have to crawl over him to get to the shower, as he undoubtedly knew. There was no other way around him and Michael made no intent to move.

"Is there a problem?"

"No."

"Good," he sighed, closing his eyes again.

There was no helping it. I swung one leg over him, careful not to put any weight on his body. Pain licked at my thighs. I gritted my teeth and glared at Michael. His eyes were shut.

I started to move my other foot. He moved quickly, like a

striking cobra, giving my leg a single disarming tug that took me off balance. I grabbed onto his shoulders instinctively to keep from sliding to the floor, half-straddling his waist. "What are you doing? I need to shower."

"Alone?" He leaned closer. "Without…me?"

My brain stuttered over his words. *No,* I thought. *He couldn't possibly — not after…*

"Don't worry. You'll get your chance to wash up." The thumb of his right hand, still on my thigh, began to move in slow, circular motions. He whispered in my ear a suggestion I won't repeat. "How about it, darlin? Doesn't that sound…fun?"

Sputtering an incoherent protest, I leaped out of his arms before his mouth could reach mine. I grabbed the bag of clothes, acutely aware of his eyes burning into my back as I scrambled into the bathroom. He'd been baiting me, yes, but there was more. He'd been almost…playful. It was tantamount to being rushed by a lion, and finding out it wanted to play fetch.

I locked the door and leaned against the cold metal surface, straining to hear his quiet footsteps over the sound of my own raucous heart. I half-expected him to beat against the door. Drastic, perhaps, and foolish, but I'd been left with the chilling impression that he was a man unaccustomed to being refused.

I scrubbed my greasy, sweaty hair with the cheap shampoo. I

wanted to lather my skin until I could no longer feel his touch, no longer smell him on me. Until I could no longer taste him in my mouth. I shut off the water and wrung out my hair. Got dressed. Jeans. Tank top. Sweatshirt. It didn't really matter what I wore. He had already seen everything there was to see.

I gripped the edge of the sink. My tired face stared back at me in the small mirror. I had a red mark on my neck where he had bitten me. I zipped my sweatshirt all the way up and sighed. No, it hadn't been so bad — but that just made me feel worse.

I didn't see him when I opened the door. Not until I looked down. He was doing sit-ups. "I had no idea you were such a quick little thing." He finished the last crunch and rolled to his feet. "I'm not going to jump you."

"Then stay away from me."

"Fine." I watched him grab something off the nightstand. When he faced me again, he handed me a water bottle and two small pills. "But do me a favor: take these."

"What are they?"

"Aspirin."

"Aspirin?"

Michael glanced me over. "I'm sure you're still sore."

"How *dare* you."

"Not like it's a secret. I could tell you hadn't been around. They'll make you feel better."

No, they wouldn't. I flung the pills at him and started to walk away but he grabbed my arm, pulling me back against him. The insult on the tip of my tongue crumbled into dust. I knew I should do something, *say* something, but I couldn't move. The effect of his proximity on my other senses made logic difficult, if not outright impossible.

"Why did you do that?" He was always most dangerous when his voice was soft. I felt my breathing quicken as he leaned forward until his mouth was level with my ear. "I thought we were past you treating me like the bad guy."

I put space between us the only way I could. I turned my face away.

He shook me. "Do you remember what happened? Because I do. I saved you. I saved your parents. I risked my life to save Richardson's whore, which nearly got the both of us killed. All I asked for in return was your sweet self, *lagniappe*, with a little bit of sugar on the side to tide me over until you can get me the money you owe me."

Michael paused, as if waiting for a response. I gave him none. "*You* came up with this arrangement; *you* put the merchandise in the store window, darlin. You have the nerve to play victim because I liked what I bought?" His face darkened. I really thought he was going to take a swing at me. "I knew you were going to use this against me...but I'm going to pretend that's the pain talking." He tossed the pill bottle over his shoulder. "This time."

It hit the wall with a rattle and rolled underneath the cot.

"Go do something useful," he said crisply. "Keep watch while I wash up. I'm going to take a shower." He looked at me again, adding, "A cold one."

Michael:

The old wives' tale about cold showers is false: blasting your body with a couple gallons of ice water doesn't make you any less horny. It just makes you horny and *cold*. I toweled myself off and grabbed a white wife beater and the jeans from yesterday. I walked on deck with the towel draped my neck.

Christina was sitting in the passenger seat, with her arms around her knees. The redness in her eyes, when she looked at me in a startled double-take, told me that she'd been crying. Probably not keeping a lookout at all.

Much more calmly than I actually felt, I said, "Did you see anything?"

"Just a helicopter."

Just a helicopter. "Did it have any markings? What color was it?" I scanned the empty horizon. "What direction did it go?"

She shrugged.

I sat down in the driver's seat. "I ask you to watch for five minutes. You can't even do that? *Fuck*." I slammed the dashboard.

She said nothing.

I tossed the towel on the floor and switched the boat into manual. "I suggest you start taking me seriously if you want to stay alive. As long as he's in charge, Callaghan has the entire IMA at his disposal — he could easily put a bounty on the both of us."

She shuddered and pulled the hood of her sweatshirt over her head, shielding her face.

I sighed. "We'll hit the state line in about half an hour. We're going to get off the boat as soon as we get to Washington."

She looked up a little.

"We'll stop to get some food and then go the rest of the way by bus. By now, somebody has probably inventoried what's left of Target Island and noticed the boat is missing. They'll probably report it as stolen to the Coast Guard — if they haven't already." That helicopter she may or may not have seen concerned me. "Are you listening to me?"

"Please," she whimpered. "Just leave me alone right now."

So I did.

A soft rain began to fall. I buttoned up my coat and grabbed her hand. I didn't trust her not to run away. Not after her behavior on the boat. "I'm not going to bite you. You need to look a little more convincing. Nobody's going to believe you're with me if you look like that."

Hatred swirled in her eyes, colored by other emotions more potent than fear and she was drawing attention with that zombie walk of hers. I saw more than one pair of eyes glance first at her, then at me, before flickering away. It wouldn't be long before some busybody humanitarian got involved and started preaching about abusive relationships.

"If you don't want Callaghan and his men to spot us, I suggest you look lively. One night with me is far less painful than five minutes with him and, unlike me, he won't care if he's hurting you. So cut it out."

She said nothing but threaded her arm through mine. Her posture improved markedly. "Better," I said. "Not great…but better."

"It's the best you're getting from me."

"For now," I agreed.

I bought two bottles of soda and two pretzels from a small stand near the docks, looking around for a bus stop as I handed over the cash. There was one right near the marina, across the street from us. "Eat your food before the bus comes."

I watched her from the corner of my eye as I munched my mustard-slathered pretezel. She barely touched hers. The arrival of the bus saved me from coming up with an appropriate threat. I shoved her uneaten breakfast into my rucksack and paid the fare before the driver could get a good look at our faces.

Nobody paid us much attention. It was rush hour, the bus was crowded. People were too busy holding onto the rail and their belongings to hazard much interest in those around them. The only available pair of seats were in the middle, in front of a man in a raincoat napping against the window. "you first," I said to her.

She made a pained face but complied. I took the aisle seat and slung my arm around her shoulders, as much to keep her from running as to keep up with appearances. She was warm. So was the bus. I leaned back and closed my eyes. *Just a brief nap,* I promised myself.

Until I heard her gasp. I cracked open an eye, then sat up straight. She was staring down at a small pile of photographs with an expression of dismay. I recognized myself in some of them, her in others. The top one showed us together.

"Where did you get those?"

Her eyes shifted toward the man in the raincoat I'd been so quick to dismiss earlier. I caught the flash of a blade in my periphery and reached for my gun — and then remembered that I didn't have one.

"Hello," the man said. "Michael, I presume?"

I knew better than to ask how he'd gotten the photographs. The angle of the shots suggested an aerial view. Probably taken with a camera that had a scope lens. The girl said she had seen a helicopter earlier — perhaps he had been aboard. He wanted me to press him for details. I didn't provoke so easily. "Who are you and what do you want from *me*?"

"Nicely framed, wouldn't you say?" he said, ignoring both questions. "Which is quite ironic, Mr. Boutilier — Michael, if I may — because that is *exactly* what I have done to you. These are only copies, of course. The originals are tucked away someplace else" — this was directed at Christina, who had started tearing up the photos with shaking hands — "so don't bother, young lady."

She looked like she would be ill.

"I was told to watch out for you, in particular. Mr. Callaghan said you are a formidable opponent even unarmed — which I presume you are, since you haven't drawn a weapon."

"Answer my questions," I said.

"I've been watching you both for quite some time." He leaned over the seat and took the rest of the intact pictures from Christina, stuffing them in a pocket. "They call me the Sniper, although as you can see, I do not specialize in guns alone. You both made lovely subjects. Particularly you, my dear." He reached out towards her, and she pressed herself against the bus.

I leaned forward. "Keep your fucking hands off her."

"Don't worry, Michael. I will leave that distinct pleasure to you. For now." Unperturbed, he rested his hand on the back of her seat. "This is a warning."

"Against what? Taking public transportation?"

"Now let's not pretend that you haven't been sneaking around behind his back. He knows you have contacts that you meet with in private. You are useful to him at the moment, which is the only reason you remain alive. But that could change if he perceives you as a nuisance — even if you are *the best*."

"You managed to catch me off guard once. It won't happen again."

"I'm terrified," the Sniper said mildly.

Cocky little shit. "What about what he's doing to the IMA? You're OK with that?"

"As long as I get paid, I could care less who the money is from," the Sniper said, proving Callaghan right. Mercenaries were mercenaries; they didn't play favorites, they played hands. "Some have resigned, yes, and a wave of insurgents were killed, but the agency remains largely intact. Mr. Callaghan is a capable man. I suggest you remember that and heed his warning."

"Callaghan doesn't scare me. Neither do you."

"Oh no? He said blithely, reaching up to pull the stop cord. Turning towards Christina in a pretend aside, he said, "I'm sure you've seen that scar on his stomach…among…other things. Ask him how he got it sometime." He smiled at me. "Farewell, Michael."

If I'd had a gun, I would have shot him.

Christina:

I touched his shoulder tentatively. He whirled around, looking like he could kill. "We have to get out of here," he said, pulling the cord. Hard. "Now."

"Why?"

"The Sniper probably isn't alone — and he could have bugged the bus."

I stumbled to my feet, gripping one of the metal support rods as the bus slowed to a stop. "So what are we going to do now? Kill him?" I hissed. "I thought we were supposed to lie low."

Michael looked like he was considering murder a viable option. "Can I get two transit passes, please?" The driver handed him two pink slips of paper. "Thanks."

"*Michael.*"

His face was flushed and his eyes were narrowed. "No, I'm not going to kill him," he said, which made me feel better until he added, "Not yet, anyway. Not until I found out what his angle is.

Now help me find a fucking payphone."

Easier said than done. Since the dawn of the cell phone age, payphones had become scarcer than two-dollar bills. We eventually found one on a deserted street corner, covered with graffiti and fliers for Seattle strip clubs. I waited on a bench, shivering, while he made the call.

"Did you get a hold of him?"

"Her. And yes, she's going to meet us here, instead."

Her?

Michael:

Shannon Luo always had a penchant for the dramatic but showing up in a red Mercedes took the fucking cake. "You couldn't have chosen a less conspicuous car?"

"I'm sorry."

I grunted, looking her over. She was wearing a tight, black t-shirt, in spite of the cold weather, and low-rise pants. A gold heart-shaped locket glinted at her cleavage. I hadn't seen her in almost two years and she still looked exactly the same. Her hazel eyes sought mine out, saying she both noticed and appreciated the quick once-over.

She glanced at Christina hovering nearby and the provocative look gave way to suspicion. "Who is this?"

"Christina." She jumped at the mention of her name. On the phone, I'd told Shannon Christina's parents were wanted by the mob and had paid me to be the girl's bodyguard. Which was true, to an extent.

Christina held out her hand. Looking surprised, Shannon shook it. I'd never realized how tall the girl was, but she dwarfed Shannon, who barely topped 5'. "I'm so sorry about your parents. That must be awful. But you're in good hands. Ed's *amazing*."

Christina's tentative smile disappeared. Her eyes swung towards me. "Ed?" she mouthed.

Oh, Jesus.

"Hmm. You're older than I expected. He said you were a child." Shannon shot me a look I pretended to ignore. "How old are you, honey? Fourteen? Fifteen?"

"I'm *eighteen*."

"Hmm," she said again. "Hardly a child at all."

"Come on," I said. "Let's go."

Shannon talked at great length over the sound of the euro-dance on her speakers. She was one of those women who can say a great deal about nothing. I barely heard a word she said, but at least she drove as fast as she talked.

I leaned back against the leather seats and tried to relax. The music was too bright, though, and the buzzing edge of the synthesizers got on my nerves. It was like listening to a fucking swarm of bees. "Hot enough for you, Ed?"

A flash of movement in the side view mirror caught my eye: Christina removing her sweatshirt. She was wearing one of the white tank tops. My mouth went dry. It was the twin of the one I'd ripped off her body last night.

My cock jumped to attention, like this was fucking roll call for it. Images began to flood my brain, a mixture of real and fantasy, I began to sweat. "Yeah." *Stop thinking about that.* I shifted in my seat, pinning it under my belt so the bulge wouldn't be obvious.

Shannon shut off the heater. "Good." I glared at her. She rewarded me with a saucy smile. "Wouldn't want you to catch cold."

Or anything else.

We stopped at a small warehouse. "Here we are!" That damned music finally turned off. Too little, too late. I could already feel the beginnings of a headache coming on. My cock returned to where it was supposed to be when I stood up, and I breathed out a little, mopping my forehead with the back of my hand.

"I got a car all lined up for you, Ed," she was saying. "And a gun, and a phone, and a couple other things you asked for." She paused at the threshold of the other room. "About the wire transfer — "

"You got the money?"

"Yes, but isn't it a little too — "

"I paid you what I owe."

"It's your money." She shrugged her shoulders and sashayed away while I waited for a bottle of aspirin to fall from the sky. Christina stumbled out of the car, looking shaken.

"Ed?"

"She thinks my name is Edward. You are not to tell her otherwise."

She nodded dizzily, leaning back against the car. "Anything else I should know?"

"Your parents are being chased by mobsters. I'm your bodyguard. Don't tell me you get carsick."

"I don't, usually. Where are we?" I watched her take in the residential/light commercial area, all of it shrouded in a thin haze of vapor. Her frown deepened. "Is this Seattle?"

"We're in the suburbs. Shannon's giving us a car."

"Lending," Shannon corrected, as we stepped into the room. She turned and her smile faltered for a brief instant, flicking to my hand around her wrist, before returning at twice the wattage. "You scratch up the paint job and I'll kill you."

"Try it. I'll have you on the floor in two seconds."

"Mm," she purred. "Sounds fun. Is that a date?"

"No." I gave her a look she pretended not to see. "I'm driving."

The rain had abated to a light drizzle by the time we got into the more heavily populated areas. I was grateful for the downpour — anyone following us would be hindered by the rain and the Sniper would have trouble orchestrating another photo shoot in inclement weather, though the tenacious little bastard probably had a waterproof camera.

The city was lit up by neon, blurring in the misty darkness, giving the shopfronts a frosty glow. I watched the girl. She never took her eyes from the window. Once, she made an appreciative sound and started to say, "Oh, look at tha — " before flushing uncomfortably and falling silent. I wondered what she'd seen that caught her eye.

"Nice area, isn't it?" Shannon piped up. There was savage proprietorship in her voice, as if in her mind she not only owned this part of the city, but was responsible for its creation, as well. "It's one of the more upscale areas," she added, as we pulled up to her apartment. "We don't have anything like Saks Fifth Avenue" — she laughed deprecatingly — "but if you want to shop in the city, this is as close as you get."

But while expensive — city housing wasn't cheap — her place, and the surrounding area, weren't quite upscale. Definitely looked as though it'd seen a roach or three in its time. I popped the lock and Shannon sighed. "You're not going to walk me to my front door?"

"I have to watch the girl. This is an upscale area, remember? You won't get mugged."

"It's *dark*," Shannon said. "And the girl's not going anywhere."

"*She* is right here," Christina said, sounding irritated. "And she has a name."

"You're eighteen, honey. You can't play by yourself for a few minutes?"

"Enough." I drew in a deep breath. *Fuck.* "I'll be right back." I twisted the automatic locking mechanism from the keyring I'd retrieved from Shannon. "If anything happens, hit the panic button. Not that anything will."

I slammed the door behind me, locking it manually, and walked up the steps. They were slippery from the rain. I held onto the rail as I ascended, wondering what scheme that woman had up her sleeve. Shannon didn't need help walking to her door. She'd gotten there long before me. Was already inside, in fact. I walked into the familiar hallway and said, "If you're so concerned about safety, you probably shouldn't leave your door unlocked."

"You should have seen your face when I pulled up." She laughed, turning around. Her shirt was unbuttoned now. "Did you really think my Mercedes was the car I'd picked out for you?"

"It's nice to see you have some sense, after all."

She moved closer. "Aren't you going to thank me?"

I cracked a smile, amused that she'd bothered. "Thank you."

"I didn't mean with your mouth." She let her lips brush against mine. Her shirt fluttered to the floor. "Well. We could start with your mouth — and work our way down."

I hadn't thought that she'd jump me in the hall, but I wasn't surprised. I wasn't pleased, either. "You almost got me fired." I held her at arm's length. "Do you want to get me killed?"

"I didn't know you were an agent."

"You still shouldn't. You pried into my personal life, finding out things you had no business knowing — until I was left with no choice but to tell you."

"I missed you." She slid her hands down my chest. I could feel her nails through the wife beater. Red polish. "I bet you missed me, too."

"I barely thought about you."

Shannon leaned closer, tugging at the lapels of my coat. "So cruel."

"It comes with the job." I pushed her away again.

"But I bet you're thinking about me now." Her mouth covered mine, her breasts pushing against my chest. I tasted a vague sweetness from her lip gloss as she slid one of her hands down my pants. "Oh, hello." She squeezed me and my breathing hitched. "Looks like you are."

"Shannon. No."

"Stay with me." Her grip tightened and I groaned. "One night. You won't regret it."

With effort, I said, "The girl is in the car." I tugged her hand out of my waistband. "I'm being paid by the hour."

"I don't remember time being an issue for you."

She was beginning to piss me off. "The answer is no."

"Why not? Is it the girl?" Shannon slipped her shirt back on but didn't button it. "Look, ditch the kid. Take here — wherever she needs to go. Then come back."

"It's not her," I said.

"Then what's the problem?" She stared at my face. "Me?"

"You're getting warmer." I started to push past her. She halted me again.

"Why? What's wrong with me?"

"Nothing. I'm just not fucking interested."

"Is it because you're giving it to your sweet-faced client, Ed?"

"I'm not discussing this with you."

"Is it the schoolgirl thing?" Shannon leaned up, to reach my ear. "Is *that* what gets you hot? Little Miss Junior Prep flashing her panties at you?"

I yanked open the door. "Goodbye."

"Wait." She held her shirt closed with one hand and hurried

after me. When she saw I really was leaving, her voice rose in alarm, sure to wake the neighbors. "Ed — come back, I was just teasing." She called after me several more times. I didn't respond.

"I thought you weren't coming," Christina said.

"Trust me, darlin. I almost did."

While she was busy puzzling that one out, I switched the car into drive and sped to my apartment.

Christina:

Michael made no effort to speak to me in the car. He was breathing hard and did not look at me, but I caught a glimpse of his face in the rear view mirror. He looked mad. When we stopped outside an inconspicuous apartment complex on the other side of town, I was getting antsy.

"I'm on the third floor." He handed me a key. "Fourteen C."

"By myself?" I repeated. "With your key?"

Michael held up a spare one. "Go," he said hoarsely.

He didn't need to tell me twice. I went. The elevator was out of repair. I had to walk up three flights of stairs. By the third floor, I was winded. I inserted the key into the lock and opened the door. The smell of musty furniture and stale cleaner assailed my nose.

All the furniture was modern, in shades of black and white with stainless steel accents. No personal touches, but the carpet looked expensive. I made my way into the kitchen. The basic appliances were shiny and new. There was a small eating area set for two with flimsy dining chairs. One of the chairs was piled high with books and folders, suggesting he didn't have much company. At least, none that ever made it as far as the kitchen.

I went back through the living room, turning around the bend that connected the living room to the kitchen and found myself in his bedroom. The obvious focal point was a large sleigh bed with black sheets. In the corner was a desk, also stacked with reading materials. Ditto the chair. I squinted at the titles. Most were reference books, but he had a couple leather-bound classics. Barely visible under the mess was an ancient set of speakers, without a single CD in sight.

I took a step back and bumped into Michael. His jacket was gone and his breathing was easier. "What do you think?"

I hesitated. "You enjoy being solitary and don't have much fun."

He almost smiled — almost — but then it faded and his face became expressionless, even annoyed. He walked past me and started organizing some of the loose papers on his desk. "Make yourself at home. It'll take me anywhere from a few days to a week to locate your parents."

"Where did you find her?" *On a street corner somewhere?*

"Shannon? Ordering equipment. It was an unusual order."

"And you became...friends...afterwards?"

"We aren't friends."

I stared at him as he lifted stacks of paper off the chair, keeping his back to me. I remembered Shannon's joyous reaction upon seeing him. The poisonous looks she'd shot in my direction. Why she seemed to hate me for no apparent reason. "You slept with her, didn't you?"

There was a pause. "Yes."

That bastard.

"Don't look at me like that," he said, without turning around. "I told her what the rules were. She didn't take me seriously."

I felt a small trickle of pity for Shannon. Not much, though. *Bitch.*

"You wouldn't make the same mistake." He sat on the edge of the bed. "You take me seriously."

Only because I couldn't afford not to.

"Did you wear a uniform at Sacred Heart?"

It took a moment for the question to sink in. "You mean at Holy Trinity? Yeah, I did. WE all did. Most Catholic schools require them. Why?"

Michael laughed, collapsing back on the mattress. I figured that was as good a time as any to change out of the bus clothes and into the flannel pajama pants. I came out of the bathroom to find him still on the bed, no longer laughing, with his arms stretched over his head. The hem of his wife beater had lifted a few inches, revealing the twisted scar that curved around his navel and intersected with the fine line of dark hair disappearing into his waistband.

Ask him how he got it.

I looked at his face, which was set with determination and something else I couldn't quite put my finger on. Something that made all the hairs on my arms stand on end. It wasn't…sexual. Not overtly, although that was certainly part of it. Whatever the thought or emotion was, it made his eyes burn. When he spoke, his words were just as unexpected.

"Would you like to learn some self-defense?"

Chapter Twenty-Four

Catharsis

Michael:

The incident with the Sniper had been an unpleasant wake-up call. Christina had spotted the man before I had but been unable to do anything. If his intentions had been hostile, we would have both been screwed. Partly, that was my fault. She was no use to me helpless and I was fully acquainted with the repercussions of getting caught unawares. I should have taught her self-defense sooner. The only reason I hadn't was because I was so used to thinking of her as the trouble-making hostage.

"You could stand to learn some basic fighting moves," I said, sitting up. My shirt settled back into place. She looked down at the ground, some color in her face.

"Aren't you afraid I'd use them against you?"

In a different world. I could easily picture her as an IMA operative. A good one. "I said basic. I am not basic. I am advanced. Even if I taught you the moves, it is unlikely that you would be able to use them against me. Go ahead. Try to hit me."

She looked tempted, but cautious. I watched her eyes flick to my face. "You'll hit back."

"I won't."

She moved closer, as I had known she would. Close enough that

I could have reached out and grabbed her. I saw the muscles in her upper arms jump as she pulled back her fist — but not with enough force for a real hit. She was going to fake it, I thought. And she did. She pulled back at the last possible second and looked offended when I didn't blink.

"I said try to hit me. That wasn't even a try. If you're fast enough to dodge me, even I'll be impressed. I doubt that's going to happen though, but you won't know until you try, will you?"

She pulled her arm back farther. I timed it, waiting. *Now.* I caught her wrist before the blow could connect with my face, jerking her arm up swiftly behind her back. Heard her gasp in pain and surprise, still reeling, as I searched for the nerve in her collarbone. I pressed it.

"Ow," she gasped, instinctively pulling backwards. Putting more strain on her arm. "*Ow.*"

"You get someone in this position, darlin, and they'll do anything you want to let them go." I slid my hand down her arm, releasing her from the pin but didn't release her straightaway. "You see? You wouldn't last five minutes against me."

She glared at me over her shoulder. "Is that a threat?"

"Only if you make it one."

"Charming," she spat. "You said you wouldn't hit me."

"I didn't."

"What *was* that, then?"

"One of your pressure points."

"Is it supposed to hurt that much?"

"No pain, no gain. I can show you…more weak spots." I kissed her neck. "I promise…I won't press them…that hard."

I didn't see the fist coming until it was too late to avoid the undercut. I managed to dodge but couldn't evade the impending attack entirely. The blow glanced off my cheek, painful, but not enough to cause damage — thank God. Either I was getting slow, or she was a lot faster than I gave her credit for. Remembering her dash for the bathroom this morning, I suspected the latter.

My hand had already shot up to catch her wrist, almost of its own accord. I was in the defensive position, ready to deliver the single, disabling twist I'd need to crack her bones.

"What the *fuck*?"

"I caught you off-guard." She had that expression that pissed me off most — lips pursed, chin up, nostrils flared. The challenging one. "Not so great, is it? You don't get to hit me, you bastard. That *hurt*."

I pushed her backwards. "*That* was a lesson. Sparring. I know my limits. Do you?" I leaned forward, centering my weight on her pelvis, making it impossible for her to get back up. It was one of the first nonviolent subduing methods I'd learned. "I'm stronger than you. Faster than you. I can endure more pain than you have probably ever experienced — or ever *will* experience — in your life. Do you really believe, for one second, you could take me?"

She squeezed her eyes shut when I whispered into her ear, "And if you tried to run from me, as many have tried, I could hunt you down. You could leave all your friends, all your worldly possessions, all of that behind. I'd still find you."

I ran a finger down her throat until I came to the place where you can knock a man out, or even kill him. I pressed down, gently, until she began to struggle, and said, "I'm a dangerous man. I've killed before, and I'll probably kill again. You still don't get what I am. I'm an assassin. I kill on instinct. Just now, when you hit me? I almost snapped your wrist. Next time it could be your neck. Don't push me into that mode, darlin. Never forget that."

"I haven't."

She turned her face away, but not before I caught a glimpse of her tear-streaked face. I'd seen it when she thought I was going to shoot her, and when she thought I was going to rape her. She thought I was a monster. *Mission fucking accomplished*. Anger surged through me as quick and devastating as a forest fire. Then the anger burned out, spent, leaving resentment smoldering in its wake. Resentment, and something subtler: something that put pressure on my chest that was as tangible as a lead weight. I didn't want her looking at me like that. I should have — for her sake and mine — but

I didn't.

God help me. God help us both.

I snapped off the light. It would be easier for her to calm down if she didn't have to look at me. I reached out, blindly, and felt for her face. She trembled, but didn't push me away. There was something childlike about her, but I couldn't put my finger on what it was, since she didn't look — or act — like one.

Is it the schoolgirl thing?

She was suddenly wearing a short plaid skirt and partially-buttoned white blouse, straddling my hips and looping her tie around the back of my neck to pull me closer. I was completely unprepared for that image and gasped involuntarily.

Christina fell silent, waiting, listening. Like a deer that just heard a gunshot, but couldn't tell the direction it came from. I shifted my hips, pulling myself partway off her. "I don't want to hurt you." I threaded my fingers through her hair and she acted like I'd slapped her. "I'm *not* going to hurt you. I just…" But I couldn't think of how to explain myself.

I could torture a man into disclosing classified information and dissemble a machine gun in thirty seconds, but couldn't comfort a frightened girl.

"I'm not going to hurt you," I said again. "Please — stop crying."

Cloak and Dagger by Nenia Campbell

Christina:

For the second time in as many days, I woke up in Michael Boutilier's arms. I felt a wave of self-loathing so strong that it nearly swept me. He'd threatened me, coerced me into sleeping with him, come close to killing me for hitting him unexpectedly — and then cuddled me afterward until I fell asleep. It was as if he had multiple personalities.

His fingers were idly stroking my hip. I wrenched out of his loose grip and was struck by the difference: the expression on his face was cold as ice. "What?" he said, misreading my reaction. "Surely you're not expecting me to coddle you again. Or did you run out of tears?"

"Fuck you," I said stolidly. "Fuck you and all your personalities, you evil bastard."

By the time he was on his feet, I was halfway to the bathroom. I fumbled to close the door but the lock was a switch and my hands were shaking and sweaty. He shoved the door open, causing the doorknob to rift cracks through the wall. "What did you just say to me?"

I stepped back from him, towards the sink, reaching behind me for a weapon — any weapon. My hand closed against the soap dispenser. "Stay away from me. I'm not your hostage anymore."

"Maybe if I tied you up and gag you, there'd be some

improvement in that shitty attitude of yours. At the very least, it'd shut you up for a little while. I'm tired of you acting like I'm the son of Satan, darlin. It's time to get down from your ivory tower."

"You *ruined* my life," I said. "After all you've done, why shouldn't I hate you? You always threaten me. You don't respect me. You're violent, and cruel, and sadistic, and — "

"Finished?"

"No — "

"Too bad. Game over. Insert new fucking quarter."

I took another step back. "You're fucked up. There is something *wrong* with you. You need medication. Or therapy. Or — " He got too close. I lashed out with the soap dispenser, which he tore out of my fingers and tossed away.

"That's not what I need."

My back hit the sink. "Stay the hell away from me."

His hands rested on either side of me, trapping me. "What if I don't?"

"Leave me alone." I was almost sobbing now. "Go bother someone who wants you."

"I don't want anyone else but you." He walked closer until our hips were flush. "You know that. You *know*," he repeated, "And you use it to goad me. Manipulate me."

"That's not true!"

"But you're doing it right now. Don't think that I don't notice when you undress me with your eyes. I'm not blind. I see the way you look at me." His voice dropped even lower, the slow drawl making the hairs on my neck prickle. "But it's perfectly all right when you slum around me, because you don't know any better. It's all my fault. Isn't that right? I'm a sinful, hell-bound son of a bitch, and you're as pure as the fucking virgin Mary — except when you're *not* — "

I slapped him.

"You want to play rough with me, baby doll?" With one quick sweep of his arm, he knocked the contents of the counter — cologne bottle, shaving cream, soap — to the floor with a crash that resounded deafeningly in the small tiled room. "Fine, we'll play your way. We always do."

"Michael — "

"Shut up." He picked me up by my butt and sat me on the counter, pinning my wrists against the mirror above my head. He kissed me, like he was trying to prove a point. The breath exploded out of me like a shotgun when he ground his hips against mine. Every instinct was screaming at me to get away, to run.

I bit down on his lip. He bit back, harder. Hard enough that my head snapped back, against the glass, causing white sparks to explode behind my eyes. I tasted blood and wasn't sure whether it was mine or his.

"Michael — "

"*No.*"

Every time I tried to pull away, he moved me back into place with a snarl and a nip. Every time he moved me back into place, the kiss got less painful until, finally, after what seemed like hours, he simply rested his damp forehead against mine. His breaths were coming in heavy pants, stirring my hair. There was a drop of blood clinging to his lower lip, which he licked away even as I watched. And his face — those *eyes* —

"I can't decide whether I want to slap some sense into you, or throw you down on my bed and rip off your clothes." A thrill of fear went through me that he could sound so calm with eyes like that. He tilted his head, as if to get a better look at me, and released my wrists. "I can't bring myself to do either of those things, though. I *don't* want to hurt you. I never did. Why do you suppose that is?"

"Because you're developing a conscience?"

"You would say that, wouldn't you? Always so idealistic — when you're not being sanctimonious, that is. But I don't really think you believe that. You still think I'm evil."

"I — "

"No. Stop talking. For once you're going to fucking listen to me. *Really* listen to me." He hissed into my ear, breath tickling, "I'm in

424

love you with, you stupid, *frustrating*, foolish girl."

I flinched. "You're lying."

"Why the fuck would I lie?"

"I don't know. Because you're a liar? Because you're pissed off at me and want to hurt me? Because you want to manipulate me? There's lots of reasons."

Michael just looked at me. The anger drained out of his eyes and he just looked...

"You're not serious." A hysterical laugh burst from my lips; I was terrified. "You aren't — "

"I'm not what? I'm not human enough to want something I can't have?"

This time, when I bolted past him, he made no move to stop me.

Michael:

I punched the wall. The plaster cracked around the area of impact, flaking to the floor. Warm blood oozed from the broken skin. I kept punching until the wall was smeared scarlet from my knuckles, wishing it was something animate. Something that could fucking *hurt*.

The telephone rang, splicing the silence with its shrill ring. I flexed the fingers on my hand and picked up the phone. *It better not be the neighbors calling to fucking complain.* "What is it?"

"Hn, you sound tense, Michael. Have you had time to consider my offer?"

"Now is *not* the fucking time."

"You *are* tense. Well, I think it's the perfect fucking time, as you so quaintly put it." He paused. "So tell me, how *is* Christina?"

"With *me*."

"That isn't...quite what I meant. Funny you should mention that, however, because I just received a call. Apparently, your girl is running towards my man. Small world."

"You're a goddamn liar, Callaghan, and I don't have time for it."

"White shirt? Plaid pants? Black hair, blue eyes?" he listed off her characteristics as casually as ordering take-out. "And in tears — I wonder why."

I cursed and grabbed a shirt off a hanger, not bothering to button it. I slipped on my boots and clumsily locked the door behind me, still clutching the phone.

"Leaving so soon?"

I froze on the steps. The hall was empty.

"Not that way, boy."

I looked up at the door frame. A camera — he had to have a camera nearby. My pulse throbbed in my temples. Fucking Callaghan and his fucking cat-and-mouse games. "You fucking watching me right now? Getting your fucking kicks? What am I doing right now, you bastard?" I flipped the bird, knowing he could see it because he laughed.

"You're a man of habit, Michael. I don't need a camera to know that. Now, are you going to join me? Or am I going to have to *persuade* you?"

"Fuck you," I said. "Tell me where she is."

"In that case, you better run, Michael Boutilier. Run, and pray you find her — before I do."

There was quiet laughter and then the phone went dead.

Christina:

I ran blindly, the alleys and streets going by in a sepia-gray blur as I raced through the outskirts of urban Seattle. I felt drained — as if all the emotions I would ever feel had been used up in one quick burst during that short exchange with Michael. As if my thoughts and feelings had been a hot sun that had suddenly and inexplicably, without any sign or warning, imploded, leaving me with a black hole in my chest that begged to be filled.

I think I'm in love with you.

I hadn't run so desperately since my escape from Target Island.

I'm not human enough to want something I can't have?

Each word pulled at my flesh like little hooks.

The cars driving by made sloshing sounds in the street, which was still damp from last night's rain. One silver car, cutting round the corner too fast, dipped into a large pothole filled with brackish water and splashed me. The cold bit through the wet fabric of my tank top with a vengeance. I barely felt it.

I kept replaying our conversation in my head. His behavior — the argument — the kiss — the *kiss*. There was an obvious conclusion but my brain wouldn't let me reach it. *You don't need that,* it said. *Just keep running. And eventually, everything will fade away.*

Sharp cramps arced up my sides. Left foot. Right foot. The buildings around me started to blur. The city was being washed away like running water colors, like the tears coursing down my cheeks.

With my eyes on the sky, I wasn't watching the pavement. My bare foot — I just realized I hadn't put on shoes — encountered something sharp and jagged. A piece of broken glass, I think. In my surprise, I stumbled and ended up skinning my knees on the cement as the sharp concrete tore through the flannel. The pain was like a hammer smashing through my brittle thoughts.

And then I was the sieve, and my emotions were sloughing through me like a burst dam. I started to cry, right there on the sidewalk. With glass in my foot, a heart heavy with wordless sorrow and fear, and scrapes all up and down my legs, I felt as small and helpless as a child. All the buildings were completely unfamiliar when I got around to looking up: I was lost. I started to cry harder, feeling stupid as well as pathetic.

Gasping, I limped to a wet park bench and tried to stop crying long enough to compose myself and figure out what to do. The street was mostly empty; what few people there were carefully avoided my eyes and quickened their pace. They thought I was crazy. If my current state of mind was any indication, maybe I was.

A photograph fell into my lap. Through my tears, I recognized myself leaving Michael's apartment. "What's a nice girl like you doing in a place like this?"

The voice, like the photograph, appeared to come out of nowhere.

Where is he? Where is *he?*

"Please, don't get up on my account." I wheeled around to see the Sniper leaning against the bench, looking down at me. "Where is your big, bad boyfriend?"

He'd taken a page too many from Adrian's book. "Michael isn't my boyfriend."

The Sniper shrugged. "You shouldn't be wandering around in such a big city all by yourself. Even if it *is* Seattle — he shouldn't have let you go off all alone."

"Who said I'm alone?"

He clicked his tongue. "Don't be coy, my dear."

"What do you want? Are you here to kill me?"

"If I was, I wouldn't have let you see me."

The chill of the air hit me like a blow.

"Actually, it's quite fortunate you turned up when you did. Especially since I just received a phone call telling me that there's been a slight change of plans. I *had* intended to get you both together, but now that I have you, my job will be so much simpler."

I got to my feet and tried to remain calm. "What do you mean?"

"Any second now, he will come looking for you." He produced a gun. "I will then escort you both to the IMA."

I wondered if anyone was close enough to hear me scream. "Stay away."

"Please, don't run. These aren't real bullets, but I would hate to knock you out. You are ever so much more entertaining awake, and I'm not sure I'd be able to carry you." His expression soured. "My partner appears to have disappeared."

Shit. He had backup.

I ran, wishing I hadn't tired myself out or paused in such a deserted place to rest. My foot ached sharply each time it made contact with the ground. A pocket of air gusted past me, followed by the sound of a small explosion. The Sniper was shooting at me. Warning shot. I didn't believe that anyone called The Sniper would miss on accident at such close range.

Run. Run until you find something to hide behind.

I ducked behind a filthy garbage can. The Sniper sighed. "You're making this far more difficult than it has to be."

"Go to hell."

"Did Michael ever tell you how he got his scar? No? He got it while he was running away. Same as you."

There was an alley up ahead, about twelve feet away. The Sniper appeared around the corner of the trash can and pointed the gun at me. "You won't make it."

I glanced at the alley. Then at him. Then I pushed off the ground with my arms, windmilling as I staggered over the wet, uneven concrete, trying to keep my wounded foot from making direct contact with the ground. He fired off a shot.

He missed.

"I told you not to touch her."

The Sniper was face-down in a puddle, spluttering. Michael was kneeling on top of him, binding his wrists behind his back. "Arrogant, *cocky* little fuck. Don't act surprised to see me."

Michael glanced up. Our eyes met, and my breathing stopped.

"You see," the Sniper said smugly. "I told you he was going to come — "

Michael kicked him in the side, hard. "You're a regular fucking mind reader. Why don't you try to predict what's going to happen to you if you don't shut the fuck up?"

The Sniper shut up.

A phone rang. Michael frisked him and pulled out a black cell, which he crushed under his boot heel. With a grunt, he picked up the struggling Sniper and said, over his shoulder, "What are you waiting for? A red carpet? Come on."

"I don't have shoes on, and there's glass in my foot."

Michael closed his eyes. "Fine. Then wait there."

Michael:

Weapons concealment was a basic technique but I was still impressed. Seattle offered the perfect conditions for the Sniper to wear his long, heavy coat without being suspect. After tying him up, I realized it would have been more convenient to remove the coat first, since I'd have to search him later. With an irritated sigh, I gave him a brisk pat-down against the hood of my car and confiscated several weapons, including his knife. He also had several different types of cameras in his possession — digital, Polaroid, and disposable. I suspected the first was his primary tool and the second two were backups, to be used in a pinch.

I sliced off his coat with the knife I'd just confiscated. The Sniper clenched his jaw and I knew the other pockets must contain something valuable — or incriminating — to elicit such a response.

From the sour expression on his face, The Sniper realized this, too.

"You're persistent," I said. "I'll give you that."

"I caught you off-guard. You and the girl."

"Shame you felt the need to gloat." I shoved a gag in his mouth, ending the conversation, and shut the trunk with a satisfying slam. I smashed the camera in my hand on the blacktop. The lens cracked. Twisted fragments of plastic, glass, and metal scattered around my feet. I kicked the pieces into a nearby puddle. The water would take care of the rest.

I pried open the backs of the other two cameras with my thumbnail, removing the film. I left the empty shells on the ground but tucked the film rolls in my pocket. Sunlight exposure had probably damaged them sufficiently, but I planned to shred them just in case.

That done, I scooped up Christina. "Where are your shoes?"

"I...forgot them."

She was deposited into the front seat. I tossed the wadded up raincoat in back. "That was foolish." She always let her emotions get the best of her.

"Where is the Sniper?"

"In the trunk."

"Oh."

I turned the ignition key. The seat belt alarm went off. I looked at her. She had her hand on the door handle. I pressed the lock button and she whipped around to look at me when she heard the mechanical thunk. "You planning on jumping out of the car now?"

I fastened the seat belt for her. It gave me an excuse to get closer. "Why did you run from me? Callaghan had a camera installed in the door frame of my apartment. He *saw* you leave. Alone — and unarmed." She flinched; I wasn't sure if it was because of me, or him, or the volume of my voice, which was rising. "You could have been killed. Where did you think you were going? You have no weapons, no money, no ID" — I let my eyes rake over her — "no shoes. You have only a rudimentary understanding of self-defense. Very rudimentary. What the hell were you trying to accomplish?"

"I needed to get away. I needed to think — "

"Clearly," I said, cutting her off, "You didn't. Think."

"But — "

"If you want to survive, you do what I say. It's that simple. And just in case it wasn't obvious before, rule number one is *don't* go running around like a chicken that just got its fucking head cut off. For your future reference."

"You also told me you didn't want anyone else but me. That you were in love with me."

"I also recall telling you that emotions make people stupid," I growled.

"Yes," she said. "They do."

Nothing could have prepared me for what she did next. She wrapped her hands around my wrists and kissed me. At first I was too startled to respond. And then I was afraid to. Afraid that any movement on my part would make her come to her senses and stop.

There was a click. She was unfastening her seat belt. My heartbeat began to race when she climbed onto my lap, and began to kiss my neck. *Oh God.* I turned my head to give her better access. Her mouth felt so good against my skin. I dug my hands into my thighs to keep from touching her and jerked in surprise when she yanked my shirt off my shoulders. "What do you think you're doing?" I panted.

"Isn't this what you want?"

She sounded curious, but there was a mocking edge to her voice that I'd never heard before. Her nails grazed down my bared chest. "No."

"But you said — "

"In your seat."

"I want to know — "

"Now."

I waited until I heard her fasten her seat belt.

"There are two things about me you should know. Don't fight me, unless you're prepared to kill me. And don't kiss me, unless you're prepared to fuck me." My neck throbbed. I didn't touch it. "I'm not a goddamn science project that you can experiment on."

"I wasn't — "

"Don't talk to me."

Neither of us said anything more after that, but I could feel her eyes on me as I drove. I didn't speak again until I stopped the car in front of my apartment. "Stay in the car until I remove the camera." I opened the glove compartment and took out a pair of leather gloves. Her face became drawn at the sight of them, which prompted me to remove the keys from the ignition. Was Callaghan watching me walking alone to my apartment? Wondering if I had failed?

I dragged a chair out of the kitchen. With a screwdriver in my mouth, I stood on top of the chair, examining the ledge for signs of tampering. It took me a while but I finally found the camera buried deep inside a knot of wood. I pried out the dime-sized device and crushed it beneath my boot heel. Then I returned to the car, picked up Christina, carried her up all three flights of stairs, and dropped her on my bed. Her white shirt was stained and she'd somehow managed to get herself covered in grime. The soles of her feet were especially filthy.

"What about the Sniper?"

"When I'm finished with you, I'll deal with him." I grabbed a washcloth and the first aid kit from the bathroom, cursing her for making me feel this way — so torn up inside and confused. After running away, and coming on to me in the car, that was all she had to say for herself? She winced as I washed off the mud. Good. I couldn't be bothered to search for any hidden wellsprings of pity and didn't expend any extra effort trying to be gentle. Once her feet were clean, I got a better look at the damage. She'd gotten a shard of glass embedded into her heel. All that walking had lodged it in pretty deep. "This is going to hurt," I told her. "Keep still anyway."

She nodded, biting her lip.

I dug in with the tweezers, trying to get a grip on the edge of the damn thing. "Almost got it." Her knuckles whitened as she gripped the sheets. I pulled the bloody shard free and dropped it into the trashcan. The wound was bleeding, which was a good sign; it meant no more foreign objects were obstructing blood flow. I swabbed the area with alcohol, working the antibiotic solution in with a Q-tip. Then I wrapped her foot in gauze. I hoped it wouldn't get infected but lately, my luck hadn't exactly been stellar.

"Thank you," she said in a small voice.

I replaced the first-aid kit beneath the bathroom sink, tossed the dirty washcloth in the hamper, and washed my hands. I walked back into the bedroom and retrieved my handgun from the bottom right-hand drawer, where it had been tucked beneath my winter clothes. I loaded the bullets with a sharp snap. "If you want to thank me, stay put right here." I let my expression harden. "If you try to run from me again, I'm going to tie you up. Understand?"

"Yes."

"Good."

I'd be lying if I said I wasn't secretly hoping she'd disobey me. I walked back out to the car. Opened the trunk with my free hand so that the gun would be the first thing the Sniper saw. "I'm going to untie you briefly," I told him. "But if you try to escape, I'm going to hurt you. Badly. Got that?"

He brought his head down in the affirmative.

"Good."

It was a nice change, having people listen to me. I missed that feeling. I left his gag on, though, just in case. There was no need to tempt fate. I grabbed the chair I had used to fix the roof, still keeping one hand on the Sniper, and positioned it in front of the TV. "Sit down."

He sat, looking defiant as I retied his arms around the back of the chair. I spread the raincoat over my lap and started going through the pockets. "What's this?" I asked, holding up a zip-lock bag of black plastic canisters. "More candid camera?"

His eyes narrowed over the gag. I returned his stare, wondering what to do with him. He could be a potential wealth of information if he decided to talk. He could also be a threat if he managed to escape. And that was a distinct possibility. Callaghan wasn't foolish enough to send one man alone — the Sniper would have backup. I could kill him, but that would be messy. I'd have to dispose of the body, the murder weapon, and all other traces of evidence, including the car. It would be a waste of precious time and resources. So would feeding him and keeping him under supervision. Decisions, decisions.

I tore the gag out of his mouth, causing him to fleck spit on the rug. "Well," I said, as he gasped for breath, "What do you have to say for yourself?"

"You have made a grave mistake, for which you will pay with her life."

"The only life here you should be worried about is your own."

"An empty threat. If you were going to kill me, you'd have done so by now."

"Perhaps." I strolled around in front of him with my hands behind my back, fingering the gun at my hip. "Or perhaps I'm trying to decide whether you hold any potential value to me — in which case, you aren't doing so well."

He laughed, the congenial front completely gone. "You have grown far weaker than we thought."

That earned him a cuff with the butt of my gun. "How many people did Callaghan send? I know you didn't come alone. He's crazy, but not stupid."

"If you want me to talk, you have to *make* me, pretty boy."

I hit him again, harder. Drawing blood. "Don't tempt me."

"He's going to kill her you know. He'll play with her until she breaks, and then kill her when he's bored. And then, when you cease to be useful to him, he'll kill *you*."

"Anything else you want to share?"

Silence.

"Nothing?" I stuffed the gag back in his mouth. "Well, I suggest you start talking soon," I said, heading back towards my bedroom. "Before I feel compelled to make you. And trust me, Sniper — or whatever the hell your real name is — that won't be fun for either of us."

Chapter Twenty-Five

Casualty

Christina:

I woke up in his bed — again. Unlike the last couple times, he wasn't in it with me. For a moment, I panicked, looking around the room to make sure I really was alone. I was. How long had I been unconscious? Not long. My clothes were still damp.

Oh, God. Michael. I squeezed my eyes shut as the memories of what I'd done flooded back. After that speech he'd given me this morning, about how I was basically a vile temptress intent on seducing him to get my way, what I had done would only serve to condemn me further in his eyes. But he hadn't taken advantage; he hadn't even kissed me back. He had just…frozen. If anything, he'd seemed insulted and — nervous. Michael nervous. It was almost an oxymoron.

Did that mean he had been telling the truth? *Was* he in love with me?

Then I had power over him. If I wanted to, I could hurt him. Badly. I could get him back for all the horrible things he had done to me over the past few months — if I wanted to. Did I want to? I thought of his intensity, his dark past, and how tired and sad his face looked on those rare instances when he let his guard down. My stomach fluttered uncomfortably, my conscience torn. Even though I still carried all that pain and anger inside of me, he had tried to redeem himself. By all accounts, he was no longer the man that he once was.

The fifty million dollar question is: Who is he now?

The door opened. It was Michael, bringing food. His face, as he approached, was careful. He was wearing the same shirt from this morning. I could see the black strap of his holstered gun running across his bare chest. His voice was as cool as his eyes as he set down a sandwich and a soda and said, "Have a nice nap, darlin?"

"I didn't realize I'd fallen asleep."

"I didn't drug you, if that's what you're implying." His eyes flicked to the door. "Don't come out of this room — the Sniper is being difficult."

"You brought him *here*?"

"I can't just leave him in the trunk, and I can't let him go. He knows too much."

Like me, I realized, with a sudden sense of coldness. "What are you going to do with him? Are you going to kill him?"

His jaw tightened. "I'm not sure."

I reached for the soda, unscrewed the cap — it was sealed, this time — and took a long drink. My favorite brand. I wondered if that was an accident; it wasn't one of the popular sodas, not the kind usually grabbed in a pinch. I was conscious of him watching me as I drank.

"Why did you kiss me?" he asked.

I nearly choked. "In the car?"

"No," Michael said, "At the fucking prom. Yes, in the car. You said you wanted to see something, that emotions made people stupid." He walked over to my side of the bed and sat down. "Were you jerking me around, Christina? Are you trying to play me?"

"N-no…"

"No?" I saw his eyes drop briefly to my mouth before returning to my eyes at twice the intensity. "What were you trying to prove? Or did you want something?"

I shook my head. Part of me wanted to move away but my body refused.

"Nothing? I have nothing that you want?" His face was so close to mine, the emotion in his voice like a taut cord about to snap.

I blurted out the first thing that came to mind. "How did you get your scar?"

"My scar," he repeated.

I didn't let my gaze stray from his face. "Yes. The one on your stomach."

Michael leaned back, letting out his breath as if he'd just taken a heavy drag on a cigarette. "Is this because of what the Sniper said?"

"He said you got it while you were running away."

"Jesus." Michael closed his eyes, rubbing at the sides of his face with his hands.

"Please tell me. I want to know. I'm curious. I want to" — my voice broke — "understand you."

"Good luck with that. I don't understand myself."

I took a bite of sandwich, figuring that meant the subject was closed. He didn't follow up with an insult, though, the way he usually did when he tried to push others away, and his mouth was a rigid line as if he was holding something back that he desperately wanted to say.

He growled impatiently. "If you really want to know," he said at last, "I'll tell you. But this stays between us — understand?"

I gulped down my mouthful of food too quickly and had to take a swig of soda to keep from choking. *He's going to tell me?* I resented the extra seconds; each one gave Michael another chance to change his mind. "I won't tell anyone."

His eyes regarded me for a long moment. "Well. I was young when I first started working for the IMA. It started when someone saw me in a gang fight — a scout. This was back in Louisiana. I was alone and cornered, and took out several men twice my size. That man was impressed enough to offer me a job. The shift from petty crime to high-pay mercenary work seemed glamorous to a kid like me."

He smiled crookedly, deprecatingly, and it rendered his face disarmingly handsome and boyish. His eyes, however, remained hard, fixed at some distant point beyond me.

"I was assigned a trainer to teach me various fighting styles designed to impair or subdue. I learned how to fire a gun, how to use knives. I learned methods of torture, and how to cause pain without leaving a bruise or breaking the skin. And I learned how to intimidate." Here, his eyes locked with mine. "I was already intimidating, because of my size. He improved on that."

"Adrian," I whispered.

Adrian had told me himself that he'd trained Michael — taught him everything he knew — but it was still strange having it affirmed. I wasn't used to Michael being forthcoming, nor to Adrian telling the truth.

Michael looked surprised for a moment, then nodded. "Callaghan is one sick son of a bitch, don't get me wrong, but he knows what he's doing. And he was the only one who wasn't turned off by the idea of coaching some street-rat gang-banger. Most of us have at least some degree of formal education. Some are ex-military. Most have been trained for this all their lives. It's unusual for someone as" — he hesitated, as if trying to find an appropriate word — "unpolished as I am to be accepted into the program."

"Adrian told me you transferred out of yours."

Michael looked surprised again. Then he laughed humorlessly. "Did he tell you why?"

I shook my head.

"He tried to kill me."

I set the sandwich down, abandoning my pretense of eating. I hadn't even touched it within the last couple of minutes, anyway. "He *did*?"

"Mm-hmm. I was doing agility training. Callaghan was teaching me to dodge and block. Size has its limitations; in a fight against someone slighter, I was at a disadvantage." He took a sip of my soda, grimacing at the sweetness. "I was getting pretty fucking cocky by that point. Callaghan noticed, and took it as a challenge. One day he come up to me and instead of beginning the lesson, he simply told me to run. 'Run where?' I said. He looked at me, just like this" — his eyes frosted over with dead impassivity — "and said, 'Away.'"

I shivered.

"I began to think he was serious. So I did run. Faster than I've ever run in my goddamn life. Callaghan chased me down six hallways and two flights of stairs before he finally caught me. But he caught me; he doesn't seem to get tired. He slammed me back against the wall and said, 'Pathetic, Michael. Ah thought Ah'd trained ye betta than that. If ye can't outrun *me*, ye can't outrun a boolet.' He pulled out his knife, and then said, 'Dodge this, boy.'"

Cloak and Dagger by Nenia Campbell

Michael ran his finger along my stomach slowly, tracing the mirror image of his scar against the front of my dampened t-shirt. "Oh my God."

"The bastard nearly eviscerated me — and he laughed. Like he thought it was some kind of a big fucking joke." He dropped his hand from my shirt and took another swig of soda. "I managed to crawl to the hospital. They patched me up. Callaghan felt like his point had been made, so he didn't come after me again — but he never let me forget, either."

I felt sick now, nauseous. "And that's how you got it?"

"Yes." He sighed.

"I'm sorry."

"I don't want your pity." He roughly set my soda back on the nightstand. "I told you because I want you to understand what you're up against. Callaghan is a psychopath. He doesn't feel pain or emotion. He lives for causing fear through sexual and physical violence. That's why he always runs down his victims before he kills them. It's why he uses a knife and not a gun. And if he catches you… I don't know what I'd — "

A heavy pounding sound came from the living room. Michael's eyes shifted unwillingly to the door. The pupils were dilated, making his eyes darker than usual, and he looked wild.

"You should get that," I mumbled.

As if agreeing, the sound repeated.

Michael:

As I walked through the living room, I ignored the Sniper's glare. It was nearly ten o' clock. Who would be at the door *now*? It was too late for solicitors. Had Callaghan decided to make good on his threats? I automatically reached for gun, making sure it was still there. It was.

I opened the door without speaking, and almost went for the Firestar when a shadowy figure lunged from the darkness. Shannon. "What — " was as far as I got before she *flung* herself at me like a child. I pushed her away from me. She was wearing camouflage pants and a black bandeau top beneath a frayed army surplus jacket. I was about to ask her what she didn't understand about the word "no" when I realized that she also had tears in her eyes. "What the hell are you doing here?" I demanded. "What's wrong?"

"A man came to my apartment. He said he was looking for you."

I folded my arms. "What did he want?"

"He didn't say, but he was a big man and," her voice dropped, "I think he might have been carrying a gun."

Big? *Shit.* "How tall?"

"Um…" She had to think. "About your height, but thicker around the middle."

Not Callaghan then. *Good to know.* But it didn't sound like anyone else I knew, either, which meant that he'd been busy hiring new recruits. That was bad. "I'll look into it," I said. "Don't go home tonight. Stay with a friend or at a hotel. One with a decent security system."

Shannon knew enough about me that I couldn't risk having her captured and interrogated. I entertained the possibility of hightailing it to her apartment for a reconnaissance mission. The soil around the complex would still be soft from the rain. I might find a footprint — and if the hired thugs were as incompetent as the Sniper, they might have left other clues, as well.

Oh shit, the Sniper. I hadn't been expecting company or I would have moved him into the kitchen. Subtly, I adjusted my posture, blocking as much of the living room from her view as possible. "Is that all?" I asked casually.

Shannon bit her lip. "I thought I could stay here."

"Not possible."

"But I feel safe with you!"

"You shouldn't!" I informed her. "Not if these men are asking after *me*."

"Why are you forcing me away?" she demanded, defiance flashing over her made-up features. Odd. She'd had time to put on her makeup before dashing over here? "Don't you care about what happens to me? I thought we were partners."

"I'm a busy man." I began to close the door. "You'll only be in the way."

"Busy doing what? Or should I say *who*?" Before I could stop her, she stood on tiptoe to look over my outstretched arm and caught a glimpse of the Sniper. Her eyes widened. "Is that a man tied up in your — "

I clapped a hand over her mouth — to my disgust, her lips were sticky with fresh gloss — pulling her over the threshold before she could alert all the neighbors. "Quiet!" She said something incomprehensible. I didn't care what it was. "Quiet," I repeated.

She went still.

I leaned back against the closed door, keeping her pinned, and tried to decide what to do. Now that she had seen the Sniper, I couldn't allow her to leave without some kind of cover story. Or keeping her here, as another hostage. I wasn't wild about either option, but I was far less wild about the latter. I released her, lowering my hands back to my sides.

"That man is the Sniper," I said, before she could demand an explanation. "I've been interrogating him, trying to find out who he reports to."

The best lies always contain an element of truth.

"One of the mobsters?" Shannon stared at the man in

fascination. He stared back. Probably because of the gravity-defying top she was wearing. "God, for a moment I thought — "

"What? That I've started my own BDSM club and your invite got lost in the mail?"

Her face flushed, but she wasn't deterred. "Why didn't you just *tell* me?"

"Because it's none of your fucking business. I don't know how to make it more clear."

"Ed…" She ran her hand down my jaw. She'd always liked doing that. I'd never enjoyed it, permitting the action only because we slept together and I'd felt obligated to. I wasn't about to tolerate that from her now. I turned my head away.

"That's enough. You should leave now, before it gets later."

Shannon yanked her hand away so quickly that her nail scratched against the skin. I winced, prompting her to start prodding at my throat. I batted her away. Her face reddened further, with anger instead of chagrin. "That teenaged *slut*. Really, Ed? With her own bodyguard?"

"I would appreciate it if you did not discuss this in front of my hostage." The Sniper was leaning forward in his restraints, watching the scene with obvious amusement. All he needed was a bowl of fucking popcorn and it'd be a regular night at the movies. "Issue *some* restraint."

She ignored me. "Don't play coy. You and I both know that you're doing a lot more to her body than guarding it." She glanced at my mouth. A small smile twisted her lips. "Is that how she's paying you, Michael? I had no idea your going rate was so low — or do you just get off on the power trip?"

A warning buzzed inside me. I was too angry to head it. "Shut your mouth right now."

"Don't talk to me like that. I'm your supplier. You *need* me."

"I need your skills, not you. And if you persist in acting this way, I'll get those skills from somebody else." I caught her hand before she could touch me again. "Which would be a pity, because when you're not burdened by foolish distractions" — I gave her a harsh look — "you're really useful. But if you *ever* slide your hands down my pants again, or touch me in any way beyond a casual, business-like handshake, I'm going to break your fucking wrist."

Shannon blanched. "You would."

"Damn right."

"So that's how it's going to be?"

"That's how it's going to be," I agreed, watching her.

Shannon tugged her hand out of mine. "Fine."

"I'm glad we have an understanding." I turned back towards the living room. "Give me a moment. I'll escort you to a hotel. You can walk yourself in — you understand."

She called me a name I pretended not to hear. I went back into my bedroom, leaving Shannon to wait in the living room alone. Christina was still sitting on my bed, pretending to drink the now-undoubtedly-flat soda. Her posture was defensive.

"Listening at doors is a bad habit," I said.

"Would you have really broken her wrist?"

Yes. I glanced at the door. "I'd rather find out. I need you to watch the Sniper while I'm gone. Can you do that?"

"You told me not to talk to him."

"You won't have to; he's gagged."

She nodded briskly. "Fine."

"I won't be gone long. I don't think I need to tell you not to untie him — or run away."

"Ed! Ed? Where did you go?" Shannon cried from the living room.

Christina looked at the door, frowning. "Is she — ?"

"I'm taking her to a hotel. She doesn't like that. But she'd like staying here a lot less." I grabbed a coat from the closet and buttoned up my shirtfront. "Don't do anything foolish while I'm gone. Just do as I say, and you'll be fine."

"I thought you died in there," Shannon said when I came back.

"Couldn't find my jacket. I have to lock up. Go wait at the car."

The sound of the lock turning was loud in the darkness. I

frowned up at where the camera had been. Shannon was being dealt with. Christina was watching the Sniper. The door was locked. But I still had that nagging feeling telling me something was wrong. I shrugged, and made myself turn away. *Nerves. All of them. Synapsing at once.*

Christina:

I waited until Michael and Shannon were gone before leaving the room. Even then, I took my time, showering and changing into some clean clothes. I doubted the Sniper would take me seriously in the stained pajamas from that morning. I pulled on some jeans and a snug black t-shirt, knotting my wet hair back with a rubber band that had held one of the clothing bags in a twist.

The Sniper leered at me over the gag as I poured myself a glass of water. It was disconcerting that he could look so dangerous while bound. I glanced at him, trying to keep my own face impassive as I channel surfed, wondering what he knew to make Michael keep him alive. I could see him watching me in the corner of my eye the entire time. Trying to intimidate me. Knowing the purpose behind his actions made them no less creepy.

The news wasn't much friendlier, and there weren't any cheery cartoons on this late. Michael had shitty cable. I turned off the TV and dropped the remote on the floor with a sigh. I checked on the

Sniper: he was still looking at me, pausing only to blink.

"Creep." *It doesn't count as talking to him if I'm saying it to myself.*

To take my mind off my sketchy charge, I took an impromptu tour of Michael's apartment. He didn't have much stuff; it was a brief tour. Soon I found myself back in the living room with the Sniper, sitting on the couch and staring at a blank TV while he watched me as if I were a mildly entertaining television program. Ten minutes went by, then fifteen. Michael had told me not to speak to him but after thirty minutes of this one-sided stare-down, I broke that rule.

"What?"

His eyes went to the gag.

"I don't think so," I said.

He shrugged and continued staring at me. If I moved, his eyes followed. He tracked my progress to the sink to refill my water glass, then back to the sofa as I sat down again, then to the corridor that led back to the bedroom as I began to pace nervously. "Cut it out!" I snapped.

If he hadn't been gagged, I swear he would have laughed.

"Fine. I give." I untied the cloth around his head, yanking it out of his mouth, and he drew in a loud, rather desperate breath. "It's off — what do you want?"

"Only the pleasure of your charming company."

"No wonder Michael gagged you. Did you taunt him like this,

455

too?"

"Michael isn't nearly as entertaining as you are, my dear."

"Bite me."

"Careful," he said mildly. "I might take you up on that later."

He is a creep. "You have a pretty good understanding of our idioms, considering that this isn't even your native language. You have to be fluent to engage in that kind of wordplay."

"Ooh. Clever girl."

"It's not a matter of cleverness. It's *experience*."

"Oh? Did *he* tell you that? Is that how he got you into his bed?"

My mouth dropped open. For a moment, I couldn't speak. The sound of his laughter made my anger rise sharply in response. "That's enough!"

"Don't pick fights you cannot win." He shrugged again, that Gallic shrug that adds a calculated degree of carelessness to everything spoken. "Besides, I am afraid that when it comes to women, Michael's reputation precedes him. He has a rather short attention-span, as I am sure you are already aware."

"Your syntax is what betrays you," I said, in spite of the strange emotions coursing through me at his words. "You spoke one of the Romantic languages originally, right?"

"I'm rather surprised he turned his shapely friend down."

I gritted my teeth. "But it wasn't Spanish."

"On the other hand, he always did like them young — and she must have been pushing twenty-five, at least. Perhaps older. Asian women age so well, it is difficult to tell."

I jabbed my finger at him. "You're Italian."

"*Si, sono corrette, mia cara.*" He paused. "*Si, es correcto, mi querida.*" His accent was flawless in both. I was visibly startled and he laughed. "Mm. You looked so pleased with yourself, too. Would you like to hear my French? I can assure you it is far more eloquent than any of the sweet nothings Michael has undoubtedly whispered to you, in the pidgin abomination of the Cajuns"

I swallowed — hard. "Do you want to be gagged again?"

"By all means, enjoy your new found power while it lasts. But I can assure you, *mon chéri* " — his eyes met mine in a deliberate challenge — "the next time you feel a gag, it will be on *you*. *Comprenez-vous?*"

"What is that supposed to mean?"

But it looked like the Sniper had finally decided to be quiet. So when somebody knocked on the door, it echoed through the silent apartment like the prelude to a storm. *Michael has a key. He wouldn't need to knock.* I checked through the peephole on a hunch, and my suspicions were confirmed: the man on the porch wasn't Michael.

"Oh shit," I whispered, backing away from the door. "Oh *shit*."

I looked around for something I could use as a weapon. Michael didn't have a fireplace, so there was no trusty iron fire-poker. I opened the kitchen drawers to find that he didn't have any cutlery, either. *Damn you, Michael. Couldn't you have left me one measly weapon?*

The Sniper twisted his head around to watch my frantic search. "Something wrong?"

My eyes flicked to him, then past him at the dining table. *The chair.* I grabbed it by the back, scattering the huge pile of papers to the floor in a white cascade. "What do you know about this?" I demanded shrilly, as a rather alarming sound began to emanate from the door.

He's trying to break it down.

The door burst open. I raised my arm as the wood fragmented into dozens of tiny splinters. The intruder was tall, muscular, and dressed completely in black. He had long dark hair tied back in a ponytail, dark brown eyes, and brown skin. Exotic, without being distinctive. He could have been anything from Filipino to Native American, and there was no doubt in my mind he could tear me apart. I took a step backwards, taking the chair with me.

He looked at me, and frowned. "This is our renegade? She's just a kid."

"Be careful," the Sniper said from his chair. "She's fast."

"Go away," I cried, as I raised the chair. It was a half-hearted effort on my part; I already knew I'd lost.

"Sorry, kid. I have my orders. Make it easy on yourself. I don't want to have to hurt you."

He might not, but whomever he was bringing me to *would*. I threw the chair at him and ran into the bedroom, stumbling in my haste. How much time had I bought? Where was Michael? *Don't think about that — and whatever you do, don't look behind you.*

Michael's bedroom had a big window that overlooked a tree. If I could tear off the screen, I might be able to jump out and climb back down to the ground. I'd almost gotten the bedroom door shut when the tall man flung it open, knocking me to the floor. I sat up, rubbing at my head, and promptly felt something sock me in the chest with enough force to launch me backwards. There was a hot wave of pain — an echoed murmur — and everything around me melted away.

Michael:

Something is wrong. The words looped through my head like a malicious virus in the mainframe of my brain, taunting me, flooding my blood with epinephrine. *Something is wrong.* I forced myself to contemplate the long stretch of road that lay ahead beneath the cloudy sky. I could not afford to do anything rash — not in such a precarious situation — but my body didn't seem to be receiving the message. My blood pressure was too high, my central nervous system was far too aroused. Sitting in a car provided little opportunity to let off the stress that came with fight-or-flight impulses.

Shannon played with her necklace, zipping the charm back and forth across the chain with a buzzing sound that grated my ears like sandpaper. Sensing my scrutiny, she turned and smiled briefly, though the smile quickly faded when she glimpsed the expression on my face. "Ed?"

The name echoed ominously in my head. *Ed.* That was important, for some reason.

"Don't talk to me. I need to think."

It was pretty warm for a winter night in Seattle, hovering in the mid-sixties. The humidity in the air was as smothering as a wet blanket and made me sweat, though I wasn't hot. I switched on the air-conditioner, wondering how many people in those expensive buildings were also wilting.

Ed.

Jesus. I was jumpier than a girl on a first date. My sense of unease grew stronger as I drove downtown. A light drizzle spattered the windshield, blurring the city lights. On the other side of the glass, the world was in motion. Chaotic. Inside, it was frozen. I could tell my silence was eating at Shannon. She was growing more rigid with each passing moment.

"Ed?"

I just looked at her.

"Do you mind?" She blurted suddenly. She was fiddling with the car radio before I had time to respond. I stared at the knobs, a feeling of *deja vu* swarming over me as I remembered twisting one of the knobs clean off my old car, back on one of the passes in the Cascade Mountains. When Richardson called ordering me to execute Christina.

Before I had been branded as a traitor.

Bursts of sound came from the speakers as Shannon continued to switch stations, finally settling on an easy-listening song from the 90s. It didn't take long for the whiny guitars to wear my nerves as thin as the Euro-dance had. "I love this song," she babbled. "Don't you, Ed?"

A flash of…something…arced through me. "No."

"But it's so happy," she protested. "Romantic."

"No, it's not. It's about fucking crystal *meth*."

Shannon looked at me strangely. "So? It's a good song. Loosen up, Ed. You're so tense."

I didn't want to loosen up. I wanted to know what was gnawing at me. It had something to do with Shannon — she was hiding information from me. *But what?*

I took a deep, calming breath, tuning out the radio, and revisited this evening. When I had spilled my guts to Christina. The memory made me wince. I'd let her see me as less than strong. Weak, even. And by telling her, I'd shown her that I didn't care if she knew I wasn't without weakness — that I even *wanted* her to know it. And that, more than anything, was dangerous. I could no longer pretend that she was a hostage or a useful tool.

I really did love her.

Is that how she's paying you? Is that how she's paying you, Ed?

Wait. She hadn't said 'Ed,' now, had she?

Is that how she's paying you, Michael?

Bingo.

My mouth tightened. I pulled the car off the main road. Shannon started, looking out the dark window as I changed lanes to turn down one of the shadowy side-streets. The traffic had thinned out, leaving the road mostly empty. "Is something wrong?" she asked in a too-high voice.

"Yes," I said, cutting the ignition. "There is."

Christina:

My head felt as though somebody had packed it with several bushels of cotton. My temples pounded steadily in time to my racing heart. My chest was on fire. I tried to sit up and felt the pain lick through my ribs — the pain of old injuries awakened. A soft whimper escaped before I was conscious enough to reclaim it as I opened my eyes, which promptly widened in horror.

I was in a moving car.

It all came hurdling back, then — Michael's confession — getting attacked by the Sniper — Michael rescuing me — Michael leaving the apartment with Shannon — the Sniper's cryptic threats — getting knocked out. I tried to touch my chest, to inspect the damage, but my arms wouldn't move. They were bound behind my back with rope; they had trussed me up like a chicken for the chopping block.

The time on the dash said 3:00 in glowing green letters. AM, I guessed. Not PM. That meant we'd been on the road for several hours. The sky was a deep indigo that bordered on midnight, sprayed with stars that looked like cheap glitter. The horizon had a disturbing orange cast from massive light pollution, suggesting we were near a decently-sized city. *Seattle? Someplace else?*

I squinted, lifting my body up as carefully as I could in order to glance out the window. Judging from the speed at which the lights were whizzing by, we were moving along at a pretty fast pace — jumping was out of the question. *And the doors are probably locked, anyway.*

The Sniper chose that moment to look over, and I saw the light flash off his teeth as he grinned. "Well, well, well," he said. "Look who is awake at last. Sleeping Beauty. Did you enjoy your nap, my dear?"

I cursed at him, but the gag rendered my insults incomprehensible. I think he got the gist, though, because he started to laugh — hard. Which pissed me off. Who was he to make fun of me? Just who the hell did he think he was? Knowing I was cutting off my nose to spite my face, I lunged at the Snpier, trying to headbonk him.

"Feisty, aren't you? Cliff—look at this face." His gloved hands squeezed my face. "Isn't she absolutely terrifying? If looks could kill, hmm?"

"I'm driving," Cliff said coldly.

The Sniper's tone turned serious. "How long until we arrive at our destination?"

"About two hours." Cliff's voice was flat, deep. His lack of affect scared me far more than anger. Anger was predictable, and could be manipulated. This was different; he was completely dissociated from the situation. Compartmentalized. Removed.

Sorry, kid. Make it easy on yourself. I don't want to have to hurt you.

What would make a man like that stoop to pity?

The Sniper pushed me back in my seat, releasing my face. "Did I not say that you would be wearing the gag next time, my dear? Was I wrong?" I wanted to hit him. Grinning viciously now, he leaned in closer and whispered, "You know, Michael didn't find *all* my cameras."

My eyes widened.

"No," he said, pleased by my expression. "As I said, I do not specialize in guns alone. And my, my — that kiss was quite the spectacle. So much emotion. It was very…titillating."

"Sniper," Cliff grated. "You talk too fucking much. You've seen those movies with the men who compromise everything because they can't shut the hell up? Shut the hell up."

The Sniper rolled his eyes. "I hope you enjoyed your time together, because bad things are going to happen to you and Michael. No more fairytale kisses or happy endings for you."

"Don't torment her."

"Her boyfriend was rough with me," he said sulkily. "I have been looking forward to repaying the favor, in full. By proxy." He wasn't so brave when Michael was dealing with him. I remembered the terror in his eyes. That hadn't been fake. Perhaps the Sniper could read the scorn in my face because he said, "No, *he* won't be saving you this time. Unfortunately for you, lover-boy isn't the only one who likes them with a little fight." He pinched my cheek and slapped me.

"She has enough problems," Cliff said. "Leave her the hell alone. I mean it."

What was that supposed to mean? The gag prevented me from

asking, but the Sniper backed off, only saying, "I can wait." And the panic that I had been swallowing down suddenly threatened to bubble over, like a tea kettle left to boil.

Chapter Twenty-Six

Vendetta

Christina:

"Everybody out." The Sniper punctuated the command with a sharp tug that had me spilling out of the car on legs that felt liquid.

The other man, Cliff, united my gag. I inhaled a lungful of the cold, sweet night air. My chest ached sharply and my breath subsided into a cough, as if I had been breathing in smoke instead of mist. "You bastard," I said, in a cracking voice, "You're going to be dead when he finds you. Both of you — but especially *you*."

"I'm so worried," the Sniper said.

I was led down a series of long hallways. Not steel, like the halls I'd grown so used to in the Oregon base and on Target Island, but paneled walls and regular tiled floors. It looked like an office building, not a prison. Though if the base extended below ground, as the others had, there could very well be containment cells. *Which they might be taking me to.*

"Where are we going?"

"The boss insisted that we bring you back to HQ when we caught you," said the Sniper.

"The boss?" My brain hit a wall. "You mean — "

The boss.

Adrian.

"Mr. Callaghan."

I stumbled.

"Oh, don't worry. I'm sure he'll want to deal with you *personally.*"

I refused to give him the response he was looking for. I *refused.*

"Can't have you knowing the way there, though, can we?"

There was a small prick. The world went gray. Then black. Then numb.

Michael:

Shannon tried to make a break for the door. I pressed the lock button, trapping her. "W-what are you doing? You're scaring me, Ed. Let me out. I want out of the car."

"I don't really give a fuck what you want. Why were you sent to my house?"

"I — I don't understand. I told you, there was a man — and he threatened —"

"That's the story you were told to parrot, yes. I'm asking for the *truth.*"

"Ed — "

"You called me Michael, earlier."

"I did?" The horror on her face was more incriminating than any slip of the tongue. "My ex-boyfriend was named — "

"Bullshit."

"I — "

"Bullshit." I grabbed her by the front of her top, nearly yanking it off as I pulled her close to me. "Where did you hear that name? Was it the man you told me about earlier, if the man really does exist, or was it somebody else?"

"I-it was him. The man. The one who came to my house," she clarified, before I could force her to elaborate. "The one who was looking for you."

I shook my head slowly. "I don't know how I'm supposed to trust you."

"It's true! He *was* looking for you! He told me you were wanted by the police or...or something. I don't remember. Ed, *please* — "

I slammed my fist against the car door, inches from her face. "Stop fucking calling me that. The jig is up — my name is *Michael*. Never mind what *he* told *you*. What did *you* tell *him*?"

Her words were hitched and uneven. "Please...don't be mad..."

"What did you *tell* him?"

"He said if I told him where the girl was, you wouldn't be hurt."

"Fuck."

"I thought I was doing the right thing. I...you're an investigative agent. She's just some *girl*."

I slammed my fist against the door again. "Bull-fucking-shit.

You couldn't stand not being the center of attention for one goddamn second, could you? Parading yourself around in a — whatever the hell it is you're wearing — claiming you're in danger. Yet you still took the time to put on your face before you fled for your life. I suppose you thought you were doing yourself a favor, eliminating the competition. That you could *console* me for my failure. Is that right?"

"Michael — " Her face was white.

"You think you fucking know me? I'm an assassin. I kill people for a living. Good people, bad people, it makes no difference to me as long as I get paid." I spoke slowly, giving each word time to sink in. "And that girl you just sold out? She's the only thing in this world that makes me even remotely human."

I tightened my grip on her shirt.

"You better pray nothing happens to her."

Christina:

I nodded awake and found myself in a stiff-backed upholstered chair. There was a jade plant to my right, the nubby leaves glistening under the florescent lights like smooth wax. Beneath my feet, covering the expensive beige tile, was an Oriental rug the color of blood. The exotic scent of tea filled the air, thick and heady, making me painfully aware of my parched throat and dry lips.

Cloak and Dagger by Nenia Campbell

"Good morning," a familiar voice lilted.

Adrian was sitting behind the desk across from me, still as a statue, with his hand at his mouth. He looked exactly the same as I'd seen him last time, except his hair was shorter and looked professionally styled. Instead of the tailored, preppy wear, he was wearing a three-piece suit. Or part of one. The jacket was hanging over his chair, leaving him in a starched white shirt and charcoal suit vest. The scarlet tie matched the carpet.

"What do you want from me?"

His faint smile was the only indication that he was aware of my terror. "That," he said musingly, "Is a complicated question with many answers. For now, consider yourself my guest. Tea?" He nodded at the silver tea service beside him.

"No." The thought of being his "guest" was almost as terrifying as being his victim. I eyed him warily as he shrugged and poured himself a cup.

"I must admit, I didn't think it would be quite so easy to capture you. I expected a greater challenge." I watched him take another sip before pushing the cup aside. The subtle movement made me notice a manila envelope on his desk.

"Sorry to disappoint." I tried to sound blasé.

"Oh, but you haven't." Adrian opened the envelope with a care that bordered on fastidious; it would have been laughable if I hadn't already known how much pain those hands were capable of inflicting. "Nor Michael, either, I imagine," he added, glancing at the photographs.

I tore my eyes from the photos. "I don't know what you mean."

"I think you do." Adrian was watching me now, gauging my reaction. "I'm sure you realize sexualization is a method of objectification. It creates distance. Debasement. Power. A common defense mechanism for those who have trouble dealing with affection or attachment."

"Thanks for the psychology lesson. Where do I enroll?"

He slapped the folder down on the desk and stood up. Part of his technique was making people fill ill-at-ease, leaving small sinister promises of worse things to come. I understood what he was doing, but I still jumped when his hand landed on the back of my chair, inches from my neck.

"You breached his defenses," he said. "That makes you valuable to me. That's why you're still alive and...unharmed." I jumped out of the chair and hit the desk, nearly upsetting the tea service. Having the chair between us made me feel a little better, but not much. Adrian glanced at his watch. "But that could change. So tell me, Christina, while I still feel like listening. Have you anything else to say to me?"

"What do you want me to say?"

"A month ago you would have done anything to hurt that boy. You would have sold him out in a heartbeat. Remember the safe house? 'I'm being held hostage! Please! Help me out! You can take whatever you want from the house — just please, *please* help me!'" He laughed.

Hearing my own desperate words being tossed back at me in such a manner made me furious. "You *did* believe me then," I hissed, "All this time."

"Of course. But having Richardson suspect you was a necessary part of my plan." Adrian walked around the chair, prompting me to back away towards the sofa on the other side of the room. "Your connection to Michael made you an easy target. I saw an opportunity, and I took it." I received an appraising look. "In that sense, I suppose we're not so different."

"That's not true!" I cried out, even as part of me wondered. "You're sick. Michael told me what you di — " Too late, I realized my mistake.

"Oh, he did, did he? Well, then you know how difficult it is to get him into a compromising position, don't you? To make him squirm? That's an achievement few can claim."

"I didn't do it on purpose."

"Didn't you, though?" Adrian said silkily. He folded his arms, glancing at a tank in the corner. A lone shark brooded at the bottom, swimming in and out of the shoals of fish. "Sometimes instinct can be enough. The locals on Target Island called me *el tiburón* because of my work, and what I do," he said absently, watching the large creature undulate through the water. The charcoal suit seemed to make his legs go on forever…rather like the streamlined tail of the shark. "Before you and Michael blew it up, that is. He's become quite the problem. I would pay quite a bit to have him brought to me. I wouldn't care how, or in what condition, as long as he was alive."

I was appalled. "You're going to kill him?"

"No, no. Not right away, at least." He smiled, but his eyes remained cold, focused on the aquarium. "He is still useful to me at the moment. But you…well, that depends…"

"I don't want to hurt anybody." Something hard hit the back of my legs. I let out a breath when I realized it was just the couch.

"How unexpectedly noble. But can you really afford such petty chivalry? I do not bargain. I will have your cooperation — with or without your consent."

My heart jumped into my throat at the suggestive way he pronounced *consent*. I tried to calm down, to keep my breathing steady. "No," I said, "I can't — "

He continued as if I hadn't spoken. "I have, in my possession, a tranquilizer in powder form. All you have to do is make sure he consumes it — all of it — and then, when he's fast asleep, you call me. I have him picked up, and let you go home…for good."

It was as if he'd picked up on my thoughts from earlier. I felt sick; despite thinking of myself as a moral person, I couldn't honestly say I thought his offer was unappealing. "What's the catch?"

Adrian lifted his eyebrows. "There isn't one."

"I don't believe you. If it was so easy, you would do it yourself."

"But he doesn't trust me — he trusts *you*."

And that was the catch: Adrian was asking me to break that trust in the worst possible way: by delivering him to the only man I suspected he truly feared. I held Michael's heart in my hands, and he was asking me to pierce it with a poisoned blade. Laid out so brazenly before me, the offer was no longer appealing; it was *wretched*. *I* was wretched.

"Screw you," I said unsteadily.

"Then let me show you something that may just change your mind." Adrian walked to his desk, pulling a key from his pocket. I watched him unlock a drawer, from which he produced a wooden display box with a glass frame. It contained such an erratic array of objects as to seem purely random, though all of them appeared to be personal items. I looked from the case of knickknacks to Adrian's pleased expression as he replaced the box in the drawer and relocked it. "I don't understand."

"The other option."

I waited, bracing myself for whatever horrible alternative he had in mind. He didn't disappoint.

Leaning so close that I ended up falling on the couch, he said, "Recognize this?" and produced a strip of rawhide from his collar. A ring dangled from it, white gold, set with a single opal. My eyes widened involuntarily and I felt the fingers of my right hand automatically brush the left.

"That's — "

"I like to keep around little somethings to remind me how much I enjoy my work. Souvenirs, if you will, from every assignment." He regarded my ring a moment longer. "You're the one that got away, Christina Parker. I thought I might keep this handy, for when we inevitably met again." It disappeared back beneath his collar. "So here we are. You and me. Do you think Michael might be persuaded to come if your life were suddenly...endangered?"

The thought of my ring being added to his collection of trophies, like a hunter displaying the severed heads of his game, made me sick to my stomach. I pulled away, and whispered, "No."

"You don't think so?" His gray eyes had an odd glint. Sick. He was so sick. I wondered if he had a trophy from Michael in there, which one might have been his.

"You're wrong. Michael doesn't love me — he never loved me

and if you can't see that, you must be…" I stared at the wall of his office for inspiration but that didn't help. All I could think about were severed heads and trophies. "I was just a convenience. He wanted an accomplice and a" — *say it* — "a quick fuck." I didn't have to feign the humiliated blush that colored my cheeks.

Adrian paused, glancing at me. It was a cold look, quick and appraising. I couldn't glean anything from it, though I hoped it meant that he hadn't believed I'd own up to what had transpired between us and that it would lend credence to my falsehoods.

"And I suppose," he said, running his fingers down his tie, "That he wouldn't be coming after you, at this very moment, because you would simply be another loose end? That he hopes I'll do the trimming for him? Is that the gist of it, Christina?"

"Yes," I said, relieved that he'd understood. "That's right."

Adrian shoved me back, hard. Hard enough to make my teeth rattle around inside my skull. "You persist in telling the most blatant lies. If you didn't amuse me so much, I'd make you pay dearly for such insolence."

I froze, a deer in the headlights. He stared back with the expression of a snake eying a cornered mouse, then pressed a button on his watch. The door opened and a guard entered the room, weapon drawn. "At ease," he said, without so much as a blink.

"What do you need, sir?"

"Have you gotten the trace on Boutilier?"

"He's on his way. One of the guard spotted him on Highway 99.'

"How soon until he arrives?"

"At the speed he's going? About twenty minutes. Sir."

"Twenty minutes," Adrian repeated, glancing down at me. "Tha is impressive."

"What are your orders, sir?"

"Guard the main entrance and prepare a welcome for the boy. We wouldn't want it to seem to easy, after all. But don't make it too difficult. I want him in here alive," he glanced at me, "and… relatively unharmed. Do what you must to make it convincing. Dismissed."

"What are you going to do?"

"It is foolish to lie to those who have the trade down to an art, Christina." He flicked open his knife. "Particularly since I have known Michael a long time." Cold steel pressed against my throat. "A *very* long time. I've never seen him act this way before. It's almost as if he genuinely loves you. And he does, doesn't he?"

I choked.

"I don't know."

"Do you love him?"

"I don't *know*!"

"And yet you slept with him, anyway. You're quite the cold-hearted little harpy." He bent to whisper in my ear, "It would be a pity to let Michael find you safe after all that effort, wouldn't it? Let's not disappoint him." With that, he let the knife slice through my shirt.

Michael:

Highway 99 was dark and empty. There were few lights, their brightness obscured further by the mist that hung in the air like a heavy curtain, which thickened as we got closer to the coast. I kept my eyes trained on the path my headlights burned into the darkness.

"Where are you taking me?"

Shannon had been silent for the last twenty minutes, and her voice nearly made me start. I debated on whether or not to answer. She had tried to escape at the gas station, when I stopped to refill the car, by honking the horn in an attempt to draw attention. The only attention she'd drawn was mine, and I was still pissed about that.

After a pause, I said, "To save the girl *you* got in this mess."

She looked relieved. "You don't need me for that."

"Nice try, Shannon," I said. "You're coming with me."

"I told you, I didn't mean to! I'm sorry! But it wasn't my fault. You have to understand that." Did I? From what I understood, she'd brought this on the both of them single-handedly. "Please, please, *please* let me go," she begged. "You can just let me off at the next stop. I promise I won't talk — to anyone!"

"You got involved in something that didn't involve you." I didn't take my eyes off the road. "Now you've got to suffer the consequences. Tough luck."

The base was on the Olympic Peninsula, a far distance from Seattle. It was the rainiest place in the country, and an ideal spot for lying low. The perpetually gray skies and an average rainfall of fifty inches per year did not make it an ideal traveling location. As I drove, a light drizzle began fall, becoming a steady pulsing rain.

I pulled up in front of the building around 5am. There were a few other cars in the lot. I unlocked the glove compartment and took out a handgun, eliciting an exclamation from the other seat. This was not the IMA as I had known it. Callaghan had likely implemented changes. Bad ones. I drew back the safety. I'd have to be ready — for anything.

"If you want to return to your apartment alive, I suggest you not do anything stupid. If you do, it won't be me you'll deal with — it'll be *them*." Her eyes flickered to the dimly-lit windows and I saw her bite her lip. "That's right."

"More spies?" she asked, trying and failing to sound defiant.

"Like you?"

"Not like me." I pressed the button for the trunk. "Worse." I got out the jumper cables I always kept around in case of emergency, and used them to tie Shannon to her seat. "It's a mob run by a man without a conscience. You've heard of psychopaths? He's the genuine article."

I picked the lock. Walked through the door. No alarm went off, which surprised me. Perhaps the alarm had been silent. I assumed it had. I walked briskly, the rubber soles of my shoes muted the echo of my footsteps as I passed through the halls.

I wasn't ambushed until I got to the staircase. Five guards: all of them wearing bulletproof vests, all expecting me. The first fired quickly. It was the move of an amateur. I went for him with my fists. I only had a couple bullets in my gun and I intended to save at least one for Callaghan.

I dodged a shot from one of the other guards and struck a hard blow on the back of the first guard's head. He went down without much fight after that, mouth hanging open, a strand of drool trickling out of his slack mouth to puddle on the title.

One of the other guards fired at me from behind. It was closer shot, far more accurate than the first guard had been. They obviously weren't trying to kill me, or I would have already been dead. Callaghan was probably still operating under the delusion that he could persuade me to work for him. This gave me a clear advantage — I intended to use it.

I landed a blow on the third guard, right under the jaw,

snapping his head back and stunning him temporarily. The second guard, who had fired the gun at me when my back was turned, made another lunge for me. I made the mistake of turning to confront the attack directly, and was grabbed from behind by the fourth guard. A swift kick to my abdomen winded me.

Grinning, the guard moved closer, readying for another attack. I aimed a kick at his knee, swiping his legs out from beneath him. The guard dropped to the floor, cursing, and the guard holding me said, "Hey — " and cuffed my temple, hard enough to make my ears ring.

Meanwhile, the third guard had recovered from my punching him in the throat and was moving towards me, his cocked-back fist and steely glare suggesting he wanted seconds. I waited, ducking my head at the last minute, so the blow landed in the face of the forth guard. He grunted in pain, releasing me from his hold, and I was free to whip out my gun and aim it at the third guard. "Where is your boss? Don't make me waste a bullet on you."

The second guard answered, "Second floor. Room three-two-seven C."

"If I find out you lied to me…"

"He's telling the truth," the fourth guard said. Both his hands were clasped to his face and his eyes were watering. The third guard had broken his nose when he'd tried to punch me.

I headed up the next flight of stairs. I had no other leads. If the guards were wrong, I could force the correct answers out of them on my way back down. The rooms passed by in a blur, only the numbers catching my attention. *There it is.*

I yanked open the specified door, which was unlocked, and entered the room. I wasn't sure what I had expected, but nothing could have prepared me for what I saw. It was an office — a nice one — but looked as though a cyclone had passed through. A tea service was scattered about on the floor with spilled tea soaking into the scarlet rug. Chairs were upturned. In the midst of this mess, Christina was trapped beneath the bastard. He'd trapped both her arms above her head with one hand. The other was out of view, hurting her. Her clothes were slashed — and her skin, where Callaghan had been too careless with the knife. She looked up, her face naked with misery. Something in her gaze made my stomach clench, filling me with fierce, wordless rage. "Michael," she whispered.

No.

Callaghan looked up, too. "I expected you thirty seconds ago, Michael. You're getting slow." Shaking his head, he got up without further pretense, leaving her lying on the floor like a discarded rag. I took off my jacket, draping it around her shoulders. There were marks on her throat where he had drawn blood and several others he'd clearly meant for me to find. I'd put a bullet in him for all of them.

"You bastard."

He slid his arms back into his shirtsleeves, ignoring me. A ring glinted at his chest, tied around his neck with a leather thong. It looked vaguely familiar, though I couldn't say why.

"What the fuck have you done?"

"I'm afraid your pretty friend will be out of commission for a while. Perhaps you should have gotten here faster, Michael."

I got to my feet. "Give me one reason why I shouldn't blow your head off right now."

"Letting passion rule you like a little boy," he scoffed. "Why am I unsurprised?"

I cocked the gun. Behind me, the door opened. I heard several clicks echo my own. With a sinking feeling, I realized my arrogance had led me straight into a trap. The guards on the staircase had, in retrospect, gone down far too easily. What if they had been instructed to miss, and threatened so that my attacks seemed like a bit of schoolboy fisticuffs in comparison?

I turned my head, and what I saw immediately confirmed my suspicions. Ten guards were standing in the doorway now. I even recognized a couple of them from Target Island. They did not look pleased to see me. The feeling was mutual.

Callaghan began to do up the buttons of his shirt. "The guards on the staircase were instructed to miss," he said, voicing my own suspicions. "These guards are under no such order. I don't think you'll be able to dodge their bullets quite so easily — unless you care to try?"

The taunt gave me pause. I knew full well who I was dealing with, and that his attempt at killing me was something he took great pleasure in lording over me, but at the same time, it lacked the usual ring of diplomacy I was accustomed to. The IMA was about the *appearance of choice*. Or had been. I said as much, privately thinking that Kent had been right all along. The IMA would have been better off with another leader. Any leader.

Adrian barked out a laugh. "Choice? I don't need to bargain with you to know you're desperate. You have no choice." He snorted. "To think you used to be the best. Pitiful."

"Not really," I bit back, "Not considering who the competition was."

The good-humored malice left his face, leaving him with the flat, dull eyes of a snake. "Drop the bloody gun, Michael Boutilier, before I let them fill your empty skull with bullets."

I let it fall to the floor with a clatter — I'd made my point. One of the guards quickly broke rank to seize the weapon and secret it away.

"You've had ample time to consider my generous offer."

Callaghan shook out his suit vest, frowning as he buttoned it over the shirt. "It's time for you to decide."

"I don't think working alongside a turncoat would be good for company morale."

"He's right, sir," one of the guards spoke up before the bastard could respond. "He already betrayed this organization once. His skills make him an even greater threat. The risk clearly outweighs the gain, in this case — with all due respect, sir."

"He also destroyed Target Island. Him and the girl."

"And killed off Agent Richardson to seize power."

What kinds of propaganda had Callaghan been spreading about me in my absence? And why did they believe it? No. That was a stupid question. A better one was, What had he done to make it so they couldn't afford *not* to?

I glanced at Christina and kept my mouth shut.

"Oh, but I intend to keep him on a tight leash." Callaghan sauntered over, reknotting his tie. I imagined strangling him with it, until his eyes popped. "If I even *suspect* he's planning on betraying us, his spirited little friend will take up permanent residence in my office and I will see to it personally that her stay is not a pleasant one." A cold smile. "For her, that is."

A few guards had the balls to laugh and jeer at that.

I wanted to kill him. All of them. Shatter the teeth in those smiles, tear out their eyes, and then rip them up and scatter the pieces to the wind. My hands formed fists at my sides. *Not now.*

"Besides," Callaghan continued, "The boy has many enemies. It would be all to easy to make them see my side of things. You may be strong, Michael, but you're human through and through. And humans are subject to certain weaknesses" — I did not look up, staring straight ahead and locking my jaw as he approached — "like death, and pain. I'm sure you remember what happened the last time you decided to get uppity with me."

"I'm not afraid of you."

"Oh no?" He leaned into my face, so close that I could taste his breath. I heard the guards shuffle uncomfortably, looking away. He placed his knife against my throat, over my jugular. There was blood on the blade. *Hers.* "Then maybe I *should* kill you."

"You won't. Not now."

"Overconfidence is a deadly trait."

"This isn't messy enough for you."

That made the bastard laugh; he was sick enough to find that funny. "You've a good poker face, Michael Boutilier." He folded the knife. "But a poor hand."

"Your men are right, though. I'll be watching and waiting."

"Spoken like a true mercenary. How very self-preserving."

"Not at all," I growled. "I'd sacrifice my life to end yours."

"Well. That makes it all the more interesting." He glanced at Christina. "I must admit, I rather had my heart set on you saying no. This compliance of yours comes as a disappointment."

I lunged towards him and was promptly restrained. The barrel of a gun dug into the back of my neck. One blast would obliterate my brain stem, causing instantaneous death. I didn't care. "If you touch her again, I'll rip your face off."

"No. What you're going to do now is get out of my sight, before my guards get careless with their aim and I decide to keep the lass." His eyes flicked towards the guards. "One of you escort them out," he said, as he strolled out of the room. "I don't care who. Everyone else is dismissed."

The guards loosened their grip. I pulled free with a shove and scooped Christina into my arms. She was conscious, but dazed. "Oh, God," she whispered. "Oh, *God.*" I opened my mouth to say something comforting in response, but nothing came to mind. I sucked at this making-people-feel-better shit and the whole situation had been caused by my lapse in judgment.

Shannon had better fucking behave.

"Come on," one of the guards said.

We walked to the parking lot in silence. I could see Shannon's shadow shifting around in the car, lit up by the guard's flashlight. If he noticed the extra passenger, he chose not to comment. "This your

car?" I nodded. He looked at the plate, memorizing the number.
"Get in the vehicle. Nice and slow. No funny business. I'll watch you
drive away."

I nodded again. *It's time to buy a new car.*

Shannon jumped as I pulled open the back door. "Michael? Is
that you? Who's…who's that?"

"The girl you almost killed," I said, taking a savage pleasure in
seeing her flinch. "Take a good long look."

"Is she all right?"

"No." I grunted. I couldn't tell the extent of the damage without
removing what remained of her clothes. I wasn't about to do that
with Shannon watching.

"What's wrong with her?" she persisted, as I got behind the
wheel.

"Assault and battery, physical and sexual. Hope you're proud of
yourself."

"You mean those men…" she trailed off. "Oh my God. What
have I done?"

She said nothing more after that. It was preferable to her brand
of conversation, anyway. I sped back towards the city, pulling up in
front of Shannon's apartment with a screech less than forty minutes
later. All of the windows were dark — I intended to keep them that
way.

"I'm going to let you out," I informed her. "But only on the condition that you *never* breathe a word about what happened tonight. To anyone. You've never seen me, you've never heard of me. I don't care if it's your mother, or your best friend, or even your fucking dog — if you tell anyone, I'll find out. And I'll come after you, and show you exactly how I earned my reputation. Are we clear?"

She nodded mutely, frantically, with such fervor that it was a wonder her head didn't snap off like a broken bobble-toy. I untied the cables. She made to get away. I caught her arm before she could quite succeed. "I mean it," I said softly. "Remember that."

Shannon swallowed hard, and nodded. I watched her go back to her apartment. She nearly ran up the steps in her haste. When the lights flicked off again, I pulled away from the curb.

Cloak and Dagger by Nenia Campbell

Chapter Twenty-Seven

Wreckage

Michael:

Change of plans. Far more pressed for time than I thought. How fast can you work? -M

I read over the e-mail. When I was satisfied, I began to translate it into a numerical encryption Kent and I had developed together several years ago. Kent had been a programmer in his time, back when computers still used punch cards, proving that old adage wrong: sometimes old dogs can *teach* new tricks.

I was finding it difficult to concentrate, though, and couldn't keep my mind on the code. Abstract reasoning had never been my strong suit and adrenaline was still surging through my body, rendering my thoughts frenetic and disconnected. After several more fruitless attempts, I came to the conclusion that I was being masochistic and shut my laptop.

A phone call might be safer, anyway. Now that I had been reinstated, the IMA would be monitoring me closely. Callaghan had made it quite clear that his regime was not going to be challenged. My cell phone and laptop were probably already bugged, as well as other devices I hadn't stopped to consider yet. I'd have to get a new phone, a new laptop, a new car. Keep tabs on them at all times. Warn my contacts about the step-up in security so their positions wouldn't be compromised — if they hadn't been already.

It had been a while since I had last spoken to Kent. Anything might have happened between then and now. I made a note to touch base with him as soon as possible. It was 10am now. Was the girl still asleep? I could run out and purchase a new phone. There was a Radio Shack within walking distance and a Fry's just a bit further down the block. If I took the car, I could be there and back within minutes.

I opened the bedroom door slowly. Christina lay motionless on the bed. In addition to my coat, she was swaddled in several sheets. As I entered the room, she stirred but did not wake. I wasn't sure if Callaghan was making empty promises; he knew I had the girl with me. If his men saw me leaving alone, he might take it upon himself to seize her to ensure my compliance. *To hurt her more than he already has.*

I turned to leave and ran into the desk chair, which toppled with a clatter. *Damn klutz.* Christina made a small sound. "Michael?"

I heard the wariness in her voice. I cleared my throat. "How do you feel?"

"Cold."

I reached up to switch off my ceiling fan and turned on the light for better visibility. The rope had left her with a bracelet rash. "How are your other injuries?" When she didn't respond right away, I added, "I can probably treat them — if you'll let me. Or I could call a doctor."

"No. You can, um, do it." She looked away.

I opened the nightstand drawer and tried not to speculate on what her initial hesitation and taciturnity meant. I gathered a handful of salves — antibiotics, topical analgesics, lotion — and a handful of gauze. I tasted blood when I sat on the bed and realized I'd bitten through the skin of my lip upon seeing the cuts and bruises that mottled her olive skin. *I'll kill him.* I squeezed the tube I was holding too tightly, getting antibiotic cream on my hand. I barely noticed. *I'll fucking kill him.* Christina winced when I touched her, prompting me to ask, haltingly, "Did Adrian Callaghan rape you?"

She stared at me in horror. I gritted my teeth at her intake of breath, trying to hold onto my slipping composure — but it was tumbling like a rock slide. *He better not have touched you. Answer me.*

I wanted to shake her from her silence. I wanted to pull her to me and have her in my arms. I wanted to stab that son of a bitch over and over in non-lethal places. The squeeze bottle fell to the floor with a clatter. Jesus. I was losing it. The only thing left to do was get out before the fallout.

As I stood, I caught a glimpse of how her face had changed. Her eyes were squeezed shut, tears coursing down her face. As if she thought *I* was going to hit *her*. The sight of that — her fearing *me*,

493

even now — slammed into my chest like a bullet. Knowing such fears weren't entirely unwarranted made the pain unendurable. I started for the door, not trusting myself to speak.

"Wait."

I paused in the doorway without turning around. I was breathing hard, winded almost. My facial muscles felt spasmodic. "What?" That sounded too abrasive. I tried again, "What is it?"

"Adrian didn't…he didn't rape me."

I whirled around. "Do you expect me to believe that? With what he did to your face, and your neck, and your body, and your — *fuck*."

"He wanted to make you angry. He wanted you to think that."

I tugged at the taut skin of my cheeks. "That sounds too convenient. You're lying."

"No! I'm not! He tried to bargain with me first. He had a drug — like a date rape drug — that he wanted me to slip into your drink… and seduce you. That's what it sounded like."

"Really." I went cold. Because we both knew I would have drunk it.

"It's not like that, what you're thinking!"

"And what am I thinking, darlin?"

"I don't know! But I'm telling the truth!" She looked at me then, with unhappy eyes. "He hurt me only because I refused to hurt you! He hurts me *because* it hurts you! Don't you get that? Don't you understand what that means?"

I stormed into the darkened kitchen, slamming the bottle of calamine against the varnished counter top. It bounced unsatisfactorily. I searched for something else, ended up settling for my fist. The pain was exquisite, but did nothing to balance out the turmoil I felt inside. I cursed, cradling my head and wishing I could squeeze out my headache with my bare hands.

He hurt me because I refused to hurt you.

He hurts me because it hurts you.

Was I that transparent? A soft shuffling sound from behind made me tense. *Yes.* I knew who it was. I could recognize her footfalls out of a crowd of fifty.

"He gave you the perfect out," I said. "Freedom and vengeance, all in one swing. Why didn't you take it?"

"That would be evil."

"Darlin, from what you've been saying all this time, so am I."

Christina shook her head. "No, you're not evil. Confused and damaged — and maybe even corrupted — but not evil. Not heartless." She paused. "You told me you loved me."

I shook my head. "I said emotions make people weak, too. Fucking look at me now. Look at *you*. Look what *love* gave us. You're worth ten of me."

The words were out of my mouth before I could stop them.

When I saw the expression on her face — pity, for *me* — I would have done anything in the world to take them back.

Christina:

I thought for a moment he was going to get angry again, but his face smoothed out and became blank. *You're worth ten of me.* His words made me uncomfortable. I wasn't so great. I'd considered taking Adrian up on his offer. Even now, seeing Michael sad and repentant made a small, dark part of me feel vindicated. "It was the right thing to do," I said uncertainly.

"Are you sure?" He sounded skeptical, as well.

"No..."

"Well, it's too late now."

"I've been thinking a lot about what you said. About...loving me." The way his eyes regarded me made me uncomfortable. With effort, I pressed on. "I'm not sure I'll ever be able to reciprocate your feelings. But I don't want to betray you, either. If you've found love..." I hesitated, about to say something about God, and how good it was that he had let Him into his heart, but decided against it. "Then that's good. It's like riding a bicycle; once you start, it's impossible to forget. It shows there's some good in you."

He shrugged. "You'd be the first to say so."

"There's a first time for everything."

"Hallmark sentiments." Michael raised an eyebrow, leaning back in the chair provocatively. "Does that mean you're not at all attracted to my body?"

I went red. "E-excuse me?"

"It's a reasonable enough thing to ask. We both know I won't be winning any Miss Congeniality contests — and you don't need to be in love with me for me to show you a good time."

Tears jumped to my eyes. "What the hell are you — "

"Joke. It was a joke, darlin. Even I have my limits." His face was torn. "First things first, though. You still have injuries you've been keeping from me." He leaned down and picked up the bottle of calamine lotion, gesturing with his hand for me to sit on his lap. "Strip to the waist."

Michael:

Her words had filled me with a warmth I didn't know I was capable of; a warmth I had been quick to suppress, because of the absent chill that would follow in its wake. I didn't think I had the capacity for affection — not the kind she wanted. I didn't say this, though. I wasn't a complete bastard. If she liked to think she saw good in me, if she wanted to take credit for it, I'd let her. She deserved that much.

I tried to remain clinical and distanced, but when she took off the remains of her shirt I got a raging hard-on, mobbed by recollections of the one night we'd had together. Callaghan wasn't the only sick fuck around here. There was a thin line between rough-and-tumble sex and outright sadism. If I'd had my way with her at the beginning, I might have done something similar to her. The thought filled me with regret and disgust.

Christina made a sound of pain, pulling away. Then she wrapped her arms around my neck and buried her face in my throat. I froze, startled, as the heat of her tears soaked into my wife beater. She was shaking with sobs. I ran my hand down her spine, as if she were a cat. This made her cry harder, and I yanked my arm back as if I'd been burned.

After a long silence broken only by whimpers, she said raggedly, "He was just like how you *used* to be."

"I'm sorry," I said. "So fucking sorry."

"That won't make me forget." She hid her face again. "It won't change how I feel. God, *why* — " Christina broke off, adding tautly, "You've changed. We've both changed."

I had certainly changed. For the worse. She probably wouldn't agree, but she'd have been safer with the old me. At least then I'd have been able to do what it took to keep her alive.

But she wouldn't have been happy. She would have been miserable, broken down until she was a mere shadow of herself.

She slept in my bed that evening anyway, curled into me, in my bed, wearing my shirt: the only thing in my bedroom that didn't belong to me. There was too much damage; Adrian had burned that bridge between us. She would forevermore associate my forcing myself on her with his sadistic abuse. And I couldn't let myself soften anymore for her sake, either, or we both would die. I was fucked, and not in the way I wanted to be.

Early the next morning I slipped out of bed, tugged on my shirt, and punched a familiar string of digits. Kent picked up in the middle of the first ring. "Hello?"

"It's me."

"Michael? I'm glad you're OK. I managed to locate the girl's parents. It wasn't easy, but since it was for you…"

"Thanks, but that's not why I called."

"Is something wrong?"

"Not exactly. I need a favor."

"I'll see what I can do. What kind of favor?"

So I told him.

I told him everything.

Christina:

I woke up alone.

His side of the bed was ice cold, which hurt me to the quick, until I remembered that this was his apartment; he had to take me home. He wouldn't just leave me alone. I wrapped myself in the blanket and got out of bed, where I promptly tripped over something. It was a bottle. I gasped, hoping I hadn't spilled any on the pristine, white carpet, but the bottle was completely dry. Had that been there the night before? I hadn't seen him drinking, and would have noticed the smell of alcohol his breath. Seeing the bottle gave me a bad feeling in the pit of my stomach.

I sat down in his armchair to watch the rain as I waited for him to come back. The black leather didn't smell like him, and now that I thought about it, neither had the sheets.

What did I really want? I didn't know the answer to that. I wasn't sure I wanted to. Thinking that all of the things I had done for him had been on a solely physical basis made me feel cruel and vain. Because when it came down to it, I was a teenage girl, impressionable and easily impressed by a pretty face and abs. Michael, the bastard, just happened to have both.

The door opened. I turned. Once again, the man wasn't Michael. It was the old guy—the one from the safe house. Kent.

I took a step back, tugging the hem of Michael's shirt down as far as it would go. "What's going on? Where's Michael?"

He took off his hat, respectfully. "Don't worry, Miss…Parker, was it?"

Cloak and Dagger by Nenia Campbell

"Christina," I said, groping on the floor for some jeans without taking my eyes off him. "What are you doing here?"

"I'm a friend."

How neatly he sidestepped the question, giving me a detailed answer without really telling me anything. Kent went right to the fridge and got a beer. He seemed to know his way around, so that was encouraging. I was scared, though. I wrapped my hand around the telephone, ready to use it as a weapon or call the police as necessary. "Kent?"

Kent inclined his head in my direction. He didn't seem surprised I remembered his name.

"Why are you here?"

"Michael sent me."

He did? "Why?"

"Because he is a young man and doesn't respond well to emotional crises."

"What...kind of crises?"

Sighing, Kent produced an envelope. "This might explain things." As he held it out to me, I noticed the seal was broken and glared at him. "He told me to read it first. I hope you don't mind."

I did, actually, but didn't say that as I took the envelope. It was a letter, addressed to me. There was no paper inside; the actual message was written on the flap.

This man will take you to your parents. Trust him, he's a close friend of mine.

And then, in much smaller writing, —

Thank you for everything.

"What is this?"

"A goodbye."

"I got that part. Why?"

"He loves you," Kent said quietly.

I crumpled the letter in my fist. "He doesn't act like it."

"He can't. He has no template for relationships. But those who know him well can tell…that he gets out of character around you. Which is why he can't afford to be around you. There are many people out there who would love to get back at that man. Families of those he's killed, rivals, clients of the IMA, many more. Michael can look after himself. But you…"

He didn't say anything else; he didn't have to. I was easy prey.

"He told me, and I quote, 'This softening she sees in me isn't enough to make me affectionate, but it's just enough to render me inept. I can't give her what she wants — virtuousness — or what she needs — protection.'" Kent shook his head. "He traveled from Michigan to Oregon with a bullet wound in order to save your life. It was rash. Reckless. Completely against his nature. I advised him against it. He insisted. He risked his life to save you and now that he's realized that you don't feel the same, he is doing it again by letting you go."

I remembered the strange expression on his face when he found out I wouldn't betray him to Adrian. The sad smile when I told him that his apartment suggested he enjoyed his solitude. I sat down on the edge of the bed and looked around at the lack of personal touches, like photographs and pictures. The apartment could have belonged to anyone. What would it be like, I wondered, to live a life without love? Maybe he *didn't* enjoy his solitude.

"He has a hard life, Christina," Kent said, reading my mind. "No family. Not many close friends. Out of those few, there's only one or two he would trust with his life. I am one of those lucky few. I'm not saying that what he did to you was justified — you are a young woman and he dragged you into many situations that were" — he coughed — "probably out of your league — but he must trust you quite a bit. Especially to confide in you like this. It's a big step for him."

I stared out the window. The cloudy sky that had been so beautiful this morning was now starting to depress me. "He's so selfish."

"I'm not trying to apologize for his behavior. But he did his best, in the end."

"In the end," I agreed. It sounded pettish.

"If you care about him, and yourself, you'll let him go. Some people," and here, he sighed, looking wistful, "Truly aren't meant to be together."

I wondered who he was remembering. "Can I ask you a question?"

He hesitated. "That depends."

"How old is he? He never told me his age...and I wondered..."

I hated the pity on his face. "He just turned twenty-four."

"He's only six years older than me," I whispered.

"I'm sorry, Christina."

I closed my eyes.

"We should probably leave soon. I suspect you may have been followed. Michael told me he found some bugs in the apartment this morning..."

"All right." I stood up. "Let me...um...get dressed first. I won't be long."

Five minutes later, I followed Kent out. I left the envelope on Michael's bed, torn into four jagged pieces. I didn't want to give him even the smallest hope. If he suspected I harbored any vestigial traces of affection for him, he would risk even more than he already had. And there would be people who would try to use me against him. To kill me. To kill him. I knew how this story ended. It was just as Kent had said, some people truly aren't meant to be together.

As we left, I did not even allow myself to cry.

Made in the USA
Lexington, KY
24 October 2012